The Crystal Feather

by

Howard Johnson

To order additional copies of this book, contact:

Senesis Word

904-687-1865 - 579-265-3386 Cell

Website: www.HJWrtiter.com

Email: Senesisword@yahoo.com

CryFthr-17507W   288 Pages, 97,400 words

THE COVER

About this image, the background behind the title on the cover:

The Hubble's 20th anniversary image shows a mountain of dust and gas rising in the Carina Nebula. The top of a three-light-year long pillar of cool hydrogen is being worn away by the radiation of nearby stars, while stars within the pillar unleash jets of gas that stream from the peaks.

Credit: NASA, ESA, and M. Livio and the Hubble 20th Anniversary Team (STScI)

In spite of its solid appearance, this "mountain" is three light years of nearly empty space with widely separated atoms, molecules, particles, and small bodies, all of many materials. There is so much of this "dust" spread near and around stars, the light reflected makes this area appear much more solid than it is.

Added to the Hubble photo at top of the front cover and directly above the **y** in "Crystal" is a tiny black "tear," the "inter-dimensional rift" in the story. At the bottom of this "tear" are the concentrating gravitational waves of the Segwah shield expending energy in an attempt to repair the rift. This tiny image is much larger than true scale or it would not be visible.

DEDICATION

I dedicate this story to my five marvelous daughters and their wonderful mothers. The inspiration for this book comes from these beautiful, intelligent, and incredibly fascinating women who shared parts of their lives with me. They taught me much about women and the workings of the female heart and mind. Of course, as a male, most of that is still a mystery to be explored in stories like this one, but never understood by mere men.

Much of what the women in this book are, is derived from my interactions with these lovely ladies. Each of them is or was a unique human being, seldom predictable, often surprising, and always beguiling. There is seldom a dull moment around any of them, and put a few or all of them together, and . . . well . . . they're a hoot!

CONTENTS

Prologue

Scentar Archon, Leandra Gordon lead a meeting of the six highest ranking Scentar on their Vega Five base in the alien universe where Humans are the only indigenous intelligent species. After the preliminaries of the meeting were over, she spoke about the looming crisis suddenly facing them.

"Humans began to conduct experiments in gravitational wave to EMF energy conversions. Their first crude experiment created a small tear in the space time fabric separating our two universes. They do not realize the danger they are generating. I call on our chief physicist, Dr. Laura Claiborne, to explain what this might mean for our future."

Laura rose and spoke. "First of all, this is a menace, an extremely dangerous menace which could result in the total annihilation of both our universe and theirs. We must do what we can to prevent this from happening. Our efforts will be limited because of our law of noninterference with other cultures. We contacted the highest Scentar officials on the other side asking for the authority to abrogate some parts of the law in this dire circumstance."

General Lairn Straglo, military commander of the base commented, "The military can take no steps other than defense without direct orders from the high command. Within those limits we will do what is required to solve the problem."

"Thank you, General. I understand your actions have limits as do ours. We must operate under those restraints until and unless we hear differently from the high command. If the danger becomes imminent and real, I will authorize actions outside of our law. Dr. Claiborne, please continue with your evaluation of the situation."

"Thank you, Archon. The Humans don't understand how dangerous their gravitational wave experiments are. The tear in the space time fabric their first test brought about has damped out after a month of frightening reverberations. They are planning to conduct a second and more powerful test in the near future. Physically, the unmodified gravitons emitted by their tests could start another, larger self propagating rift or tear. Should this rift reach sufficient size, the different dimensions of space/time that hold our two universes apart would *fold* into each other through the rift. The eventual result would be the annihilation of both universes. This would take several years of Human time, so the opportunity exists of time to work on and solve this before it gets out of hand."

Doorla Mark, head gravity scientist/engineer on Vega Five, asked, "What did Humans do that differed from the initial Scentar forays into gravity/EMF conversions? Why did it create such a problem? We had no such problems with our earliest research, at least none I can remember from our studies of its history. The best solution would be to convince them to modify their equipment and test procedures. Is there a possibility of our doing so within the law's restrictions?"

"Whatever we do, we will be pursuing some questionable actions that push the legal limits. Any interference at all is strictly against our laws of contact," Archon Gordon reminded them. "However, we must take whatever steps we can reasonably take, or those laws will be meaningless. I believe we should develop several plans within and outside of the law, in case we are authorized to act in ways the law now specifically prohibits. As a last resort, I will authorize any corrective action regardless of the law should such a rift pose an immediate and serious threat."

"Our information is they are planning another test using more power than the first." Dr. Claiborne continued, "We should direct our first efforts at preventing or changing the test. If this doesn't work and the test creates a bigger problem, we will deal with the situation when it presents itself."

Chapter 1 - Trip to Stentor Seven

From force of habit I carefully studied each passenger who came through security and into the waiting area for the shuttle. The years as undercover security for various highly sensitive projects taught and trained me to look for anything unusual. On my first vacation in years, I was headed back to my favorite place in this quadrant of the galaxy. Officially "on vacation" I remained, as always, an active though currently relaxed agent for the Eegis project.

My mind came to instant alert when a tall, exotic redhead strode catlike into the waiting area and flowed into a seat. From the feline way she moved, I was sure she was a Scentar, a rare variant of homo sapiens from the old earth. I'd heard about this advanced human subspecies, but had never seen one. Her simple, dark, reddish-amber dress clung to her like a second skin, moving flawlessly, enough to show it was not attached.

When she sat, our eyes met and locked for a moment. A sudden, intense feeling of pleasure ran through my body as I imagined her moving sinuously against me. The feeling was more emotion than thought and caught me off guard. I am **never** caught off guard. The thought, *something is not right*, sent a chill through me for an instant and was gone.

When they called my group to board, she stood and walked toward the gate right in front of me. She appeared slender, almost fragile, as she stepped fluidly up the ramp and into the shuttle. I never saw anyone whose body flexed so smoothly with such sensual, liquid movement.

This is my lucky day, I thought to myself as she slithered into the seat next to me. She turned and looked into my eyes.

"I'm Leura Clauson. Who are you please?"

Her directness and musical voice surprised me even more than her exotic appearance. "Uh Draxel, Draxel Syl—call me Drax." I was quite ill at ease, certain my words betrayed my discomfort.

"Were you ever on Stentor Seven before?" her silky voice chanted softly. "This is my first visit to the Vegan star system."

"Been there several times," I struggled to say.

Her breath was like warm milk. She wore a fragrance that hung on the edge of awareness. The aroma was there, but as soon as I thought how delicious it was, the scent was gone, returning only when the thought died. I had never experienced such a woman. In unfamiliar territory, I struggled desperately to find a mental foot hold.

"I'm going on my first vacation in years, and this is a spectacular place to visit. Are you on vacation?"

"No, I'm a botanist on a research project. I plan to study plants growing in the low gravity and artificially controlled atmosphere."

The lilt of her speech was enthralling, not an accent, simply different and quite musical. "A scientist! I'm impressed!" I smiled as I spoke, thinking that a vast understatement. "How long will you stay, on your project, I mean?"

"At least one stellar year. My grant may be renewed for an additional year. This is my first major assignment. What was that little smile about?"

Her perception was unbelievable. "Just a little private joke—on me."

"A secret?"

"No, just a laugh at myself." Her directness, too, was a surprise.

"Tell me."

Now I was getting a bit irritated. "Let's say it's something I'd rather not tell someone I've just met."XXXX

Completely disregarding my irritation, she switched the subject smoothly. "What's your profession?"

"I'm a gravity propulsion engineer. Do design work on the propulsion systems on craft like this one we're on." I was merely repeating my usual cover story. Suddenly, another uneasy feeling hit me out of the blue, like a *deja vu* experience. *I met this lady before*, I thought to myself, *but that's impossible*. My mind scurried to find something to say. "This vacation is long overdue, and Stentor Seven is the one place I most love to visit."

"Tell me about it. I've seen the digirecords, but those are quite bland. No beauty or poetry. You said you've been there?"

"Yes, and the place is beautiful, spectacularly beautiful."

The hum of the shuttle's engine increased as the craft rose slowly from the pad to start the two-hour trip. The motion was noticeable, but would disappear as soon as we cleared the atmosphere and the main drive kicked in.

"How did the planet come to be? The records were sketchy about the planet's origins; they merely mention it was artificially created with no explanation. What does that mean?"

I was becoming more comfortable, since I was now on familiar territory. "Originally Stentor Seven was a small, sterile planet a bit larger than the planet Mars, but with a smaller mass. It lies precisely the right distance from the red dwarf star, Stentor, for a life supporting environment. Focused gravity beams were used to tow huge ice planetesimals in from the nearby ring. They melted and became the oceans and created the atmosphere, mostly carbon dioxide. Special vegetation was introduced to consume the carbon dioxide and add oxygen to the atmosphere. A wide spectrum of biota from earth-like environments was also introduced. After several hundred years of a chaotic profusion of these plants on the land and plankton in the seas brought the atmosphere to its present mixture, much like earth's. The atmosphere had a bit lower content of nitrogen and a much larger argon component. Temperatures, pressures and many other properties were adjusted for human habitation and the biota thrived. Since then, many larger life forms were introduced and soon flourished. The combination of optimal rotation rate and distance from Stentor, along with lots of work over the years gave us a semitropical paradise covering the entire surface."

"It sounds wonderful."

"Because of the low gravity, plants grow to immense size and spectacular proportions, but you understand all of that. Right? I trust this will be the focus of your research project."

"You are correct. Please tell me more."

"Stentor Seven is different and must be experienced. No description can do the place justice. I wouldn't want to clutter that discovery experience with inadequate descriptions. A little patience and you will enjoy this surprising experience for yourself."

"I will take your word for that. How exciting," she said as the main drive took over, and the hum and vibrations ceased. We had cleared the atmosphere and were on our way.

Over the next hour I relaxed as we spoke about families and friends. She drew pleasant experiences out of my memory and shared her experiences as a child growing up. There was an unusual quality to her stories. They were softly emotional. Incredibly, I felt her joys and pains as she described them.

After a rather long pause in our conversation, I realized she had fallen asleep. Her head against my shoulder brought on pleasurable sensations, as did her snuggling down against me several times during the flight. I examined her closely. Her hair was extremely fine with individual hairs growing unusually close together. It was dark red with no hint of a color change near the roots. If it was dyed, it was a perfect job. She turned a bit and put her hand gently on my right arm. Her pale amber skin was baby-soft and unflawed. Her hand felt like satin, nearly frictionless. By now I realized she was too perfect to be a normal human. The "Scentar," as those rare advanced humans were called by some, were reported to posses unusual emotional abilities. She seemed to possess those.

A crystal pin high on her dress caught my eye. It was the only adornment she wore of any kind. It appeared to be a feather, about an inch long and fragile. It was shaped like a real feather, but was crystal clear. When it moved, it sparkled with the many colors of the spectrum, quite difficult to describe. One moment clear, the next flashing color, and another catching and reflecting or refracting any light source. The pin was so vibrant it seemed alive.

Chapter 2 - We Arrive on Stentor Seven

A slight bump was followed by vibrations and the hum of the landing drive. Leura sat upright without the slightest hint she had been asleep. "We must be arriving."

I stared blankly at her. "You slept the last hour without moving. I wish I could do that."

"Concentrate on pleasant thoughts and close your eyes. You'll go right to sleep."

I smiled at her easy answer, still concentrating on the lovely crystal feather pin. "What's the pin your wearing? It's beautiful."

"A gift. My mother gave it to me when I completed my studies. It's the only jewelry I ever wear and signifies fidelity."

"That's one I never heard before."

"A special kind of fidelity. Fidelity to a common, usually treasured experience with someone you love. My mother loved me very much, as I loved her. It's about the wonderful life we spent together before I left home. Specifically, it's commemorating our last day together. That experience will never happen again."

"That's beautiful, sad, but beautiful." My unhappy feelings were intense and undeniable for a moment as those words were said.

"Yes, my twin sister and I gave her a similar pin. It's a family custom. We both knew we would never see our mother again."

I'm sure my shock showed. "Why not?"

Her voice was full of pain. "It's a bit complicated. We knew our paths would never cross again."

The sorrow within me became overpowering. "How can you be so sure?"

Leura had the tiniest hint of melancholy for an instant. "Please, I'd rather not talk about this anymore."

I experienced an intense change to terrible anxiety which was overwhelming. Then, as fast as it struck me, it was gone. I felt fine. "What was that all about?" I said out loud in reaction.

"What was what all about?" her clear, silky voice had returned.

"Sorry. I had a strange feeling for an instant and it startled me."

Once more Leura shifted mental gears without hesitation. "Would you be able to help me to my hotel? This is all so new to me and I'm a bit nervous about going there alone."

With my luggage scheduled to be delivered, I was free to go where I wished. "I'd be pleased to."

"You're sure this won't be an inconvenience?"

"Positively. I'd love to take you to your hotel." Once again I could hardly believe my good fortune.

*　　*　　*

The air car dropped us at level 196 of the hotel, landing smoothly on the cantilevered plaza. Leura picked up the one small bag she carried and danced across the plaza right to the edge. She was a little girl running with excitement from one side of the outside walkway to the other as I led her to her room.

"I've never been up this high in the hotel. How'd you manage such a room? I thought the upper floors were reserved for foreign dignitaries?"

"And foreign botanists," she quipped as she flipped her hair and, with a flourish, hand-printed the door which slid soundlessly into the wall and then closed silently behind us after we walked inside.

I was dumbfounded. The room was decorated in shades of the same color as Leura's dress and hair. "This can't be an accident. How'd you persuade them to decorate your room to match—you?"

Her appearance and demeanor changed. She laughed in a sensuous, lyrical way, no longer the little girl. Her voice had the timbre of a flute or muted violin.

"I plan on being here for at least a year, so they let me choose my own decoration. Do you like it?"

"The decor takes some getting used to, but certainly is beautiful." Once more, an intense feeling of warmth and pleasure flowed through my entire body. A soft "Wow!" escaped my lips.

After stowing her luggage, she pranced out of the bedroom and walked up to me. "Now, Mr. Syl, since you wouldn't tell about the wonders of this place, how about showing me? Could you possibly help me **experience** Stentor Seven as you said I should?"

Once more a delicious, warm sensation flowed through me. "I'd be delighted to do so, even if my time was limited. How about a little mountain climbing for starters?"

"Isn't that a bit strenuous for starters?"

"There's an elevator at the end of your floor. It will take us to the roof. Come on," I said as I guided her out her door, around the corner of the building, and to a glass enclosed elevator doorway.

"Oh my," she exclaimed when she spotted the huge mountain hovering over the hotel. "Is that the one we are going to climb?"

"Positively! In this gravity, those stable mountains rise seventy thousand feet with sheer cliffs you can see from here. Step into the elevator and we'll start our climb."

"An elevator? We go up in an elevator?"

"No," I said with a gentle laugh. "The elevator takes us to the roof where we catch a cable car for the ride to the top and an inconceivable view."

Once in the cable car she reverted to the wide-eyed little girl once more. "This view is amazing. I can see all the way to the seashore. Look at those waves breaking. They seem to take forever to cover the beach."

"Do you realize the beach is at least thirty kilometers away . . . and down below us at least a dozen?"

"The view is so beautiful . . . and appears much closer." The cable car reached the summit and we got off. "I thought the air would be much colder up here," she said.

"That's another result of the low gravity and the depth of the atmosphere. The air mixes vertically and doesn't form layers. You must go extremely high to reach cooler air."

We walked over to an open-air restaurant, ordered drinks, and took a table with a panoramic view. After sitting and discussing the spectacular scenery, I pointed to another cable car on the other side of the peak.

"Would you like a ride down to the beach? The cable car goes there nonstop."

"All the way to the beach?"

"Yes, all the way to the beach. It's an open car, so you can hear and feel as well as see."

"Let's go!"

As the open car dropped, the sounds of the unbelievable, mountain waterfalls were all around us. A wide-eyed Leura skipped from one side of the car to the other. "I know now what you meant about experiencing it, and words would be inadequate. The muted sounds of those slow waterfalls and of the unusual rivers are a chorus of musical mumbles. and look . . . there is no spray. The water forms huge drops, balls of water, why is that?"

"That's because they fall so slowly air doesn't blow them apart. Rain falls the same way, in huge mushroom-shaped drops. The warm rain is unbelievable. Because of the low gravity, raindrops fall slowly, congealing into those large blobs. Eventually they are blown apart by the air as they fall through it, only to coalesce into blobs once more. It's a most delightful feeling to be softly pelted by the big blobs of warm water."

"I heard about the rain. I can hardly wait to experience it. I want to run through those big drops freely, without clothes."

I would surely like to be there, ran through my mind, but I didn't say so. Her next comment drew vivid, erotic mental pictures in my mind.

"If the chance comes up, could we run through the rain together? I'd like that."

It was said so innocently, so matter-of-factly, she caught me speechless. I was struggling for composure. "Uh - yeah - sure. That sounds like a great idea."

By this time the car reached the beach station. As soon as the car stopped, Leura bounded out and raced onto the beach. She froze as a huge wave rose up then slowly crumpled onto the beach. She outran the slowly moving surf to where I stood.

She kicked off her shoes and grabbed my hand. "Come on. Dive into the surf with me."

"Can't! I'd ruin my clothes."

"Waterproof," she shouted, grabbing her dress to demonstrate as she ran down the beach and dove into the next huge wave.

My momentary fears for her safety were soon relieved when I saw her body surf right up to the beach. After doing this several times, she walked up to me a bit breathless, peeled off her dress, squeezed the excess water out and then slipped her damp dress back on. This was all done with complete abandon and innocence.

"Take off your clothes and dive in. You'll be so exhilarated."

"This public beach is not clothing optional."

"How parochial," she said as she picked up her shoes. "This was fun, but I should probably go back to my room and unpack soon. How do we go back?"

"We can walk, call an air car, or climb the lift."

"What's the lift?"

"It's a hand ladder used to climb straight up in the atrium of your hotel. The light gravity makes climbing the ladder practical, easy for most people."

"Oh! Let's climb. Sounds like fun."

Chapter 3 - Soft Music, Soft lights, Surprise

When we entered the hotel, I showed her the lift. It's a simple knotted rope that slopes across the atrium from the first floor to the tenth and from there, crisscrosses the atrium, ten floors at a time all the way up.

"Isn't it dangerous? I mean, what if you accidentally let go? The gravity may be low, but a fall would still do some damage."

I laughed and showed her the safety strap. "Slip your hand through one loop, pass the strap over the lift and then do the same to the other hand. Should you let go or tire, the strap will hold you as you dangle from the lift until you start climbing once more. Go ahead, try it."

Soon Leura was scampering up the rope like a monkey with me in close pursuit. Watching her unusual body flexing as she climbed was pure pleasure.

"This is fun," she said as she vaulted onto the fiftieth floor landing. "Some time I'd like to try to climb all the way, but it would take quite a while. How about we catch the elevator from the next landing?"

"Good idea. I'm beginning to be a bit winded," came from me through breaths that were laboring a bit. She didn't seem winded in the least.

"I'll bet you would soon be conditioned if you climbed this every day for a while."

"Probably, but it will never happen," I said as we headed for the elevator.

"And why not? I thought you said you were on vacation."

"Well, it's a sort of working vacation. There are a few things I must do while I'm here."

"Tell me."

"It's supposed to be confidential."

"Secrets?"

"Proprietary technical information. A description would bore you to death," I said, hoping to be vague and not answer.

"Now you piqued my curiosity."

"Trade secrets we are not to divulge to anyone. You may be a spy for a competitor. After all, you are a complete mystery to me."

"Well, I'm not a spy," she said as we arrived at her room. "Can you come in for a while? I can play some lovely music you've most likely never heard."

Good fortune was still smiling on me. "I'd love to hear some of your music."

Leura stepped lightly to the entertainment console and turned it on. She was right. Such music I had never experienced. In unique tones and mixed rhythms I sensed more than heard, the plaintive cry of a loon, the rustle of pine trees in the wind and the crashing of waves on a rocky shore. The sound bordered on being visual and somewhat dreamy. Leura smiled as she switched the glass outside wall from clear to one way. We viewed the beauty of Stentor Seven stretched out before us, but no one outside could see in. Once more I became aware of her delicate perfume. The aroma stimulated all of my senses when she walked over and gazed straight into my eyes. The warm-milk-like fragrance of her breath caressed my sense of smell. It was intoxicating. She reached up and gently placed her wrists on my shoulders. Her hands hung loosely, touching my back. I hated the shirt that lay between her hands and my skin.

"Now, Dr. Syl, I want us to dance together, all right?"

I was now out of my league and rapidly losing any hint of control. *What the hell is happening?* I wondered to myself as she slipped her silky fingers around my neck, took my hand and moved to the music. As I looked into her eyes, I realized they were a dark blue with a hint of red to the black of her large pupils.

"Pull the little ring at the back of my collar," her soft voice commanded.

With a slight pull, her dress changed from the amber-red to an iridescent blue-green. She began moving rhythmically against me to the hypnotic beat and sound of the strange music. The sensation penetrated my whole body which flushed with warmth.

"Now, dear Drax, I want to show you my appreciation for what you are going to do for me."

She pulled me gently into the bed where cool satin sheets caressed my skin. I hardly felt the difference between those sheets and her silky dress. Something akin to an adrenaline rush of fear surged through my being. I was perceiving everything with intensely heightened senses and enjoying every delicious moment.

"Lie on your stomach. I want to give you a massage," she urged.

Ecstatic, I complied. Her long, slender fingers were soon working up and down my spine, around my shoulder blades and neck and down the back of my legs. I had never felt so sensually stimulated, so aware, in my entire life. When my body turned to jelly, she stopped the massage and began dragging her fingers lightly over my bare arms. I felt her lips moving up and down the back of my neck. The stimulation to my skin was electrifying. Finally, she stopped and lay down on her stomach beside me.

"My turn."

I was overcome with passion and amazement. "What do you want me to do?"

"Do to me what I did to you. Don't you think that's fair?"

I remembered and uttered a line from the distant past under my breath, "Resistance is futile."

I began in the middle of her back. The fabric of her dress seemed like a second skin. Unbelievably soft and satiny, it moved smoothly to my touch. She had no taut muscles. I continued to massage her for a while until she rolled over on her back and faced me. Those dark eyes bore into my essence.

"Tickle me, please. Slide your fingertips slowly and gently over my skin. Barely touch me, like I did to you. You liked it didn't you?"

"I prayed you'd never stop."

"Continue until I can't bear any more. Then we can weep together."

"Weep? What do you mean, weep?"

"Weep for joy. Ultimate joy."

"I don't understand your meaning, but I'm game. Joy sounds good right now."

"You're doing wonderfully. When both of us are out of our minds with joy, then we will weep."

I felt as if I would explode. Every touch of my fingertips on her skin drove me to new heights of ecstatic pressure. After what seemed like hours Leura rose slowly, slid over beside me and began brushing my hands and arms with her fingers as I continued touching her. Then, because I was almost paralyzed, I stopped moving my hands.

Leura sensed the change and rolled ever so slowly onto her back pulling me down with her.

Those dark blue eyes continued to bore into my soul while her soft voice hummed quietly, "Weep my love. Weep for all time." Her voice trailed off into silence.

My mind and senses virtually exploded, a long, delicious explosion of complete abandon. I lost my sense of gravity and seemed to float in the midst of the continuing soundless explosion. I had never before felt such intense pleasure. The center of my being separated from my head and floated through my body. I was in my arm, then hand, foot, leg, abdomen and back to my head in rapid succession. Intense feelings ricocheted between joy and melancholy, pleasure and despondency, never remaining for long in any single state.

After what felt like an eternity, Leura's near whisper floated through my head. "Thank you, dear Drax. Thanks for life and love." I opened my eyes for an instant. I was surprised as a narrow stream of tears flowed from the corner of her eye. My eyes again closed, and I drifted once more in complete, all-engulfing, feeling-filled silence.

Then things changed, drastically. Normal gravity had returned. When I reached for her, all my grasping hands found was a slightly damp, rumpled cotton sheet. *What the . . . I* thought as I opened my eyes to the shock of a bright, sunlit window in a beige room. I was alone and in a different bed in a different hotel. Outside, the sun was rising over the unmistakable skyline of Cleveland, Ohio. "My God!" I said out loud. I was incredulous! "I never—almost forgot who I was," came stumbling out of my mouth as reality crept back into my senses.

A flash of realization brought me to check my watch. There was barely enough time to make my breakfast meeting with Arlo Trippy, the engineer who was my NASA counterpart, working with me on the Eegis project. I dressed quickly, grabbed my suit coat and headed for the dining room. Arlo was waiting as I walked in.

"Right on time. I like people who are punctual."

"I nearly wasn't. You wouldn't believe the wild dream I had last night, or maybe this morning. At least, I think it was a dream. The experience seemed so unbelievably . . . alive."

"Sometimes dreams can seem quite real."

"This one sure was." I shook my head, still bewildered. "Well, let's get down to business. That's reality."

"Certainly," Arlo paused and gazed intently at my coat lapel. "What's the pin you are wearing? You weren't wearing it yesterday."

I glanced at my lapel. Firmly attached was a tiny crystal feather.

Chapter 4 - Was It or Wasn't It?

I felt an instant of absolute disorientation as I tried to concentrate on the business at hand while facing the unbelievable reality of the crystal pin in my lapel. The crystal feather was pinned where my small Mensa logo pin usually was attached. What a jolt the sight of the feather gave me.

"What's the matter, Drax? You look almost—terrified."

I struggled desperately to come up with a plausible explanation for Arlo's ears. Trying to explain the dream was clearly out. "I– uh– realized– uh– I forgot to tell my boss about something important before I left."A lame little lie, but it would work—for Arlo.

"Well why don't you use your cell phone and tell him now? I can't believe the unflappable Draxel Syl could be so- well- freaked out over anything."

Sanity and control were slowly returning, responding to my I-can-handle-anything attitude about life. "No need to call right now, and it's a her, Ms. Mendrex to be exact. She's a career administrator and hasn't a clue about what we do at the research level. Still, she has a lot to say about who does what."

"Do I hear a hint of resentment?"

I was becoming more comfortable by the minute while recovering from the initial shock of seeing the feather. "No, nothing like that. Actually, I like the job she is doing. She keeps us on our toes and makes us justify the time and money we spend yet doesn't meddle in what we do. She's one of the best superiors I ever had."

"Then why the white knuckle reaction?"

I was stumbling mentally. Lying like this was not in my area of expertise. I was uncomfortable and wished Arlo wasn't so curious. "Let's go back to what we met to discuss. I remembered my error and can correct things with a call after our meeting. No harm done."

"You still appeared for a moment as though someone had hit you right between the eyes with a two-by-four. Are you sure you're okay—you don't need to contact her right away?"

16

"Positively!" *Come on Arlo, let go.* Drax thought to himself.

As if in an answer to my unspoken plea a waitress appeared. "You boys ready to order or do you need a few minutes?"

By the time breakfast and our discussion of the status of the Eegis project ended, Arlo seemed to forget the incident which still gnawed hungrily at my thoughts. Then, as Arlo left, he gave me this admonition, "You'd better remember to call your boss pretty soon. Whatever you forgot seemed quite important."

I nearly lost it, but managed to control my reaction. "Thanks for reminding me. I'll call when I'm back in my room."

Chapter 5 - A Visit with an Old Friend

As I walked back to my room, I knew the reality of the feather was going to dog my thoughts for a long time. There were many jewelers in the Schofield building on Ninth Street and one particular jeweler I wanted to ask about the feather. Victor Bump and I were close friends since attending Case-Western Reserve University years ago. I wanted Victor's opinion of the feather. He would tell me at least something about the pin if anyone could.

I walked across the square from my hotel, up Euclid Avenue to Ninth Street past stores and buildings substantially changed since I last walked that way.

It was about eleven thirty when I walked into the tiny office on the eighth floor. "Hi Victor," I called as I walked up to the open half door separating the tiny reception area from the work room. "How's the jewelry business these days?"

"Drax! Is that you? How are you and what are you doing? I haven't seen you in years."

"I don't remember for sure, Victor, but at least three years ago was the last. I left Cleveland right after you made those special earrings for me to give to Stephanie. It seems impossible she's been out of my life for three years."

"I never did think she was right for you. A bit too mercenary for my tastes and for yours, I'll bet."

"You got that right. How's your family? Your boy is out of college now, isn't he?"

"Yes, Chris is doing quite well. He's working for NASA now on some kind of hush-hush project. He won't even tell his old dad about what he does—top secret he says."

I gulped at his revelation. *I wonder if he is involved in the Eegis project?* I thought, but of course remained silent. "That's great. You are extremely proud of him, justifiably so."

"Yes, I am proud of him—and the other one as well. Sheila will graduate from dental school in two years. That's all well and good, but you didn't come up here to chitchat about my kids. What can I do for you?"

"Actually, Victor, I brought something—a piece of jewelry I want your expert opinion about."

"Oh? Where is it?"

"It's this small pin in my lapel. What can you tell me about it?" I asked as I removed the pin from my jacket and handed it to him.

Victor took the pin and started his examination with his loupe. "That's a high quality piece, carved and not cast."

"Any idea who might make such a piece or where this might be from?"

"Hmm!" emanated from Victor's mouth as he examined the pin, but otherwise, he remained silent.

After a few minutes, he placed the pin carefully on the counter and said, "This is an unusual and high quality piece of workmanship. I've never seen any remotely similar and couldn't even guess who or where it originated. It is obviously carved, but there are no carving marks, none at all. One cannot carve any kind of crystal without leaving tiny marks from the carving instrument. This piece has no marks of any kind. In fact, there seem to be no imperfections at all. It's startling. How did you come to possess such a piece?"

"It was a gift from a friend, an unusual friend."

"Well, I'd like to know where your friend got it. In my experience such detail and accuracy are impossible, as if someone took a feather, turned it into an unusual crystal material and then shrunk the piece to its present size. That's impossible, but there it is. Can't you ask your friend about it?"

"I doubt I'll ever see her again."

"Her, you say? Drax, are you still hoping to find that one special woman? They don't really exist."

"You'd better not let Martha hear you say that."

"Well, there are those few exceptions," he said with a grin. Then seriously, "I'd still like to know where she got this and how it was made. Nothing I've ever seen even comes close to this kind of workmanship. Your feather is a master work of art."

"If I ever run into her, I'll ask."

Victor gazed intently at the pin, turning it this way, then that. "I wonder," he said slowly.

"Wonder what?"

"Would you let me examine and test it a bit more thoroughly? I promise not to hurt it."

"What kind of test?"

"I am suspicious about the material it's made of. There are few materials so clear which refract light the way it does."

"And what materials would those be?"

"Glass, cubic zirconium, quartz, moissanite, and diamond. Let me use my little magic analyzer to find out which."

I handed the pin to him and soon he had it mounted securely in his little machine. "What does it do?" I asked.

"It will provide us the refractive index, heat conductivity and hardness. Each of the materials mentioned will show a different combination of those three properties. In a moment or two the analyzer will give us an answer."

Several flashes of light, a click, a hum and then a small piece of paper scrolled out of the machine. Victor picked up the paper, glanced at it, and turned to me with an amazed questioning face. "What?" I asked.

"That's hard to believe, Drax, hard indeed."

"Tell me."

"Before I do, I want to examine it closely through a magnifying glass more powerful than my loupe," he said as he transferred the feather to another examination instrument.

After several minutes examining it in silence, he gave me a stare of incredulity, and finally spoke, "Your pin is technically impossible, but the feather is a flawless, clear white, diamond."

"Diamond? Are you sure?"

"Absolutely! I could never even imagine such a piece. Your feather is a marvelous piece of art, absolutely priceless. Where did you meet this woman? Where is she from?"

"You wouldn't believe me if I told you, which I won't."

"Okay Mr. Mysterious, whatever you say I will pry no more. Your feather is spectacular and belongs in a museum under 24 hour guard. I can't imagine it's worth—hundreds of millions to the right buyer. I'm sure."

"You're kidding!"

"Never more serious in my life."

"What do I do about it?"

"Seriously? The best thing you should do is keep wearing it on your jacket. If this were a known art or jewelry object, I would remember hearing of it. If you keep this information to yourself, I doubt anyone would even have an inkling about it. Remember, sometimes the best place to hide an object is right in plain sight. Oh yes, don't lose or leave it anywhere. I wish I could refer you to someone else for help, but I wouldn't have the slightest idea where to start."

"How can I be casual about a pin with such a value?"

"Drax, if anyone can do that, you can. Your secret's safe with me, but don't describe or even mention it to another person—ever!"

"Okay Victor, and thanks for the exam and info, even if it did blow both our minds. You're still the best there is at answering such questions. I'm glad I was in Cleveland and came to you when I got this feather."

"Thanks for the compliment. Is there anything else I can do for you?"

"That's about it. If I ever do find that one woman, I'll ask you to make some special jewelry for her."

"Stop in anytime. It's nice to chat with an old friend, especially one who did so much for my kids when they were little. Any chance you're here long enough to stop over for dinner? Martha would love to see you, and Chris lives close enough to drop over."

"Unfortunately, my plane leaves in about two hours. I came to town for a meeting that couldn't be handled over the phone or Internet because of prying eyes and ears."

"Well, try and come back for a real visit with us before my grandchildren are grown."

"I'll try! Say hello to Martha for me, and remember me to both of your kids, will you? I keep some wonderful memories of times spent with them."

"You remember, of course, you are Chris's idol. He went to Case and got his engineering degree because you went there."

"Yes, I knew, and consider earning his respect one of my greatest achievements. I hope he keeps up with his dream of making a scientific breakthrough. I didn't realize he works for NASA. Of course, I haven't seen any of you for several years while I've been working in California."

"They'll be glad to hear from you. I assume you're still working on those far-out things you can't talk about."

"Yeah! It's a living."

"Are you still associated with Cal-Tech? The physics department wasn't it?"

"No, I left there more than a year ago to join a small, private research group working on some quite revolutionary stuff."

"I suppose that too, is hush-hush?"

"For the most part, yes."

"You and Chris seem to share secrecy too."

"Yeah! It's a dirty job, but somebody's got to do it."

Victor laughed. "Get out of here, but come back soon. Best of luck on whatever you're working on."

"I'll try, but no guarantees."

"Sounds like the Drax I've known for so long. One last thing, if you ever decide to sell or otherwise get rid of your pin, let me help you. I won't take a penny, but there are enough problems associated with such an item I would save you a lot of grief."

"Victor, you are a jewel. I will definitely contact you if ever I decide to do anything like that."

I headed out his door, and walked across the old black and white checkerboard marble floor of the hall to the elevator. Many memories of Victor and his family ran through my head as did the many times I walked that hard floor during those happy years.

Chapter 6 - The Trip Home

My mind suddenly switched back to the feather. I was at a total loss as to what my next effort to find out about the pin would be, or where and how it came to be on my lapel. There was no rational explanation. Maybe my dream was not a dream but a strange reality? The thought, together with the knowledge Victor provided, was bugging me—driving me crazy. I could hardly think about anything but the feather and the beautiful and exciting Leura.

I grab a cab to my hotel, pick up my small overnighter, and head for the Rapid Transit to go to the airport. I hurry to catch my flight. The feather, Leura and the dream fully occupies my mind. They are becoming an obsession. No matter what I think about, I am led to the same dead end. By the time I drop into my seat on the plane, I am on the verge of becoming a basket case. My Delta flight is by way of Salt Lake City and will put me into LA about quarter to nine. Whenever I fly, I usually read, sleep, work on my PC or all of the above to occupy my time. I try reading, but can't concentrate. PC work is impossible and I doubt I could sleep. Thank God the tiny, elderly lady sitting next to me is deeply engrossed in a book. I am not up to small talk with anyone.

My mind reels all the way to Salt Lake—no ideas, no anything. I am without answers, even lacking intelligent concepts to think about. I decide to down a couple of drinks—and I don't drink. Maybe then I might sleep some. By the time the plane touched down in Salt Lake City, I had managed a few short naps, but still little relief.

I wandered aimlessly around the terminal 'til departure time, taking my seat in the plane with about fifteen minutes to wait. At the last minute, a young woman with a high collared coat and a large head of hair black as midnight walked in and sat down in the seat next to me. She had two carry-on bags. One she placed overhead, the other she opened in her lap and removed several large books before placing it under the seat. I was so preoccupied, little about her registered with me. One thing I did notice was her face was virtually hidden by hair which was styled in that carefully coiffed, seemingly messed, just-got-out-of-bed hairstyle.

"Are you from Salt Lake?" she asked.

"No!" I said, not wanting to start any conversation. She obviously understood my feelings and immersed herself in one of the large books in her lap.

I went to sleep and was only awakened when the pilot announced our landing at LAX. My deplaning habit was to remain in my seat until most passengers were gone, then walk out. The young lady next to me took some time putting her books into her carry-on before standing and taking her bag down from the overhead bin. To my great surprise she reached over and pressed a tiny envelope in my hand before hurrying down the aisle. I opened the envelope and found a card with a phone number and the words, *call me.* The number placed its location close to where I lived in Pasadena. The thing that about blew my mind was the other item in the tiny envelope, my Mensa pin. *What the hell is this all about?* I said silently to myself.

I hurried off the plane searching for her, but the young lady was nowhere in sight. The mystery was getting complicated. This was a new and real contact. The experience with Leura now seemed less and less like a dream. There was no doubt about either pin. Both were quite real as was the woman in the plane and the note. Those concrete facts gave me pause to wonder if my *dream* had been a dream. I had no choice but to follow up.

In the limo between LAX and my apartment in Pasadena, I studied the envelope and the note. The note seemed ordinary enough, a simple, plain, personal note like those boxed notes sold in office supply stores. There was, however, something about the way it felt that bothered me with unidentified familiarity. Something hung just out of reach of my memory like a name one can't seem to remember. I would call the number in the morning. I tried my cell phone, but the battery was discharged. It would be too late to call by the time I got home.

Once I was in my apartment, I watched the late news from my bed and mercifully dropped off to sleep before the program was over.

Chapter 7 - The Mystery Deepens

I awoke to the morning news which merged seamlessly with the news that had put me to sleep. I had finished dressing after my morning shower when the door chime announced a visitor.

"Who's there?" I said to the entrance intercom.

"This is Lieutenant Corbett, Pasadena police, Dr. Syl. I'd like a word with you."

"What's this about?"

"It's important. You either need to come down here, or let me in so I can come up there."

What the hell is this all about, I wondered. "C'mon up," I said as I entered the door release code in the keypad.

Five minutes later I welcomed the lieutenant into my apartment. He was fortyish with an athletic body and tousled, curly brown hair that clung to his head like a knit hat. He was definitely a guy you wouldn't want to mess with.

An extended hand and friendly "I'm Jim Corbett, Pasadena police," made a favorable first impression. I liked this man immediately.

"Draxel Syl, call me Drax. I realize this isn't a social call, What's this about."

His first question was a shocker. "Do you know a Leura Clauson?"

Add this to what happened earlier and I became even more confused. "Uh—yes—sorta," was all I thought to say.

"Sort of? What kind of an answer is that? Do you or don't you know her?"

My mind raced to find a reasonable answer that wouldn't paint me as an absolute kook for the lieutenant. I found it. "Yes, I do in an unusual way I'd like not to try to explain until I learn more about why you are asking."

"Well, can you explain this?" He handed me a bound notebook about five by eight. "Check inside."

When I glanced through the notebook, I saw pages filled with neatly written information about me, my travels, and my meetings—the ones I had yesterday along with a number of previous days. It went back at least two months. "Where in hell did you find this?"

"I thought you might be interested. We found this a block down the street in the apartment of one Leura Clauson. At least that's the name on the tenant list and on the lease. That's why I asked if you knew her."

"Why were you in her apartment? Has something happened?"

"Take a look at this and tell me what you think," he said, handing me a digital camera showing a photo of a badly damaged room.

"Is that blood all over everything?"

"Yep! Lots of it. The apartment, her apartment, had been torn up more than any I ever examined before. That's why homicide was called. Folks in the neighboring apartment called 911 to report a violent fight about two this morning. When our guys arrived, they found her apartment virtually destroyed. Furniture was broken, and the main entrance door was torn off its hinges. There was blood everywhere as the photo shows, but there was no one around, alive or dead. The people who called in had barricaded their door they were so frightened."

"Did anyone else see anything?"

"I don't think I should answer yet until we can explain what the notebook was doing there. We found it on the floor, under the bed. That's why I'm here."

"I wish I knew, Lieutenant, I really wish, but I'm dumbfounded by the notebook and I don't believe I ever met the Leura Clauson who lived in that apartment."

"But you do know a Leura Clauson, right?"

"I was afraid you were going to ask that. How are you on bizarre stories?"

"I checked you out before coming here and you don't seem the type to tell bizarre stories, so go ahead, tell me your story."

"Well, basically, I met a Leura Clauson in a dream, a strange and yet realistic dream I had the other night. I've never met anyone by that name in real life, never. Believe me, I would remember her."

"I asked several of her neighbors to describe her, say what she looked like to help us search for her. Only one remembers ever seeing her clearly, and she has lived there for six months. She seems very private. No one remembers having spoken with her."

"What did your witness say she looked like?"

"Tall and unusually slender, youngish, maybe mid-twenties, and with a large, coal-black hairdo."

Click—a match! "She sounds like the woman who sat next to me on the plane from Salt Lake last night. She handed me a note and asked me to call her."

"Did you keep the note?"

I picked up the envelope from my desk and handed it to him. "Not much on the note."

The lieutenant removed the note and read it. "Can I keep this? It might help us out."

"Sure, for a while, but I want it back."

He scowled at the note, then checked his own pocket notebook. "Well isn't that interesting? The phone number is for the one in her apartment. I don't think you need to call. I believe you met our Leura Clauson. Does she match the one in your dream?"

More complications. I thought. "Not really. The one in my dream had straight red hair, but the rest of the description fits, sort of."

The lieutenant became tediously official. "Where were you around two this morning?"

I grinned. "You had to ask, didn't you?"

"Just doing my job. I'm sure your apartment security will tell us, but how about it?"

"The limo dropped me off about eleven. I was so exhausted from my quick trip east I went right to bed, watched the late news and died. I got up a short time before you arrived."

"You're sure?"

"Positively! By the way, Lieutenant, how about breakfast? I'm starved and usually eat at the little deli across the street. Would you like to join me? Cops do eat, don't they?"

The lieutenant relaxed visibly. "Usually I eat on the run, but we can continue our conversation over breakfast."

I slipped into my shoes, grabbed a jacket, and we headed for the deli.

Chapter 8 - The Lieutenant Asks Questions

In a corner booth over ham, eggs, toast, and coffee, we continued our conversation. "In my report I'm not going to mention anything about your meeting this lady in your dream. I'll mention you met her on the plane. This may be an interesting story, but I don't really want to hear any more. Dreams don't make good copy in a homicide report."

"Homicide? I didn't hear you mention a body."

"Honestly? No body, but there was so much blood we are sure someone died. I'm quite sure a homicide occurred. We're treating it as such, even without a body." The lieutenant brought out his notebook. "Do you know a Charles Hruby?"

"No."

"How about Sigmond J. Frawley?"

"Another blank."

"Maria Mendrex?"

Click! Again. "That's my boss's name," I said in wonderment. "Why do you ask?"

"Your boss? Those three were listed on a single page in her notebook along with phone numbers. I hoped one of them would be familiar to you. We'll be running them down for questioning soon."

"I've worked for Maria for two years now. She's a straight arrow and sharp. I'd like to talk to her about this myself."

"At last a positive link, weak, but definite. Otherwise, you're no fount of information about this lady. What did you two talk about on the plane?"

"We didn't."

"You sat next to her for two hours and never said anything to each other?"

"She asked me if I lived in Salt Lake and I said no. That was the whole of our conversation."

"Then she gave you the note and left the plane, right?"

"About right."

"What do you mean, *about*?"

"I didn't tell you about the pin."

"What pin?"

"My Mensa pin was in the envelope with the note."

"She had your mensa pin? How did she get that?"

"That's a mystery I'd like an answer to myself."

"Are you sure this is your pin?"

"It's mine because it has the ID number I scratched on the back."

"When did you lose it? How long it has been gone?"

"It was on my coat lapel when I left for my trip to Cleveland a week ago. The morning when I went to breakfast with Arlo it was gone."

"Did I understand you to say you lost your pin in a hotel room in Cleveland? Then an unknown lady gave it back to you in an envelope she handed you before you exited a plane from Salt Lake City. In the envelope there is a note to call her. Is that what you're telling me?"

"When you put it that way, it sounds kind of goofy."

"Impossible, I call it. How in hell do you expect me to believe you? What happened?"

"You wouldn't believe me if I told you, so I won't."

"Try me."

"Not a chance."

"Sounds like obstruction to me. You might be arrested."

"Suppose I told you a little green man walked through the wall of my hotel room, took the pin for a day and then walked through the side of the airplane in flight and gave it back."

"Now you're being ridiculous."

"My point is made."

"What point? You tell me a ridiculous, nonsensical story, and that's supposed to prove a point?"

"It did to me. If I told you what actually happened to me, you would think my story even more bizarre than the little green man story. Believe me. You would react in the same way. If I ever figure out what happened about the pin, I'll tell you, but not until."

"No matter what?"

"No matter what!"

"You are one stubborn son-of-a-bitch."

"I've been called worse."

"I guess I can't use a rubber hose and beat it out of you, but if you're involved in this young lady's murder or disappearance, I'll nail you. Count on it."

"Lieutenant, if I knew anything real that might help you out on this case I'd tell you. Believe me! I've told you everything I can reasonably suppose. For the sake of my sanity, I want those answers at least as much as you. Right now you know one hell of a lot more about Leura Clauson than I do, so get off my case. How about telling me what you have on this lady for a change."

"I want to believe you, but it's hard to keep those doubts in check. You must admit it sounds a bit shaky."

"Shaky, Lieutenant? Hell, what I seem to remember happened—no, what did happen to me in the last week is impossible and I'm on the inside. Your doubts are minor compared to mine."

"Okay, I'll cut you some slack. I'll even tell you what we learned about Ms. Clauson."

"It would please me to no end."

"First of all, we ran a check on her early life and didn't turn up anything. It was as if Leura Clauson didn't exist until she shows up on the faculty of the University of Florida. Then we tried searching under similar names and came up with a long list, most of which were dead ends of one sort or another. Besides Leura, there was but one other woman on the list we decided was a possibility. Both seemed to come out of nowhere. Leura Clauson, Dr. Leura Clauson, is or was a professor of botany at the University of Florida in Gainesville. She did all of her undergrad work and got her advanced degrees at Florida. She is the youngest PhD in botany in the country, twenty-four years old. Her records say she was a child prodigy originally from some little town in Minnesota."

"That's intriguing."

"Why do you say that?"

"My brother is working on his masters in botany at Florida. He never mentioned any young female professors in his department. I can't imagine him not telling me about a botany professor such as you describe. Ori always talks about the young women he meets."

"Well, he missed this one. Anyway, Dr. Clauson disappeared about a month ago—vanished without so much as a trace. Her clothes, her PC and the project she was working on at the university all disappeared with her. No one has heard from her. At least, no one has admitted to any contact. We've got photos coming, but I've not seen them yet."

"I'd certainly like to see those photos."

"I'll try to get hold of them, possibly this afternoon."

"I'll be available."

"The other name is even more interesting. Laura Claiborne has an equally sketchy background. She appeared out of nowhere as an adult woman four years ago. We found no records of any kind about her before the time she walked into the studios of public TV in New York and auditioned for an opening as an interviewer on a new science show. She said she was a physicist with an advanced degree from somewhere. They were so impressed with her knowledge they gave her the job and a one year contract in spite of her lack of any resume. That was four years ago. She claimed to be a Kurdish political refugee from Iran. In spite of her dark skin, hair and eyes, she was more Italian than Kurdish and spoke perfect English. In any event, she soon became a regular on public TV."

"Yeah! I remember seeing her several times on TV. Didn't she also run a show of her own on the science channel?"

"That's the one."

"For all I saw of the lady on the plane and remember of the TV program, She could be the same woman—with a big, black wig. Now that I think about it, the TV gal did resemble the Leura Clauson I met—resembled her a lot."

"Well, she disappeared about the same time as the other one, without a trace also. She had been on a shoot somewhere in the desert in Chihuahua, Mexico. She had a complete mobile unit and two technicians with her. According to the technicians, they took their jeep and went back to town to pick up something they needed while she stayed in the large van that served as their mobile unit. When they returned, the van and everything in it had disappeared, including Ms. Claiborne. The van had been parked on rocky ground, and there was no trace of a trail. Funny thing, the road they took to town about forty miles away was the only road anywhere in the area. If she drove out, she had to go past them, but they never saw her or the van. How something as big as a van could disappear, even in such a remote area, is a real mystery. Not a trace of the van has ever been found. Ms. Claiborne has not been seen either."

"You're giving me lots of questions, but no answers. We need answers."

"Oh yes, and the names of the two technicians? Charles Hruby and Sigmond J. Frawley, were the other two names in her book. That's not the worst of it. The van they were using?"

"What about it?"

"The PBS station said it wasn't one of theirs as all of their mobile units were accounted for."

"Sounds like your answers are few, maybe none at all."

"Lots of questions, with no answers. I was hoping you might fill in some of the blanks."

"Guess not."

"It's early on in this case, too early to worry about a lack of answers—a normal situation. Finding those answers is what we do, and we will." Lieutenant Corbett took a last sip of his coffee and stood up. "I need to go back to my desk and find out if those pictures came through. I should also be getting the preliminary DNA report from the blood by late this afternoon. Call me if you think of anything you didn't tell me. We've a body to find, and my people are still investigating the crime scene. I'll check with them before heading in, in case they found something I should see." He handed me his card and said, "Call me if you think of anything."

"Good luck! And I mean that," I said as we left the deli. "And please keep in touch."

"Don't worry, I will. I'm counting on lots of help from you on this case."

"Why so?"

"I read your complete background, remember?" was his parting shot as he headed for his car. As confused as ever, I headed back to pick up my car and drive to my office. Hopefully I can clear enough confusion out of my mind to do some work. First of all, I wanted to ask Maria a few questions.

Chapter 9 - Will it Never End?

When I walked into the Eegis Center building, Manuel, the guard, greeted me with a strange, worried face.

"Good morning, Dr. Syl. I'm glad you're back."

"Good morning Manuel. Is everything all right? You seem troubled."

"Didn't anyone call you about Ms. Mendrex?"

"No, what about her?"

"She didn't show up yesterday—no call, nothing. That's not like her."

"Didn't anyone try to contact her at home?"

"Marty called her home and cell phone, right from my desk here. Her home phone didn't answer, not even her answering machine. Her cell phone was off as all he heard was her voice mail request. He was worried."

"Where's Marty now? I'd like to speak to him."

"I believe he's in his office. I can call him for you."

"Please, and let me talk to him."

Manuel picked up the phone and after a few words turned to me. "He says for you to come to his office ASAP and never mind the phone."

"Tell him I'm on my way."

"Okay!"

Marty Cohen, our Research Coordinator, is the one who keeps all of our research on track and the group in communication. An experienced research scientist in his own right, he is one of the top people in material physics and engineering. Marty is one of those rare people who inspires others with his enthusiasm and leadership. The sparkplug of our research engine, Marty is the heart of the Eegis project and the reason I came on board. I hurried to his office in the middle of the second floor where he had easy access to the leadership of every section of the project. As I walked through the second floor, everyone I passed was in a somber mood. The usual friendly greetings were subdued. A wet blanket seemed to be thrown over the entire place.

Marty met me at his door, his face unusually serious, his hand extended. "I'm glad you're back. We're in a mess since Maria disappeared. You knew about that, didn't you?"

"Manuel told me. Why didn't anyone call me?"

"We've been trying to contact you since a day after you left. Your cell phone didn't respond. All I got was your voice mail. Then we tried the GPS in your phone and got no response either. I assumed you had turned off your cell phone, but the GPS cannot be turned off. We were getting concerned as we had no idea where you were or what happened to you. By the time we got around to calling your hotel in Cleveland, you had checked out. We caught up with Arlo at NASA, but he had no idea where you went after your meeting. At least you were all right. Arlo said you were acting strange, something about needing to contact Maria."

"My cell phone battery died. I didn't turn it off."

"That's not possible."

"Why not?"

"All our cell phones use built in live-loop chargers. We designed them ourselves, right here. They constantly recharge from ambient electrical fields generated by all electric wires, everywhere."

"Damn! You're right. I forgot all about that." I pulled my phone out of my pocket and tried to turn it on—nothing. "Well for whatever reason my phone is dead. See?"

"Let's take your phone to Chen Yu right now. I believe that's the first one to fail. I'd like him to find out why," Marty said as he reached for the phone.

While he talked to Chen Yu, I began organizing my questions. *Had Maria truly disappeared and if so, how and why? Was her disappearance related with the disappearances of those other women? Why did my phone quit at this particular time?* I realized I was becoming suspicious of every even slightly unusual happening.

Marty hung up. "Drax, Chen Yu is sending an aid to pick up your phone. He will set up a new cell phone for you with your same number. He wants to keep and test this phone to find out what happened. He'll bring the new one to you as soon as he can, as late as this afternoon."

"He solves the phone problem for me, but what about Maria? It doesn't sound good at all in light of something I learned this morning."

"Oh? What's that?"

"First, tell me about Maria. Disappearing isn't in her way of doing things. Something happened to her—something bad I fear."

"The police won't consider her a missing person for another twenty hours since there was no sign of violence at her home."

"What about her home?"

"When she didn't show yesterday and we couldn't reach her, we sent Terry Gross to her place to find out if something had happened to her there. He called me to report she was not in her apartment. When, after a great deal of persuasion about ill health possibilities the building manager let him inside her apartment, he found her uneaten breakfast was sitting on the kitchen table. Nothing seemed disturbed. Her car was still in the garage with a cold engine. Terry's thorough."

"You say you called the police?"

"As soon as Terry told me what he found. They said they couldn't do anything under the circumstances, but they did send a patrol car and two uniforms to check things out. They found nothing as of now."

I pulled Lieutenant Corbett's card from my pocket, grabbed the phone, and dialed his number. "I think I might be able to start some police action going."

"Oh, who are you calling?"

"Lieutenant Jim Corbett, please. Tell him Draxel Syl is calling." I put my hand over the mouthpiece. "He's a cop who will definitely be interested in Maria's disappearance."

Another cop came on the line. "I'm Jim's partner, Forrest McNulty. Jim's not here. Can I help you?"

"I remember some information that might relate to the bloody apartment for him. Tell him to call me as soon as possible."

"The Leura Clauson case? If it's important, I can contact him."

As soon as I told him about our missing lady he said, "Give me your location. I'll be there as quickly as possible. I can catch Jim on the way as he'll want to check this out. I'll grab the report of the two uniforms and may send them back out there. Thanks for the call."

"I'm in Marty Cohen's office here at the Eegis building, second floor. Know where it is?"

"About half hour away. See ya in a short!"

Marty, a bit stunned, asked, "What the hell was that all about? What bloody apartment? How would it relate to Maria's disappearance?"

I gave Marty a brief rundown of my conversation with the lieutenant leaving out the dream sequence and the pins of course.

Marty shook his head, "That's scary. Do you suppose Maria is involved in—in whatever is going on?"

"I wish I knew!"

"It's a growing mystery to me. I hope we can at least start finding answers. I am busy keeping a major project on track here. At this point in time, things don't sound so good. Our second run created a whole new set of problems. My chief administrator disappeared and my chief engineer vanished for a week. Now he is somehow involved with several other women who seemed to vanish as well. Now I'm expecting a police investigation."

"When you say that, it sounds serious."

"You're damned right it's serious, and that's not our only serious problem. Let's head down to the test lab. I will show you what happened during the second run after you left. You won't believe it." Marty got up and we headed down the hall at a rapid walk.

As we walked, I asked, "What about the second run? Wasn't that run like the first one we did six months ago but with double the power input to the coils?"

"It's the way we set up the experiment, but the results were, well, unexpected. As we seemed on the verge of a breakthrough on work with tremendous significance, all hell breaks loose. I don't know what caused it, but you'll see for yourself what happened."

Chapter 10 - Finally, Some Recognition

We arrived at the lab and walked over to the test apparatus. Marty asked, "Now do you know what I mean by unexpected?"

"The damned table appears to be cut in half by a saw, and an unusually fine saw at that. How did it happen?"

"You tell me. If you examine the table carefully, you'll notice the side of the cut is glassy smooth. We measured the top and determined about two inches is gone. The shelf is missing about an inch and a half. Now look at the floor underneath."

"The hole was cut clear through the floor. How deep did it go?"

"The space is an inch or more wide at the center and tapers to the ends which are a bit more than eight feet apart. The missing material cut clear through the duct, the electric conduit, the wires in the conduit, and the ceiling of the floor below but did not reach the floor. It's like a thin disk of material simply disappeared."

"Were you here when this happened?"

"Standing right over there at the input console watching the coils as the power was applied."

"My God, Marty, tell me what you saw."

"When we reached full power, I closed the circuit to the coils. Then the lights dimmed and there was a brilliant blue flash accompanied by a tremendous, loud thump like someone dropped a heavy object on the floor. For an instant there was a loud rush of air. The sound was as if the space in the table was a powerful vacuum. The test drew so much power the protective circuits blew, plunging the entire building into darkness. The air movement was powerful and blew all the notes and papers off the recording display and everything off of both desks. The emergency lighting came on, so we saw papers and dust swirling around the setup. When we picked things up, we discovered a few of the papers were missing—gone!"

"That's incredible!"

"Not only incredible, but impossible. That's not all."

"No?"

"Remember the stool?"

"The heavy steel stool? Of course. What about it?"

"It's gone too. We set it atop the table next to one of the coils and used it to hold the ammeter to tell us how much current we were using. The ammeter was connected to the coils and was still there, but the stool was missing."

"The damned stool must weigh at least sixty pounds."

"It's listed at 85 pounds in our inventory. I checked."

"That's crazy!"

"And one more thing, when we checked out the void in the table and floor, we discovered their cross sections were perfect ellipses."

"How perfect?"

"Too Goddamned perfect. The edges of the hole were also too perfect—far too smooth for any known cutting method. Draw an eight-foot long perfect ellipse on the work surface of the workbench right between the two coils, then rotate the ellipse about the short axis and remove every atom from inside the resulting disk shaped space, bingo, the void."

"Can you think of any reasonable explanation about what happened? This makes no sense to me."

"We're working on several theories. We called Crazy Charlie for help since we thought a particle physicist might be able to help. You were going to visit him while he was in Indiana before you met with Arlo. He said you never showed. What happened?"

I thought for a moment and drew a complete blank. "Uh—damn! Marty, I don't remember trying to go there. In fact, now that I think about it, I don't remember anything since I finished setting up the second trial run of the free current coils for you. It was Wednesday. I was supposed to fly out Thursday morning to Indiana and I don't even remember doing that."

"C'mon Drax. That's impossible."

"No—seriously, Marty, I realized I can't remember anything between Wednesday afternoon and Tuesday morning—nothing! I lost a whole week."

"Drax, if anyone but you made a statement like that I'd trot them off to the looney bin."

"With all of the improbable things I experienced in the last few days, nothing seems to be impossible."

"This is bizarre! What else happened that you haven't told me about?"

I had no choice, so I told Marty all about the dream, the feather, the lady on the plane—everything. He was stunned and shook his head when I finished. Then Manuel called to announce McNulty was here.

"Are we ready to talk to him?" Marty asked.

"I'd say it makes little difference. This is one impossible mystery after another."

"Manuel, Show Officer McNulty to the small conference room and tell him we'll meet him there in a few minutes." Then turning to me he said, "Are we going crazy? What are we going to tell the police that makes any kind of sense?"

"I think all they'll be interested in is Maria's disappearance. Let's not confuse the issue with conjecture about what happened in the lab."

After his comment, we headed for the conference room. Marty asked, "Did you tell them about your dream?"

"Hell no! I don't want them to think I'm a nut case. I will say one thing."

"What?"

"We've enough unanswered questions to last a long time."

"Amen for sure. There has to be some logical explanations, but I doubt we will find them any time soon."

By the time we reached the conference room both Forrest McNulty and Jim Corbett were there waiting. After introductions, we sat around the small table and talked. Jim handed me a photo.

"That's Laura Claiborne," Jim reported. "Do you recognize her?"

I tried to hide my surprise as I recognized the face of the Leura Clauson of my dream. The photo was fuzzy, but there was no mistaking who it was. "She doesn't look like the lady on the science show," I complained. "Her hair is different. Still, she could be a relative, a sister maybe, but not she, not exactly."

"It's not," Jim said with a grin. "I wanted to see your reaction. You've seen her before, I can tell?"

"Who is she?" I asked.

"Where did you meet her and what is her name?" Jim asked while displaying a smug, superior face. "And no song and dance, I want some straight answers."

"You first."

"C'mon Drax. It's obvious you recognized her. Who is she?"

"When I met her, she gave me her name as Leura Clauson."

"And where did you meet her?" Jim said with an all knowing smile.

"On the shuttle between Vega Five and Stentor Seven," I answered without batting an eye.

"Where on Earth is that?"

"It's not anywhere on Earth. Vega Five is the fifth planet out from the star Vega. Stentor Seven is the seventh planet out from the star Stentor in the Vegan star system."

There was a prolonged dead silence before Jim said, "Don't give me any of your smart-ass nonsense, damn it. I'd run you in for lying if it were legal. Now, once more, where did you meet her?"

"I told you before that you wouldn't believe me if I told the truth, and what I said is the absolute truth. Now, who is she and where did you pick up her photo?"

Jim handed me another photo saying, "This is a blow up of the full photo of your friend, Leura, and another woman, taken Monday morning by the security camera at the apartment complex where Maria Mendrex lives. Who is the other woman in the photo?"

Right beside Leura and obviously walking freely with her was Maria. "Wow! This puts a new twist on things," was all I could say.

"Still want to stick to your nonsense?"

"Damn it, Jim. It's the truth. If you'll say you believe me, I'll tell you the whole story."

Marty held up his hands. "Wait a minute! Drax told me what happened and I for one believe him. There are some strange things happening around here, things that defy logic and reason. We are both scientists and not prone to telling or believing outlandish tales, so think about it. If you want to continue this conversation, you must accept what we say. Then we may find some answers. Otherwise, gentlemen, this interview is over!"

McNulty grimaced. "Damn it. You guys are both nuts."

"Hold on, Forrest," Jim said, extending his hand to keep him seated. "There may be something we just learned about that is in the same stripe."

"What the hell can that be?" Forrest said with disgust.

"In my hands is a report on the blood DNA found in the busted up apartment. Like the story Drax told, the report makes no sense and says the blood is definitely primate, but not exactly human."

"So what?" Forrest asked belligerently. "So somebody slaughtered an ape. I've seen worse."

"The blood is not from any known primate either, yet closer to human DNA than even the Bonobo. The DNA comes from an unknown species of human. We also found out the DNA is male, so it rules out any of the women as a source of the blood."

There was dead silence. All I could think about was my "knowledge" of the advanced human subspecies from my *dream*. I was not about to relate this information—at least not yet.

Jim spoke slowly. "We should pool our information and try to make some sense out of all this without beating on each other. The real answers might be *outside the box* thus making us blind to those realities."

"That's the most intelligent words any member of this group has said so far," Marty said. "If we accept some things that don't make sense as facts, maybe we can find a reasonable explanation. Something happened in our lab that make no sense either, but it did happen. Now we're trying to understand it. Perhaps these strange happenings are connected."

Forrest acted a bit sheepish. "Hell, I'm no scientist, but I know a lot about getting to the truth and sometimes things are not what they seem. When that happens it's always because somethin' nasty is goin' on—some bastard's lyin' or stealin' or cheatin' on his wife. You can count on it. All this crazy info is bull shit. When we solve the problem, it'll be somethin' simple—some lousy bastard like I said before."

"Don't be too sure Forrest," I warned. "That kind of thinking could preclude our finding the real answers."

Over the next few hours we listed and discussed as many happenings as we could find and think of, trying to find links—putting things in some sensible order. Together we were painting a sketchy picture with few relationships and numerous unknowns. It was a start. We decided it was crucial to find Maria and Leura. They were our best chance and most recent sighting were only a few hours old. Forrest agreed to contact rental car agencies with a copy of the photo of the two women. Jim would continue investigating the bloody apartment. Marty and I would concentrate on the strange void in the floor and table.

"Well, gentlemen," Jim said, "We've all got things to do, so let's do it. We need all we can find on Maria from your personnel files. I assume it's okay if we look here."

Marty was a bit startled. " I—I—maybe. Personnel files contain sensitive information. We're not supposed to let anyone see them."

The lieutenant was exasperated. "Damn! You're not going to make us get a warrant are you?"

Marty thought for a moment. " I don't think there is any sensitive information in her file, so I'll okay it. But let me check first."

"Damn it Marty, all we want to do is find the lady and the personnel info might help. We're all on the same side aren't we?" The lieutenant was irritated.

"Shit, Lieutenant, we can't chuck all our protocols without a word. I said it would be okay, didn't I?"

I didn't like seeing this conflict. "Cool down you two. We've enough problems without adding internal conflicts. The first important thing is finding Maria. Besides, it's after noon, and we had better take a lunch break."

Jim stood up. "Forrest and I must do some things now, so why don't we meet back here at say, four o'clock. That will give each of us some time to mull over what we know, check for any new information, and then compare notes. I doubt we are going to find any solutions in a few hours, maybe not for several weeks or longer."

"Why don't we put off our meeting until tomorrow morning at ten? It will give us all a chance to think through what information is at hand and do a little individual investigating," Marty suggested.

After a general nodding of heads in agreement, we all headed for our individual destinations.

Chapter 11 - More New Information

Marty and I headed for the lab with but a single thought between us. "Are you thinking what I'm thinking?" I said as we walked.

"If you mean to check out our equipment and set up another run, you're dead on," was Marty's reply. "There's one other bit of information I'm missing."

"What's that?"

"I'm going to contact Terry and ask him to check your flight to Fort Wayne last Thursday to find out if you were on it."

"Damn! I had forgotten all about that. Good idea."

"Drax, you forgot many important things in the last few days. What the hell is going on?"

"If I knew or even had any idea, I'd tell you. Honestly, I'd like those answers as much as you—maybe more. Dammit, Marty, I'm the one who can't remember, and that bugs the devil out of me."

"If I didn't know your record, I doubt I would believe you. Something's going on here neither of us understands. Hell, we don't have the faintest idea what."

When we reached the lab, Marty called Terry and asked him to check on my flight. Then we started examining the pile of equipment. We pulled the two halves of the table out and stood them together.

After staring at the table for a few minutes, Marty said, "Let's measure the damned thing and learn exactly how much material disappeared. The table was thirty-six inches wide when in one piece"

A quick measurement of the table standing straight with its sides leaning against each other and we discovered the top was four inches narrower. The gap in the center measured five and a quarter inches, and the height of the center of the coils was twenty-six inches above the table top. This gave us a disk diameter of ten or twelve feet. When we had the number, we both looked at the ceiling above the cut in the floor. There was a neat flat ellipse cut out of the ceiling right next to the fluorescent fixture and directly above the one in the floor.

"Damn!" Exclaimed Marty. "I wonder why we never noticed that before?"

"I got up on a step stool and peeked into the hole. "The void barely missed a big bundle of telephone and power cables, but cut through ceiling tiles and T bar supports. That's weird."

"What is?"

"It missed all the wires supporting the T bars, so nothing fell down. That's why we didn't notice it. That plus, why look up? All the equipment was lying on the floor in a heap."

The phone rang and Marty answered. "That's interesting. Terry said you were not on the flight nor were you on any other flight until the ones you used to fly back here from Cleveland. How in the devil did you get from here to there?"

"I wish I knew. Damn, do I wish."

"You went home from here Wednesday and packed a bag for your trip. Do you remember doing that?"

"Marty, for years I've kept an overnighter in my briefcase with underwear, shirt, socks and a toilet kit. That's for those quick trips I've had to take frequently at the last minute. I remember setting it out by my doorway before I went to bed on Wednesday. I don't remember even getting up on Thursday. Hmmmm? Wait a minute. Now I seem to remember a bit. I grabbed my briefcase and headed over to the deli for breakfast. Then I walked down the street toward the limo pickup spot. I remember passing a large gray van parked at the curb. Then—nothing. It's like, zappo—not there."

"I wonder if we should check with the people in the deli, or the limo driver? They might remember something."

"I can do that right now, but there's something else that puzzles me."

"Oh?" Marty exclaimed, "What?"

"Why didn't I recall that before and not until this moment? Earlier I tried to remember the day, but with no results. Why do I now remember?"

"Don't ask me. I am clueless."

"So? What else is new? I can't seem to answer even the simplest of questions about the last few days. It's driving me crazy."

"Why don't we go to work resetting up the last experiment? Working should keep our minds occupied for a while. At least it's something we can do. I'll grab two thirty-six-inch angles from the shop. We can use those to put the table back together, so we can mount the coils."

"Okay, boss. While you're doing that I'll check out the coils to see if they're okay. I'll ask Terry to help me. Those buggers are hea—vy!"

By the time Marty returned with the steel, Terry and I had separated the coils, laid out their connecting wiring and checked them for continuity. They were both without a flaw. The three of us attached the steel angles to the cut ends of the table with bolts and nuts making the table top precisely thirty-six inches wide with a gap down the center.

It was six by the time we finished assembling the apparatus and connecting the wires. Marty said, "We've put in a full day. Let's run all of the operational tests in the morning, starting around seven. Then we can run a third experiment in the afternoon."

"Sounds good to me. I plan on stopping at the deli for breakfast and asking about that Thursday morning."

As we walked to the door, Marty said, "I wasn't questioning your honesty earlier. I wanted to make certain you understood some of this is hard for me to swallow."

I laughed. "Hell, Marty, It's even hard for me to swallow and I'm in the midst of all these impossible happenings. I took no offense. We've worked together for so long we often even think alike. It's hard for me to believe all this myself."

I stopped to pick up a pizza and headed for home. As soon as I got there, I grabbed a beer from the frig, turned on the TV and watched the early news while devouring the pizza. Soon after finishing a second beer, I hit the sack and crashed. I was glad to get some solid sleep after all the confusion.

My alarm went off at five fifteen. I hopped out of bed, did the shower thing, dressed, and headed for the deli. Myron was working the counter. We always passed pleasantries. "Myron, do you remember a week ago Thursday when I had breakfast here the last time for a week I would be here."

"Yeah, Drax, I remember. You told me you were headed for Indiana, right?"

"You got it. That's the day. Do you remember anything else about that morning, anything unusual, even if nothing had to do with me?"

After thinking for a while, Myron shook his head no. "I don't remember anything unusual, nothing at all. Just a normal Thursday morning."

A bit later when I was finishing my bagel and coffee, Myron called me over to the counter. "There was one strange thing happened that morning. My regular bakery delivery guy came in bitchin' about a large gray van parked in our loading zone. Said it didn't belong there and he wouldn't be able to deliver my bakery 'til it was moved. I went out to tell the driver to move and as I did, he drove away. Problem solved. It was right after you left."

"Thanks Myron. You confirmed one thing."

"What's that?"

"The van was real. It's the last thing I can remember seeing for a week."

"C'mon. You're kidding."

"I'll tell you about what happened some day, but right now I've got to go to work."

"Pleasant memories." Myron said with a grin. He was good at sarcasm.

As I walked past the loading zone, another hazy memory flashed through my mind. I remembered seeing the back door to the van open as I approached. I tried desperately to remember more, but all I drew were blanks—nothing more.

"Marty's waiting in the lab," Manuel said in reply to my good morning without taking his eyes from his paper. Manuel was economical with words.

"It's about time you got here," Marty said.

The time was only five to seven, but Marty seemed to enjoy being earlier than I for these special jobs. This little game I played with him regularly.

"Oh, I thought we were to start at nine. I came in early to try to beat you, and lost again."

Marty displayed a Chessie cat grin. "You say the sweetest things."

Friendly jabs over, we went to work running the tests on our equipment. "With luck we'll be ready to go by the time of our meeting," Marty said.

"That is if we breeze by all these tests without a glitch," I said, sure we would experience at least one.

Everything went smoothly until we started the last electronic alignment test. "I can't believe those coils aren't aligned properly," Marty said in disgust as he handed me the alignment tool. "Put this on the east coil. I'll do the west one."

A quick check and I announced, "They're definitely out of physical alignment now. How could they change since we set them earlier? The physical and electronic alignments must be within tolerances or the system won't function at all."

"Maybe we didn't tighten them, but let's do it right this time. You use the mallet and I'll tighten the locks. Ready?"

"I'm ready. Here goes." A gentle tap or two with the mallet, a careful tightening of the locks and the physical alignment was complete. The electronic alignment was a bit more tricky. With a weak current flowing in the coils, the four test ammeters must indicate exactly the same current flowing at each point.

"The damned meter readings are way off, Drax—not even close. How'd that happen? We didn't move the secondaries."

"I'll readjust the primaries to bring the meters to the same readings. Then we'll reset the physical alignment and start over."

We wrestled with an uncooperative test system until it was obvious we were not going to succeed in time to start the run before the meeting.

Marty said with disappointment, "Let's give up for now. We can barely get to the conference room in time. We can return to this later."

*   *   *

We were the last ones to enter the conference room. The two cops were already there.

"We thought you guys forgot us," Jim said with a grin.

"How could we possibly forget our city's finest?" Marty replied, always the diplomat. "Anything new on Maria?"

"Nothing!" was Jim's immediate reply. "We're right where we ended up yesterday."

"Yeah! Nowhere!" Forrest said in disgust.

"I do possess some new information, not much, but it's something."

"Spit it out Drax!" commanded the lieutenant.

"I remembered having breakfast at the deli a week ago last Thursday. I also remembered seeing a large gray van parked outside the deli. Then my friend Myron, who runs the deli, told me about a similar van he was about to run out of his loading zone the same morning. The driver pulled out before he got to him. After he said that, I vaguely remember seeing the rear doors of the van open as I walked by."

Jim asked, "And?"

"That's it—all I can remember."

In a loud, agitated voice, Forrest asked, "How in hell is that going to help us find your Maria?"

"Did I hear my name?" came from the opening door as Maria walked in as if nothing happened. Her entrance blew us all away.

"Where the hell have you been?" came out of my mouth automatically. Similar exclamations from the others echoed my sentiments.

"I'll explain in a minute, but who are these two gentlemen?"

Introductions and a brief explanation brought Maria up to date.

Jim Corbett stood and handed Maria the surveillance photo of her and Leura. "While you're at it, would you please explain this to us?"

Without batting an eye, Maria answered, reacting coolly. "That's my friend Leura and I, as we walked out of my apartment building a few days ago, why?"

"We'd like to speak to your friend and find out what happened at her apartment."

"That would be difficult."

"Why?"

"I lack any idea where she is or how to contact her. Besides, you wouldn't believe me if I told you what happened or where I was."

Jim grimaced. "Gawd! Now we're back to weird stuff again. I've heard more bizarre stories involving the young lady, Leura, than I want to deal with. Go ahead, Maria, tell me some more that I won't believe."

Chapter 12 - Maria's Revelation

Maria glanced quickly at each of us in turn. "I know. I know. I must explain. First, what is this all about and why are the police involved?"

Marty answered. "Well, for starters, the police are here because of your disappearance and because another woman, your friend, Leura, disappeared under somewhat similar circumstances at about the same time. Add that to her apartment being wrecked and bloodied, and there are several overlapping mysteries. Now that you're okay and not abducted, their search for you is over. That leaves us wondering about Leura and how she ties in with all this other stuff. I think I can speak for Drax and the two officers in wanting you to tell us exactly what happened to you and how Leura fits in. For you to disappear is out of character."

The five of us sat around the conference table while Maria launched into her story.

❊   ❊   ❊

I had just sat down to breakfast Monday when the doorbell rang. "Who is it?" I asked through the intercom.

An obviously young woman with tension in her voice replied, "I must tell you something important, right away."

I never let unknown people in. I was apprehensive and told her, "I'll be down to meet you at the door." I'm on the second floor, so I didn't take long to go there.

I saw her clearly through the glass door as I walked into the foyer. She was an unusual appearing young woman, striking in fact, with long dark red hair. As I approached the door, I felt the most unusual and powerful sense of urgency.

"Please come with me. My name is Leura Clauson and I'm a friend of Draxel's. It is important to all of us that I speak with you," she said as I opened the door.

At her request, I accompanied her outside. We walked a few car lengths up the street to a large van parked at the curb. I was a bit concerned when she asked me to enter the back of the van. She sensed my concern.

49

"You don't need to go inside. I can show you what I want through the open back doors," she said as she stepped inside the van and began rearranging things inside.

I was soon viewing a computer display showing a surprising video of our test setup right before the second run was started. It also showed Marty adjusting the ammeter, so it could be seen from across the room. Feeling reassured there was no danger, I stepped into the van and took the seat Leura indicated.

I asked her, "How did you take that picture? There were no TV cameras in the room."

She launched into an explanation I soon interrupted saying, "I can understand a bit about remote video imaging, but the rest of your comments are way over my head."

"Suffice to say it's a real video of an actual happening," She said as we watched.

The video was taken at extremely high speed because she slowed it down as I watched what happened when Marty applied the power. At first there was a faint, disk-shaped bluish glow right between the two big coils mounted on the rack above the table. The disk brightened until the light obscured the screen and I could hardly see anything. Then, in an instant the brilliant light turned cold black. The stool popped out from beneath the timer and flew straight into the black disk along with a bunch of papers and a lot of dust. It looked more like a void than anything real, or like the business end of a large vacuum cleaner the way all that stuff was sucked into it. Then the blackness disappeared, the table slowly fell apart, and the entire apparatus gradually collapsed on top of the remains of the table. The power went off because everything went black for a few seconds. All of this happened quickly, leaving papers and dust swirling slowly around the apparatus after the lights came back on.

After the video ended, I looked around in the van. There was stuff in there *like I never saw before*, lots of electronic equipment and several things that looked like LP gas tanks. Under the tanks and secured to the left side wall was a small motorcycle, a dirt bike. Mounted on the right inside of the van was a large circular apparatus at least seven feet in diameter. It looked like a large, thin donut made out of shiny metal. Though I'm educated in the sciences, I was hired by Eegis for my administrative skills and training. I had no idea what any of the stuff in the van was.

Noticing my looks of curiosity, Leura smiled, "All that electronic equipment is needed to operate our portal. It's the ring there on the wall. I'll show you how it works when we are at a safe place to operate it."

"What do you mean?" I asked, apprehensive once more.

Leura sensed my fear. "Please don't worry. I will explain everything and won't do anything without your permission. That's one of our basic laws of contact."

"Laws of contact?"

"I must tell you a lot—if you'll permit me. I'd like you to go with me out to a remote place in the desert near Palm Springs. We will be where we can operate the portal in about two hours. I'll explain things as we go." She was reassuring and persuasive.

"What the hell—nothing ventured, nothing gained," I said as I stepped forward and dropped into the passenger seat. "Let's go!"

Leura grinned, patted me on the shoulder, and took her seat behind the wheel. "You'll be amazed," she said as she steered the truck away from the curb and headed down the street. "Be prepared for a big and pleasant surprise. In fact, there will be lots of pleasant surprises."

"So, what's all this about, all these *surprises*?"

"Maria, you were a bit nervous at first, but now you seem, well, confident and interested."

"I can hardly believe I'm heading out into the unknown with someone I've just met. I haven't a clue what this is all about, even after seeing your video. I don't understand what I saw, but I certainly am curious."

*   *   *

She told me a fascinating story about a parallel universe, and how our experiments posed a great danger to that universe, and to ours as well. She said those experiments could cause a self-propagating tear in the fabric of space/time through which our two universes would be pulled together and annihilated. I didn't understand much, but was frightened.

I blurted out, "My head is spinning, my brain is in power gear and making little headway. It may be more than this practical and orderly gal can handle. I'm beyond disbelief. A van filled with strange equipment, a beautiful driver from another universe, blue flashes, black voids, disappearing stools, split tables, and now strange parallel universes. All this oddball info is creating confusion in my mind. I'm a bit overwhelmed."

Forrest stood up angrily. "I'm not going to listen to any more of this nonsense. Let's leave here now, Jim."

Jim responded sternly. "Sit down, McNulty. Listen and keep your mouth shut. Try to open that closed mind of yours. Maybe you'll learn something."

Forrest glared at Jim, and sat down defiantly. He would remain an extreme skeptic. I continued my story after the interruption.

✻   ✻   ✻

Leura answered, "That's often how it seems in new and radically different circumstances. I felt the same way right after I went through the universe portal and first set foot in your universe. It was different—frightening in fact. I think it's often beyond any of us at first—extremely different situations I mean, so don't feel bad. My head too is sometimes sent spinning from new situations, particularly those beyond what we imagined. We must accept what our senses are telling us and try to find ways to understand how this all fits together."

"Much of this is beyond me—on the verge of being unbelievable. Still I can sense the seriousness of what you've been telling me. Let me say what I understand from your story thus far. Our first experiment some six months ago caused a tiny, short-lived *tear* in the dividing *fabric* separating our universe from yours. Sensors in your universe detected it and raised a red flag when the danger was assessed and you realized what could happen. Understanding the reason for the danger is beyond my current understanding, but the danger itself is not. Then you told me another tear in this *fabric* could become self propagating and grow large enough that our two universes would *fold* into each other. If it happened both universes would be annihilated."

"Actually, that's a good, basic understanding. You at least realize the scope of the danger and that you must stop experimenting for the present."

"Why didn't you explain this to the experimenters? Why go to the trouble of all this mysterious subterfuge?"

"At the time it wasn't so critical. We were going slow to comply with our rules of contact. Since then, drastic new developments brought about by your second experimental run changed the situation from mildly dangerous to drastically crucial."

"And why is that so?"

"It would be difficult to explain to people not from our culture who lacked our knowledge base. Our people hoped they would be able to offer training in the near future, training that would take some serious time. Then your experiments would continue safely."

"I think you underestimate our intellectual abilities," I said a bit ruffled. "As a matter of fact, I'm a bit ticked off at your attitude of superiority. Why couldn't you give us the information and let us deal with it? The more I think about it, the more it pisses me off. What do you know about us? I mean really? When and how did you reach us from that other universe? All you seem interested in is that we are threatening your existence—and ours as well. Wouldn't you be a bit concerned about providing us with a lot of new knowledge if our situations were reversed? I certainly would."

Leura laughed. "Don't be upset. We know a great deal about you, your world and your universe. We visited your universe and world for thousands of your years."

"I find that hard to believe," I said disdainfully. "If things are as you say, why haven't we ever had contact before? Surely there would be some kind of interaction we recorded."

Once again Leura laughed her friendly, musical laugh. "One of our rules of contact with another intelligent being or group of beings is we do not interfere in any way with our knowledge or technology. We can act only as observers."

"Why are you interfering now?" I asked, then added quickly. "Act as if I didn't ask such a ridiculous question. That should be obvious to even the feeblest of minds."

*　　　*　　　*

Jim interrupted Maria. "That's all interesting if it happened that way, but how does it tie in with the bloody apartment? That's all we are interested in."

"I'm sorry. I forgot why you two are here. I haven't a clue how Leura ties in. She never mentioned an apartment or any kind of conflict or crime."

Jim stood up. "Maria, I think your story does not concern us. Since you are okay and there doesn't seem any crime was committed, I think we'd better return to police work. Also, we're unable to find any connection between your friend, Leura, from your wild tale and the bloody apartment. If anything comes up that may concern us, please tell us about it."

Chapter 13 - Maria Tells of Her Trip

After we drove and talked for about an hour she asked, "Would you go on a trip with me? It's a long trip in distance, but a quick one in time."

"And where would we be going?"

"To the Vegan star system."

I gulped because from my amateur astronomy I knew where Vega was. "That **is** a long distance."

"Would it blow your mind to find out we can travel there in a few seconds?"

"At this point in time I don't think anything would blow my mind and I happen to know a little about the Star Vega. It is a type A0 star 25.3 light years from us, has three times the diameter of the sun, has twelve times the mass and shines 50 times as bright as our sun."

"I'm impressed. How did you happen to know that?"

"I'm an amateur astronomer and our astronomy class recently spent time studying about Vega."

"Well lady, in less than an hour we'll be there, in the Vegan star system. Vega has a habitable planet about five and a half AU away from the star. The planet's orbital period is approximately ten of your years, and it rotates once every 25.6 hours making 3,424 rotations or "days" in one orbit. We divide each orbital period into ten periods that are almost exactly the same length of time as your year so we call these periods, years. Vega 5 is a tiny bit larger than your earth. We built a portal base there, our universe portal to this part of your universe."

"A **universe** portal?"

Leura smiled as she drove. "We use two kinds of portals. The one we will be using is a normal portal and can be powered by even a truck engine as you will see. This type of portal only works within a universe and has range limited by the power available to run it. A **universe** portal on the other hand is a much more sophisticated apparatus requiring immense amounts of power and can transport between universes. It also requires an isolation building to prevent contamination of any kind between universes. Both the base and portal on Vega five were in operation for more than five thousand of your years."

"My God, that's before the pyramids. It's difficult to accept."

Leura slowed down. "I'm looking for a road, actually, it's not much more than a path, to take us out into the desert away from prying eyes. It should be right about here."

After driving slowly for about a quarter of a mile she spied the road. "We're headed for the other side of the hill over there," she said pointing. "There we'll be out of sight of anyone except a desert wanderer and there are few of them."

"Why?"

"What do you think would happen if someone reported a truck glowing blue and then disappearing?"

"People would think they were crazy."

"Maybe so, but we can't take the chance. You'll see."

By the time we reached our destination half an hour later the *path* had virtually disappeared. We were driving across the desert. Now I understood why the truck had those huge wide tires. Leura positioned the truck level and facing due north. Then she went into the back with me following.

"Now I will run a scan to learn if there are any life forms within sight. If any of them show a human signature, we won't be able to use the portal. That's a rule." She turned on what looked like a radar screen and soon there were tiny yellow, green and blue dots showing, some of them were moving.

"The scan is set for fifty miles and shows all life forms bigger than a house cat. The yellow dots are small animals, probably jack rabbits. The green dots are larger animals and the blue dots are humans. Any man made objects show up as purple, a camera for instance, or a plane, or a car. The row of purple and blue dots moving in a line is of course the highway we were on. The purple dot with the blue number 128 is a commercial airliner with 128 people aboard. If any of those blue dots representing humans would be in sight range within fifteen minutes, the dot would be red and we couldn't use the portal. If any of the purple dots represented man-made objects moved or changed mass signatures since the last scan, they would show as red dots until I identified them."

"Wow! What are those two red and blue dots over by the highway and why are they red?"

Leura punched in a few commands on the keyboard and the red changed to purple. "Those are two vehicles that pulled off the road. I entered a command that analyzed their mass signature and identified them."

"What happens if you do that and the object is not identified?"

"Then I hop onto the dirt bike and check it out."

"Any problems with people out there?"

"One time I found a guy with a camera about three miles away. I knew he had a camera from its mass signature. I took a bike ride out and found a naturalist taking wildlife photos. He was beyond a low rise and couldn't see the truck, so there was no problem. I had to be sure."

Leaving the scanner operating she turned and picked up a small device resembling a cell phone and pressed a few icons. "This little gadget will turn on the portal and control where we go. Be prepared for a surprise."

The truck engine labored for a minute or two and the ring began to glow with blue light. The light grew brighter and brighter until I could hardly bear to look directly at it. Then the light vanished. What had been the solid side of the truck was now an opening into a large room.

Leura grabbed my arm and helped me through the opening and out into the room. "Welcome to Vega Five."

I turned around and there was the truck sitting on the floor of the room and with a round opening in the side. I was flabbergasted.

Leura explained the obvious. "The side of the truck is the portal through which we, the truck, and the portal itself could move instantly to many parts of this universe. We are now on the planet Vega Five. We must hurry as there is another trip to make."

We walked across the room to a large doorway that opened into a domed enclosure where eight or ten squat, bus sized objects stood on fat legs. A short stairway led from the ground into each of these craft. She led me to one of them and we walked up five steps and took seats together on one side of the craft.

When we sat, Leura commented, "We got here in time. This shuttle will soon be leaving and the next one doesn't leave until four hours later."

There were ten rows of eight seats served by two aisles. Most seats were filled. The occupants were both male and female and with earth-like clothes. There were twice as many females as males. I realized they all appeared a bit different, like the subtle differences in appearance between Leura and me. Suddenly, a musical sound repeated several times, the steps folded up into the craft, the door closed with a swish and a hum and vibration began. The hum increased in pitch and intensity and the craft slowly lifted off.

"That's the shuttle's lift off engines," Leura informed me. "We're on our way. The hum will cease once we clear the atmosphere and the main drive engines take over. We will take about two hours to reach our destination."

I was curious about this unusual woman. "I've heard about enough of the technical stuff. What I'd like to learn is more about you and your culture. Things of a personal nature must be different in your universe. Tell me about you and your family."

Leura laughed that musical laugh. "Actually, other than a few major differences, a Scentar's family life is much like yours."

"Oh? I find that hard to believe."

"One difference is the ratio of males to females. You probably realized there are about twice as many females as males. That's because our births are different. Each female birth is a set of identical twins, while male twins are extremely rare."

"That's a major difference."

"We call our twin our Maia and with her we possess a powerful emotional connection. We are as you might say, extremely close. We do not use what you call mental telepathy, but we are able to communicate some things without words. It's hard to describe and just happens."

"Wow! That is different."

"Occasionally identical triplets are born, again, female. These are called laia, and possess the same close ties as maia but with three identical females."

"I can imagine some real difficulties with male/female relationships. How do those work out?"

"Our social, moral, ethical, and legal male/female relationship standards are different from humans. We use no such thing as your marriage. Most Scentar experience a number of sexual/romantic relationships during their lifetime although many maintain a single, personal relationship. There is no stigma to either path. In nearly every case, a female's maia will become involved with the same male. If and when a female becomes pregnant, she, her maia, or laia as the case may be, will *bond* with the father into a permanent family unit for the purpose of rearing the child or children. In about half of these bondings, the maia will become pregnant as well, usually within a month or two after the first pregnancy. Accidental pregnancies are rare. The average bonded Scentar family has three children."

"That is **quite** different from humans."

"Other than our sharing of the male, our family life and child rearing are much like yours. We experience problems of course, but a lot less than most humans. Our families are less likely to break up—much less."

"I guess you can't argue with success, but all of that would be a big cultural shock to most humans," Maria said.

"Look around when we land. Few families made the move to this outpost, but there are some. Meet them and find out what you think of Scentar family life."

Maria paused to let her story sink in.

Chapter 14 - Drax Comes to Grips with Reality

I realized what was happening and no longer had any doubts about Maria's words. "Maria, would you like me to say where you were headed?"

Marty was startled, first glancing at Maria, then at me. "Drax, this sounds a lot like the story you told me about your dream. Can you now doubt what happened?"

Now Maria seemed befuddled. "What do you mean by that, Drax?"

"You were headed to Stentor Seven, weren't you?"

Maria grinned and replied, "You believe me because you made the same trip. Leura told me about it."

I started becoming concerned. "What all **did** she tell you?"

"Only that after you had received training and indoctrination, she was supposed to make sure you returned to earth with no memory of being gone. Then she nearly blew the whole thing by falling for you. She explained that Scentar are emotional and form strong emotional bonds quickly—and permanently, I might add. You surely did mess up her life. She did not provide the gory details." Maria grinned as she added those last words.

"What did you think of Stentor Seven?" I asked, trying to change the subject and nail down what had happened to me there.

"I only received a six-hour tour, but that's quite a place. Did you know the base is their final training and inoculation base in our universe, their only one?"

I was flabbergasted. "You said it was their training and inoculation base. What do you mean?"

"That's all Leura told me that I understood. She talked about *jump* distance limitations for their portals, the rapid evolution of micro biota in both universes and the great danger that poses for most large creatures. I understood most of it, but when she started on folding dimensions of space and universes annihilating each other in a dimensional collapse, she lost me, and scared hell out of me at the same time."

"Did she say anything specific about their portals?" Marty asked.

"Only that they were related to the experiments the Eegis gravity team was conducting, but were precisely configured so they would be safe. She was concerned those Eegis experiments had *wide ranging effects*, as she put it, and the lack of precise controls made them dangerous."

"Why didn't she come to us and tell us this? We're not stupid. We would understand." I was getting a bit angry once more.

Maria shook her head. "Their civilization is much older and more developed than ours. She explained their laws against interfering with more primitive civilizations. These laws define clearly what can and can't be done or revealed. Only after the second experiment did they considered the threat level high enough that some of those laws would not apply."

"Why did she tell you and not one of us?" Marty asked.

"That's easy. I'm the head administrator. First they decided to track Drax since he sets up all of the equipment for the experiments and they wanted to follow where he was at all times. They considered giving him information, so the next run would not be so dangerous. After they analyzed the results of the second run, they decided to contact me and stop all experiments until they find a practical and legal solution. I do possess the power, to stop the experiments."

"What do we do now?" I asked.

"We wait," Maria said firmly.

"Wait for what?"

"Leura said she would contact me when they decided what to do. They are still working on repairing the damage done by the second run. There was quite a bit of contaminated material that slipped through into their universe from ours when we created that temporary uncontrolled rift or *wild portal* as she called it. They simply cannot take the risk of alien biota becoming established in their universe. It happened once before a long time ago and millions of them died before they got it under control. Since then, they used strict protocols about universe portals."

"So, what else did you learn? I mean, virtually anything would be new information. What did you see there? What about your trip back? How did you get here?" My mind reeled with questions.

"Leura told me the Scentar on Vega Five and Stentor Seven are all dedicated people. They are trained for years before they make the journey from their universe to ours. It's sad, but they can never return to their universe. Reversing the adaptation process they go through, so they can survive in our universe, is more dangerous than the original process itself. As a result, they can never go back."

"Never?"

"Never! So joining their New Universe Service is a lifetime commitment. They can never live a normal life—never even return to their families. Once they enter our universe, they are kept isolated from our bugs while their DNA is rebuilt to cope with them. This is the adaptation process I mentioned. This process takes about ten months, and during this period some of them die of infections. Their biological complex on Vega Five is a complete isolation and treatment system. They use special viruses to reorganize the DNA in every cell in their bodies, even mitochondrial DNA."

Marty was incredulous. "Wow! That's mind boggling. They change their DNA, so antibodies are made to fight off our diseases. That's some biological technology."

"Yes, but it's not as you said. As I understand her, they change the DNA, so the cells themselves possess the ability to adapt to our alien bacterial and viral attacks and create their own natural antibodies, like our bodies do. The DNA change takes place in a few weeks. The longest part of the adaptation process takes place after the DNA change when they are transferred to the inoculation center on Stentor Seven. It's the inoculation for so many dangerous critters that takes so long. They even need protection against many infectious agents that are relatively harmless to humans. There are some in each group who die because their bodies don't adapt quickly enough. Like us, they can still become infected from critters that mutate and bypass their antibodies."

I was beginning to understand some of Leura's sadness about her mother. "But couldn't they reverse the process and be able to return to their universe?"

"Leura explained the risks of such a procedure were too dangerous to take. These risks include danger to the individual's health as well as possible contamination of their universe. She said her words were a simplification of the reality, but fairly accurate."

"That's sad," I said. "Cutting yourself off permanently from all the people you love. I doubt many of us would make such a sacrifice."

Maria replied, "I think you might be surprised at how many of us would jump at such a chance. The adventure, the excitement of new worlds, the unknown, that all could sound inviting to many young people. You of all people, Drax, should understand that. You like to push the envelope—well don't you?"

"Yeah, but I have no family. My parents died when I was young, so I have no siblings or even cousins. The foster parents who raised me were no great shakes. They did so for the money. I guess that's why I'm so against forming any kind of attachments. I'm free to take whatever risks I want without fear of hurting anyone."

"What about friends? Certainly at the university and among us here at Eegis. I'll wager you have some elsewhere as well."

"A few professional colleagues. I meet with them and talk with them, but they're acquaintances, not really friends."

Maria had a strange mischievous grin as she said, "What about Victor Bump and his family?"

I was shocked. "How in the hell do you know about Victor Bump? He's from a part of my private life no one here could possibly hear about."

With a know-it-all grin on her face and an impish sound to her voice, Maria replied, "I learned a great deal about the private Dr. Syl from our friend Leura. She has an unbelievable dossier on you. It goes back to your school days, and I mean grade school. Those records include details of all of your movements after she pinned the feather on your coat."

"Damn! I don't like that. You were quite nosey to look through that dossier. What else did you learn? and what about the feather?"

"Let me back up a bit, and give you the whole picture," Maria pleaded. "It's not at all what you might think, but I did learn things about you even you can't remember."

I was beginning to steam. "And what the hell might that be?"

"How about the week you lost a few days ago. Would you like to know where you were and what you did and why you can't remember it?"

"How in the hell would you know that? Maria, you'd better explain yourself before I am pissed off."

Maria curled her lip with disdain. "Keep your wounded little boy temper in check will you? You should try not to act like a pre teen. This is serious business. She has a similar dossier on virtually everyone here at Eegis including yours truly. Here's what I learned about your missing week.

"Your dear little Leura was waiting in her van as you left the deli after breakfast. As you went past, she opened the back doors, called you by name, and invited you into the back of the van. You took one look at that gorgeous redhead and followed her like a puppy dog. Those are my words, not hers. She was much more gracious. Once inside the van, she showed you a video of your experiment setup with you in it. You were so dazzled by that video and by her charms you jumped at the chance for adventure, and headed out into the desert with her, abandoning your other plans."

Marty stared at me wide eyed. "Is this true? Did you abandon your plans to meet with Crazy Charley and go off with this woman?"

"How in hell would I know? I don't remember. Though it is something I might do considering the circumstances."

"Don't worry, Marty. He's being honest with you. They did a hypnotic memory block on him from the time he started past the van until the morning he woke up in Cleveland. Thanks to the soft heart of one young lady there was one part of his memory that was not blocked. That part was intended as a test to learn if the new information and hypnotically implanted memories worked. They worked like a charm."

I was pissed. "Yeah! That little bitch used me in some sort of experiment. I was a guinea pig to her, a Goddamned guinea pig."

Maria bristled and raised her voice. "You've got it all wrong, Drax. Your memory will all return slowly over several months. Then the whole story will reveal itself. The little lady is in love with you. That's why she didn't block out the one experience, so you would remember her. She's one of the most decent people I ever met. A real angel."

I remained adamant. "Fortunately, I didn't fall into her trap, close, but no cigar. I kept no feelings for her whatever. She's simply another bimbo who uses men for her own purpose as far as I'm concerned."

"If that's what you think this conversation is over. You gentlemen can figure out this situation without me—if you can."

At this point, Marty stood up and said, "Will you two please shut up, simmer down and quit shouting at each other? Grow up and quit this petty schoolyard bickering. We've important work to do, maybe the most important in human history. You two are letting petty, personal opinions interfere with making serious decisions with far reaching consequences."

I was still steamed. Maria had fire in her eyes. Lots of effort would be required to calm either of us down. I was so pissed at being used by that little bitch.

Marty continued sternly, "Here are my new rules for you two until you are civil again. You will address all comments to me in first person and without reference to anyone else. I don't want a single word to pass between you two without my expressed permission. and if you continue to glare at each other I will erect a screen between you, so you cannot see even a part of each other. The first one to break my rules is fired—immediately. Maria, you may be chief administrator with a lot of power, but this is still my organization and I could fire you. Such a thing would damage your reputation in the scientific community with all it might mean to your future, so sit down and shut up. Drax, the same goes for you. Do you understand?"

After hearing two yeses, Marty continued. "Maria, I would like to hear your full story which was so rudely and unnecessarily interrupted. Drax, I will record Maria's remarks and provide them to you when you calm down. Until that story is finished, you are excused. Don't stand outside to try to hear what is being said. That's an order!"

Once more I was furious, but I had no recourse, so I sulked off to my office.

Chapter 15 - Maria Completes Her Story

This is the rest of Maria's story as recorded . . .

"I think I should explain something about all Scentar. They are incapable of lying. True, they can hide their thoughts and refuse to answer a question, but if they do answer you can bank on it being the truth. This took a bit of getting used to for me, but I'm sure it's true."

Marty interrupted, "Aren't you being a bit naive? To believe such a thing, I mean. I assume she told you."

"Actually, Marty, she did explain it to me, but not until after I had figured it out on my own. There were many things she said that brought me to ask her. She never volunteered the information. She definitely understands about human duplicity as well and has been trained not to accept what humans say without confirmation."

"Wow! They certainly are ahead of us on that."

"You got that right. Anyway, they spent five days brainwashing—that's my term—Drax with information about the planet Stentor Seven. They also indoctrinated him with a background as a gravity propulsion engineer. They made the planet seem to him like a favorite, old familiar haunt. He did all the things he talked about experiencing in his dream, skin diving, sailing, surfing—everything. Those were real memories. Only his personal history, his job as a gravity propulsion engineer was fake. I did many of those same things. Leura explained to me real memories will last a lifetime while implanted ones will fade fairly quickly. His memory block will fade over a few months.

"Then Leura confessed to me that on the last day she seduced him, because she was and is in love with him. She told me that she started to fall while reading his dossier. Our Dr. Syl turns out to be an honest and forthright person. At least that's what came through from his dossier. He's done some kind and generous things for friends and acquaintances, even strangers, people in need. I never knew that, but I know it now."

"In spite of how he blew up at you? and at Leura?"

"His ancient male ego fired up by testosterone is the cause. He'll get over it."

"I'm not so sure. My guess is Drax is stirred up by deceit, and he's convinced himself he was deceived. I doubt that will go away easily."

"Well, he damned well better get over it, or they'll both miss out on what could be a special relationship. I think so in spite of my temper tantrum. I lost it because he's so damned blind. He might throw away a fantastic relationship because of a little ego glitch. Stupid! I hate stupidity."

"You didn't help any."

"No, and I'm genuinely sorry I blew up. Now I wish I knew how to patch things up."

"That will take some doing, I'm afraid. Now, let's return to your story."

"Okay! After she had seduced him—she did not provide the details and I didn't ask—she took him out with a sort of sleep-inducing, hypnotic device. He was sound asleep anyway. She woke him up enough to dress him and put him onto the shuttle back to Vega Five. Then she used the portal to move them and the van to near Cleveland. She drove to the hotel where he had a reservation, checked him in using his credit card, and put him to bed. Then she used their hypnotic memory block for the time from the hotel on Stentor Seven to when she put him to bed. She assures me he will regain all his lost memories within the next few months, a bit at a time. He will also remember the things they placed in his memory as if they really happened. This may prove confusing to him on occasion, but rarely so. You might check with the hotel. I'm sure that check-in is recorded on their security cameras. Oh yes. She wore a disguise all the time she was with him at the hotel, so security tapes wouldn't catch her face."

"Then how come she was on that security tape with you. She wore no disguise then."

"That's easy. Once the second run was made and created a near catastrophe, secrecy was pushed onto the back burner. Their first priority was to stop the tests, at virtually any costs. She was unaware the situation had changed until after she dropped Drax at his hotel."

"I can't believe all of this is cleared up by your explanation. What a relief if we are willing to accept all you've explained.

"Marty, it's not that simple. There are a few other problems Leura learned about on the day I went with her. Problems that might be even more serious than the dangers our experiments posed."

"Another unknown problem? That's all we need. and what might that be?"

"She did not explain the problem. Said she would need to learn more about the extent of the danger before she could tell us. She emphasized we must believe her when she said it was serious. I for one believe what she said. and there's one more thing I hesitate to tell Drax."

"Oh? What's that?"

"The last thing she did after putting him to bed in his hotel room was to inject an ID tag into his butt, so they would be able to track him."

"I think we'll keep this between us for the time being. No need to do anything else to raise his ire."

"You got that right!"

"So what do we do now? Hell, I've got a major research project to run here. I can't shut down everything because of some possible unknown danger."

"Leura said she would be back to me within the day. My guess is we'll hear from her sometime this afternoon. If we're through here, Marty, I'd like to go back to my desk and see what catastrophes happened in my absence. That okay with you?"

"Good idea! I think I'll go take a stab at warming up Dr. Syl. I can't believe how angry he was. I've never seen him like that. He's usually so even-tempered and unflappable."

"I believe Dr. Syl experienced the emasculation of his personal control and manhood by a little wisp of a girl. That injured his male ego tremendously. I doubt you will be able to reason with him for some time. I believe cold, irresistible, brute force will be the only way the facts will ever persuade him. Good luck!"

Chapter 16 - Drax meets Segwah Captain Woolgah

As I walked toward my office, I tried to calm myself. My anger was a raging bull charging willy-nilly through my mind. Thoughts of angry actions, scenarios of vengeance, plots of revenge, all coursed through my head. There was no room for rational thought as those primal juices drove out all reason. Leura was the enemy and Maria her confederate. I stormed into my office and plopped down at my desk without a single thought about what I was doing.

A knock on my office door snapped my mind back into the immediate present. The hairs on the back of my neck stood up. No one *ever* knocks on my office door. My "Who's there?" was greeted by two burly men bursting in my door.

"Draxel Syl?" One of them asked.

"Yes, I'm Syl."

"You will come with us."

My "Not until you tell me what this is about," was no sooner uttered than they grabbed my arms, picked me up and headed for the door, my feet dragging on the floor. They were exceptionally strong. The thought *Neanderthals* went through my mind as they were shorter than I but much heavier and more muscled. They both had lots of coarse, dark facial hair. While one of them held me securely, the other peeked out the door then motioned for his companion to follow. A quick trip down the hall and into the elevator was followed by a descent into the basement. Once in the basement I was hustled to the back of the long-term storage room. We stopped near a large circular object, a metallic donut of about six feet in diameter attached to a square metal cabinet the same height as the ring and about four feet wide by four feet deep.

The one not holding me pulled out a control of some sort and began pressing a few buttons. Slowly the ring began glowing blue and getting brighter and brighter. When the blue light went out, I could see through the ring into another room with chairs and a table where another one of them sat, waiting. I was unceremoniously carried through the ring and dropped down in one of the chairs. When I turned, the ring and control box were sitting on the floor in the room.

"Dr. Syl. Welcome to the realm of the Segwah! I am Captain Woolgah of the star ship Gelwah. I'm sure you realize to oppose us or try to escape would be foolish, so consider yourself as our guest, as you might put it."

The captain was a bit taller than the others but equally burly. His facial hair was reddish brown and not unkempt. He was obviously the one in command. When he sat down across from me, my two abductors went out through a door on my left.

"I would not use the term, *guest*. *Prisoner* is a more accurate designation. Why am I here and what do you plan to do with me?"

"Do not be concerned. You will not be harmed as long as you cooperate with me."

"In other words, as long as I am useful to you, I won't be killed."

"You understand the realities of your situation. That's good for us both. Now let's discuss what I want you to do."

"And if I refuse?"

"Your refusal is highly unlikely. We do not use the supposedly *civil* limitations of our enemies the Scentar. We do not use their brain altering techniques on helpless humans as they do. Let me add, we possess no animosity toward humans. You gave us no reason, so we are happy, as you say, *to live and let live*."

"That's no comfort. So who must I kill or betray to take myself off the hook?"

"Now Dr. Syl, please do hold your sarcasm until we can tell you what we want."

"Well, it has to be something I know that you don't, or something I can do that you can't. There are not many options. My bet is that once you have what you want, I'll become so much dead meat."

"You've no basis for such a belief."

"Just good old human instincts and experience. That's good enough for me. I grew up with a whole bunch of apes like you. If I survived them, I can understand and survive you."

"My but we hold some anger issues from the past. That's good information and can be used to control you should it become necessary.

"I wanted you to know, so you don't miscalculate. One slip could be a mistake I wouldn't want you to make, and might be costly for me."

"You are an unusual human, Dr. Syl. I judge you a worthy adversary in any conflict other than physical. As you can see, we hold a two for one strength advantage over you, so physical combat would not be fair."

"I don't think being fair is high on your list of priorities."

"Sadly for you, that is true. Enough of this mental jousting contest. Let us return to business—why you are here—what we want, as you so vividly described.

"We, the Segwah, are at war with the Scentar. The war started when they invaded our universe about six thousand of your years ago. As warriors, we fought valiantly against them and their determination to destroy our culture. Their technical superiority, their portals in particular, gave them an enormous advantage. But for some among them who sympathized with our plight, we surely would be wiped out by now. These *friendly* Scentar arranged for us to obtain a hundred portals such as the one that brought you here plus two universe portals. With these portals, we were able to pursue and fight the Scentar on a more equal basis and the tide turned. Within a thousand of your years, they were mostly driven out of our universe. At this point, we took the war to them using the two universe portals to conduct surprise raids in what you would call a *hit-and-run* manner."

"What about contamination with micro biota between your two universes. Wasn't that a constant danger during your incursions?"

"Aha! That is only a problem between you and the Scentar. Our chemistry is such that we are immune to both your micro biota and that of the Scentar. They do not grow in our bodies nor does ours grow in theirs. Our genetic researchers tell us Humans and Segwah are close genetically and use similar micro biota. For this reason, neither poses a significant threat to the other. We came to your universe accidentally and established a colony of about twelve thousand Segwah shortly after we obtained the universe portals. This colony was on your planet. Unfortunately, once we withdrew the portal, we could never establish portal contact again, so our colony was lost. We lost track of what happened to them. Universes and locations within any universe express unique signatures. These must be provided for the portal to operate. We never had the signature of your universe because our first contact was purely an accident. That is why we couldn't come back once the portal was withdrawn. Our people did not understand this at that time."

"I may know what happened to your lost colony."

"Very interesting! I will want to pursue that later, but for the moment I must continue the explanation. For thousands of your years, the war between us flared up occasionally.

We would invade them, and they would retaliate. Then, a few months ago, your experiments caused a rift that triggered our universe portals and gave us the signature of your universe. Now we have your address, so to speak, and here we are."

"And what does that portend for the future of humans? And, by the way, how did you learn our language so quickly?"

"We do not covet any part of your universe. First of all, your universe has few habitable planets compared to ours by a factor of at least a few hundred. Our universe contains less than half the habitable planets that are in the Scentar universe. So you see, there is no real incentive for us to expend much effort here in yours. In fact, our laws are strict about interfering in the affairs of less developed cultures and societies. The language thing is a technology we learned from the Scentar. It's a mental imprint process. They had information on your languages in the data we received along with the imprint technology. Like the Scentar, we can gain the knowledge and use of any language in a few hours once the data is available to us."

"This is all leading up to something you want from me, so what is it?"

"You are right, of course. I will admit there is an object in your universe we do covet, an object that would provide us with a greater ability to defend ourselves from the Scentar. Possession of this by Segwah would enable us to fight the Scentar on a closer to equal footing. The portal alone could tip the balance, so we would no longer be subject to their dominance in our own universe."

"And what might that object be and why am I the only one who can help you? And, by the way, precisely where am I at this moment?"

"The object I speak of is the Scentar base on Vega Five. Possession of that base would be of immense value to Segwah. If you help us accomplish that, your reward would be beyond your imagination. We see you as the most likely one capable of doing so at the moment."

"And why would you believe that?"

"We recently attacked a Scentar operation in your city and held it long enough to copy some of their digital records to our central database here. Those records describe you, your position in your research facility, and your contact with the Scentar, Leura. From this information, we determined how you could deliver control of their base to us. Unfortunately, the brave Segwah who conducted the raid were killed by Scentar, who also lost at least two of their members. Fortunately, our brave fighters held out until after they had sent the data here. The data also contained information about your building. This information enabled us to capture you without being seen."

'Where's here?"

"You are our guests in the Segwah star ship Gelwah under my command. We are near the edge of your solar system."

I did some quick calculations. I was certain the Scentar would be able to scan space for a considerable distance and find any ship not well hidden. "How do you escape detection by their sensors? Surely they must be able to find you."

The Segwah captain laughed. "An astute observation. You are indeed much more intelligent than I at first supposed. Let's say we are hidden like a *needle-in-a-haystack*, to use one of your colloquial expressions—difficult to find."

I took his cue and decided we were in the Oort cloud near to or maybe even attached to one of the many large planetesimals in that sphere of objects surrounding the solar system. Such a ship would be virtually impossible to find. A *needle-in-a-haystack* indeed. I was not about to tell him I knew.

"You're probably hiding behind one of the planetary moons in our system. Maybe Phobos or Deimos."

"Very good, but a bit off I must admit. I promise to tell you when our business is finished, and now let's return to that business. Our time is limited."

Chapter 17 - Drax Gets Orders for a Segwah Mission

Itook quick mental stock of what I knew. I assumed they decided they couldn't take over the installation by direct attack. They would use trickery to go inside, possibly with help from someone already inside. Their flagship might be hiding in the Oort cloud a great distance away from Earth. They are certain to use a portal in the ship capable of letting *it jump* anywhere in the universe. and they are under time pressure for whatever reason. I had to stall for time and find a way to learn more about the ship, its armaments and how many were aboard. He obviously had an enormous ego, so I planned to play on that.

"Are those two goons your crew? I mean, you must keep at least a few others aboard."

"The Gelwah has a complement of more than three hundred and sixty including ground troops and is not a small ship as you might think. I served as captain for twenty of your years, a relatively long time for a Segwah captain of a star ship."

"How long have you been in our universe?"

"A short time. I think that's all the information I will provide. Now you will learn how you are going to help us and why any deviation from our instructions will be dangerous. From the data we received, we know you will be going to Vega Five with Leura and your friend Maria soon. That's why we must take you back before anyone discovers you are missing. You will accompany them to Vega Five where you will place this little homing device on the floor against the outside wall in their portal building. I suggest you remove yourself as quickly as you can from the vicinity of the device. We'll then finish our mission."

The homing device was an American dollar coin. "Very clever. Then what will happen?"

"Inside the building their protection is useless. There are but a few armed guards around the perimeter. For protection, they rely solely on barriers and weapons outside the building. From inside our thirty-five man force can secure the building in a few minutes. By the time they learn what's going on, all their defenses will be manned by

Segwah and turned against them. We will be impregnable. We will not let anyone in, especially with a homing resonator beacon for portals," he added with a broad grin.

"And what makes you think I won't sound an alarm?"

In his fingers he held out a tiny cylinder, not much bigger than a toothpick. "This little device will let us hear everything you hear and say. It will be implanted beneath the skin behind your ear. Should we hear anything in the way of an alarm, anything suspicious, I press this little button and, POP! You are out of it, gone. Crude, but effective don't you think. We'll be watching and listening from nearby. Any questions?"

"What if I make a mistake?"

"You will not make any mistakes."

"But if I do?"

"Any mistake will be your last."

"What if I don't believe you possess the capabilities to pull this off, that you're going to blow me apart inside their compound to make problems between Humans and Scentar. Why should I believe anything at all you've told me? You offer no proof."

"Aha, Dr. Syl. You are a skeptic."

"You're damned right I'm a skeptic. I'm a scientific researcher. I need understandable proof." I couldn't imagine anyone with such an ego would miss the opportunity to show off his pride and joy.

He arose and extended his arm toward the door. "I believe we can take a quick tour of my ship. This way."

We entered a dark corridor, walked straight for about twenty meters and then turned a sharp right. There were windows on the left and a solid wall on the right. There were no hand rails. Out the windows were a large number of stars with one bright one down and to the left.

"The bright star is your sun. We are far from your planet, which cannot be seen with the naked eye. Off to our right if you look carefully, you will see a small natural object which is gravitationally bound to a much larger object on the other side of the ship."

I had been correct. We were in the Oort cloud shielded from sensors by a much larger planetesimal. This was a standard and clever military maneuver. What amazes me is combat maneuvers used in the days of sailing ships, still work with modern, star ships.

"How big is your ship?"

"The Gelwah is about two hundred of your meters long and fifty wide at its widest part. It's main engines are used only to power the main portal. With this portal, we are able to move virtually anywhere within a universe and also between universes. This is one of the two universe portals we received from the Scentar."

"Then this is a Scentar ship? I mean, they built it?"

"No, the ship was built in our shipyards. The portals are from the Scentar and were built into the ship during construction. This is the thirty-fifth ship these particular portals were part of. Regrettably we never learned how to build portals though we tried many times. Portals do not lend themselves to reverse engineering. Though we took a few of them apart, and destroyed their usefulness in the process, we never learned how to put them back together, let alone build new ones. Of course, the Scentar are not about to show us how. That's why it is so important for us to capture their base on Vega Five. Such a coup would give us another universe portal as well as five basic ones, and provide us a greater defensive capability."

"And also a greater offensive capability."

"Your background is military? This was not mentioned in our data about you."

"I served in the US Navy for five years. I was on an aircraft carrier."

"Oh yes, one of those little waterborne surface ships, one that launches aircraft. It's rather primitive, but useful on your world."

"It's twice the size of this tub."

"Ah, but it can't travel in space or between universes and could be destroyed by a single blast from our smallest impact weapons."

"I doubt that." Hopefully I could egg him on to show me his weapons.

"Oh? When we reach the fire control center, I will show you what we can do."

As we walked forward toward fire control, I smiled to my self. My ruse was working perfectly. He may be a Segwah, but his ego was humanlike.

"Notice the object off to the left?"

"What about it?"

"It is about a kilometer in diameter."

"What is it made of."

"It is a loose agglomeration of ice and a few pieces of rock,. typical of these bodies, not a solid."

"How far away is it?"

"About sixty kilometers. When we reach fire control, I will fire a small blast from our forward impact guns to demonstrate. These are mostly anti-personnel weapons used in support of ground forces."

"You use a ship like this in support of ground troops? Isn't that a bit of overkill?"

"We rarely use impact weapons, but they are light and take up little space. Also, they are capable of being dismounted and used by ground troops. Ah, here we are."

He called a few commands into the intercom then turned to me. "Look."

There was a minor vibration from forward in the ship. The entire top portion of the object exploded in a shower of white and some fiery sparks.

"Now lets see what a disrupter will do."

"What's a disrupter?"

"Excuse me, I forget. A disrupter is a high energy weapon that dissolves molecular bonds and reverts compounds to basic elements. Some of those elements recombine instantly releasing that bond energy as heat, and the whole object explodes into molecule sized particles. You'll see."

A few more commands to fire control were followed by a soundless thud, felt rather than heard. At the same time, the remains of the object expanded quickly to at least twenty times its size like a white cloud. The cloud then dissolved slowly, and the object was gone.

"As you can see, molecular particles are invisible once they cool."

"What would be the result if the object was another star ship like this one?"

"That object was mostly water ice and so reacted quickly. A star ship is made of metal alloys and dense ceramics. The surface would disappear slowly while the heat would soon turn the hull incandescent. Eventually the hull would be breached, and the ship would be destroyed, but that would take a relatively long time, slightly more than a minute of direct fire. During that period, any combat ship would maneuver and respond with fire from its own weapons. Holding a disrupter on any spot for that long on any enemy ship would be impossible unless it was disabled, a derelict. For ship to ship combat we use what you might call torpedoes or guided missiles. We call them *tolos*. They use several types of explosive devices from chemical to fusion that are designed specifically to penetrate a hull and expend energy into the hull penetration. Your anti tank weapons use a similar principle on a much smaller scale . They are effective anti ship weapons and can destroy a ship with a single hit in the right place."

"You've studied our weapon systems?"

"Yes! Actually, most of our information comes from Scentar records we acquired over many years. They keep extensive records collected over the long period of time they studied your world. As a warrior, I naturally concentrated on those military records that might be of most use to me."

"Amazing!"

"Scentar are open with their records. By making them easily available to all of their own, they make them available to us. I must confess, this has advanced our knowledge and technology tremendously."

"I think you would both benefit from peaceful coexistence rather than constant warfare."

"Probably so, but how do you stop a war of annihilation that has been going on for thousands of years?"

"Then you considered ending combat?"

"Of course. Any warrior worth his salt would prefer not to make war. I hate seeing my men, my people, die, even those brave individuals who are my enemies. Sadly, we are forced to try to correct the unnecessary and often ridiculous mistakes political rulers make—mistakes that frequently lead to warfare."

"That is an interesting viewpoint. An intelligent viewpoint I might add. I am impressed."

"I thank you and consider that a sincere compliment, especially from a—guest."

"Another question about those disrupters. How do they work against buildings, fortified buildings?"

"Actually, much better than against moving targets. Against fortifications, we use a combination of tolos and disrupter fire. Fortifications do not normally move, so concentrated disrupter fire works fairly well against them. After significant disrupter fire, a tolo or two will usually break through any fortifications."

"What protections do you use against tolos?"

We use computer controlled counter fire from both guns and missiles. It's effective, but not fool proof. The accelerating co-development of offensive and defensive arms determines the result. Doubtless even your primitive weapons systems followed the same pattern."

"That's true all the way back to the spear and shield."

The captain laughed as we turned and headed amidships. "I had never thought in those terms, but you are correct. Enough of this interesting but useless banter. We must take you to the health treatment center, or is that hospital in your dialect? We need our doctor to inject that little object behind your ear. Then we will send you back, so you can make that trip for us."

"No need to hurry on my account."

"You show quite a sense of humor, Dr. Syl. I like you."

"I'm afraid I can't reciprocate."

"I understand perfectly. Ah here we are. Time for a little surgery."

Insertion of the object didn't take long and was fairly painless. As I sat on the table after the insertion, the captain walked to the door. "Goodbye Dr. Syl. I do not expect to meet with you again. I wanted to hear your theory about what happened to our lost colony, but there is no time. Pleasant journey." He left the room.

The doctor placed some sort of injector against my arm, and gave me an injection. The room began to swirl, and then everything went black.

Chapter 18 - The Planned Attack on Vega Five Revealed

y head was throbbing, my feet were cold, and I realized I was laying on cold, hard concrete. I opened my eyes. I was on the floor of the long-term storage room in the basement of the Eegis building, right where I sat when I was taken through the Segwah portal. I checked the time on my watch, seven o'clock. I had been gone at least eight hours. I walked forward to the elevator and punched my floor. The car stopped on the main floor. When the doors opened, I was greeted by Herb, our late night security, gun drawn and aimed in my direction.

"I'm sorry Dr. Syl, but you gave me a start. Supposedly there was no one left in the building but me. Where in the devil did you come from?"

"It's a long story, Herb, but I awoke in the basement storage room a few minutes ago."

"How could they miss finding you? They've been searching for you since about two. When you disappeared, they combed the entire building from basement to roof because you hadn't signed out and there was no record of you leaving. I'd better call Marty."

As Herb picked up the phone, my mind raced trying to think how I could tell them what had happened without blowing my head off. I wondered about writing out the details. I had been told they could hear me, but would they if I wrote the info? I guessed they would, so that was out. Then it dawned on me if I wrote the info out and didn't look at the paper, how could they possibly know. I had to go back into my office. By this time Herb handed me the phone with Marty on the line.

"Marty?"

"Where the hell did you go?"

"I can't tell you."

"Bull shit!"

"No, Marty, I can't, and I can't explain why over the phone."

"Okay, I'll be down there in fifteen minutes."

"Meet me in my office."

"Your office?"

"That's right. In my office."

"Gotcha!"

With that, he hung up. I only hoped Marty remembered our old code from Cal Tech days. As I headed for my office, Herb asked, "Where are you going, Dr. Syl. I must enter that information in the log after hours."

"I'll be in my office. Marty will be coming to meet me there in fifteen minutes."

"Okay Dr. Syl."

I walked into my office without turning on the lights and closed the door. My office window faced east away from any city lights, and was pitch black. I felt around and located the printer and removed a handful of papers from the tray. I then searched for and found a felt tip pen. I was in business. I spent a full fifteen minutes writing the entire story of my trip and what had been done to me including the *bomb* behind my ear. I only hoped my words written in the pitch black were readable. The last thing I did was find and stick scotch tape to the top of the sign I made for Marty. I hoped he would read it before entering my office. I opened the door and without looking at the sign, slipped around the door and taped the sign to the outside at eye level.

I didn't wait for long.

Damn! Don't give me away! I thought as Marty rushed down the hall shouting, "Drax, I hope this isn't one of your little games."

He stopped in front of my office. . . nothing but silence. I was greatly relieved. He was taking the time to read my sign. Marty played the scene perfectly as he opened the door. "Why are you still here? You remember about the appointment with those electronic security people in half an hour. We definitely need better internal security, and they're the best in the business. Let's go!"

By this time, I had managed to pick up all the notes I had written and placed them inside a folder. "I'm sorry Marty, I forgot. Here's the file on our existing system," I said, handing him the folder. "I'm ready."

We rushed to the elevator and went down without speaking. After signing out with Herb, we left the building and got into Marty's car. We exchanged meaningless small talk nervously as we headed toward Marty's apartment.

"I must stop and pick up some other papers," he said loudly as we stopped in front of his building. "It may take a while, so please be patient."

Things were progressing well. Marty had my requests down to a T. As I waited, he was reading all the information I had written about the Segwah plot and my part in it. After about twenty minutes, a large gray van pulled up behind Marty's car. I was not surprised when Maria walked up with her fingers to her lips indicating silence and held out a sign that read, *We think the bomb behind your ear is a fake. Leura is preparing her equipment to check it out. Please wait.* Thinking about Leura, the hackles stood up on the back of my neck. I was still furious with her. All I thought was she and the Segwah captain were two sides of the same coin, warriors in a mortal battle who would use any trick to win. I would eventually get over it, but I wondered, *Was I picking the wrong side to help?* I also wondered why I held no anger for the Segwah but despised Leura. This didn't make much sense to me until I realized I had no personal involvement with the captain. We were only mental combatants—unemotional.

Maria was joined by Leura holding an object about the size and shape of a hair dryer and wheeling a cart to which it was attached by a cable. When Maria motioned, I stepped out of the car and walked to where Leura was and turned facing away from her. I was glad I didn't look her in the eyes. She placed the object which I assumed was a detector of some sort against my head behind my ear.

After a few minutes she announced, "Just as I suspected. It's a fake. You can relax."

"Maybe some junk they stuck in my head with no actual function?" I asked.

"No, it could be a real bomb with a remote triggering mechanism, and if so, would kill you if exploded. Included is a remote sensing beacon, but there are no audio or video devices or any kind of transmission device. That means that all it tells them is where you are, and they must be within the relatively short distance of less than fifty kilometers to receive the data. Of course, they might be watching us right now. I'll check with the scanner to find out for certain."

"If not removed, I will probably die, right?"

"Most likely, but not until you've completed your purpose or they think you've defected from their plans. We'll remove the object in a secure location. I didn't find any triggering mechanisms or temperature sensors, but that doesn't mean there are none. I suggest we wait until we are inside the building on Vega Five before we remove it."

"What if they decide to blow me up in the mean time? That bastard told me one little glitch and, **bang!** That doesn't leave me with a secure feeling."

Leura looked softly at me. "Drax, whatever decision is made about where and when to remove the bomb is entirely up to you. I think the key is in that coin. I'll wager a portal beacon will be part of the internals and a triggering device that will explode the bomb soon after you place it on the floor. I imagine he told you to leave quickly after placing it on the floor, right?"

"Exactly. I'll bet he wanted me away from the coin when I blew. So no one would find it."

"Now lets take a closer look at the coin."

I handed her the coin and said, "Could your scanning of the coin trigger something in it? I mean, they might set up a booby trap of sorts in case of a scan or other close examination."

"Our scanners are equipped to handle such a possibility. Those types of booby traps provide a definite and recognizable mass signature. Our scanner will work without triggering a response. It will counter any internal command. The technology's a bit complicated, but rest assured it will work. Our technologies are far ahead of theirs. That's why they try to capture technology of ours. They cannot make these things themselves."

"The captain even said as much to me," I said with a chuckle.

Leura placed the coin on a small platform atop the box on wheels and brought down a thick plate from the raised back pressing lightly on the coin. After a few minutes, the screen lit up with a number of symbols and some writing I did not understand. Then she turned to face us.

"Well it's not as bad as it could be, but a bit worse than I hoped. Contain a portal beacon, a temperature sensor connected to a triggering mechanism, and a scan sensor, the mechanism shows a fair degree of sophistication, more than we've seen before. The scan sensor was countered, so your bomb didn't go off. All of these devices are based on Scentar technology acquired during one of their raids. It has another device, crude and of their own creation, but unknown to our database. More analysis of the logic patterns will be required to find an answer. So far the computer has searched without results, but our device will find those patterns and tell us the function. In the meantime, I suggest we plan how we are going to proceed."

Marty spoke up. "Leura, shouldn't you notify your people on Vega Five?"

Leura smiled. "I sent them a complete copy of all of the papers Drax wrote us along with my report. I expect to hear what they would like us to do shortly."

"I don't understand how your communications work, but I trust you used a secure means."

"Drax, we continually fought the Segwah, as they call themselves, for thousands of your years. We developed both communication systems and portal transfer systems that they cannot intercept, or even detect when they are going on. Rest assured the message was secure."

"Checking! Just checking!" I replied a bit sheepishly.

"And, Dr. Syl, I appreciate your concerns and don't mind your checking at all. In fact, I'm glad you do so. One little mistake and we could experience some big-time troubles."

"Oh? I assumed you didn't make mistakes."

"I'll ignore the sarcasm and admit we do make mistakes. We're only human."

"Oh, please!" I said, emphasizing my disdain. "That was too pathetic."

Maria was furious. "At a time like this, you turn an accurate and even humorous comment into a battle cry because of a past imagined slight. You're the one who's pathetic, Drax. For a man with a bomb in his head to treat so viciously the only one who can save his life, is nothing short of insanity—it's plain suicidal. If I were in her shoes, I'd consider walking away from you and letting your head blow. I've lost all respect I once had for you unless you offer Leura a genuine apology and right now."

"Not a chance. You may be taken in by that female, but not I." I did all I could do to control my anger as I spoke.

Marty intervened. "If this nonsense continues I'm going to sack both of you. I did not say I would ask for your resignation. Being fired from a project like this is tantamount to a termination of any career in your profession. I will do so at the next temper tantrum for either of you who sound off or egg the other one on to do so. Leura, please accept my apology for Dr. Syl's unwarranted and inexcusable behavior."

Leura said, "No apology is needed. Objectively I understand his anger is based on faulty judgement of the circumstances resulting in an injured male human ego. I remain convinced Drax is a kind, considerate individual and personally, I still care for him. His attitude toward me is painful for me but does not change my opinion. I only hope I can change his mind. In the meantime we still have a serious problem and the life of one of us is in imminent danger. I am prepared to do what I can to prevent injury to Drax, thwart the planned attack at our base on Vega Five, and prevent damage to the people and structure of both of our universes. I was dedicated to this purpose when I joined the NU Service, the purpose of my life. I need your permission and your help to do my job. Please! Let us go on with it. Time does not wait."

By this time I felt sheepish because of my actions and attitudes. Indeed I was selfishly thinking only of my own small picture and not the big one I was in the midst of.

I hardly believed I was apologizing. "Leura, I am indeed sorry for how I behaved. I will do everything I can to control my temper from now on. Do not construe that as a change in my belief that you used me for your own purpose. I will trust that Vega Five is the best place to remove the bomb and also permit your forces to prepare a reception for the Segwah attack which they will not expect. Now, how do we pull this off?"

Maria turned to me and had the last word. "I'm glad you came to your senses, at least partially. Unless I'm mistaken, we will now go into Leura's van and head for Vega Five. What about it, Leura?"

"Yes, as soon as things are ready. Then we'll go for a two-hour drive before we jump. Marty, I ask that you stay here in case something goes wrong. We are not, as you say, out of the woods yet. Should something happen to us, you are the only person who will know about this entire situation other than the Scentar. They will be in touch with you if something does go wrong. Remember. No news is good news."

Leura wheeled the cart back to the van, up the ramp, and secured it to the side wall. Then she turned on the scanner. After a minute she turned toward us. "There are no Segwah within five hundred kilometers. That's the limit of this scanner's range. Now we can proceed as they only know where Drax is, nothing else. Let's go."

Marty said, "Good luck!" and headed for his car after we said our goodbyes.

We closed the van, took our seats and headed out for the desert.

Chapter 19 - Off to Vega Five

The walk through the terminal on Vega Five triggered memories of my previous visit. I wondered which memories were real and which were not. We were greeted by two men, obviously military and known to Leura who introduced them.

"This is General Lairn Straglo who is the military commander here on Vega Five, and this is Chief Kropa Delgo, head of station defense," she said and then completed introducing us to them.

Obviously Scentar, they were much alike to me. Both were tall, well over six feet, and slender. Only a close study of the way they moved would reveal them as other than human. Not as fluid of movement as Leura, they seemed relaxed by human standards, and for military men. Their hair was dark with a reddish hue and shoulder length. Their uniforms were smooth, skin tight, dark gray, and seamless. They each wore a wide, black belt. There were wide flaps or pouches hanging on each side like thin black leather attache cases. They had no ornamentation or obvious weapons. Their caps were like berets, but with a narrow, square bill in front. Their long black boots with square heels seemed more like women's fashion footwear than military.

General Straglo spoke to us first. "Welcome to Vega Five. We are truly pleased you are here. Because of the urgency of your visit I will dispense with the usual formalities and conduct you to our hospital to take care of the item behind your ear, Dr. Syl. We can talk while en route."

A small, van-like wheeled vehicle pulled up and we were soon moving rather quickly out of the terminal building. We drove onto a wide roadway leading over a small hill and out of sight of the terminal. The roadway looked like a highway on Earth.

The general continued. "After this is over, I hope we have the opportunity to show you around Vega Five, and are able to explain what we accomplished here and why. Now we must concentrate on the military defense of our base. I examined the information you, Dr. Syl and Leura provided us. I know Captain Woolgah by reputation. Years ago Chief Delgo met him in combat. He is indeed a clever man. We are also familiar with the type of ship he has, an impressive weapon with strong defenses. Under the right circumstances, he could capture our universe portal."

"With at most two hundred combat troops and a total complement of three-hundred and sixty on his ship?" I asked. "That seems a bit small in comparison with your obvious numerical superiority and, I assume weapon technology superiority as well."

General Straglo laughed. "Those facts may be true, but suppose he has a hundred Gelwah class ships and six thousand men, or even a hundred times that number, men and equipment that could be thrown into any attack. Then it might not be so easy."

I was suddenly apprehensive. "If that were so, wouldn't you have some evidence, some results of scans, some knowledge of their capabilities and possible tactics?"

"We battled them for thousands of your years, defended against their hit-and-run tactics and usually won, but there were casualties. We find we must be constantly adapting to changes in their tactics."

"He said his ship and one other were the only ones with universe portals. How would he be able to move many ships into our area?"

"A shrewd observation, Dr. Syl. Our hope is they do not hold many ships nearby. My guess is there might be forty to fifty at most. Unfortunately, Vega Five was not designed as a defensive military outpost. Until recently the Segwah were not aware your universe existed or rather they had no way of linking a universe portal to it, so they posed no danger to us here. Because of this, we were virtually without defenses against their type of attack. Once we learned they could come here, we made plans to bring in defensive armaments and warriors to protect the base. These plans are only partially completed."

"That doesn't sound good for our side. What is currently in place?"

"We installed a large complex underground on the opposite side of the main base from our permanent portal installation. It's deep underground to escape detection by their sensors or probes. My guess is they believe we possess no defenses and will be easy to capture. Unfortunately, all military personnel that come here must go through the complete year long genetic conversion and inoculation process. Those new ones here the longest are only in their fifth month as we speak."

"You mean we are without any military personnel? Defenseless?"

"Far from it. We keep more than two hundred trained military on our base. They are a small number among the hundreds of thousands of nonmilitary who live here and operate this base and Stentor Seven. We are now training several thousand of these civilians on defensive weapons and tactics. Many are ex-military who only need their skills upgraded. We are far from defenseless.

"What about weapons and defensive fortifications?"

"We received several substantial shipments of weapons, many of which are already installed. All of our weapons and military personnel are in our underground complex. Our training and operations take place underground in the same large facility I mentioned. The Segwah are completely unaware of our defensive build up or if we even have those capabilities at all."

"Wouldn't they suspect you did and were hiding them? Wouldn't they be able to track your shipments and learn you were placing them underground?"

"Ah, Dr. Syl, you underestimate us as I hope the Segwah do. The first thing we did was construct a second universe portal system underground, energy source and all. Since we had a duplicate portal as backup to the main one, all we needed to bring in on the surface was the power source. We made it appear as though we were merely expanding our basic energy system. Their scanners cannot tell the difference. Once the new underground portal system was in operation, we began receiving shipments of men and materials from our universe completely undetectable. That was four months ago. Currently, we should be able to thwart all but the most massive attack by the Segwah, one much larger than they will be able to mount at this time."

"What if you're wrong? What if they do mount a massive attack, one large enough to overcome your defenses?"

"We will fight valiantly, but if all is lost, the entire base will self-destruct. There is no way the Segwah will capture any of our equipment or technology."

"I think you told me more than I wanted to know."

"Oh? Why is this so? I don't understand."

"It's a joke, General. A joke."

General Straglo laughed heartily. "Believe it or not, Dr. Syl, I understand."

We were approaching a rather large building complex, lots of glass with hexagonal domes over each separate section of the building.

Leura announced, "That's the portal building. We'll enter it and then move quickly to the hospital through underground tunnel connections. We don't want them to find out you are not staying in the portal complex. The tunnels and the portal complex are all shielded from scanners, so the signal from your little capsule will be blocked. They should be aware that they will lose the signal as soon as you enter the building."

General Straglo spoke first to Leura. "The surgical team is awaiting us. They are in the room at the end of the hospital tunnel still within the shields. Dr. Syl, we should remove that little bomb from you within a few minutes. Then we need to move quickly to a location we prepared for you to place that signal coin."

We all hopped on a little motorized cart and headed into the tunnel. As we rode, the general's communicator buzzed.

"That's good!" he said after he listened for a few minutes and then closed the communicator. "That's the final information about that third part of your little bomb, Dr. Syl. Its logic is set for processing in the instant before the trigger goes off. That logic triggers the portal signal in your coin and also triggers the coin to emit another signal in their communication frequencies. My guess is that will be the signal for the balance of their forces to attack. The ships carrying those forces must now be close to the Vega system, or the signal would not reach them."

We reached the surgical room at the end of the tunnel. I was soon laying face down on a comfortable operating table and surrounded by medical personnel. One press against my head with a flat black tool and my head went numb; I felt nothing. The next instant, I was sitting up, and Leura was showing me the object I remember being in Captain Woolgah's fingers.

"Wow! Careful with that."

Leura laughed. "Don't worry, the trigger mechanism has been disrupted. It's harmless. Everything else is intact."

General Straglo urged us on saying, "Lets move! We don't want our attackers to become impatient."

We climbed back on the cart and were soon headed down another tunnel—a much longer and darker tunnel that sloped downward.

General Straglo spoke. "We are now headed for the new underground defense complex. In about fifteen minutes we will be there. This complex is a newly dug room some distance away from the old complex and much farther from the surface. From there we will head up close to a special place we prepared for receiving the Segwah. There we will leave the coin and make a hasty exit back to the defense complex a safe distance away."

We burst through an opening into a mammoth lighted cavern with a floor covered with shipping containers of many kinds and sizes. "These are the newest arrivals of equipment and arms for our defense. As you can see, they are rapidly being unpacked and taken to their place of installation," Chief Delgo said. "Installation and operation of these weapons is my responsibility. I wish we had more in place, but those that are ready are quite powerful. I think we will surprise the Segwah if they attack. Our present support troops trained for four months and should be ready for combat by now. Their small weapons are superior to those of the Segwah and their protective armor can handle most anything Segwah ground troops can hand out."

"Damn, Chief. I hope you are on the money with that comment. You're not exaggerating things a bit are you?"

"Not at all if the attacking force is as we suspect. A ten times larger force would overwhelm our defenses but is unlikely. Those are the facts. Besides, surprise is on our side, and that can amount to a major asset."

"I'll take your word for it," I said as the cart dove into another tunnel on the far side of the cavern.

The only lights were those on the cart which only lighted about fifty feet ahead. This tunnel was sloped decidedly uphill. The motor in the little cart strained against gravity to pull its load. After about five minutes, we burst into a small, lighted, bright white, square room about the size of a four-car garage. There was a door at each end. The opening we had used to enter had a large doorway with a sliding door to close the opening. The hope was the Segwah troops would come through the portal into the room and be trapped. The doors on each end led into short dead-end tunnels. Once in the room, sensors would trigger explosives in the floor and walls and the room would collapse on the Segwah, burying them under tons of rock.

"Now Dr. Syl. Place your coin and let's leave here," the General ordered as the driver turned the cart around and aimed for the tunnel.

I dug the coin out of my hand, ran over to the side wall and placed it on the floor as Captain Woolgah had directed. I ran back and jumped on the cart which dove into the tunnel. The door closed behind us, and the darkness of the tunnel closed in. We were going downhill at an increased pace, bouncing along on the uneven surface.

Suddenly there was a loud thump followed by what felt like several muffled explosions. A loud, grinding sound followed, and the tunnel shook as we burst into the weapons cavern. Something had not gone as planned.

"Control center! Now!" Shouted the Chief to the driver.

We headed across the cavern in a new direction at a high rate of speed.

"Everybody off here!" shouted the Chief when we stopped near the center of the complex. "Someone will come for you soon." were his parting words as the cart rushed off.

Chapter 20 - The Gelwah Arrives on Vega Five

General Straglo searched desperately for another cart. "I should go to my command post as soon as possible and find out what has happened. I don't like the sound at all."

Two carts were seen headed our way. The general jumped on the first shouting, "Follow me! I can lead you to a safe exit."

We jumped on the second cart and were soon careening across the floor of the huge cavern following what appeared to be a road. Unintelligible commands were soon booming throughout the cavern.

Leura interpreted. "All personnel were ordered to their defensive battle positions. We experienced a perimeter breach. There are invaders inside the defensive perimeter. That's all they are announcing."

"Shit! Now what?" I was on unfamiliar ground on an alien world knowing we were being attacked, but without a clue as to what was happening. My combat experience took control. *Find a weapon! Any weapon!* Beat through my head.

"Leura! Are there any hand weapons in all this junk? Could you find them if there are?"

Leura grabbed the driver and pointed toward a large stack of small boxes. "Look for boxes with a circle around a hand symbol. These boxes will contain LK's or Galbo blasters. Both are excellent hand weapons. The Galbos are deadlier, but take a bit of recharge time before they are ready to fire again. The LKs are stunners, but can be fired repeatedly. They are also smaller and easier to hide."

It only took a few minutes to find some boxes with the hand symbols.

"How can you open these?" I asked in frustration as I examined the metal boxes that seemed to be without openings.

"It won't be easy," she replied. "They require a code to open."

Then the driver stepped over to one of the boxes, a small black control in her hand.

"This will do it!" she said as she punched the keys. "That's one of my jobs."

The box on top split down the middle and opened flat.

"LKs!" Shouted Leura as she grabbed a few of the small boxes and began opening them. "Take as many as you can hold, at least four. Once they run out of power, throw them away and use another. Driver, do you see any Galbos?"

"Yes Ma'am! There's a box right behind you. All of these weapons are fully charged, too," she said as he punched more keys.

The box of Galbos split apart as Leura said, "You'll only need one of these. They will self recharge indefinitely."

The LKs were tiny, about the size and shape of a flip phone. They resembled small TV remotes. Galbos were more my style of weapon. About the size of a Glock 40, they had an extendable stock, a muzzle rest and a sighting mechanism that appeared to be a scope. I took several of the LKs and two Galbos, tucking one in my belt. The driver did the same. Then we all got back aboard and asked the driver where we should go.

She grinned and asked, "Do you want a safe hiding place or action?"

Maria and Leura were both holding a weapon in each hand and replied, "Action!"

"Hang on!" she shouted as she whipped the cart around and headed toward a nearby tunnel. Soon we were headed steeply upward toward a small, bright light. After going upward for a long time, I realized the reason the light was so small was because it was far away.

"What is that light and what are you planning?"

"The light is the opening right next to the portal building. My battle station is manning the personnel scanner that is hidden inside the opening. From inside there is a good view of the south side of the portal building. It also provides an open line of fire from inside the tunnel right down the side of the building. There are no weapons installed yet, but our hand weapons will do."

"How long were you on this post?"

"Two weeks. It was just finished and opened. I've only tested the scanner once, but it works."

"I hate to keep calling you driver. What's your name?"

"Sylvia. Gopher First Class, Sylvia Zymas at your service."

"Gopher?"

"That's right, Gopher. It's an honorable rank given to those who qualify in making tunnels and driving these carts through them. I believe it's after a little animal on your earth that lives in tunnels underground."

"Well Sylvia, it's an honor being here with you. Thank goodness we're on the same side. Incidentally, my name is Drax and that's Maria who is my boss. The other lady is Leura, one of your people."

"I am familiar with Leura. She's famous here. You and your friend, Maria are from this universe, right? Well, you are the first Earth people I ever met. It's a thrill. I'm pleased to meet you."

We were approaching the opening, and Sylvia slowed the cart to a crawl.

"Let me check outside to find out what's going on," Sylvia said as she jumped down from the cart and crept to the opening. "Nothing going on right here. Things are quiet. I'll warm up the scanner and see what s going on elsewhere."

Sylvia stepped over to a scanner console near the opening and sat in the operator's chair. I went to the opening and peeked out. As I did, I heard a strange Fzzzt sound. The sound was bouncing off the flat surface of the building in front of me and obviously came from behind the tunnel opening where I couldn't see. Leura grabbed my arm and pulled me away from the opening as I heard another Fzzzt. She called Maria over with us.

"That was the sound of Galbo firing, and not far away," she warned. "One shot from a Galbo and you're reduced to hot dust. Let me show you both how this works."

She took out the Galbo and pointed to a lever. "This is a safety lock feature. It must be turned forward to activate the weapon." Pointing to a sliding lever with several dots of increasing size, she said, "This is the power control. Small dots, low-power, big dots, high-power. The middle setting will cut a man in half at one hundred yards. The tiny dot setting will do the same at ten yards. The highest setting will burn a hole in six inch steel in about ten seconds. It's a distance setting and controls the power and the spread of the effective pattern. Using the sight, it is accurate to a long distance controlled only by how steady the weapon is held."

Sylvia called out, "Look at this. It's a view across the center of the compound toward where that small underground room was near the surface. That's where we were less than half an hour ago."

The egg-shaped hull of a large, gray vessel, its front third buried in the ground and the rest covered with earth, rock, and vegetation, lay at the surface with smoke rising all around. It was messy but intact. I guessed it was the star ship Gelwah, Captain Woolgah's. It was clear his entire forward weapons bank was buried with the front of the ship under tons of soil and rock. It didn't take me long to figure out what had happened. Woolgah did not portal his troops for a surprise attack as we thought. What he did was portal his entire ship into that tiny underground room thinking to severely damage the real portal building and gain access at the same time. The sudden intrusion of the ship burst through the surface with a tremendous explosion of rock and dirt. That was the large thud we heard. This set off the explosives that bounced harmlessly off the skin of the ship and blew more soil and rocks out of the ground.

Sylvia cursed. "Of all the rotten luck. All of our weapons capable of dealing with the ship are aimed outward. I don't think there is a single hyper-disrupter or hyper-Galbo that could safely fire on the vessel. It's far too close to use any of our tolos. The collateral damage would be too great. I wonder what the chief is planning to do?"

I watched a small vehicle on tracks work its way between the boulders and piles of earth toward the ship. When it reached the hull of the ship it stopped moving and placed an extended arm against the hull.

"What's that little machine and what is it doing?" I asked.

Sylvia replied, "I haven't the slightest idea. I've never seen one of those before."

"That is a field communications unit. It is used to send data from remote field observations to the research center when it is impractical to do so in person. It's a scientific data communicator. I don't understand what it is doing here," Leura said coolly.

"Do you use any communication links with the Segwah?" I asked Leura.

"None. We do not communicate."

"Then how do you negotiate a surrender?"

"We don't and they don't. We destroy them and they destroy us. It's that simple."

"Then how do you back away from a stalemate?"

"We've never had one," was Leura's answer.

"Well, you do now, and it may be that someone's trying to find a way to negotiate. Sylvia, can you communicate with your central command?"

"Sure! There is a com link right here on my console."

"Then let me talk to them. Now!"

In less than a minute after she handed me the com input I was talking to the Chief's communications officer.

"This is Draxel Syl at your forward observation point . . ."

"B Sylvia," Sylvia said, catching on quickly.

"B Sylvia," I repeated to the com unit. "What are you doing with that field com unit?"

"I am not authorized to tell you," came back.

"Then contact Chief Kropa Delgo on the com unit. He'll tell me."

"Just a minute."

After several minutes, another voice came on the com unit. "This is com unit officer Greelo. Who are you please?"

"This is Draxel Syl of the Eegis project on Earth and I want to use your data unit to try to communicate with the ship."

"Impossible!"

Leura took the com input and spoke sternly. "This is R8 Leura Clauson at B Sylvia. Please comply with any and all of Draxel Sil's requests as quickly as possible. Reply!"

After a moment of dead silence, a contritely voiced officer Greelo replied, "Yes R8 what can I do?"

The power of Leura's R8 status, whatever that was, impressed me. "Does that data unit possess two way audible communication ability?" I asked.

"Yes! We are trying to use it to hear what's happening inside the ship."

"How can I tap into it and use this com unit to try to communicate with the captain of that ship."

"That's never been done before."

"Try it! . . . Now!"

"We'll try! We can connect the unit directly with your com. Your voice should reverberate within the ship. I'll tell you when it's ready, sir. I will need a few minutes."

Chapter 21 - Aboard the Star Ship Gelwah

Captain Woolgah sits at his command post, his brow furrowed with worry. The signal should have gone off some time ago. He turns to his first officer seated at the helm control.

"Jemrah, prepare to jump to orbit around Vega Five. We will jump in precisely fifteen minutes if we don't receive the required signal. Tell the other ships to follow our lead and prepare to jump on my order."

Jemrah glanced at the captain, a sneer on his face. "Yessir! It's about time we moved on them. We suspect they installed few defenses. We should have made a frontal attack days ago. Our conquest of their base would be all over by now."

"That's a brash and unwarranted statement, Jemrah. Supposing they installed a massive disrupter array hidden around the portal complex. A direct attack would be suicide."

"Why would your human not tell the Scentar, warn them of our planned attack? They could be waiting for our men and cut them down as they step out of the ship."

"Because he believes that if he does, he will die."

"You can't be certain of that."

"The beacon showed us he did precisely as we ordered right up to the time he entered the portal building. Then the beacon was shielded by the building. I'll wager he is approaching the point of placement of the beacon right now. His effort took a bit more time than we supposed."

"What if the beacon doesn't turn on for any reason?"

"Jemrah, No more what ifs. We attack in thirteen minutes or on the beacon signal, which ever comes first. Now quit your nay saying and check all attack preparations."

"They're all checked and ready to go."

"Check them again."

By the time Jemrah had run all of his checks, only four minutes remained before the jump. Suddenly the scanner on his console lit up. The portal beacon on Vega Five had turned on.

Captain Woolgah issued several quick orders. "Signal the fleet to jump as planned. Lock portal coordinates on the beacon. When the connection light goes on, operate our jump sequence. We'll be inside their portal building in a few minutes. Announce the attack sequence to our ground troops, so they'll be ready."

"Yes sir!" Jemrah said with a smile, his hand poised over the actuate control.

The connection light glowed green. "Now!" said the captain and Jemrah pressed the jump control bar.

The ship glowed with a soft blue light which grew steadily brighter and then disappeared. Inside the ship, the crew felt a strong jolt as it materialized in an underground room much too small to hold it. Most of them were knocked down. The ship entry created a loud thud felt more than heard. Several loud explosions then rocked the ship, blasting its hull from outside and battering the occupants. The displaced rock and soil mounded up around the ship which ended up nose down, the entire fore section buried in rock and soil. This was not what the captain expected.

"Damage report!" he shouted over the com unit.

The reports came in one after another.

"Hull integrity maintained, but all forward scanners are inoperative."

"Local guidance control systems are not operating."

"Forward view ports are all blocked. We are at least partially underground."

"The only way out is through the front and rear emergency hatches topside. The bottom and side ones are blocked."

"Forward weapons ports are all blocked. Rear topside impact weapons are all that remain in operation."

Jemrah said to the captain. "Sir, we are trapped. I tried firing various control jets and we didn't move."

"Can anyone see anything outside?"

"Sir, the rear fire control station says they are observing a clear view out the right side. All they can see is a large field of low vegetation and several buildings about a kilometer away from their position. They cannot see forward or to the left at all."

"What kind of field of fire can they cover?"

"They report only a limited range of movement for the guns. The jolt partially jammed their aiming control."

"Weapons maintenance! Can we ready any weapons to fire? Report."

After a few minutes, weapons maintenance came on. "Sir! We should be able to have those impact weapons operating in about twenty minutes. The guides were jolted off their tracks and must be pried back in place. Fortunately, the shell feeds are all working, and the outside sights are in good shape."

"Get on it. What about the forward weapons?"

"The main disrupters are all jammed into rock and cannot be fired without damaging the ship. The lower impacts are virtually destroyed, but the upper ones will be functional if we clear the debris that is piled on top of them."

"Can we fire those guns to clear the debris?"

"Not without a good chance of a blowback that would destroy the entire forward emplacement. No, we must send a crew outside to clear the debris."

"What about access to the exterior?"

"We can access the outside from the maintenance hatch above the impact turret."

"Wouldn't anyone going out the hatch be open to enemy fire?"

"Yes! We could send a few troops out first with Galbos and Denbo shields to suppress enemy fire. They would be vulnerable to snipers or major weapons fire."

"Do so now! If some weapons are not on line soon, we'll be blown to pieces anyway."

"Yes sir!"

The captain thought for a moment then spoke through the com unit. "Portal control. Is the portal charged and useable?"

After a few moments a reply, "Captain, without the main engines to charge the portals they are both inoperative. The impact so disrupted the engine stack we will need at least an hour to put it back in operation. Sorry, sir, but we're already working on it."

"Do it in half that time. We desperately need some power."

Captain Woolgah turned to his first officer. "Situation assessment! Now!"

Jemrah frantically input information and requests into his console. "We will need about a minute for results, sir."

"Open the view screen. Let's see what we can see."

The screen was blank. "Forward imager must be blocked. I'll switch to the right side."

The viewer lit up with a bright scene visible over soil and rock pushed up by the impact of the ship.

"There's a clear view of several buildings about a kilometer away across the field, Sir. Do you know what they are?"

"No, Jemrah, I don't. My guess is those are the portal buildings, where we wanted to attack. This is the first visit to Vega Five for the Gelwah, and scanner input is all we can use. Do a sensor sweep and let's find out what's out there."

"Sir, the top scanners are not yet back on line. Maintenance said it will be a few more minutes."

"Damn! Damn! Damn! Can anything not go wrong?"

"There's one good thing, Captain."

"What's that?"

"They have yet to fire on us with any kind of weapon. Maybe our suspicion this base was without defenses is correct."

"Jemrah, you are a prince! Thank you for calling that to my attention."

"Sir, the situation assessment is complete," Jemrah said handing the report tablet to the captain.

After examining it carefully, he turned to Jemrah. "Status of the forward weapons?"

"They will soon be ready, sir. The gun crew reported maintenance has cleared most of the debris. The guns will be ready to fire in less than five minutes. Wait, there's more. They began taking small arms fire—galbos. They're covering with the shields and retrieving one wounded. They are returning fire."

"Keep on that link and give me a step by step. Tell me the minute those guns are ready to fire."

"Yes sir!"

After a few minutes Jemrah reported, "Good news, sir! The top side scanners are on line. The forward gun crew reports debris cleared and all personnel inside. The guns should be ready to fire any minute now."

"Good! Now lets see what the scanner can find starting forward."

All the screen showed forward was a pile of dirt and rock. As the scanner rotated toward the rear, a field with dirt and rocks up to the side of the ship stretched out toward a series of cream colored buildings. Nothing was moving in the field of view. Then there was movement close to the side of the ship.

"What the hell is that machine coming toward us?" the captain shouted.

"It's a small mechanical device on treaded wheels."

"Contact the forward gun crew and ask if they can take a shot at it?"

After a minute, Jemrah reported, "They say it's in range, but the guns are not ready to fire."

"Tell them to fire the instant they can."

A moment later he reported, "Sir, they say the guns are now ready, but the target has moved so close to the ship they can no longer hit it."

"Damn, it's right up against the hull."

"Sir, the scanner sensors detect no weapons of any kind in the object. It's a simple data transmitter, bi-directional. It poses no threat."

"What the hell are they doing with that? Can it be they are trying to listen to what's going on inside our ship?"

"That's about all it would be able to do," Jemrah answered.

What sounded like a voice seemed to come from the area of the ship where the data transmitter was parked.

"Turn up the sound pickup from the right side passage way. That's about where the sound is loudest."

Chapter 22 - Peace Within an Extended War

Drax's voice came through the com system clear enough for the captain to understand. "Captain Woolgah, this is your earlier visitor, Draxel Sil. Do you hear me?"

The captain shouted through the com system. "Yes, Dr. Syl, I can hear you. What do you want?"

"I'd like to try to negotiate a peaceful solution to the little problem at hand."

"And why should I negotiate with you? We are in the middle of a Scentar base far from your world. I would suggest the best thing for you to do is pack up and go home. Our quarrel is not with you."

"No? My quarrel is certainly with you. That little bomb in my head was set to kill me soon after I placed your beacon. I'd say that was more than a quarrel."

"Is that what they told you was in your head? Actually, that "bomb" was a small syringe designed to deliver enough anaesthetic into your system to knock you out for a few hours and was otherwise harmless. We had no intention of killing you. As I explained during your visit, we have no quarrel with humans, none at all."

His words did not jibe with what I had been told. I looked at Leura.

"Is that true? Was that a bomb or an anaesthetic syringe?"

"You said it was a bomb. I think we took your word. We can check it out as we still hold it."

I was not convinced, but I did remember saying it was a bomb.

"Dr. Syl? Are you still there?" came over the com unit.

"I'm sorry, Captain, I was distracted for a moment. How about working with me to resolve this peacefully. Let's find someplace to start."

"How can you guarantee my safety should I even agree to negotiations? and how do you know I am not at this moment planning a massive attack aimed at destroying this base?"

"First of all, I cannot guarantee you anything right now. Second, I am certain you are at this moment planning to continue your attack and capture this base, not destroy it. What I can guarantee, is to help you and the Scentar hold off starting to kill each other long enough to try and find an agreement to prevent that carnage. At this moment, Humans have no quarrel with either of you. There is no history of warfare or even the slightest conflict with Scentar or Segwah, none! Surely that would be a good place to start."

"Can you offer anything as a good-faith gesture? Anything that we can confirm?"

"Yes, and do you?"

"I think we do, but who lays down the first weapon or the first revelation? That is a dangerous situation."

"I think your ship is mostly, if not completely disabled. You don't appear to possess any useable weapons or you would be firing at something."

"Actually, we can use our impact weapons. I believe we demonstrated some of their capabilities to you. Would you like me to prove that?"

"No! I'll take your word for that. Your revelation was at least a beginning. The negotiations began, and now I shall give you some information."

Both Sylvia and Leura shouted, "No!"

Leura continued. "You have no authority to give them any information. None! You can't do this."

I'd had about enough of this, so I shouted at them, "You are invaders in *our* universe. Both Scentar and Segwah are aliens here. If military power makes you right, then you can stop me, but don't you follow some universal laws that prevent your interfering with our lives?"

The silence spoke volumes.

"Captain Woolgah!"

"Yes, Dr. Syl."

"Do you follow any laws that protect alien species like we humans in our own universe from interference by Segwah?"

"Yes, we do. They are the basis for our actions in your universe. I believe I hinted at that during your visit. However, there are exceptions in cases of imminent danger to the Segwah universe. Your abduction and use as an agent of ours is one example."

"If there were no danger to the Segwah you would not be able to interfere with our actions, correct?"

"That's correct."

"And Leura, doesn't the same thing apply to Scentar?"

"As long as there is no immediate danger, that's correct."

"Then I am requesting that both sides stand down and cease any planned hostilities. That's ALL planned and unplanned hostilities."

"I don't think that is possible," Leura said.

I glanced at Sylvia and said, "Open this broadcast com unit to all channels. Now!"

Sylvia pushed a few buttons. "It's now open to the entire base, sir."

"Captain Woolgah. Will you open your communications to your entire ship?"

"I'm a bit nervous about doing so, but yes. The entire ship can now hear your words."

"Thank you all for listening. This is Draxel Sil, a native resident of the universe you are all in as guests, or invaders. I am accompanied by another citizen of this universe, Maria Mendrex. You are to cease any combat activities in compliance with your laws and at the specific request of two native humans. We are the entire group of humans on this planet. To do otherwise would be to interfere with our culture and society and that is strictly against your law. I hereby direct any official to take all necessary steps to assure my orders are carried out. Do I make myself clear?"

The voice of General Straglo came on the com. "Am I to understand that Captain Woolgah has agreed to stand down?"

Captain Woolgah's deep voice replied, "Yes, General Straglo, I agreed and I believe you must as well."

"As much as I fear doing so, I have no choice," General Straglo replied.

There is one problem we Segwah must deal with soon, Dr. Syl."

"And what is that?"

"There is an attack fleet approaching. They are under orders to make a three pronged frontal attack on this base. Our little collision has destroyed our deep space communication system and we are without a way of contacting them. It would be greatly appreciated if you connect this com system to your own DS signal system, so I can contact the fleet and stop the attack. The frequency is 1074.044 the directional coordinates are180.23.56 and I believe time is of the essence."

General Straglo came on line. "We will place that link in operation in less than a minute, Captain. Our antennae are being redirected to 180.23.56."

"Thank you General. I will let you know when I confirm that the fleet has called off its attack. Their jump should be completed by now and they will be approaching at sub-light speed."

A stream of pops and tones was soon coming from the com unit. About a minute after the message stopped, another, answering message was heard. It was a much weaker series of similar sounds. This was followed by two more short series of each level.

Captain Woolgah's voice replaced the pops and tones. "I received confirmation. The attack has been called off. Our ships are well within range of your scanners if you care to confirm for yourselves."

Chapter 23 - Drax Gets His Way

I took charge of the com system and made this announcement, "This is Draxel Syl. I want to thank all of you for honoring my request. Now, I would like to set up a meeting where we can negotiate what to do from here on. Maria and I will represent humans, and I suggest Scentar and Segwah each select six individuals for the negotiations. Since this is a Scentar base, I suggest General Straglo as the host and negotiations leader. General, we will await your organization and scheduling of the first meeting."

As Drax walked away toward the cart, Maria followed him and asked, "How did you come up with that? It was a masterpiece. Your effort took a lot of brass, but you pulled it off. I would never believe it had a chance."

"Elementary, my dear Maria. Consider the players, all relatively junior officers in a highly structured organization with tight and strict rules. We hold all the cards. As long as we can keep them beholden to their laws and from killing each other, they're as docile as lambs. Even their warriors fit that bill."

"Drax, you're crazy! Where'd you ever learn that stuff?"

"Maria, I grew up in several foster homes in neighborhoods with bullies and pimps most of whom could break me in two and would at a moments notice. To make things worse, I was an Anglo in an Hispanic world. I developed the skill of being a peacemaker between guys, gals, and groups that routinely wanted to kill each other and hated Anglos. In the process, I learned how to earn the friendship of many who had no friends and didn't want any. There was a hierarchy of bullies from the top dogs to the lowly grunts. Each one bullied the ones lower and was bullied by the ones higher up in the hierarchy. Because of the special skills I developed as a peacemaker, they left me alone most of the time.

"I considered the Scentar and Gelwah as members of rival street gangs with a fairly strict code of ethics. That's how I treated them, and I succeeded. I even told Woolgah I grew up with guys like him. He didn't take it as an insult because I didn't belittle him. You got to give the devil his due."

"Now what will you do? You don't think any of those petty politicians on Earth will let you speak for them with these other universe people do you?"

"Don't need to. Who will ever hear about it? We'll be protected by their law about noninterference. That's the best protection ever. Once this gravitational tear problem is solved they'll all be history anyway. That's all they care about."

"I think you're wrong there. I do not share your cynicism. Anyway, I'd like to go home and back to work. This gallivanting all over the galaxy can wear you out. I've had about enough excitement to last me a long, long time."

I called Leura over. "Leura? Can you think of where we go from here? The immediate crisis seems over, and we're still in this damned tunnel."

"I'm sorry you two. We're waiting for the porter they are sending to pick us up. It will be right outside in a few minutes."

"What's a porter?" I asked.

"It's one of those little vans. We rode out here in one earlier. Remember? Let's go out to meet them."

We said goodby to Sylvia and followed Leura outside. The porter was bouncing across the field toward us. When it pulled up, we were surprised to see General Straglo seated in the back. When we entered he began talking.

"Dr. Syl? I hope you won't mind my asking, but we would like you to lead our negotiations. I'll gladly host, but after a few words with my staff, we decided you would be much better as the leader of the meeting."

"I am complimented, but wouldn't everyone want to appoint someone to lead who is more familiar with the problems?"

"We don't think so. We and the Segwah fought each other for thousands of your years, nearly six thousand, in fact. None of us has any real idea precisely how or why the conflict started. There are stories, of course, but no one seems able to sort myths from real knowledge. For this reason, we would like you to lead us and provide an objective view as moderator. I've not had a chance to suggest this to the Segwah, but I'm certain they would prefer you to me."

"There is much I must do back home. I need to be home soon."

The general turned to Leura. "You explain to him your plan about the portals."

My ears picked up. "What about portals?"

Leura took out a book from the small case she had been carrying and handed it to me. "This is an explanation of the dangers associated with your gravity experiments and how to protect against them. The book contains an outline of a proposal to teach you how to conduct those gravity experiments without danger of creating a fault in the fabric of space/time. This is not a simple subject to teach and to understand. You will need to learn a few different concepts in both math and physics. We think this will take at least four months. During the process, you will also learn something of our culture. This is essential to the learning that is to follow. Once the cultural training is complete, the next step, training in the use of many new instruments, will take at least another four to six months. The training will take place both here and on Stentor Seven. It's a bit unusual. We're not sure how quickly you can adapt to radically new knowledge and techniques that our people often learn at an early age. The process could take a lot more or a lot less time than we expect. That remains to be seen."

"What do I do with this book?"

"Read through first and then ask about anything that doesn't seem clear to you. You'll realize, we will not only be teaching you how to safely conduct your experiments, but also how to teach the same information and techniques to others. That is even more important. Once you read and understand the information in this book, you will realize how important stopping what you did that started this whole process is. I mean stopping things immediately."

"What about the Eegis Project and the work Marty, I, and our group are doing? I would be gone for a long time from that."

"You'll learn more during your studies here than you would in a hundred years of stumbling around on your own. The answers we will give you will do that. You will also continue contact with your group and share some of your new found knowledge with them. The Eegis project will benefit immeasurably."

"Doesn't that go against your basic laws of contact? I thought that kind of interference was strictly forbidden."

"Drax, you must realize that in a case where the existence of two universes is at stake, those laws would be abrogated."

"Just checking. I wouldn't want to break any of the rules, your rules that is."

Maria spoke up. "Drax, sometimes you can be so brilliant, and others you are as stupid as a log. I can't believe you're still carrying all that garbage around with you."

General Straglo spoke up. "Did I understand you to say Dr. Syl is stupid? That cannot be true. You must be mistaken."

Maria grinned. "General, human men, brilliant men, men with superb education and experience, men of great scientific achievement, all of these can experience moments of extreme ignorance and stupidity about women. It's as if their brain shuts down and their liver or some other even worse internal organ takes over their thinking. My guess is Scentar, male Scentar, overcame that little throwback to the lower animals thousands of generations ago."

The general was shocked and incredulous. "I'm afraid such a thing is beyond my comprehension. We admire our ladies and enjoy their company. Our families are usually close and share much with each other. They are quite different from Human families because of our twin females. All of these things we give up when we make a commitment to the NU service, family, children, close friends. It's a call of tremendous dedication and sacrifice. The service neither encourages nor discourages male/female relationships. A few of us find mates among others in the service. Some even bond and raise families, but most do not. Because of both instincts and culture, we form permanent and long-lasting emotional connections with those mates who share our values. This can be sad for those who find such an attraction toward one who does not feel likewise. Fortunately, that is an extreme rarity."

Maria sighed. "That, General, is a gross understatement."

I got the message but was not swayed. I did not feel as angry toward Leura as I had, but I had no warm feelings. I wished Maria would leave things be. Then we pulled up to the portal building and headed inside. General Straglo led us up an elevator to the fifth floor where we were greeted by several Scentar, both men and women. I could see several machines working around the Segwah ship through the huge glass window. They were digging the Gelwah out. Behind the Gelwah another identical ship stood on the ground.

Six sturdy legs supported the ship, and a stairway led up to a hatch in the nose. There were a number of both Scentar and Segwah on the ground near the ships.

Spotting this, General Straglo said. "I never thought I would experience such a day, Scentar and Segwah together and not trying to kill each other. I wonder if this will last?"

"I hope so. I said.

Then our friend from the tunnels, Sylvia, walked up with a big smile on her face. "They asked for someone to be your guide around the place, and I volunteered. I jumped at the chance. So they've assigned me to show you to your rooms and then be your guide."

"That's great, Sylvia, so where are we headed?" Maria asked.

"To the base hotel. It's a rather long walk, so a porter is waiting outside. I'm supposed to tell you to relax and rest in preparation for tomorrow and the start of planning for the negotiating sessions that will start in two days."

I was dumbfounded. "Wait a minute, a planning session? Tomorrow? Who says?" I didn't see anyone who could organize such a meeting so quickly.

Sylvia smiled. "I'll explain the schedule as we are on our way to the hotel. Follow me."

Maria and I were soon on our way to the hotel.

Chapter 24 - Drax and Maria get an education

Sylvia explained as we rode along. "You must understand, our communication system here is such that virtually everyone on the base is kept informed of all important happenings as they occur. Our civilian head—our Archon is the word in your language—controls and arranges all nonmilitary matters as well as all civilian/military interactions. The Archon is the ultimate decision maker, our chief executive when there is any question of what action to take."

"And who is this Archon?" I asked.

"Her name is Leandra Gordon. She was elected by all the citizens of Vega Five and Stentor Seven. Her maia, Louandra is her assistant."

"That's interesting. I didn't realize you use a democratic form of government as we do."

"Well, it's not quite like yours. One has to earn citizenship in order to vote. I for instance am not yet a citizen."

"You're in the Military and you're not a citizen?"

"No, I still must earn citizenship."

"What are the requirements to become a citizen?"

"There are many, but the most common is education. In our education system, one must be an R3 or higher before citizenship is granted. I must attend the university for at least another complete series to be eligible. A series is roughly comparable to one of your semesters or quarters. Even then there is an examination to learn if R3 status has been reached. Few do so before they reach full maturity."

"Okay, now what does than mean, reach full maturity? It has a nebulous meaning in our language."

"One must reach the age of nineteen of *our years* to be considered, mature. Nineteen is usually the earliest age when our bodies mature, and we are able to conceive. A major physical change takes place at this time. It's an important and specific change of both our appearance and our body chemistry. Until that change, I am considered a juvenile with much less authority than one who is mature. I will reach eighteen cycles on my next birth anniversary. That's roughly twenty of your years. At least one cycle will pass after that before I could possibly go through the change, or pass the test for that matter."

"Interesting! I didn't know any of that about you. What is this, R3, you speak of? Is it an arbitrary education level like college graduation or a bachelor's degree in our world?"

"There are some similarities, but many differences."

"For instance?"

"We use no grade level system in our schools after our primary education is complete. After that, one takes an entrance exam on any subject or service one wants to study. The result of the entrance examination determines at what level one enters school and also what school one enters. The R plus the number indicates the number of special courses of study, courses beyond the basic, where one has successfully passed the examination for that level. I completed one special course of study equivalent raising my status to R1. That would be somewhere between a bachelor's degree and a master's in your system."

"Then your R3 would be equivalent to our doctorate?"

"No, an R3 is much more like your master's degree. Your Doctorate would be more the equivalent of our R4. Of course there are numerous differences. The only real equivalence is the time and effort required to achieve any level. In addition to education, experience in any field can lead to an increase in R level. For instance, my military service has raised me one level to R2. Long periods of service in any field can also lead to advancement, but even then there are examinations one must take. Every advance must be earned by work and qualifications."

"I understand that Leura is an R8. Isn't she rather young to obtain so much education and experience, and why does that status give her so much power as when I wanted to use the data unit?"

"The important thing in our culture is education and achievement. Leura has not reached R8 by education alone, but by her achievement as well. She is a famous individual to all Scentar, because of her work on plants on Stentor Seven. She is undoubtedly the highest ranking botanist that has ever been here. In addition, she is an accomplished Human cultural scientist and one of if not **the** highest authority on Human cultures from our universe. That is why she works with you Humans. Early in their lives she and Laura, her Maia, were similar to what you might call child prodigies. Actually, their entire family earned similar records and are all high-level Scentar. The Maias' commitment to NU service was unusual and unique in their family. Leura and Laura are the only ones of their family to do so."

"So all that makes her a powerful person here? One who commands respect and whose orders are obeyed?"

"That is a rather coarsely drawn comparison. There is a lot more than what you say. One would need to understand more of our culture to learn the reality of our actions. I am certain you will receive some inculcation of our culture during the course of study you will be taking."

"Is everybody here aware of more about what I'll be doing than I am? That gives me a rather uncomfortable feeling—like my life is out of my control."

Maria spoke up. "Drax, lately you developed a fragile ego. Don't you recall Sylvia explaining how information is communicated to everyone here instantaneously? That explained a lot to me. Naturally Sylvia, as our guide, would know these things. I even knew that from being in the vicinity when Leura was telling you about it. She also said something about you deciding whether or not to take the course of study. You would still maintain that precious control you are so sensitive about."

"Damn it Maria, why do you keep hitting on my ego? I don't think it has been bruised. I guess I'm sensitive about losing control of my actions. Could be it's a mental throwback of my younger days when I was constantly on edge, on the defensive, trying to stay alive. Those were tense times for me. I was alone in a culture that had a tendency to destroy anything and anyone who was alone or strange."

"Well, mister sensitive, that was an amazing revelation. Maybe you are now coming to your good senses. You are not alone now. You are among real friends who care about you—big time. Why don't you relax, and ignore all those demons from your past? The little lady you seem so suspicious of would give her life for you. It's obvious, but you seem oblivious to it as a reality."

"All right, Maria. Maybe I am a bit suspicious because of my past experiences and that made me super sensitive about some things, but that's who I am. Those instilled cautions are difficult to dislodge. I'm a hard sell, but once sold I stay sold. You for instance. How long have we known each other, worked together?"

"Two years at Cal Tech and three at Eegis as I count it."

"What does that have to do with anything?"

"Don't you remember how we started off? Shall I repeat what you said about me to Marty about two weeks after I was put in charge of your section?"

"Hell, Maria, that's not fair. I didn't know you then."

"And what is the difference? I mean the real difference? I believe you said you resented me because I was taking control of your life. Sound familiar?"

"You didn't seduce me to persuade me to do your wishes."

"No! I didn't. But neither did Leura. She seduced you because she cared for you and wanted to share intimacy. Unless I miss my guess, that little activity had nothing whatsoever to do with getting you to do anything but make love with her. This was an emotional and cultural thing, pure and simple. Can't you understand?"

"Hell, I don't know."

"Yes you do! Admit you were wrong and remove that stupid ego stuff from your head."

"I still feel used. I still don't trust her."

"You're an idiot!"

"I'm reacting the way most Human males would react."

"And that's the big problem. Leura is not a Human. I'll wager one thing that is bothering you is the way she and all Scentar deal with love and sex. Their way is uniquely different from how humans handle those significant drives. When Leura explained how their culture viewed them, I had a typically human reaction. Since then I thought a lot about the realities of how we behave. I'm beginning to think their way may be infinitely better. It would take some getting used to, but the lack of stigma alone would make life better for many individuals."

"Maybe so, but get off my back. Give me some time to think about it."

"Okay Drax. I guess I am a bit pushy. But that's because I think so much of both of you—and that's the whole truth.

Chapter 25 - The Luxury Hotel

Sylvia, who had been hearing the entire conversation, had something to say. "Excuse me, I am listening, but I understood virtually none of your conversation. I concluded it was a Human cultural thing beyond my understanding."

Maria laughed. "Sylvia, you are not alone. Much of what we were discussing is beyond even our own understanding. Some Human behavior is clearly beyond rational explanation, confusing even to other Humans."

"I think I would like to study Human culture. From what you say it must be complex, intriguing."

Maria and I both laughed heartily. The reply, "Good luck!" came from both of us.

Maria said, "If you ever gain an understanding, please teach us, will you?"

Her brow wrinkled in question, Sylvia said, "You are definitely confusing me. Your culture must be different from ours, very different."

"Truer words were never spoken," I said with a smile.

The porter pulled up in front of our hotel.

"Here we are," Sylvia proclaimed as she opened the doors, "Here are the key cards for your rooms. You'll find appropriate clothing in the cabinets and the closets. All services are available by voice command. Anything you want simply ask out loud. That includes lights, water, shower temperature, windows, blinds, and food or drink. There's a com console and entertainment center in both rooms. It operates by voice commands. If you are confused or want a question answered, ask the com unit. The display will explain virtually anything you might ask it. Should you want to speak to anyone, their name will cause the system to attempt contact."

I was impressed. "How is all this ready for us? and so quickly?"

"Leura made the arrangement some time ago. She was certain you would be coming here. This whole Human/Scentar interaction project has been in her hands for several years. The latest development, the problems related to your gravity experiments, has greatly expanded the scope of her responsibility. Now she has help from the other side. Many in her family are now involved in the project. Of course, except for her maia, they all work from the other side."

"What's this *other side* you keep referring to?" I thought it must refer to their universe.

"I'm sorry, sometimes I forget you are not Scentar—and that's a compliment. We refer to our home universe as the other side. This refers to the other side of the universe portal. A place where we dare not go."

"As I suppose, and I'll consider your words as complimentary. Indeed, you seem as an old friend to us. I think Maria would agree."

Maria nodded her head in agreement. "Yes, Sylvia, you act as if we've always known you. As a matter of fact, all Scentar seem to become as friends rapidly, at least to us. Are you trained this way?"

Sylvia laughed. "Guilty! Everyone here has had training in relating to Humans. There is much emphasis on being *genuine* as you might say, and relating as equals in every way. You must remember, once we are here there is no going back. We are committed to being as *human* as is possible. I hope that came out correctly. I would not want to be misunderstood."

"Sylvia, you are priceless," Maria said giving her a soft pat on the shoulder. "You are kind and considerate, a lot more so than most humans would be. Now I would like to go to my room and stretch out for a while. This has been a busy and tense day. I think Drax will agree, eh, Drax?"

"Absolutely! Where will you go now, after delivering us here?"

"My home is in an apartment not far from here, about twenty minutes away by porter. Should you need me, call my name and I'll answer. You two are my responsibility as long as you stay here. I am pleased to serve you."

"Well, Sylvia, we are pleased you are taking care of us. When will we see you again?"

"I will be here at eight o'clock to pick you up. You should learn that we divide a day into twenty four hours and each hour into sixty minutes here because that is how you act on Earth. But realize our time periods are all a bit longer than yours since Vega Five takes twenty-five and six tenths of your hours for a single rotation. Timepieces of several types will be provided as needed. Your own will show at least one hour and thirty-six minutes earlier each day compared with our time. Several weeks will be required for your circadian rhythm to adjust to the change. You may suffer from what you call jet-lag for several days, but it should go away in no more than a week."

"Oh my!" Maria exclaimed. "I don't handle jet-lag well. I never thought about the differences in our times."

"You'll get used to it, Maria," I said grinning broadly. "Now let's head up to our rooms."

After sending Sylvia home, we took the elevator up to the twentieth floor and found our rooms. We were right across the hall from each other.

Maria opened her door, turned and said, "Good night Drax. I plan on some serious shut-eye and soon. See you in the morning."

My "Goodnight Maria," was barely spoken before she closed her door.

I walked into a room that was a bit larger than the average hotel room on Earth. Two chairs were at a small table in front of a large window facing what I took to be north. There was a large, open closet with a built-in chest of drawers on the right. There were several suits, mix and match, and a nice robe hanging in the closet. A check of the drawers revealed shirts, socks and underwear. At the bottom was a shoe rack with several pairs of shoes and some slippers. Opposite the closet was an alcove with an office sized desk and chair with a large display screen above the desk. The words, *Welcome Drax* were displayed on the screen. The desk was against the wall. As you sat at the desk, your back would be toward the closet. The alcove was open on the right side to the main room.

The main room had carpeted floor and the table and chairs I mentioned before. On the left and beyond the desk was a door I assumed led to the bathroom. Beyond the doorway, there was a wall covered with a large ceiling to floor tapestry with wispy geometric designs in reds, greens and browns. Everything was pleasing to the eye. The wall ended at the window which I assumed was a sliding glass door. There was a balcony on the other side of the glass. Against the wall with the tapestry, was a simple couch big enough for at least four people. There was no more furniture in the room. *Where is the bed?* I wondered. I decided to ask and see what happens.

"Where's the bed?" I asked aloud.

I was answered by a soft female voice that sounded much like Leura. "I am at your service, Dr. Syl. Please call me Tillie. The bed is behind the couch. Would you like to use the bed?"

"Yes, Tillie." I wanted to find out what was going to happen.

The voice warned, "Thank you, Dr. Syl, and please stay clear of the lighted section of floor." At the same time, the floor in front of the couch lit up in about a six-foot square section. The tapestry-covered wall tilted out into the room and the couch folded up and back into the wall beneath the bed. In a few seconds, a queen-sized bed was in place with pillows where the couch used to be. The wall opposite the bed parted, revealing a display screen displaying the words, *Welcome Drax!*

After testing things like the lights, the sound system, the temperature control and how to use the bathroom facilities, I decided to try a bit of fun.

"Tillie, can I order a massage?"

"Yes. There is a massage room on the second floor. Would you like to arrange for a massage?"

"Can't I get one here in my room?"

"Yes, but that is an extra cost option. The massage room is included in your room rate."

"Are you sure?"

"I will check. One moment, please."

In less than a minute Tillie replied. "George from physical therapy will be glad to come and give you a massage. There will be no extra charge."

"How about a female masseuse? Are there any of them around?"

"I will check. One moment please."

Leura appeared on the screen. "Drax, Tillie reports you are making some strange requests. She was directed to contact me for any unusual requests or activities. Can I be of help?"

This was an unexpected turn of events. "No, not really. I was testing to see how this thing worked. Tillie is a machine, right?"

"That's right, a machine programmed to do and explain ordinary things. Tillie is resourceful, but she has limitations. Anything out of the ordinary is referred to a person on duty. I was checking to find out if you or Maria needed anything. Tillie got me as the one on duty. Are you certain you don't need anything?"

Oh how I was tempted. Memories of the time on Stentor Seven surged through my brain. Then the old anger kicked in. "No, Leura. I don't need anything. This is one fancy place. A guy could become accustomed to living like this."

"Well, don't get too used to it. Once the negotiations are finished and you start the learning process, things might not be so fancy. So good night."

"Good night Leura."

I wondered what she meant by those comments, especially those words, *things might not be so fancy.*

"Dr. Syl. Do you want George to come and give you a massage?"

"No, Tillie. Forget about the massage. Fix me a nice hot bath in the Jaccuzzi, or what ever you call it. I'd also like some soft lights, soft music, a glass of good scotch on the rocks, and don't let me fall asleep until I go to bed."

"Yes, Dr. Syl. and that's called a therapy bath."

The results were fantastic, unbelievable in fact. The therapy bath turned me into mush, the lights were low and soft, the music was Dave Brubeck and George Shearing, and the scotch was twelve year old Chivas. Somehow Tillie had learned about my favorite things. By time the warm air drier had blown me dry, I was barely able to drag myself up onto the bed. A sip, the last sip of the Scotch and yours truly was off to dreamland on the wings of Ferde Grofe's "Grand Canyon Suite." I'm sure I never slept more soundly.

Chapter 26 - Peaceful Negotiations

Midday of the second day of negotiations things changed dramatically. Communication portals linking the highest levels of both Segwah and Scentar governing bodies had been added to the negotiations. The Segwah had a council of thirteen elders who had selected one as the council representative for the negotiations. The Scentar were governed by a triumvirate who presided over a rather large body of representatives. All three of the triumvirate were included in the negotiating group. Several hours of procedural negotiations were needed to accomplish this during which time all but two members of both original negotiating teams stepped down. We now had ten members with the triumvirate acting as a single individual for all intent and purposes making the group eight strong.

Vraga, the spokesperson for the triumvirate, was a striking woman with long dark red hair sprinkled with white. She was a bit taller than the other two members, and was the senior member of the three Scentar. The other two, one male and one female, would not speak during the negotiations but would confer with Vraga. The left wall of the negotiating room was a display screen where the triumvirate appeared as if they were seated in the room. The right wall held a similar image of the Segwah council representative, Wolkah.

Wolkah was obviously an aged Segwah. Though his advanced age had made him much smaller both in height and bulk than Captain Woolgah or First Officer Jemrah, he was obviously still vital. His facial hair was white and he was well groomed. The exposed part of his face wore the weatherbeaten lines of one who has experienced a full life.

He stood and addressed the group with the strong voice of one in authority, even through the changes of the automatic translator. "I believe we all understand the situation there on Vega Five. This unique set of conditions has brought about extraordinary events, and is a first in a long history. I must say I feel a great deal of difficulty restraining a lifetime of animosity as I am certain do the Scentar present. That we are all governed by virtually the same powerful body of law has been a major revelation to our council. We did not until this time learn that Scentar had a similar law covering interaction with other species and cultures less advanced than their own. This new knowledge has shaken the foundation of our governing principles and the actions those principles bring about. Because of this we, the Segwah council, took action. We ordered all of our field operations to cease initiating attacks and take only defensive actions. This is a unilateral decision we made without any preconditions. We will, of course counter all attacks on any of our personnel wherever they may occur. We will first learn what new ideas or concepts this group brings up before changing this new policy."

When he finished and sat down, the Scentar triumvirate were seen to confer rapidly with each other. While this was happening, Leura turned to Maria and me saying, "I can hardly believe what I'm hearing. I never knew the Segwah had such laws or that they could bring about such remarkable results. It's incredible."

I remained skeptical. "I hope this *truce* goes farther and does last, but I fear that some goof with an itchy trigger finger will mess things up, and soon. Look at those warriors out there near each other by those ships. They've been killing each other all their lives. They must be harboring resentment for the past. One misstep and I'll bet they'll be back to killing each other in a second."

"Drax, You may fail to comprehend the power of our laws of contact." Leura tried explaining. "That is our most powerful controlling force. It is constantly drummed into us from when we were young. What amazes me is that the Segwah enacted a similar law and they obey it. I was never aware of that. That changes things substantially and also gives you and Maria a lot of power. You realized that power and used it to create an astonishing situation. One with powerful and far-reaching possibilities."

Vraga stood up and faced the group. "We communicated the words of Wolkah to our governing body and respond emphatically that we respect and admire the actions of the Segwah. We also recommended that they, the governing body, take all steps necessary to stop our military from attacking any and all Segwah outposts or forces anywhere. That applies to forces in both of our universes as well as this one. I am certain to receive confirmation shortly. I must say that I am overwhelmed, indeed that all three of us are amazed and heartened at this turn of events. This is without precedent in our entire history. I will inform you all as soon as I receive a response." The group relaxed and began talking to each other while waiting for Vraga's people to respond. I looked at the faces around the room. All appeared positive save one and that troubled me. Jemrah, First

Officer of the star ship Gelwah, was sitting back, arms crossed and with a defiant scowl. He had an expression on his face best be described as disgusted.

Captain, you had better pay attention to your first officer. I thought to myself. I had a bad feeling about this, but would wait to see if anyone else had the same kinds of thoughts. I decided to share my feelings with Captain Woolgah at my earliest opportunity. Actually, I thought Jemrah had a murderous look in his eyes, and that did not portend well for the new found affinity between Scentar and Segwah. Our eyes met and locked. He seemed to sneer before turning away from my gaze. *That bastard is up to no good,* I thought.

I turned to Maria and said quietly, "Look out for Captain Woolgah's first officer."

"Why do you say that?"

"Just an instinct. He's up to some kind of mischief, of that I am certain. Try to observe him without being obvious. I'd be amazed if he's a happy camper. All these warm fuzzies between Scentar and Segwah obviously made him uncomfortable and wary, maybe even angry. One pissed off Segwah might lead to several more. We should see who his buddies are, keep track of them as well and particularly learn where they go. I plan on making notes."

"You **are** suspicious. I'll keep an eye on them when I can and see if I agree."

I called the group to order as Vraga was ready to speak.

"It is confirmed. All Scentar attack plans against the Segwah are now on hold pending the results of this meeting. I can also confirm that as far as we have been able to determine, Segwah attacks on us also ceased. This confirms Captain Woolgah's words. I want you all to know that for the first time in thousands of our *years*, there are no ongoing combat operations between Scentar and the Segwah. This is an impossible turn of events I hope can be extended well into the future. Who knows where that might lead us? I believe a round of applause should be given to both Captain Woolgah who was brave enough to take the first step and to the creative genius of Dr. Draxel Syl who had the audacity and wisdom to apply our own law to the situation."

With that the entire group applauded. I carefully watched First Officer Jemrah whose applause was far from enthusiastic and whose face was carefully emotionless. Maria was also watching him. It was long past the time when the group was supposed to adjourn for the day.

I stood up and announced, "We stayed long past our closing time, so I suggest we adjourn until tomorrow morning unless there are any objections."

Captain Woolgah stood and addressed the group. "Before we leave, I would like to thank Vraga for the fine compliment she paid me. It was appreciated. I would also like to thank the other Scentar, our human friends, Chairman Wolkah and our Segwah council for the creative thought and prompt actions that brought us to this singular achievement. We made a significant step. Now we must create new ways of thinking about and acting toward each other, so this small step can grow into a new tomorrow for all sentient beings."

Another round of applause echoed through the room, but Jemrah seemed less than enthusiastic once more. As we headed out of the room I went over to Captain Woolgah and took him aside back into the room, just the two of us.

"Captain! I think your first officer is less than enthusiastic about all this. I would watch my back if I were you."

"My friend Drax. I am well aware of the shortcomings and lack of vision of Jemrah. I believe there are good reasons for his reaction. Not long ago he was in a major battle with Chief Delgo. At the time, he was captain of the star ship Remlah, a ship of the same class as the Gelwah. In the battle which had not been going his way, then Captain Delgo pretended severe damage and limped away from the battle, drawing Jemrah away from the other ships in his formation. Jemrah was thinking to finish him off and return to the battle, a foolish move. Delgo quickly portaled his ship behind Jemrah's vessel and opened fire with all weapons. Though he fought valiantly, the first disrupter volley destroyed his maneuvering thrusters and left him virtually helpless. Seeing this, several of our ships broke off from the battle and came to his rescue. Captain Delgo portaled back to his battle position and reentered the battle. As a result, the crew of the Remlah had to be transferred to our other vessels. The advantage provided the Scentar enabled them to drive our fleet from the battle in disarray. This resulted in the Remlah being abandoned and lost. Fortunately, the self destruct system destroyed the Remlah before the Scentar could board her."

What happened to Jemrah then? How did he end up on your ship?"

"He was of course demoted, a relatively minor punishment for such a foolish and damaging action. He had several subordinate positions after that and was troublesome in each. He had been my first officer earlier, and a good one, so I stepped in and asked for him when my first officer was given a command of his own. He has been with me for three of your years now, and with few complaints. The still seething resentment he harbors is understandable because of his loss of rank and status, not to mention the humiliation. Yes, he is one troubled Segwah. I doubt this will affect his performance under my command, but if it does, I will deal with him swiftly and decisively."

"That's quite a story. How ironic that Chief Delgo would be here at this time, ironic and unfortunate. I hope Jemrah doesn't make serious problems for you and the rest of us. We are dealing with enough as is."

Captain Woolgah reassured me as we walked out of the room. "I'll keep a close watch on him while we're here. Should I see any signs of danger I will act swiftly."

I was not convinced and remained concerned as I hurried to catch up with Maria.

"Where did you disappear to?" She asked. "We walked out of the room and suddenly you were gone. Our hosts are waiting to take us to our rooms. When you disappeared, I was beginning to worry something had happened."

When I explained my conversation with Captain Woolgah she said, "You certainly are concerned about him, aren't you?

"I'm afraid he's going to cause trouble, big trouble, in spite of the Captain's reassurances. Actually, I don't think he was completely honest with me. The Segwah don't seem to use the compunction about deceit that the Scentar possess—if indeed they do. I'm still not sure about that."

"Well, Drax, I am and I came to that conclusion all on my own."

"Are you sure about that? I mean they posses the obvious talent to mess with your mind. They surely did with mine and I'll not soon forget it. Anyone who can implant memories in your brain can deceive. That is truly deceit. I don't appreciate it one little bit."

"I know where you're coming from, Drax, but I still think they are honorable and treat us with respect and honesty. I also think you judge the little lady all wrong and you're going to suffer."

"Ha! We'll see. I wouldn't be too sure if I were you. Maria, we're involved with two humanoid species far more developed intellectually and technically than we are. Think Europeans with their guns, books, and factories and native Americans when we Europeans arrived. Think about what our ancestors did to those poor bastards."

"Your comment is a poor comparison. We are greatly advanced from those Europeans emerging from the Dark Ages. They had none of the humanitarian consideration both the Scentar and the Segwah expressed in their laws about less advanced cultures or societies. You see what your own reference to those laws got us—Peace!"

"I'll concede your point. I'll also concede my ego took a buffeting. That said, I still don't trust them—none of them. Some of this stuff is too pat—too contrived not to be deliberate."

"You think this war thing is not real? That it's all put up? If so, what could be their purpose? They've gone to an awful lot of trouble to convince two people, well, three including Marty, about all this."

Chapter 27 - A Terrible Surprise

Tillie called, "Dr. Syl—Dr. Syl! Time to wake up." Her musical voice awakened me at precisely seven. "There are sixty-four of your minutes before Sylvia will pick you up. Would you like a cool shower?"

"No, Tillie. I'd like a luke warm one."

"As you wish."

By seven twenty I was ready, and none too soon. Maria's face on the video accompanied by her voice invaded my delicious solitude. "Drax! I'll meet you at your door for breakfast in one minute. You are ready, aren't you?"

"Yes, Godzilla. I'm ready and opening my door."

After breakfast in the hotel dining room, we headed for the main entrance. At exactly eight o'clock, Sylvia herded us into the porter and headed out around the fountain on the way to our meeting. Suddenly things went terribly wrong.

There were several loud tearing sounds, and I felt a flash of heat on my face. The porter turned sharply to the left and crumpled into the fountain. One moment I was in the air. The next moment I was in the water of the fountain. The porter was cut in two and was hanging with the opening above me, upside down and slowly rolling down on top of me. Half of Sylvia's body was still strapped in the driver's seat. I couldn't see Maria anywhere as the remains of the porter slowly pressed me down into the pool. I had glimpsed bright red water in the pool before my head was pressed under the water. I heard voices shouting in an unknown language punctuated with the repeated Fzzzt, Fzzzt of Galbos firing as I struggled to reach some air.

After what seemed like forever and when I knew I was going to die, I felt the weight of the porter being lifted off me. As my face broke the surface, I desperately gasped for air and got a mixture of air and water. I choked and sputtered until I was lifted by my legs, upside down and clear of the water. In this position, the water ran out of my lungs, and I slowly regained my breath. All I saw were some stocky legs in black combat boots. I recognized them as Segwah boots. I was being held upside down by two Segwah. That was not encouraging. When I looked beyond the boots, I saw the wreckage of the porter, and several bodies and pieces of bodies draped over the edges of the fountain. The bodies were all Segwah. *What in hell happened?*

I finally gained enough breath to speak. "I can breathe! Please put me down."

"Are you all right?" a familiar voice asked. "You look like Segwah hell!" The voice said as I was lowered and helped into a sitting position on the edge of the fountain. I looked up into the face of Captain Woolgah.

"Captain. Should I be glad to see you?"

"You should be. We saved you from being executed."

"By whom"

"About a hundred renegade Segwah. Many of them were damned good soldiers. Even some were friends."

"Where's Maria?"

"I'm afraid she's among the dead. Hit in the abdomen by a Galbo blast. Sorry my friend. I realize she was close to you. Several Scentar removed her body from the vehicle and were carrying her off the last I saw of her."

"Damn! Damn! Damn!" I ended with some big time tears. I realized how important Maria had become to me. The pain I felt was much different from that of losing a colleague, or even a friend.

"Who else?" I managed to ask after I regained some control.

"Your driver, two attendants from the hotel, one bystander, four good Segwah fighters from my combat troops and ninety renegades: including Captain Letchwah of the star ship Reechlah. That's all I learned from the report here in my hand."

"What in hell happened, Captain?"

"You remember warning me about my First Officer, Jemrah?"

"Was he involved?"

"Yes, but to his credit, he's the one who realized the renegades were going to attack and where. He became suspicious of several of the crew of the Reechlah when he overheard some of their conversation. At great personal risk, he hid near their ship. Using a listening device, he heard them plotting. He took most of the night to work his way out of his hiding place and reach me without being caught. He was then powerfully persuasive to convince me to mount an action against them.

We led our entire combat group out to try to arrive here before them. Unfortunately, they were not only ahead of us, but they kept a rear guard which we ran into some distance before we could reach their main force. Destroying that rear guard cost me three good men. By the time we caught up with their main force, they were within range of the hotel and were set up to wait for your appearance. They obviously had someone on the inside tell them where you would be and when and how you would be heading out. So we're not out of the woods yet.

"Jemrah and two others volunteered to try to flank them and reach your vehicle by running around their force barely out of sight. They hoped to do this before the porter was cut to pieces. They nearly made it in time. As we caught up with them and started our own attack, your vehicle started to leave and they opened fire. The battle was over quickly. Galbos at close range can kill a lot of men in a short period of time. Because of our vantage point behind a hill and with them all out in the open it was a slaughter. We only lost one more. With the three on the other side of the fountain and the rest of us on this side, we set up a vicious cross fire as your vehicle started around the fountain.

"Unfortunately, they managed to fire off several blasts that hit your vehicle. I think the fact that the porter turned into the fountain was what saved your life as both the vehicle and the fountain were between you and the Galbos that fired. Jemrah reached you first. He and his two comrades lifted the remains of the vehicle off of you. When he realized you were under water, Jemrah and another picked you up by your ankles to try to clear the water out of your airways."

"I guess I owe your first officer an apology and a sincere thank you."

"Not only you, but I as well, as do all Segwah and Scentar. I hope that his unbelievably brave and selfless actions will gain for him full reinstatement in our military. I plan on using all the influence and persuasion I can to make such a thing happen. He will also be a candidate for our highest military honor, the Order of Cheemah."

"What do we do about the mole?"

"The what?"

"I'm sorry, the inside contact who provided them with the information."

"There are still twenty-two members of the crew of the Reechlaw back with the ship. My men are now on their way to take over the ship and question the crew. We also captured five members of the attacking force who were not killed in the battle. My men will learn all they can from them before they are executed."

"You're going to execute them without a trial?"

"They will be asked what was in their minds. If we find they were forced to act with the renegades under threat of death, they will be released to face a less severe punishment. Otherwise, they will be executed immediately."

"How can you tell if they speak the truth or not?"

Captain Woolgah laughed. "Our interrogation techniques gain truth. We merely open the minds of the accused. There is no way they can hide the truth from us."

"Torture?"

Again the captain laughed. "No need for that. Our equipment reads thoughts without pain or discomfort of any kind and only takes a few minutes. With any luck, we will discover your *mole* as well. I'm afraid the one or few possessing that knowledge are dead."

"Amazing! Couldn't you use that to find any traitor?"

"Our equipment can be used only on those found involved in illegal or traitorous activity, and accused by two reliable witnesses. It is used both to convict and exonerate the accused. Those who make the accusation are also subject to such examinations, so accusations are never made falsely. It's an effective and humane system."

"Sounds to me like it would be hard to beat. Don't you use lawyers?"

"Of course, but they too are subject to examination. No one can lie to our system. Deceit is impossible."

Chapter 28 - A Military Standoff

A loud voice was heard over some kind of speaker system. "Segwah! You are surrounded by a large force with superior weapons. Lay down your weapons and stand together in a group. Now!"

"Shield!" Captain Woolgah shouted. There was an immediate loud crack, like the first sound of a close lightning strike. Everything went black, then silence.

After checking his men to see if they were all right, he turned to me. "Drax, we are now protected from all but the most powerful weapons by a new Segwah technology, a portable shield generator of great power we brought with us in case of such a development. Unfortunately, the shield stops any outgoing weapon fire as well. They cannot hit us, and we cannot hit them."

As lights came on from portable lamps carried by each Segwah, I asked Captain Woolgah, "So what happens now?"

"That my good friend is a question with no answer. This is the first time our shield has been used in a combat situation. As I said, our shield is new."

"Could I run through it?"

"No! Both energy and matter are stopped completely."

"Could you shut it off long enough for me to run past it?"

"That would be risky."

"But not impossible?"

"We would be exposed to enemy fire while the shield is down."

"Suppose I started running at the shield, and you turned it off before I hit it, then turned it back on when I passed it. Could you risk that?"

"I'm certain there would be no danger to us as I doubt they could react quickly enough to aim before the shield was back in place, but you would be out in the open. However, if you didn't clear the width of the shield before it was turned back on you would be obliterated."

"Well then you'll wait until I'm clear before throwing the switch."

"I suppose that is possible."

"How can I communicate with you from the outside?"

"Difficult, but not impossible. The system that powers the shield constantly monitors all energy use. Any energy striking the shield would register as a variation in that energy use. A blast from any weapon would be countered with a surge of energy from the shield power source which would register in a way we could read. Even a hand Galbo blast would register."

"Great! How about three short blasts followed by two long ones signals okay to drop your shield. Two long blasts followed by three short ones could indicate there is risk, but it may be okay. Silence or any other series would tell you to hold the shield in place."

"That would work. I'll ask Jemrah to monitor the power indicator and shut down the shield on your signal. Don't worry, we'll be prepared for combat when the shield goes down in any case."

"Good! Make sure no one has an itchy trigger finger."

Captain Woolgah chuckled. "Draxel, I do enjoy your colloquialisms. Did you plan what you will do when you are outside?"

"Sure! Try to convince everyone to listen to reason."

"I like your courage and optimism. I hope you can pull it off."

He handed me his prized Galbo, slapped me on the back and said with a grin, "Be sure this is returned!"

"I promise!" I said as I tucked the Galbo into my belt and checked to make sure there was nothing to hinder my dash at the shield.

Captain Woolgah shouted a few directions to his men who formed an open aisle from where I stood some thirty feet from the shield, shining their lights so I could see the way clearly.

At his shout, "Now!" I took off running down that aisle.

At the last minute, the silver gray of the shield was replaced by daylight brilliance and the sounds of outside. The sharp crack of the shield being reset told me I had made it. No more than thirty yards ahead of me, a group of at least fifty Scentar soldiers behind Denbo shields came to life and took aim at me. Fortunately, no one fired. I shouted my name to identify myself.

Recognizing me, Chief Delgo stepped out and shouted, "Over here Dr. Syl. Don't worry, they will not fire unless I give the order."

"Thanks, Chief! You don't need to worry either. They can't fire at you while they're inside that shield."

"That must be a new defensive shield of some type. I've never seen anything like it. We fired at it a few times, but it seemed to absorb or reflect any energy that struck it dispersing it over a wide area."

"You're right about one thing; it reflects any energy that strikes it over and above what it is able to absorb. Captain Woolgah says it is a new technology they developed. This is the first time they used the shield in a combat situation. I haven't the foggiest idea how it works, but the power source is small, small enough to make the system portable."

"Why did they let you out?"

"So I could do something to stop this nonsense and restore peace and cooperation."

"I doubt that can be accomplished since they started the fight. We could never trust them again."

"Why do you think that? Did you learn what really happened."

"Only what our officer at the hotel reported to me."

"Who is your officer and what did he tell you?"

"Lieutenant Kholban of our security force reported that a group of Segwah attacked you as you were leaving the hotel and that a few brave Scentar soldiers fought them and killed all but those now inside that shield. They lost several soldiers in the battle."

"For one thing, your Lieutenant Kholban is a liar and fabricated the entire story. I also suspect he and his group are the traitors involved in creating the action in the first place."

"Those are serious charges, Dr. Syl. Scentar do not lie except under extraordinary circumstances. Do you have any proof?"

"I don't need any proof. I was right there in the middle of things and saw exactly what happened. Your lieutenant is a damned liar no matter who or what he is. As a matter of fact, he or his companions must have leaked the information about where Maria and I were going to be and when we would be there. This enabled the rebel group of Segwah to make the attack. The Segwah inside the shield attacked their own men and clearly thwarted the attack. They killed more than ninety of their own trying to prevent going back to the state of war. If not for them, I would be dead along with Maria and Sylvia. Also, the Scentar and Segwah would be back at war. Captain Woolgah's first officer personally saved my life at great risk to himself. He also prevented a resumption of the war."

"That's a disturbing story, Dr. Syl."

"Captain, there are some enemies among your own who want the war to continue for their own reasons, like those renegade Segwah."

"I'm finding this hard to understand, but I will get to the bottom of it."

"I'm concerned about how deep this may be. For whatever reasons, there are those on both sides who want the war to continue and seem to be willing to do anything to destroy the peace process. Captain Woolgah says they have ways of determining the loyalties of any of their people. Can you use the same capability?"

"Yes, we can, but there is no one here on Vega Five with the authority to use it."

"Could I use it? I believe you will find I not only possess the authority, but would be derelict in my duty as a citizen of this universe if I didn't."

"I will speak with General Straglo about that. He would be the one to make the final decision."

The captain's communicator crackled with General Straglo's voice. "Chief Delgo."

"Yes General."

"We found a new problem. I received an urgent communication from Roylar Waalo, communications officer of the Segwah star ship Kallwah. He says they tried to contact

Captain Woolgah or his ship for some time without success. Their Captain Mirklan is concerned, and asking about his whereabouts."

"Tell him Captain Woolgah and his men are safe, but are presently unable to communicate."

I blew my stack. "Damn it, Delgo, Mirklan's the second in command of their entire fleet to Captain Woolgah. They'll never buy that. Let me talk to him."

"General, Dr. Syl would like to speak to you. Here he is," Chief Delgp said as he handed me the communicator.

"General, tell Captain Mirklan that Captain Woolgah and his men are currently protected under their new energy shield and that I hold the key to their shutting down the shield. Use my name as I'm sure he is aware of who I am and what I can do."

In a few minutes, the communicator came on with a new voice. "This is General Straglo's communication officer Ghee. The General is on his way there by air car and should arrive in less than a minute. The Segwah star ship Kellwah and three others will set down near the other two Segwah ships. They announced they will not fire unless fired upon. Captain Mirklan would like to talk to Dr. Syl as soon as possible. General Straglo will personally take Dr. Syl to meet with them in the air car."

The air car landed and the General stepped out. "Climb in, Dr. Syl."

"Not until the General issues an order to all Scentar telling them not to fire on any Segwah unless and until I personally issue the order. Is that clear?"

"I cannot issue such an order. It would be suicide. Now step in!" the General replied.

"If you want peace, issue the order. If not, keep doing what you've been doing for thousands of years, killing each other off for no understandable reason and in direct defiance of your own law. You don't happen to be in agreement with those who are trying to restart the war, are you?"

General Straglo fumed but issued the order. As soon as he did, I aimed the Galbo at the shield and fired the release code. Within a few minutes, the silvery dome that had been the shield disappeared, and about thirty dazed Segwah stood there in the bright sunlight. We all watched as four star ships settled to the ground down the slope near the other two. I hopped into the air car and asked the pilot to stop and pick up Captain Woolgah. Within a few minutes, we were all gathered near where the ships landed right in front of the Gelwah. There were now six fully armed Segwah warships on the ground in sovereign Scentar territory, but in our universe. No one was firing at anyone. I prayed this would hold.

After a short discussion, the military officers decided on two specific rules. The first: anyone or any group firing a weapon will be arrested and imprisoned. Scentar will arrest Scentar and Segwah will arrest Segwah. The second: all members of the military will voluntarily submit to loyalty testing when the means are arranged. Any who fail the test will be imprisoned. The two Segwah captains asked for the death penalty, but I explained that would not be allowed in our universe. Once the orders were issued by the military, I headed back to the negotiations room in the portal building.

Chapter 29 - A Big, Joyous Surprise

Leura met me as I walked into the portal building. "Chief Delgo said I'd find you here. Come with me. You will be surprised, very pleasantly."

"Oh?"

"Follow me."

"Where are we going?"

She smiled as she led me out the door. "You'll find out when we are there, so be patient."

"The negotiation session is supposed to start in half an hour. I can't miss being there."

"Because of the disruption, negotiations are rescheduled to start at one tomorrow afternoon. You have plenty of time, so don't worry."

We talked as we walked across the grass toward a building on the other side of the complex. Leura asked, "What do you think are the chances this truce will turn into a lasting peace?"

"I think there is a good chance if both Scentar and Segwah can keep their respective stupid idiots under control."

"I can see the Scentar doing so, but I wonder about the Segwah. They are so warlike, so fierce and aggressive, so—unpredictable."

"From what I've seen and heard, those words would describe the Scentar as well."

"That's because you haven't lived your entire life in fear of a Segwah attack."

"Isn't that exactly what all the Segwah fear from the Scentar? After all, you did invade their universe and start this conflict in the first place. All they've been doing is defending their own. I think their response has been just and proper."

"After we gave them portals and much of our advanced technology, they began raiding our outposts and killing our people. They started this whole war."

"As I understand it, some of your people provided those things in defiance of your government and laws in order to help the Segwah and promote peace. What happened to those people?"

"I never learned that anything happened to them. That was a long time ago. Why does it matter?"

"According to my information the entire Scentar group who tried to promote peace spent the rest of their lives in prison while their families were disgraced and had their citizenship revoked. Sounds like the Scentar powers were anything but magnanimous. It sounds as though they wanted to keep the Segwah under their control."

"Where did you hear that?"

"From Captain Woolgah whom I found to be a fine and honorable person. But for him and his men I would be dead and the Scentar-Segwah war would be raging."

"But he's a Segwah and can't be trusted."

"He's been more honest with me than you , and you are supposedly a friendly Scentar. Whom would you trust more if you were in my shoes?"

There was a long silence, then she stopped walking, took both of my hands in hers and looked straight into my eyes. "Drax, you opened my mind to information virtually the opposite of what I was told my entire life and believed. I never considered the Segwah as people, only as warriors and attackers. Any thoughts other than those never entered my mind. The origin of the war, how and why it started are never questioned by me or anyone I knew. It is obvious we knew, but never examined it. That was never discussed in our history studies."

"You were propagandized."

"Remember, Drax, those things happened about six thousand years ago. Your history only goes back five thousand years at most and think how sketchy it is. Don't be so judgmental. Besides, your record for fighting wars during your history is not so pure either."

"Leura, you're right on the money. I assumed the worse when I first met Captain Woolgah. After talking with him, I began to like him. Now I not only like him, but I admire him greatly. He is a truly honorable person."

"Let's talk about that later. I want some answers about the Segwah, but for now, I want you to see your surprise." Leura turned and we once again headed across the grass. Eventually we entered a building identical in appearance to the portal building.

"What building is this?"

Leura smiled. "It's our medical research facility. Some fantastic things are done here in both preventive medicine, injury repair and reconstruction of damaged organs."

"And why are we here?"

"You'll learn in a minute," she said as we entered the elevator.

We stepped off on the fourth floor. Leura walked briskly down the hall with me in tow. We then entered a large room with lots of strange equipment. In the center was a large cylindrical object made of silvery metal. It was about eight feet long and four feet in diameter. Tubes and wires ran from one end of the object. When we came close, I heard it humming softly. Leura walked around the other end of the object and held her hand up to indicate I should stop.

"Wait right there at the rear of the womb for a moment, Drax, until we're ready."

I stopped in my tracks. "Did I hear you say womb?"

Leura was talking to someone at the other end of the *womb* as she called it, but I couldn't understand her words. When she finished talking, she turned and motioned me forward saying, "Here's your surprise."

There was a head with shoulders and arms sticking out of the end of the womb. "Maria!" I shouted and promptly burst into a torrent of tears, and I never let my emotions do that. I bent down and kissed her, smack on the lips.

"Careful, Drax. Those kinds of actions might change a girl's mind about you." After that soft reaction, Maria returned to her old ways. "Come on now, you didn't really think you could be rid of me so easily, did you?" she said weakly but clearly.

Still emotionally shaken I managed to say, "I was told you were killed in the attack."

"Actually, I was. The first Galbo blast cut me apart from my diaphragm down destroying all of my abdominal organs and severing my legs below my hip joints. Maybe Leura should fill you in on all the gory details. I'm still a bit weak and can't breathe very well yet."

I took one look at Leura, threw my arms around her, picked her up and danced a circle with her.

While I still held her in the air she said, "I knew you would like my surprise. If you'll put me down, I can explain."

I was still elated as I put Leura down. I kept looking from Maria to Leura and back in utter disbelief and grinning from ear to ear. As I stood there not knowing what to do or say, Leura retrieved two chairs from against the wall, and placed them so Maria could see us.

"Sit down, Drax," she said, indicating one of the chairs and taking the other. "You seem in shock. Do I detect some uncommon emotion from the normally controlled Dr. Syl?"

I chose to ignore all the mixed ramifications of her little comment. When we were seated, and I had gathered up my emotions, I let loose a torrent of questions about Maria, her injuries, what the womb was and what it did.

Leura stopped me. "Hold on, Drax. Please let me answer one question before deluging me with a dozen more. Maria is on full life support. That means her body functions are at least partially being handled by the womb. Her heart and lungs were undamaged, so they are fully functional. She lost all but a small portion of her blood, so we replaced it with synthetic blood. That was the first thing we did or she would not survive."

"How about the rest, her legs, her organs, her skin? What is her prognosis?"

"It's complicated, but stated simply, we will rebuild her body and replace, actually regrow, all the missing tissue. That's why we call this machine the *womb*. It works in ways similar to what the womb does for a developing foetus except it develops only the missing tissue."

"What about her legs, her bones, blood vessels and all those severed nerves? Those are all extremely complex."

"Once the doctors established circulation of the synthetic blood she was placed in the womb. Once inside, her legs were properly positioned and held in place, so they could be reconnected. All other salvageable tissue was also placed inside the womb which was then filled with a different kind of synthetic blood. In this material are millions of what you might call nano machines of many kinds. These tiny machines rebuild everything cell-by-cell. Some of them search out the ends of severed nerve, muscle and other tissues and reconnect them. Others rebuild missing bone and tissues of all kinds, finding and using existing similar tissues. Still others use the body's own cellular replacement mechanisms to regrow all missing tissues and replace even missing organs."

"My God! That's amazing. I can understand what the womb does, but how is another matter. I see now what a few thousand years of advancing technology can do for medicine."

"It still amazes me even though the techniques have been around for a long time. Fortunately for Maria, her brain and spinal cord were not damaged. Even our technology cannot restore the neural network that is the person. We doubt that will ever be possible. We can repair and replace the physical, but the memories and neural connections of thought and personality will never be repairable."

"When will she be, ah, finished—able to come out of the womb?"

"Unfortunately, she must remain in the womb for from six to eight months. After that, there will be several months of rehab. She will learn and retrain her body to respond to her brain. There's much she must relearn including how to walk."

Maria spoke up. "Hey you two. I'm right here. Can I take part in the conversation?"

Leura smiled and took Maria's hand. "Of course! Only don't over do it. You're still weak and are supposed to sleep a lot, remember?"

"Yeah, I'm a head with arms only. I can't feel anything else. It's like the rest of me doesn't exist."

"Well, most of the rest of you doesn't," I said as I took her other hand.

"Drax, you really know how to cheer and encourage a person."

"You've only been conscious for a few hours, Maria. Did anyone explain the com system to you?" Leura asked.

"Yes, but how do I eat?"

"You don't. In fact, you won't be using any of your bodily functions except breathing for a long time."

"That's a bummer. Of course, that's positive considering the alternative."

"They will start letting you drink water in a day or two. You can swallow, can't you?"

"Yup, I tried and it seemed to work."

"They also explained about the sleep system didn't they?"

"Yes, and I don't like them to be able to put me to sleep whenever they want. That's unnerving."

"They will give you plenty of warning so you are prepared."

At a small chime, Leura turned toward the womb. "I see the monitor says we've been here long enough and you must sleep. We'll stop by again, soon." Leura leaned over and kissed her on the forehead.

"Okay, boss. I guess they're tossing us out so behave."

"Drax, you say the nicest things."

"Maria, I'm so damned happy to see you alive I can't express it. If I say much more, I might begin to blubber." I squeezed her hand and kissed her, this time on the forehead. Still those warm fuzzies were unnerving me, making me dizzy.

"Thanks for caring, Drax. Your words mean a lot. Now get out of here, so I can sleep," she said with a smile. The look on her face said much more than her words.

We walked silently out of the room and down the hall, each engrossed in our own emotions and thoughts. As we walked out of the building, I remembered Sylvia.

"What about Sylvia?"

"Leura stared straight ahead when she replied, "As I explained inside, some damage is too severe to repair."

We continued across the grass toward the portal building in silence once again. The moment was too powerfully emotional for conversation. I could feel Leura's sense of both awe and pain of loss, a feeling I shared. There was something else there, tense and undefinable.

Chapter 30 - A New Challenge

A week of relative quiet passed after the attack. The negotiations were going well as all sides seemed to grasp the unprecedented opportunity for new, peaceful relationships. Chief Delgo invited me to his office to explain what his investigation of the rebel attack had discovered. When I arrived, Captain Woolgah was there as well and greeted me with a sound slap on the thigh, a Segwah friendship greeting.

"Greetings, my good friend Drax. I must say I was pleased to hear that your friend, Maria, survived the attack. I learned of her survival a few minutes ago. Having witnessed her being extracted from the porter and carried off after the attack I was certain she was dead. As you might say, it was a miracle."

I returned the gesture. "Yes indeed. I am not only overjoyed, but impressed with the medical science used to save her. It was miraculous."

Chief Delgo pointed to some chairs and spoke up. "Gentlemen, please sit here. I will update your knowledge about the Scentar dissidents and their plot."

"I will do likewise regarding those Segwah traitors," Captain Woolgah replied as he sat.

The Chief began. "An active cell of about forty dissenting Scentar was discovered by our investigators. They and their leadership, Lieutenant Kholban, were brought before a judging panel of Scentar. The panel determined most of them could be rehabilitated and returned to normal activities. Only four, including Lieutenant Kholban, posed any threat. These four will remain in prison until their disposition can be determined. We are certain those four represent the only serious Scentar threat to the peace between us, at least here in the Vegan system. All of these renegades refused to provide us with any helpful information."

Captain Woolgah responded. "Thank you, Chief Delgo. Only the five Segwah rebels not killed in the fighting were found to be a danger. We imprisoned them. Only some of the soldiers of the Reechlaw were involved in the revolt. All of the remaining soldiers and crew were found free of involvement. Captain Letchwah was the leader of the rebel

Segwah and was working with the Scentar lieutenant. The five surviving Segwah conspirators refused to explain their reasons for wanting the war to resume. Given enough time we will find an answer to that. I still think we should execute them."

"Not in our universe or while I can prevent it," I answered sharply.

"Drax, my friend, I bow to your authority. Your name will always command respect among the Segwah. I will see to it. I consider you a worthy adversary who has turned into a close friend. I also must commend you on your guidance of the negotiations. They are going well, and we accomplished much. I am enthused about the growing promise of a possible permanent peace."

The com unit came to life with three long beeps, the emergency signal. Then a voice said, "Attention all scientific personnel! This is an emergency command. Please proceed to the portal building as quickly as possible and gather in the assembly room. This is **not** a military emergency. I repeat. This is **not** a military emergency. However, all military personnel should stay on alert in case they are needed. This emergency command applies to all personnel from all universes, Scentar, Segwah and Human." The announcement was followed by the same commands being repeated in the Segwah language.

The command began once more to repeat in English. I stood up. "Gentlemen, I'm sure that command included a request for my presence, so I must leave. The portal building is right next door, so I won't take long to go there."

I bolted out the door and headed for the connection to the portal building. When I arrived and went inside of the building, I saw at least a dozen Scentar heading toward the elevator. Leura was waiting for me by the elevators.

"Good, you got here quickly."

"What the hell is happening? What's the emergency?"

"Wait until we are in the conference room on the third floor," she whispered as we entered the elevator.

"You look grim. It must be serious."

"Yes, and we desperately need your help."

When the doors opened, she guided me off to the left while all of the others headed in the opposite direction. "Where are you taking me? The others are not going this direction."

"We're going to the small prep room off the main conference room. Several of our gravity scientists want you to answer some questions about your experiments. What's happening doesn't make sense."

"Help me out here. What doesn't make sense?"

"I'm sorry. The small rift started by your second experiment is now continuing to propagate. We thought we stopped the rift, but unexpectedly it started up again. If we don't stop it soon, within less than one of your years, the possibilities of peace and war will be meaningless."

We entered the prep room and joined two grim-faced Scentar. The tall woman spoke as soon as we walked in. "Good! You brought him." Then she turned to me. "Dr. Syl, I'm Doorla Mark and this gentleman is Karl Woodley. We're working with several people on the other side trying to repair the damage to the space time continuum caused by your experiments. We need you to provide us as much detail as you can about your work and in particular about the magnetic frequencies your equipment was using. We need your information as quickly as possible."

For the next hour I provided everything I knew about the second experiment. With each explanation, Karl entered data in his computer input device. During our conversation, I said I wished Marty was here to provide what I couldn't remember. About half an hour later, the door opened and Marty walked in.

"How in hell did you get here?" I asked in amazement.

"I was working at my desk. There was a flash of blue light, and a portal appeared right in front of my desk. A man stepped through the portal and asked me to go with him. The next thing I knew I was walking down the hall toward this room. He roughly explained what was happening and that you had asked for me, so here I am."

Doorla interrupted our conversation. "Gentlemen, please hold your conversation until we receive some answers. Need I remind you we could be on the verge of annihilation?"

With Marty now able to fill in the blanks in my information, we worked feverishly to assemble the needed data. After about two more hours, Doorla stood up.

"Gentlemen, I thank you for your efforts and for the data you provided. Your data has been portaled to our people on the other side who will use it to try and find a way to stop the rift from growing and eliminate the threat. We've done all we can from here. Now all we can do is wait."

I was curious. "What are they doing—to stop the rift I mean?"

Karl tried to explain. "Before I try to explain that, I would need to learn how well you understand multiple space-time dimensions and the associated universes."

"Not well I'm afraid. Until you people came along, everything about it was theoretical. We dealt with the math a bit, but we never thought of it as a reality, especially not with flesh and blood people."

Karl smiled. "I'll give you a short course on the subject. It will help you to understand better."

"Okay, teach, shoot!"

Karl screwed his face into a question. "I beg your pardon?"

"It's a colloquialism, Karl, and means go ahead, please."

"All right! Imagine a box, a six sided cube, and consider only the surfaces. Now fold the top of the box down onto one of the four sides and then fold the four sides down onto the bottom. Now fold two edges of the resulting surface in half an infinite number of times into a line. Do the same thing with the line and you end up with what?"

"A point."

"Exactly! A point with no dimension, only position. That's a rough approximation of what will happen to our universes unless we can stop the rift or tear from propagating. They will fold into and annihilate each other."

"That's scary! How long would it take for that to happen?"

"Any answer would be pure guess work. Maybe a simple example would help. Imagine a small round ball rolling into a funnel with a hyperbolically curved surface. The ball would roll around the surface in a helical path until it dropped through the hole. Gravity would be the driving force exactly as it would be when the two universes collapse in on each other. Unlike the ball in the funnel, the fall would be a cascade. It would go from four dimensions, to three, to two, to one, rather than from the three-dimensional funnel into the three-dimensional hole."

"That still doesn't indicate how long it would take."

"Consider the possibilities. If the ball were released with no horizontal motion, it would roll straight down the surface into the hole. In such a case, it would happen virtually instantaneously. Should the ball contain enough horizontal momentum, it would spiral round the funnel for a long time before dropping through the hole. In such a case the collapse could take many years during which time parts of each universe would catastrophically annihilate each other. Also, both universes would be grossly distorted as the time-space interface collapsed."

"That doesn't sound like a fun thing."

"All this is highly speculative. The physics involved makes for an extremely complex situation. We have no idea what an observer would experience as the two time sequences cancelled each other. Time dilation would also affect anyone within the universes who might experience nothing in real time. For instance, we might not feel a thing here, yet a trip through a universe portal could be vastly different, dropping a passenger into a void or even far into the future—millions of years."

"In other words, it could be happening as we speak and most individuals wouldn't even be aware of it, right?"

"Precisely, but it hasn't gone that far yet. We can still work out a solution in time."

"And there would be no way for us to know other than by using a portal?"

"Our gravity wave sensor equipment accurately shows the extent and location of the rift, but other than that you are correct."

"How weird!"

"That is theoretical. Naturally we never experienced such a phenomenon and have no idea how it would affect us."

"Isn't there anything we can do about the rift? Stop it or reverse it, so the collapse wouldn't happen?"

"As Doorla explained, our people on the other side are working on it, trying to find a solution. So far they haven't finalized anything. Perhaps the information you and Marty provided will help with a solution."

"That's not encouraging. I hate being out of the loop—not knowing anything about what is being done."

"All I can tell you is they are working on a method to damp those gravity waves started by your experiments. They are what is causing the defect to grow and cause such a danger."

"That's something Marty and I do know a bit about seeing as the entire project was our concept. We were responsible for the design of the machine that started all this mess. Could you obtain for us access to what amounts to the basis for their efforts? In English, please and use our math systems."

Karl scratched his head in a human fashion and looked at Doorla who said, "I see no problem with that. Karl, start things going to obtain the information they requested." She turned to Marty and me. "I'll arrange for a suitable place for you to work."

"I feel much better. At last we will be doing something positive and not just waiting."

"If we are lucky," Marty said. "We might come up with an answer."

Chapter 31 - A Romantic Reality

Two days later we were checking out the lab assigned to us, learning to use all the equipment, and adding a bit of our own stuff to the mix. Once the equipment was checked out and tested we sat down at a table with the first sketchy data from the Scentar. Weeks would pass before the bulk of the data would be worked out. At least that is what Doorla explained to us.

"Damn!" Marty exclaimed as he went through the first data. "We were on the right track with our gravity experiments, at least theoretically."

"Seems so! Obviously the Scentar are now on the right track as well. Whatever system will work will involve a powerful and focused gravity wave generator of some kind. That's clear, at least to my thinking."

"It will take a powerful device, one that will need to be designed and built from the ground up with virtually no previous experience."

"Sort of like our experimental setup that caused the problem."

Marty laughed. "We created the monster. Now let's create the monster's nemesis."

We had been working steadily for more than a week with little rest or diversion. We were frazzled. Our days of intense effort were without much progress and we needed a break. Besides, the bulk of the data had not yet arrived and wouldn't for a week. Captain Woolgah had invited us to join him and his number one for dinner on the Gelwah and we decided to take him up on it.

I wanted to visit Maria on our way, so we headed for the medical research building. I checked ahead of time to make sure she would be awake and able to see visitors.

As we approached the building, Marty stopped me and faced me directly. "Do you realize you've been talking about Maria nonstop since we left the lab? What's with you two? Do I get wind of a budding romance?"

I was a bit surprised—befuddled is a better word. "I like Maria a lot, but romance? . . . not a chance."

We resumed walking to the medical building. Marty suddenly stopped and faced me. "Drax, I've worked closely with you for a number of years, and your last comment was pure BS? If you're not at least beginning to fall for Maria then I don't know you at all. She's all you talked about for at least the last half hour, and none of your words were professional. My guess is you've got it bad"

"Am I so very obvious?"

"Like the grin on that ugly puss of yours it's written all over you. If you haven't admitted so yet, hint to Maria you might be a teeny bit interested in her in a nonprofessional way and see what happens. My guess is there will be tears and mush all over the place."

"I couldn't do that."

"You will, or I will flat out tell her you are in love with her."

"You wouldn't!"

"Try me!"

"Okay Mr. Trouble maker, but suppose I hint and she cuts me down?"

"Nothing ventured, nothing gained. Actually, I would be amazed if she didn't grab you and kiss you on the spot. After I saw her in that contraption for the first time, I had the feeling something was going on from her side. Then you bombard me with little things about her on our walk here. No, whether you two will admit anything or not, you are definitely becoming involved."

"You keep your damned mouth shut!" I managed to blurt out as we entered the building and headed for the womb clinic. By the time we reached Maria, I was close to being a basket case—a blithering, love-struck idiot. Marty displayed one of those pleased-with-himself grins as we walked up.

"Am I ever glad to see you two," Maria said with obvious pleasure. "It can be lonely stuck in this damned coffin."

After Marty gave her a hug and a kiss on the cheek, Maria turned her head toward me. "If you don't give me a real kiss, I'm going to drag myself out of this monstrosity and attack you."

We kissed with no holds barred. "WOW!" was all I could say.

Marty, still with that Chessie cat grin, asked. "Would you two like to be alone?"

"Not on your life, Marty," Maria said smiling. "I want witnesses to everything that goes on here. I can't escape from this damned thing to protect myself, so I need you."

"It seems to me you are doing well from your confinement, at least verbally," Marty remarked with a grin.

"I don't have any idea how well I'll handle the months ahead. I think I've seen or read half the library already. I've even begun writing stories of my own."

"A budding author? How about that?" Marty said.

We launched into a discussion of writing, how Maria could best deal with her confinement, and all that had happened during the last few months. This lasted the better part of an hour.

Marty checked the time. "Hey now, I hate to break this up, but we have a dinner date with Captain Woolgah."

"There you go, deserting me again," Maria said, smiling.

"I don't want to leave, but duty calls," was about all I could muster up. "I'll be back to see you every chance I get."

"Don't worry. Anytime I am bored I hit the *sleep* button and drift quickly off to dreamland. The doctor tells me to sleep as much as I can, up to a point. The womb operator says he will tell me if I'm sleeping too much. So far that hasn't happened."

Soon we were aboard a porter and headed toward the Gelwah and Captain Woolgah's dining room.

When we arrived, Captain Woogah and First Officer Jemrah greeted us in what I assumed was full dress uniform, a simple yet striking outfit. Dark blue, pleated, kilt-like skirts were worn over flaming red tights. These were set off by short, blue boots the same color as the kilts. Over a simple, white turtleneck shirt, they wore an open jacket that was a cross between an Eisenhower jacket and a bolero. It was the same red as the tights. Around their waists they wore a wide gold belt with the symbol of the Segwah space military in the front. The only other insignia of any kind was their symbol of rank on the collar of the jacket and on their caps. Their caps were exactly like a typical Greek fisherman's cap, even to the dark blue color. I was impressed.

"You look elegant," I said to them in greeting.

"We thought you might like to see us in something other than our gray combat outfits," the captain said as they both gave us their arm across chest salute in a friendly, informal manner. "We are honored for you to be our guests and wish to show our respect."

"I don't believe I've seen a more hand some pair on any occasion. I say so with utmost sincerity." Marty was rarely so complimentary. He was impressed as well.

"I'm sure I can speak for us both in saying we appreciate your kind and complimentary remarks. We both appreciate them, especially coming from such highly regarded friends. Enough of this effusive patter. Come join us for fine food, drink, and conversation," Captain Woolgah said as he motioned us up the ramp toward his ship.

First officer Jemrah smiled a rare smile. "My captain has indeed expressed my sentiments. At the top of the ramp, a steward will show you to our dining room. We will follow."

The steward led us down a long passageway to a lift taking us to the ship's bridge level. A short distance to the left took us to the captain's private dining room off the bridge. The room was tastefully decorated without frills. A table and six chairs was comfortably centered between one side wall and a serving counter that ran the length of the room. At the end opposite from the entrance, was another door I assumed led to the kitchen. The room was designed to serve the twenty bridge and staff officers, so there was plenty of room around the table for servers to move easily.

"If you gentlemen will take the two seats on the far side, my first and I will sit facing you. This table normally seats my staff and has been used for planning many a military action. If my good friend Drax, here has his way, we might never use the table as such again. That would indeed be a blessing."

Marty spoke up. "It is said in our universe, at least on our planet, that most wars are caused and then promulgated by power hungry politicians and despots. These idiots then rely on military men to bail them out of the messes they created. This applies to small wars and major conflagrations in equal measure. What say you, Captain?"

"That certainly has been my experience. My experience also tells me some of those types of politicians are in the military. This can create big problems."

Jemrah said, "The recent flare up is a perfect example of exactly that, power hungry politicians embedded in the military."

After a fantastic meal, a few glasses of wine and some quiet reminiscences from each diner, Jemrah posed a question to Drax. "What exactly is being proposed to try to solve the problem of the self-propagating rift in the space-time continuum? This is a problem transcending all others."

"You sound as if you understand something about the problem, or are at least interested," Drax said with some surprise.

Captain Woolgah replied, "Jemrah was one of the top scientists at our military university before he went into mandatory service in the war. His field was and still is, the physics of gravity energy. Perhaps he could be of some assistance."

Drax smiled. "I will at least listen to any and all interesting ideas on the subject. One never knows who might present a viable solution. What are your thoughts on the subject, Jemrah?"

"As I understand it, your experiments with a standing gravity wave generator started a self propagating rift in the space time fabric that defines the boundary between the Human and Scentar universes. I believe it is growing in spurts as the standing gravity wave resonates, then builds and amplifies the forces generating the wave. This causes the rift to expand in an ever growing process. It continues to grow because, like a *snowball,* it is rolling *downhill* as far as gravitational forces are concerned."

"I sort of understand what you are saying," Drax said. "What we need is a way to stop the growing rift."

Jemrah continued. "Consider a two-dimensional example in three-dimensional space of what is a three-dimensional condition in four-dimensional space. Take a square piece of flat material—a sheet of cloth, paper or even thin metal. Clamp two parallel edges and apply force to pull the edges apart. As long as the force is equally distributed, it would take a strong force to pull the two edges apart since the force is distributed along the entire piece. That is the normal condition of the fabric of space/time. Make a minor change in the positioning of the force by setting the edges at an angle rather than parallel and everything changes dramatically. All of the force is now concentrated in a small section of the piece and it begins to tear or rip apart. This relieves the force and the edges return to being parallel. Once this happens, extreme stress is relieved and the rift stops growing. The fabric is stable once more until a new change of position again concentrates the force in a small area. I believe the type of gravity waves your experiments generated are bringing about such a phenomenon in the fabric that defines the common edges of the two universes. The harmonics of the gravity wave are reverberating and causing the tear to propagate in a dangerous manner. That's why the waves must be stopped."

Drax and Marty looked at each other in amazement. Marty spoke first. "Jemrah, the new first order of business is to let you become active in our planning group. From what I heard, you may know more about this problem than either of us. My next question is, how do we stop the tear?"

Drax looked at the captain. "Captain, can we borrow your first officer to help us with this problem?"

"I would consider it a great honor for my first officer and good friend to be called for such an assignment. By our military protocol, such a request must originate from my first officer himself. What say you my friend?"

Jemrah at first was surprised, then seemed a bit embarrassed, then smiled confidently. "I respectfully request assignment to the emergency research group with Marty and Drax."

"Done!" Captain Woolgah said. "I'll do the paperwork later. Now, what is the next step?"

"As much as I would like to dive into how to stop the tear, I believe we should do so at the lab where we keep all the facilities," Marty said to Jemrah. "Why don't you come to the lab tomorrow morning, and bring with you whatever pertinent records you need? Let's not turn this pleasant social event among friends into a business meeting."

"Well said, my friend," Captain Woolgah said with a wide smile. "A gathering of good friends is too precious to waste on business, even the business of saving universes."

We tried talking about other things, but kept drifting back to the major problem. By the end of the evening, we had fairly well mapped out our goals for the first few days at the lab.

As we walked down the ramp to the waiting porter, I said to our hosts, "Thank you for a superb meal, and for being such gracious hosts. It was a genuine pleasure."

"I echo those comments," Marty said.

"We must do this again, soon. It was a pleasure having you as our guests—real guests this time," Captain Woolgah said with a grin. "So much better than the first time you were on my ship, eh Drax."

"We've come a long way since then, Captain. A long way."

Chapter 32 - Attacking the Problem

We spent the morning discussing the rift and sharing what we each knew or at least hypothesized about the entire problem. Near lunchtime Marty said, "From our discussion and the new information you gave us, Jemrah, I'm more certain than ever it will take some kind of powerful gravity wave device to will damp and disperse those standing gravity waves creating the problem."

Jemrah sort of chuckled as he told us, "We may already possess a device to do what you described. After our exchange of information this morning I am convinced it should at least be investigated. Let's discuss it over lunch, away from the lab. Then after lunch we can set up some tests."

"Can't you tell us now?" I was curious, and asked, "Does it involve your new *shield* weapon?"

"Drax you are quite astute. Yes, it does. Let's go to lunch. I'll explain about the shield and what I think it can do."

"Shield weapon? What's that?" Marty asked.

"Sorry boss, you weren't here during the short revolt when the new Segwah shield was used. It saved a lot of lives. In fact, it was essential in bringing about the Segwah-Scentar peace that we are working so hard to hold on to."

Jemrah refused to say any more until we were at lunch, so we headed for the restaurant in office building five, nearby.

When we entered, a hostess asked what kind of seating we wanted. At our request, she directed us to four chairs in a corner away from traffic where we could relax and converse. The chairs were fixed to the floor and there was no table There was a round pole at the center point between the chairs. Atop the pole at about table height, was a flat, round plate about a foot in diameter, much too small to be a table. When the hostess discovered this was our first visit, she explained how to use the menu and how our meal would be served.

Marty glanced around as we sat. "Not elegant, but not sterile either. It's a bit upscale from the office cafeterias I'm used to. Definitely quieter."

When we were seated, menu displays dropped down from the ceiling. A woman's pleasant voice came from the display, "Please make your selection by touching your choice."

None of us had seen this type of ordering before, so the instructions from the hostess were appreciated. Still, it was a while before we pressed the 'order complete' button.

In a few minutes, a voice said, "Look up. Your meal is being delivered."

A round table at the end of a pole descended from the ceiling. Our meals were set up and ready when the table settled slowly and attached itself to the plate atop the short pole.

"Now that's what I call service," Marty exclaimed. "No waitresses scurrying around. Lunch was delivered quickly and efficiently."

Jemrah said, "This type of service is common in our universe as well. It is efficient and clean."

"Okay, let's get down to business," I said. "I'm anxious to learn how your shield weapon works and will solve our problem. We'll eat while you talk."

Jemrah began. "Our shield is a special kind of standing gravity wave, actually, two standing waves in opposition. These waves are generated by a device with some similarity to the crude one you put together that started all of this. Each wave is the surface of a sphere of opposing gravitational force. The inner surface pushes out. The outer one pushes in. The two surfaces are close to each other, but do not touch. This creates a barrier to all kinds of energy. Gravitationally, they act to the force of gravity much like a capacitor acts to electrical force. They store energy, gravitational energy. Any physical object striking either surface, inner or outer, will cause that surface to absorb the energy, then reverse it, bouncing it back in much the same way a rubber ball bounces. When the energy is radiant EMF energy and not from mass inertia, it is absorbed and stored. Up to a point, the shield will store large amounts of energy. Whatever energy is stored can be converted by the control system into heat or electrical energy."

"What happens when the capacity to store energy is exceeded?" I asked.

'We don't know since it has never happened. We proposed a number of theories, but we just don't have the answer."

"Is the size of the sphere controllable or always the same? And how do you turn it on and off?" Marty asked.

"The size of the sphere is a function of the wave frequency and is easily set by the computer in the control system. It is turned on or off by applying or shutting off power to the wave generator, a simple switching system. Also, the more power available, the larger the sphere can be without reaching the breakdown point."

"Okay, what is the breakdown point, and what happens when it is reached?" I was beginning to realize where all this was headed.

"The breakdown point is simply where the energy supplied by the power source is not enough to maintain a sphere of a given size. The larger the sphere, the more energy is required. When that point is reached, the sphere will grow no larger or will simply collapse as the power source is overwhelmed. That is precisely what happens when the shield is turned off."

"Couldn't you use the power generated by the gravitational capacitor effect to at least partially power the shield? What power source do you use anyway?"

Jemrah laughed out loud. "I can see you gentlemen have much to learn about gravity and gravitational force conversions. My observation should not be construed as any kind of negative comment or criticism."

"No offense taken. We are aware of the limits of our knowledge. That's a simple fact," I replied.

"The power source is a Kenli fusion generator, a safe and powerful energy source used in many applications, and yes, it would be possible to use the energy generated by the shield. Unfortunately, it would require equipment making it impractical to use as a weapon of defense."

"What makes you think it would work to fix the rift?"

"The shield should place a powerful damping effect on any gravitational resonance of any frequency passing through the physical shield. If we could generate one big enough, it should neutralize the standing waves causing the rift. This would fix the problem. At least I believe it would."

"Wouldn't a monstrous power source be required? And how could we move such an object into the proper position to do this? Can we pin-point the location of the rift?"

"The power source itself is not much of a problem. The main drive engines of a star ship could supply the power. Designing and building a control system to direct all the power and convert it into a shield configuration is another thing entirely. Once we work out the basics, Scentar engineers should be able to produce such a control device. As for moving it into the proper position, that is a navigational problem. We do know the precise location of the rift."

"Why didn't you come forward with this earlier?"

Jemrah sighed. "Though I studied and read much in this field of science, I am not recognized for this knowledge. To the intelligentsia I am an ordinary Segwah. Who would listen to what I say when there are many lettered scholars of this science in our universities? You two and my Captain listened to my ideas at dinner and gave them value. The possibility I might contribute to the effort to stop the rift made me feel good. My hope is this effort might result in a solution. That is the important thing."

We all were eager to return to the lab to work on the project. At a verbal command, the table retracted into the ceiling, and we headed back.

It took about a week for us to complete the basic outline for scaling up the shield generator and control system. They would need to be installed in a star ship and connected to the drive power source. This daunting task was then to be turned over to Scentar engineers to design, build and test.

At the first meeting with Doorla Mark, the head of the Scentar science and engineering group, two of Doorla's high level project managers were in attendance. Jemrah explained what we had outlined in our planning session.

Doorla spoke. "We examined your outline and the detail plans of the gravity power generator provided by the Segwah military. Incidentally, we are appreciative of the effort of the Segwah council to provide us these plans in view of their great military value. That is another powerful building block in the new peace accords. Jemrah, not only do we think your ideas are well thought out and will work, but we would like you to join our engineering group to help us design and build the necessary hardware. Is this possible?"

Surprised, Jemrah hesitated, then responded. "I would greatly appreciate the chance to work with your group. I see no reason it would not be possible. What do you think, Drax and Marty?"

I looked at Marty, we each shook our heads affirmatively in unison, and I said, "What a wonderful suggestion. It was your idea that started us on this track in the first place. You being involved will provide continuity to the project."

"Then that is settled," Doorla said. "We'll start by showing you around our facility and introducing you to our team." Doorla's two associates immediately stood and welcomed him. Jemrah beamed.

Within a few days, Doorla contacted me and said they estimated the project should be completed in about six months. Leura explained they had set up the first section of my training to be done at their education campus on Stentor Seven. Marty was to head back to Eegis to try to reorganize the project to fit the new knowledge we were receiving.

Chapter 33 - The Guys with the Money

It was early Sunday evening when Marty was portaled back to his apartment in Pasadena. He had been gone for ten days, leaving Terry Gross in charge with about an hour's notice and instructions to put the Eegis gravity project on indefinite hold and shift the people to one of the other two projects until he returned. Fortunately for Terry, Marty also sent a memo with these instructions to each project head.

He stepped through the portal into his bedroom and into bedlam. His answering machine was beeping, his emergency phone was ringing, and someone was pounding on his apartment door.

He answered the door first to a red-faced and distressed Terry Gross.

"Where in hell were you? A week ago last Thursday you put me in charge with short notice then disappeared with no information about where you were going, how to contact you, or when you would return . . . nothing. Drax and Maria disappeared a week before that—same scenario. Then last Wednesday the shit hit the fan. Henry Sheldon called and wanted to speak to you about progress with the gravity project."

"Henry, one of the Sheldon brothers? Our New York backers? They never call me. I haven't heard from them in at least two, maybe three years. What did they call about?"

"Henry is the quiet one. He called first. Wanted to talk to you. Said he had received some disturbing information about Eegis, and wanted your reassurance everything was on track. I assured him things were going well. Then he insisted he talk to you. What could I say? I told him you were unavailable for a few days. Then he asked to speak to Maria or Drax. He was upset when I said both of them were away with you. When he pressed me for your location, I told him I didn't have it, but that you were working on something holding great promise for Eegis. He wouldn't let go. When I wouldn't tell him where any of you were, or even when you would be returning, he became furious. Then he asked me for your cell numbers. He went ballistic when I told him your cell phones couldn't be reached."

"Then what did he say?"

"Nothing. He hung up."

"Hung up without a word?"

"Yep. Then about half an hour later, the other brother, Joseph, called me. He was seething. You know how he talks rapidly and a blue streak?"

"Yeah."

"Well, he talked slowly, not his usual rapid-fire way. He sounded tense, 'Our flight will take us to Pasadena Sunday evening,' he told me in terse language. 'Get everyone together to meet with us at nine o'clock sharp on Monday in the conference room. We will want a complete rundown on who is where and what they are doing.' Then he hung up. He sounded angry and upset."

"Those jack asses. One of the terms of their funding agreement was that they would not interfere with our work as long as we provided accurate progress reports every two months. We did so with reports even more detailed than they requested, and on time."

"They seemed to have heard about the three of you being absent and out of contact several times. This all happened since the last report, so how did they obtain that information?"

"I'm beginning to smell a rat. They most likely placed a spy in the organization, someone who tells them what's going on all behind our backs."

"That's damned sneaky. I wonder who might be the spy?"

"My bet is some support person, one with little authority who can learn what's happening and not be noticed."

"Manuel . . . I'll bet it's Manuel. He's in a perfect position to note all the comings and goings. It's either he or Herb or one of the other guards."

"You might be right, Terry. Manuel and the night guard, Herb, work twelve hour shifts, four days a week. The other two do the same thing Fridays and over the weekend. One of the four of them is always manning the front desk."

"I wonder how we can find out? It might even be all of them. Who hired them anyway?"

"Too bad Maria's not here, she'd know. Wait . . . Now that I think about it, they are furnished by a guard service. They don't work for Eegis. The security company providing them works for the building owners. Guess who owns the building?"

"Since you put it that way, it must be the Sheldon brothers."

"The gentleman wins a cigar. No wonder they find out everything going on. This gives me an idea of how we can force their hand."

"Oh. How's that?"

"Did you tell anyone about the Sheldon's coming, or set up the meeting for tomorrow as they requested?"

"No, I was waiting and hoping you would return. We can tell everyone about the meeting Monday morning when they arrive for work."

"Perfect. Let's both be here around seven and say nothing to anyone, nothing about a meeting, or visit, nothing. Act as though it's another normal day. That should smoke out any spy or spies. They will expect us to panic. I'm betting our actions, or lack of any, will cause them to panic, or at least do something to reveal them to us."

"But what about the Sheldons? Won't they be upset?"

"Hell, Terry. They've gone ballistic already. We can send everyone down to the meeting in a few minutes if we must. I'd like for you, me, and the brothers to be in the meeting first. I placed a few aces up my sleeve for the Sheldons, aces with teeth."

"I hope you know what you're doing. You wouldn't want to jeopardize the financial backing for Eegis."

Marty laughed heartily. "With what we now know, and they don't, I guarantee we will experience no financial problems, none at all."

Terry grinned. "That's good to hear, but I haven't a clue as to what you've been doing, where you've been, or what it means for Eegis. Add that to the mysterious movements and disappearances of Drax and Maria, and it's unnerving. If I didn't know you so well and trust you, I would be skittish about now. Hell, I'm still a bit skittish."

"I understand fully. I'm sorry, but things happened so fast, big things, overwhelming, unbelievable new things. I hardly had a chance to catch my breath, let alone share my knowledge with anyone at Eegis. Do you realize this all began three weeks ago when Drax left on his trip? Rather than even try to explain, I will show you some video I made while I was away. Then we can discuss where I've been and what Drax, Maria and I ran into."

"Damn it, Marty, you sure lay a lot on a guy. After your explanation, my curiosity is boundless. How soon can we view those videos?"

"I'll show them to you in a few minutes. First let me deal with the panic alarm phone and my phone messages. Then you can view the videos. Then we'll need to plan for our meeting with the Sheldons tomorrow morning."

"Probably most of those phone messages are from me."

"I'll check them anyway, just in case."

I picked up the emergency phone and heard the caller's phone ringing. On the second ring a disturbed Jim Corbett answered.

"Drax?"

"No, this is Marty Cohen. Drax is not available."

"Okay, Marty, I need desperately to talk to Drax. We found some new evidence in the bloody apartment case I've been trying to confirm for more than a week. How can you people accomplish anything when you are gone. It's as if you vanished from the Earth."

I laughed at his comment. "I'll ask Drax to call you soon, maybe within the week."

"Damn it Marty, I can't wait that long."

"Meet me at the Eegis building at eight in the morning. I can help you then, but right now we're up to our butts in alligators."

"That's not a good response. How about right now?"

"Can't do it. Tomorrow morning's the best I can manage."

"How about fifteen minutes of your time if I come right over? I can be there in about ten. Please. I'm desperate."

I checked with Terry. "You okay with a fifteen minute interruption? This is Lieutenant Corbett who sounds desperate."

"Why not? We're in a messy fix anyway. Sure, let him come. I can wait."

"Okay Lieutenant. Come on over as long as all you need is fifteen minutes."

"I want to show you a photo of a body we found, and ask you if you recognize it. Be there shortly."

Chapter 34 - Lieutenant Corbett Gets the Message

All but two of the phone messages were from Terry. The other two were from Henry Sheldon. In his last message, he said that if I didn't respond by Friday, August 31, they would pull the plug on Eegis and withdraw their financial support. I thought, *boy, Henry, have I got a surprise for you.*

Terry winced on hearing the second message. "He sounds like he means it, Marty."

"Don't worry a bit, Terry. I'm loaded with ammo for him that will blow him away."

"I sure hope so. I rather like this job."

"I wonder what body Corbett wants Drax to identify?"

"Is that what the lieutenant wanted? Someone to identify a body? Why Drax or you?"

"I won't worry until I see the photo. Let's talk about tomorrow 'til Corbett gets here."

It was no more than ten minutes before the persistent ringing of my doorbell announced the lieutenant was anxiously waiting outside.

When I opened the door, the lieutenant fairly burst into the room, photo in hand.

"Take a look at this," he asked, even before the formality of an introduction to Terry. "What do you think? Can you identify it at all?"

The photo was of a dead Segwah wearing civilian clothes. Choosing my words carefully I answered, "That is one dead Segwah."

"A what?"

"A Segwah."

"And what in the hell is a Segwah?"

"Another primate species, related to humans, but from another universe."

"Gawd. This is like the conversation I had with Dr. Syl a couple of weeks ago, pure nonsense."

"Do you remember the conversation?"

"Most of it. The part that made sense."

"Remember telling us about some unusual DNA?"

"Yes, now that you mention it."

"I'll wager if you compare that DNA with the DNA from this body it will be a species match. I'll also bet both will be a species match for Neanderthals if you can find those records."

"You must be kidding."

"Never more serious in my life. Try it."

"Are you serious? This isn't a stall, is it?"

"I'll bet a month's pay on it."

"You are serious. What does that tell us though?"

"It will tell you that the blood, the body, and Neanderthals are all the same species."

"How will that help us to find the killers?"

"I doubt you'll find them. They are Scentar, who are at war with the Segwah."

"And who in hell are the Scentar?"

"Another alien primate species from still another universe. It's a bit complex, at least for humans to understand."

"This is all a bunch of hogwash. You can be in trouble messing with a police investigation this way."

"Lieutenant, let me show you a video I was about to show Terry to explain where I was for the last week. It will blow your mind. I suggest you hold your questions until the video finishes."

The video took about ten minutes. Shown were several shots of the Scentar buildings on Vega 5. Some included the Segwah star ships with both Segwah and Scentar military moving about beneath them. There were shots of Karl, Doorla, Marty and Drax together in front of Research Lab Building 1 and another of Drax and Leura next to Maria in the womb. There were two shots of Drax walking with Captain Woolgah and several of mixed crowds of Segwah and Scentar. Jim and Terry both looked on in amazement.

"For your information gentlemen the entire video was shot about a week ago at the Scentar base on Vegalan, the fifth planet out from the star, Vega. It is about 27 light years distant from Earth. The slender individuals are Scentar, and the burly ones are Segwah. The rest are, of course, the humans. I assume you now want some answers."

The two of them sat in stunned silence. Terry was first to break the silence.

"You mean, that's where you were when you were away? How did you go there and back and what was the thing Maria was in? Were those spaceships sitting on the ground? My God, Marty, questions are coming faster than I can ask them."

"Terry, we go there and back using what they call a *portal*. It's a gravity wave space distortion device. An hour ago, I stepped into a portal in the portal building you saw in the video and then stepped through a portal directly into my bedroom. The device Maria was in is an advanced healing machine called a *womb*. Maria was in a terrible accident and would be dead without the use of Scentar medical technology and the womb device. She will be in the machine for several months while her damaged body is slowly repaired and regenerated. She'll come out good as new."

After a long silence, Jim spoke. "I don't think I had better put any of this in my report. They'd furlough me and send me to the PD psychiatrist in a minute if I did. Unbelievable . . . Is that video real?"

"I took most of it myself, all but those parts I was in."

"Unbelievable . . . Unbelievable," Jim kept saying over and over as he shook his head in amazement. "Those burly guys sure resemble the body we have. Videos could be fake, but that body is real. I must conclude the video is also real."

"I don't think we should tell the world about this yet, do you?"

"I'm going to act as if none of this ever happened, and I never saw your video. I don't want to be labeled a looney and dragged off to some police psychiatrist. No one is going to hear about this from me. Hell, I won't even tell my wife. She'd react as if I went off my rocker also."

Terry rolled his eyes. "I wonder how, in the name of heaven, we will ever be able to explain this to the world in general. It will most definitely be a problem we will eventually need to face. I can hear all those news commentators and politicos falling all over themselves to claim to be the first to learn anything about this. Those media news apes and bimbos will go bananas. It will be the biggest media circus of all time."

"Yep. That will be a big problem. I'm glad I won't be required to deal with it," Jim said with a big grin. "I think I'll see about those DNA comparisons and leave it at that in my report. Good luck, guys. I'll leave you now and act as if this evening never happened."

After Jim left, Terry asked to view the video again. We ended up viewing it several times. Each time I identified more of what was shown as Terry asked questions. I felt good about his acceptance of my explanations, and that he now shared some of our off-world knowledge. Terry is a decent guy, a friend for many years. He can handle it.

"Here's some magic the Scentar gave me. It's my portal beacon. It's much like an iphone, acts as one too. In addition to being a cell phone, GPS and camera, it contains a homing device for a portal beacon. I can contact the portal building on Vega 5 with it, and request a portal to go there or text a question and receive an answer. The portal for texting is a tiny device inside the phone. The one for transport of a person or persons is a large machine sitting in the portal building on Vega 5."

"That's over 27 light years away. How is that possible?"

"It's a bit difficult to explain, but actually, one side of the portal is there and the other side is here. There is zero distance between them. The portal warps space time to accomplish this. All of this is way ahead of our most advanced technology and involves systems and devices we can't even imagine. Think radio and TV to someone in the fifteen hundreds."

"Wow!"

"I don't think we need any more planning about tomorrow. Let me do the talking. Not that you couldn't contribute, but there are some definite things I plan to say depending on how the Sheldons come at us. I don't want to tell you because it would be best if you were genuinely surprised. If you are, it will contribute to the success of our meeting, your genuine surprise."

"Okay, Marty, I trust you, always will. Getting used to what your video showed is going to take me some serious thinking time. I think I should head for home and let you do whatever you need to do. I'll spend time thinking about the video and all it means for the future."

"Won't we all? I've only scratched the surface myself, so I'm not far ahead of you. Knowing you, you'll undoubtedly be catching up quickly after you take that trip with me. See you tomorrow at seven, okay?"

"Definitely okay."

After Terry left, I worked at my responses to whatever the brothers might throw at me. I anticipated the meeting with pleasure, for lots of reasons.

Chapter 35 - All Hell Breaks Loose at Eegis

At quarter to six Monday morning I took a quick shower and headed for the IHOP down the street from the Eegis building for my usual breakfast. I walked into the Eegis building at quarter to seven. Herb greeted me as I sauntered in.

"Good morning Mr. Cohen. Good to see you back."

"Good morning, Herb. How are things going?"

"Pretty quiet, the weekend and all."

"Isn't the weekend guy supposed to be on duty now? I thought you started on Monday evening."

"We traded off, so I could take off Thursday for a family visit. We do so frequently. Any special requests for today?"

"None come to mind. Gotta go to my office and catch up on my work after being gone for a week. See ya."

Herb seemed a bit surprised. Score one for probable confirmation of suspicions. I stopped and turned around. "Oh, if Terry comes in while you're on duty, tell him I want to see him, will you?"

"Sure, Mr. Cohen. I'll tell him. I'll leave a note for Manuel to do the same. He'll be replacing me in a few minutes."

"Thanks, Herb. I appreciate that."

Once in my office I sent Drax a short message about what was happening and asked him to stand by to portal to my office in two to three hours if requested. I asked him to confirm receipt of my message and let me know if it would be possible for him to make the trip. Then I got busy contacting several big time local investors about a possible opportunity with an unbelievable breakthrough technology.

At seven sharp Terry walked into my office. He winked as he said, "Manuel told me you wanted to see me, so here I am."

We both laughed. I told him, "All my ammunition is in place in case we need it. Now I will call and ask my attorneys for some big time and immediate assistance, and if so, could they send someone here at 2:30 this afternoon. It's convenient they are located in the building across the street. Excuse me while I call them. It should only take a minute or so."

When I explained to my attorney what I needed he said he would send two of the firm's contract and investment specialists over at the requested hour. If possible, they would be the two who helped put the original contract agreement between Eegis and the Sheldon brothers together.

"Okay Terry. All we need do now is wait to see if the brothers' spies take the bait."

A little after eight the phone rang. It was Manuel. "Mr. Cohen, did you plan anything for this morning?"

"No Manuel. Why do you ask?"

"You've been gone more than a week and I thought you might want a staff meeting to bring people up to date."

"That's thoughtful of you, Manuel, thank you. There is so much to catch up on I'll be too busy for a staff meeting today. Maybe tomorrow or even Wednesday. I'll know better by this afternoon, but thanks anyway."

Understanding what was being said from my side of the conversation alone, Terry burst out laughing. After managing to stifle his laughter, he said, "They bit hook, line, and sinker I would say. I must hand it to you, Marty. That was artfully done."

"Now I wonder what will happen when the Sheldons arrive. My guess is they will be here about five of nine."

"Should we go down to meet them?"

"Hell no. We are playing a power game for big stakes. I want them to come to us. Manuel will call my office shortly after eight. He'll say they are upset and wondering why the meeting they requested hasn't been called."

My cell phone beeped. It was an answering text from Drax. "Okay your request. I will be standing by to portal to your office as requested, once I figure out precisely when to be there in our local time."

Precisely at five past nine the phone rang. "Mr. Cohen?"

"Yes, Manuel."

"The Sheldon brothers and several of their lawyers are in the main conference room wondering why there is no one there for the meeting. They are terribly upset."

"I wonder why they should be upset. Ask them to move to the small meeting room. Tell them I'll be down in about ten minutes."

"Yes, Mr. Cohen. They won't like that, but I'll tell them."

"Okay Terry, let's go down and pull the roaring lions' claws, shall we?"

"Whatever you say, boss. Do you suppose we might need bullet proof vests?"

"We won't, but they might."

We walked into the room, and two angry men stood up and began yelling at us.

"Gentlemen, Gentlemen," I said quietly, holding my hand up to indicate a request for silence.

This was greeted with still more angry words from the Sheldons and their attorneys. Finally, the man whom I assumed was their lead attorney, was able to speak. He handed me a large packet of legal papers, puffed himself up, tipped his head back with a superior, haughty attitude, and then began to speak.

"I am John Beresford, attorney for Sheldon Brothers ITC. We had hoped for a reasonable negotiation in a meeting with all Eegis personnel. Since this obviously did not happen, we are now faced with this disturbing confrontation. My clients instructed me to respond with their last resort to your obvious belligerent and non cooperative attitude. These papers contain notification of a court order. This order will terminate all contractual and financial assistance agreements between the Sheldon Brothers Investment Trust Company and the organization known as the Eegis Project, LLC. effective immediately. Also, you must turn over to Sheldon Brothers ITC, all data, documents, and records including all computers and computer hard drives, as well as any other records in whatever form: electronic, paper, film, or other media from such project. You, Mr. Cohen, your entire staff, and all employees of Eegis will also vacate the building by noon today. You will leave without taking any kinds of material other than your clothing and empty personal briefcases. The private security force we retained will supervise and control your exit."

"Are you finished?" I asked.

Beresford exuded disdain and superiority as he pronounced, "Yes, I think we are finished."

"My first response is to say it is clear that you and the Sheldon brothers are the ones who present, and I quote your words, 'your obvious belligerent and non cooperative attitude'. At no time has there been any kind of such attitude shown by any member of the Eegis Project. We were always friendly, courteous, forthright, and prompt in all communications with Sheldon Brothers ITC from day one to the present. We have filed all reports in a timely fashion and done everything precisely as our financial agreement requires. We didn't break any rules, legal or otherwise. The Sheldons cannot present a single reason to ask you to hand us a termination directive. We plan to ignore all of whatever is asked for in those papers on the grounds they are illegal and falsely based. Might I ask if you read all the contracts the Eegis project has with Sheldon Brothers ITC?"

"Yes. Of course we have."

"I mean all agreements and entirely, including the fine print, the real meat of those agreements?"

"We went through it thoroughly."

"Then you read the section about the buyout option?"

"Of course, but how would you or anyone come up with the amount of money to buy out the Sheldons. Such action would be impossible."

"To the contrary, I possess a letter of intent from a group of well-financed investors. This letter should be delivered here in the next few minutes. Accept the letter and you will walk away with a handsome profit on your investment. Turn it down and you will face numerous lawsuits based on the facts of one little part of our original agreements. A part you either didn't see or chose to ignore."

"And what is this part you are referring to?"

"Find it yourself, or wait until all those suits are filed."

"You are bluffing."

"Okay, then call me. Call my bluff."

A man appeared at the door to the room.

"Gentlemen, my buy out offer has arrived. Please excuse me while I consult with this member of my investors group before we present our offer. After hearing Mr. Beresford's ridiculous statements, I plan on making some major changes in our offer. Terry, will you please run these papers across the street to our attorneys?"

Beresford gave me an angry look of knowing superiority before turning to the Sheldons who seemed in a state of shock. I had not reacted to their challenge as they thought I would.

As I started for the door, Terry grabbed the sheaf of papers and headed out with me. "Be back in a few minutes, Boss. I don't want to miss what happens next," he said with a broad grin.

Chapter 36 - Turnaround for the Money Folks

Outside the room, I spoke with a man who introduced himself as Ramon Maxim, attorney for the investment consortium most interested in Eegis. The principal of the investment group was Herman Gold, a longtime friend and colleague who understood a lot about what we were doing at Eegis. Their group had not been in a position to invest when I first put the Eegis project together. Since then, their situation has changed. They are now interested and in a much better position to invest. After the formalities of introductions, we delved into the business at hand.

"Ramon, I request a single change be made in the proposal. I'm sure you can pen it in. I'm also sure there will be other changes from their side."

"That's the way it usually goes. What do you want changed now?"

"Reduce the total amount of the offer by half. Make sure the changes do not obliterate the original offer."

"Are you sure that is wise? It's a significant change."

"After what happened a few minutes ago, I still consider it a generous offer. The Sheldons and their attorneys are hostile. Out of ignorance and misguided recommendations, they took an uncalled for action. I will be negotiating from a position of strength, so there is no need to start with more than a minimal offer. Should they balk, I may even reduce the amount even more."

"Mr. Gold told me you knew what you were doing, so I'll support your position. Is there anything else I should learn about?"

"Of course. I don't care if they turn down the offer. They may even decide to sue. It will be their funeral if they do. In fact, if we gave them all of our data, all of our experimental work results, everything, they would receive nothing of value they could use. The Eegis Project would still be a viable entity and still own everything needed to be unbelievably successful. Our most valuable asset is the minds of our scientists and technicians and will remain so no matter what happens. Also, the name, *The Eegis Project* is my personal property. This is clearly spelled out in their personal agreement with me which they forgot. It is separate from their financial backing agreement. I suspect they forgot to mention that to their attorneys as well. Here's another little piece of information: the building lease agreement is between the Sheldons and me personally. The Eegis Project is not even mentioned in the lease. We still have about five years to run on the lease and I doubt they could break it. They'll be eating their own words expressed in the order their attorney read to me."

"Maybe you should tell me about the order. Is it a court order?"

"Yes, issued in New York. My attorneys are dealing with it as we speak. I doubt it has any teeth. Honestly, I see this whole mess as a result of a temper tantrum by two guys who should know better. I stepped a bit on their egos, unintentionally at first and then deliberately. Their reaction was a ridiculous loss of temper."

"Okay. I understand most of the picture, at least it is clear enough we can properly handle any negotiations. Let's present them with the offer. I think I'm going to enjoy this."

"That's the spirit," Marty said as they walked into the conference room grinning.

"Gentlemen, I am presenting an offer to buy out your interest in Eegis. It is a generous offer, so I hope you will accept it and do away with this ridiculous order to throw us out. If you do, we will all have a lot less of grief."

Mr. Beresford accepted the papers solemnly. "It will take us some time to examine these. We may not be finished until after the noon deadline."

"Mr. Beresford, your clients obviously neglected to inform you that I personally hold the lease on this building. Since I honored, and will continue to honor the requirements of the lease, there is no legal way you can throw any of us out."

Beresford turned to the Sheldons. "Is this true? Does Mr. Cohen personally hold the lease?"

The Sheldons answered sheepishly and quietly allowed it was so. Mr. Bereford was not pleased.

"You gentlemen can use this conference room as long as is needed for you to examine and discuss our buy out offer. You may also want to adjourn to a place of your own choosing. Please call me when you are ready to proceed with Mr. Maxim and me regarding the offer. Notify Manuel so he can call us. We will be in my office. I would appreciate knowing how long you think this will take as I am busy catching up on my work after being gone more than a week."

Beresford now showed great concern. "If you will wait for a few minutes while we examine your offer, we will provide an estimate of how long it will take."

"Certainly," I agreed. Maxim and I both sat down to wait.

Terry came in and bent down to whisper in my ear. "Did I miss anything?"

"Let's step out in the hall."

Once outside I brought Terry up-to-date on Maxim and the offer. He chuckled when I told him about the lease. We went back inside as Beresford arose.

"Why did you cut the cash offer in half? That makes it far less attractive to our clients. Obviously you thought it worth the full amount or you wouldn't have made it in the first place."

I looked straight at Henry Sheldon. "As I said before, we didn't start this mess, you did. We are perfectly satisfied with the original agreements. You decided you wanted to change things for whatever rational reason escapes me. Your decision to come down on us like you did reduced the value of Eegis in the eyes of the investors. Mr. Maxim has agreed with me the offer will be substantially reduced once more if not agreed to by noon tomorrow."

"I don't think it fair," Beresford whined. "We will want to go through the offer in detail, and may want to change some of the provisions. We will need more time."

"Twenty-four hours after noon tomorrow the offer will be withdrawn. End of options. After noon you will deal with the law suits now being prepared by our attorneys across the street. I don't think you want to go there. You'll lose."

"Our record in court is excellent. You could lose there."

"Mr. Beresford, Sheldons, all of you gentlemen, you cannot conceive of what you are up against. We will **not** lose, you will. I will gladly bet any amount you name on that, literally."

Henry Sheldon spoke up, "You are bluffing again."

"Henry, if you will come with me to my office for a while, I will show you what I'm talking about. Come by yourself."

He looked at his brother and at Beresford. "Should I go?"

Beresford shrugged his shoulders. "What's the harm? We can go through the offer while you find out what Mr. Cohen is talking about. What do you think, Joseph? Should he go?"

Joseph was obviously uncomfortable but said, "Go ahead. Maybe you'll learn something, but don't be gone more than an hour."

"I promise to bring him back by eleven. That's about an hour from now."

Chapter 37 - Henry Takes an Unexpected Trip

I decided to prepare Henry for a shock. "Henry, we've spoken several times and I consider you a stable person. Let's forget about all the current crap and act as friends. I promised Terry I would take him for a tour of a distant place we can visit easily. Would you go with us?"

"What's this? Some sort of game? I can't go on any trip now. You said we were going to your office." Henry was suddenly a bit apprehensive.

"That's where we **are** going. You will not be asked to do anything you don't want to for any reason."

"Sounds a bit fishy to me. I'd better return to the conference room," he said as he stopped walking.

"Suit yourself. We won't force you, but if you don't go, you will miss something unbelievable, something pleasant that you'll never learn about if you don't come with us."

"You're sure I will be okay?"

"I guarantee it. I promised you would be back in the conference room by eleven. I intend to keep my promise."

"Marty, until this blow up I had nothing but respect for you. I can't see as that has changed, so I'll go with you. I hope I'm not being foolish."

"Any time you want to leave you can, okay?"

"Okay."

While walking down the hall to my office, I sent a text message to Drax. I told him to portal to my office in five minutes, or as quickly as he could after five minutes. I also told him to be prepared for a couple of visitors.

When we entered my office, I closed the door and spoke to the visitors. "Would you please sit there? In a few minutes there will be a blue glow which will expand into a circle with a portal. Dr. Draxel Syl will be on the other side, so don't be startled."

"Henry looked at me with wide eyes. "A portal? What's a portal?"

"It's a kind of doorway, an unusual doorway. You'll see soon."

Okay, Drax it's been seven minutes. Where are you? I thought as we waited.

The reassuring telltale blue glow formed near the wall away from the chairs where we were sitting. Soon it had expanded to the full circle with Drax standing on the other side. Henry seemed a bit frightened and stood up.

"Wha - - What's that?" he stammered.

Drax stepped through the portal and greeted Terry and me.

"Henry, I would like you to meet Dr. Draxel Syl. You know of him, but here he is in the flesh." I saw Henry reluctantly move to shake Drax's hand.

"Pleased to meet you, Dr. Syl," he said peering through the portal into the hall of the portal building on Vega Five. "Where in heaven's name did you come from . . . and where is that?" he said, pointing through the portal.

Drax answered, "Step through the portal and I'll show you around."

A wide-eyed Terry joined Drax and me as we stepped through the portal. Henry remained rooted in my office.

"Come on, Henry," I chided. "We are quite sort of time as we must be back in the conference room by eleven."

A group of Scentar technicians, mostly female, walked by as we waited for Henry. He watched them intently.

"Who are they?" he asked as he stepped carefully through the portal.

"Those are Scentar. A race of individuals quite different from humans. This is their base. It's on Vega Five, the fifth planet out orbiting the star we call Vega," Drax explained as he directed us toward the main entrance.

"They are aliens? Where did you say we were? Where exactly?"

"Vega Five, the fifth planet out from the star, Vega," Drax replied. "It's about 27 light years away from Earth."

I thought Henry was going to pass out, but he merely swayed a bit, looked pale, and managed to keep walking toward the main entrance following the rest of us. Drax led us straight through the main entrance and out onto the wide expanse of lawn. It rather resembled a college campus except for the two Segwah star ships parked on the far side across a quarter mile or so of manicured grass lawn. Terry was busily absorbing everything like a sponge, an excited sponge. He looked like the proverbial kid in a candy store.

Henry stopped, pointed at the star ships and asked, "What are those?"

"Segwah star ships. Would you like to take a ride in one?" I asked."

"Are you serious?" Henry was incredulous.

"There is an air car approaching" I explained. "I'll wager there are some local officials coming to greet our guests. Let's wait right here until they land."

I could see Leura piloting the craft through the clear front window as she set it down carefully about four meters away from us.

"Drax, you put together an impressive welcoming committee," I said as Archon Gordon stepped out of the car. She was followed by General Straglo, Chief Delgo, Captain Woolgah and his First Officer Jemrah, Leura and her maia, Laura. It took some time for introductions which Henry handled well. He seemed to be getting over the initial cultural shock of the trip, and of meeting aliens for the first time. Leura and Maia guided us all into the air car for a tour of the base and nearby support center.

"I understand we can spend less than an hour, earth time, so we won't be able to go inside any of the buildings. When we fly over it, Maia and I will point out the various features of our base. We will then set down for about fifteen minutes in the plaza where we will be centrally located and can view most of the complex. While there, we will try to answer your questions."

After the tour, we stepped out on the plaza. Leura pointed to the sky. "Three of our moons are visible in various phases. Our largest moon, Cephus, is below the horizon. Look carefully above the tree tops. Our smallest moon, Perre, which is full is right there.

There are five moons total orbiting Vega Five. At least one is visible at most times. There are those rare times when none are visible and others when all five are visible."

We were near the Segwah star ships squatting on their six fat legs. Terry and Henry both had questions about those ships. Captain Woolgah described as much as he could to answer their questions.

"The ships are nearly identical and much larger than they seem from this vantage point. In cross-section they are about the same size as one of your aircraft carriers. In length, slightly less than half. They are much lighter, less than 12% of the weight of a carrier, but of course, everything about them is different. We use three means of propulsion. Micro drive is used for maneuvering at slow speeds like landing or docking. Welt drive is our main and most consistently used long distance power source. For extremely long distances in short time periods, we use one of two types of portals built into the ship. All systems are based on gravitational energy and energy conversion. This is a technology you are barely beginning to discover. We used it for thousands of your years."

After dealing with several other questions, all of us but two boarded the air car. The two Segwah bade us good bye and headed for their ship. Drax, Terry, Henry, and I were dropped off at the portal building where good byes and well wishes were exchanged. As we walked through the building toward the portal, Terry and Henry had an animated conversation with many utterances of, "beyond belief," and similar expressions.

Chapter 38 - The Sheldons Gain a New Perspective

After stepping through the portal into my office, Drax handed me a fat envelope. "Here are some instructions about ending the lease on my apartment and storing my stuff. I think it will be a long time before I return. If there are any problems, text me, okay?"

"Of course. We will keep in touch."

Then he addressed Henry and Terry, "I must stay on Vega Five. I hope your visit was informative and did not overwhelm you. All of this requires a massive effort to understand important new things, a drastic change in one's reality, and acceptance of whole new worlds. It will take time to digest. Good luck and good bye."

After our responding farewells, he pressed a button on his control and the portal disappeared in a faint blue flash. My office was back to normal.

Henry was excited. "I must hurry to tell my brother about all this. He'll never believe me."

"You've got that right, Henry," I said. "In fact, we are going to ask you to tell no one about your experience."

"What do you mean, no one?"

"Just what I said. No one. Not a single solitary person."

"How can you expect me to do that? It's impossible."

"On the contrary. I think you will want to keep it to yourself. Otherwise, those you tell will think you are crazy as a loon. Think about it. Do you have any proof? . . Any confirmation of any kind?"

"I saw those things with my own eyes. That's all the proof I need. My brother will believe me."

"Even if we say you were so upset you became delusional in my office, ranting about things that couldn't possibly be? Things like air cars, star ships, aliens, and multiple moons in the sky. Are you beginning to get my drift?"

Henry became quiet and sullen. "You wouldn't ... yes, you would. You bastards. You planned this to happen, didn't you? Now I don't have any idea what to do."

I felt a tiny bit sorry for him. "Henry, here's a deal for you. Consider this. The Eegis project has no power over the people and things you saw. We could all walk away and leave you and your brother holding a worthless organization. The total value of the Eegis project now lies in the minds of those members who are aware of the things you discovered in our trip. Those individuals include only me, Dr. Syl, Maria Mendez, and now Terry here. You also have the knowledge, but without our confirmation and access, your knowledge is worthless. Your organization has no power or control over those four minds. You and your attorneys can file and win all the lawsuits you want and that will change nothing, nor will it gain a thing for you."

Henry was beaten. His shoulders sagged, his face looked bedraggled. He appeared on the verge of tears. "You say you can offer us a deal. What kind of a deal? You hold all the cards."

"I'd like some information about this fiasco with your attorney."

"Oh?"

"Who instigated all this crap anyway, the meeting—all the legal hogwash? I'm certain it wasn't you who created this mess? Until this flap, we've gotten along famously, like old friends. Who hired the guards to spy on us and report whatever they reported that triggered all this shit? Tell me."

"Actually, Joseph's wife kept pressing him, asking what was all this money going to return them, what were you going to do. She asked even before the agreement, when we were still negotiating. She was the one who talked Joseph into using the security company to spy on you. I thought it unnecessary paranoia, but Joseph did it to shut her up. She's the one who screamed bloody murder when your people began disappearing. All she could think of was employees taking paid vacations away from business. When you were AWOL for more than a week, she blew a fit. Oh yes, our lead attorney, Beresford? He's her brother. He's the one who tried to stop the investment in Eegis in the first place. Said there was nothing concrete to invest in. He doesn't think far out science is worth anything."

"That explains a lot. Thanks, Henry. Maybe we should make a deal with you and leave your brother and his wife out of it."

"I wouldn't do that to Joseph. We've been business partners, and good friends besides being brothers as far back as I can remember. I'd like to keep it that way. This is the first time his wife has ever interfered with our business and I'll make certain it's the last. I wouldn't be surprised if her brother wasn't behind all this in the first place. He's one of those stir-up-trouble-so-I-can-earn-a-fee attorneys, a greedy one at that."

"Henry, you've given me several ideas of how to deal with this situation. I will ask my attorney to set up a new agreement between Sheldon Brothers ITC and The Eegis Project to replace the old one. I think you'll like it and so will Joseph. There's one caveat."

"Oh? What's that?"

"It's a personal agreement between you and me regarding our little shared secret. It will state if you should divulge any of our trade secrets to anyone, the agreement between Sheldon Brothers ITC and The Eegis Project will be void with no financial compensation. This will be so stipulated in the agreement. Also, the agreement will remain private. Copies are not to be made public. Should the agreement be made public without the written agreement of all parties, it will be void. Our attorneys will draw up the agreement which will be an enforceable document as soon as all parties sign. All parties will include you, your brother, and all current senior members of the Eegis Project."

"I doubt Joseph will sign such an agreement."

"You will give him no choice and I will back up those conditions. Otherwise, there is no agreement. You know what we can access. Joseph does not. I will leave it for you to convince him. Otherwise, it will not be a deal. I'll give you twenty-four hours to convince Joseph. I also suggest you fire your attorneys for improper conduct. Our attorneys should present the agreement by then. You two stuck your financial neck out on the basis of a shaky theory and our reputations as scientists. We are appreciative of your confidence. The demonstration of your faith in us is why this offer is being made."

We walked into the meeting room with minutes to spare. "Joseph, your brother wants to talk to you," I announced. "I suggest you listen to him and follow his directions. We'll meet you back here in 24 hours, eleven o'clock tomorrow." as I turned and walked out the door I turned and said, "Oh, and Beresford, you'd better search for a new job."

Terry smiled and shook his head as we walked down the hall and headed for my office. "I've gotta hand it to you, boss. You handled a difficult situation well."

"Elementary, Terry, and it was easy. We held all the cards."

"This has been a time full of surprises. Things were in constant turmoil, a veritable circus, since I went to your apartment yesterday afternoon and found you there. My head is still reeling with all this. I need to relax a bit and catch my breath, try to figure out where we are and what to do next. What do you say, boss?"

"Well, we both need to catch up on what's happened since I left a week ago. First off, why don't you bring me up to date on the two nongravity sections. I'll explain where we are on the gravity section, and how the information you gathered during our little trip bears on that. We have a lot of ground to cover. It will be tomorrow by the time we finish. We hope to do so in time for our meeting with the Sheldons."

✳   ✳   ✳

The next day, the Sheldons alone showed up to meet with Terry, our attorney, and me. The agreement presented by our attorney was examined and signed. Joseph didn't say a word but did not seem troubled or angry. Obviously, Henry had convinced him it was the prudent thing to do.

Henry took Marty aside and quietly asked, "Would it be possible to take Joseph on the trip I took? I would appreciate that. Don't worry. I didn't even give him a hint."

"I think it can be arranged. We're sending two of our people there for training in a few weeks. I'll make arrangements for both of you to go for a visit then. I'll give you the precise time when it is firmed up."

"That would be wonderful. and again, I'm sorry for the blow up. None of us needed that."

"Maybe not, but you did enjoy the trip, didn't you?"

Chapter 39 - Meanwhile, Back at the Ranch

A week after I escorted the visitors from Earth back to Marty's office it was time for me to head for Stentor Seven and the training. The trip there brought back bittersweet memories. The shuttle ride was a deja vu experience with Leura in the same dark red dress seated beside me. I had no idea what to expect from her or from me for that matter. I had gotten over most of my anger because during the passage of time, most of my memories of what happened had come back. We talked about two things during the entire trip. The efforts to stop the rift using the Segwah shield, and the training program I was about to undertake.

"There will be four of you taking the special course we designed," Leura informed me.

"Oh?"

"When we asked Marty, he declined saying there was too much going on at Eegis for him to be away. He suggested two members of the Eegis project and an associate of yours from Cal Tech to take the course with you. You worked with each of them before."

"My guess is Glenn Smith and Elsa Svenstrum from Eegis. I wouldn't guess who it could be from Cal Tech."

"You're right about the two from Eegis. The one from Cal Tech is Professor Samantha Grundig, the gravity specialist."

"Not Sam! Damn! She might be trouble."

"I was told you two worked well together at Cal Tech."

"We did, too well, at least as far as I was concerned. We had a strictly professional relationship for at least two years. A few weeks before I went to Eegis, we had a little romantic fling. Besides being one of the best in her field, she can be an aggressive woman. She's not my type. Shortly after we became involved, things got a bit sticky. I tried to deal with her in a kindly way, but she mistook my efforts to mean I wanted to continue the relationship. Things ended up a bit messy."

"My, how you do find trouble with aggressive women," Leura said with a bit of fire in her eyes and a big grin. "I'd better look out for her."

In an instant, those eyes, the warm milk smell of her breath, and the strange fragrance of her, all unnoticed before, combined into an intense emotional reaction—a warm, overpowering sensation for less than a minute. I sat silently, staring intently at her, overpowered by emotion. Then it was gone as quickly as it came on.

"I'm sorry, Drax. I didn't mean to let my feelings take control of me like that. I could see and feel your reactions."

"Don't be sorry. It was a wonderful feeling. How do you do that? I mean—well—those feelings, they are so intense. That's one thing I remembered so clearly from our first meeting. Those were obviously your feelings, but how am I able to feel them?"

A feeling of soft warmth came over me as Leura explained, "You, and I assume most humans, possess what you call subliminal emotional sensations. They are triggered by mostly subliminal sensory stimulations. Any of the senses could be involved. For example, are you familiar with the common human reaction to seeing enlarged pupils of the eye?"

"I seem to remember an experiment where the subjects chose between two identical photos except in one, the pupils of the eyes had been enlarged. Virtually everyone chose the one with the enlarged pupils, without knowing the difference, or why they chose."

"Precisely! There are literally thousands of other sensory factors which result in similar emotional reactions. This has evolved in Humans as a survival instinct. Scentar evolved this same quality to a considerably higher sensitivity than Humans, both from a sending and receiving sense. It is somewhat analogous to the sensitivity of an EMF receiver and emitter. A strong sender signal can trigger a significant response in a receiver of limited sensitivity."

"Beautiful! What a clear explanation. It also explains many unusual and unexplainable, to us, reactions to people and circumstances. Someone newly met who one instantly likes, or even falls for, with no apparent reason. Wow, we learn something new every day."

Leura laughed her musical laugh. "Drax, I do love your colorful colloquialisms."

By the time we had reached my little apartment near the campus, all my lingering animosity and suspicion had vanished. As we stepped inside, Leura's face morphed into an impish expression. "As you can see, this is rather stark compared to your room in the hotel on Vega Five as I promised. Still, it has a lot of nice features. No Tillie, no automatic food or drink dispenser, and no hide-away-bed, but all the amenities of a modern, slightly upscale, one bedroom apartment on Earth."

A quick walkthrough confirmed Leura's explanation. What a comfortable place.

"I will be staying in a similar place about a kilometer away, at least during the part of your training in which I am your teacher. Now, I had best let you unpack and settle in. Should you need anything, give me a call."

With those words, she turned to leave. "Wait a minute," I said to my surprise. "I believe I owe you an apology for the way I felt—for the things I said."

"I understood why you felt and reacted as you did. In your culture, that is the way things are. Apology understood and accepted," she said as she turned to face me.

I felt, and I'm sure she felt, a sudden, powerful warm surge of passion. What happened then was our first visit to Stentor Seven all over again, only even more intense. The big difference? When I awoke the next morning, she was still there beside me.

Chapter 40 - Life According to Leura

After a shower and a hearty breakfast from my fully stocked larder, we sat at the table and talked, or should I say Leura talked. I listened.

"Drax, I would like to explain to you a number of things about our culture and physical nature that are quite different from those of Humans. Some of these differences could pose problems and misunderstanding. I know how important your understanding of how we think about and deal with love, sex, personal loyalty, physical attraction, and all similar ideas is to you. My in-depth studies of your culture provided me considerable understanding of the emotions those factors can bring about in Humans. I don't think you learned much about us, so consider this your first lesson in Scentar history, culture, social activities and living.

"I gave a similar explanation to Maria shortly after we met, so she would gain some understanding about what happened to you and me on your first trip to Stentor Seven. She seemed to understand how we feel about such things, but doubted Humans would ever accept such, even in another species, let alone culture."

"Maria's a sharp lady, and I believe, a good judge of character. She would give you good counsel."

"She certainly did, and we quickly became dear friends. She was surprised when I explained that other than a few major differences, a Scentar's family life is much like yours."

"And what are those differences?"

"The ratio of males to females for one. I'm sure you noticed there are about twice as many female Scentar as males. That's because every female birth is a set of identical twins, while male twins are rare."

"I am aware of the different ratio, but never thought about the reason. That's amazing."

"We refer to our twin as our *maia,* and we experience powerful emotional connections. We are close, as you might say. We do not enjoy what you call mental telepathy, but we are able to communicate many things without words, mostly emotions and feelings. It's hard to describe, but it does happen."

"That is different. However, I heard similar comments about identical twins among Humans. We may not be as different as you thought."

"Our views on social, moral, ethical, and legal male/female relationship standards are dramatically different from humans as are our common practices."

"I never even thought about that possibility. I think we assumed all humanoids operated on the same basis."

"For instance, we do not follow an equivalent to your practice of marriage between one male and one female. Our *bonding* is the closest thing we use, and that involves three individuals, two female twins and one male, and their children."

"Wow! How different. It's hard for me to conceptualize and brings up lots of questions."

"Other than our sharing of the male, our family life and child rearing are much like yours except there are two mothers. We do experience problems of course, but less than most humans. Our families are less likely to break up—much less."

"Scentar family life must be a lot less traumatic than human. Of course, what would I know? I never had a family, only keepers."

"Yes, I read about your growing up, and how you became who you are. That's one of the reasons I was so attracted to you. Scentar females possess strong mothering instincts, different from Humans, but at least as strong. Incidentally, though we are physically compatible for sex, we believe there is little chance conception will take place ?"

"I wondered about that, but who would I ask?"

"Well, now you have your answer. According to our scientists, our species are most likely too divergent genetically for conception to take place. Did you know that all three intelligent species, Human, Scentar, and Segwah, evolved from the same root? For instance, we are genetically more closely related to the great red ape of your planet, the orangutan, than to humans. You and the Segwah are closely related and, we think, could interbreed successfully. The nearest species to Humans on Earth is the Bonobo."

"If that's true, why do you appear so much like humans? You are more like us than are the Segwah. Since we are in different universes, how can we be related?"

Leura laughed. "There are two answers. First, parallel evolution caused by similar genetic mutations often produce taxonomically similar, even identical results. The other is because of naturally occurring portals between our universes. These portals occur frequently during thunderstorms and solar flare eruptions. They resulted in transfer of many life forms over millennia. For example, the Human and Segwah universes contain similar life forms closely related genetically. That is why micro biota from either universe does not threaten life on the other much more than their own. The Scentar universe has had numerous catastrophic occurrences of invasive life forms, micro biota in particular, from the human universe. This is a cause for great concern and is why, like all Scentar here, I can never go home."

"That is so sad, so terribly sad." as soon as those words were out of my mouth I felt an intense pang of sadness. When I looked at Leura, the pang disappeared.

"I'm sorry," she said. "I sometimes forget how my feelings affect you. I never knew even a Scentar man to react as strongly as you. It is unusual, and my only personal experience as you are the only Human male I am attracted to. It is so sad we could not produce children. You, Laura and I would make for a wonderful bonded family."

"Laura? How would she be involved with it?"

"I think I had better talk to you about Maia. She will be here in a few weeks and will take part in some of your training, the physics part, her field."

"Why would you need to talk to me about her?"

"Didn't you hear what I said about a Scentar's maia? For one thing, she will feel a powerful desire to seduce you. A powerful, instinctive desire beyond any reason because it's genetic. I hope you understand this, or you will be surprised."

"You don't want that to happen, right?"

"To the contrary. Nothing could make me happier. It is a female Scentar's most powerful desire, that her maia make love to her man. It's our instinctive way, and is quite beautiful."

"I'm terrified. It goes against everything in my Human experience. We do not normally do such things. I will be at a complete loss as to how to deal with your maia."

"Consider us as one person, not two. This would help."

"I don't think I could do that."

"Did you hear anything I told you when we started this discussion? We are different from Humans."

"That was merely conversation. Now I will be facing a real live female I've never met, and you tell me she will be determined to seduce me. This situation will be a real live problem."

"Okay! I think I found a solution. Let me think things over for a few days. When I work them out, I'll tell you."

"That's it? You'll think about it and then tell me? What if it doesn't work?"

"It will work if I think enough about it, I promise. Now it's about time we made a few decisions."

"About what?"

"About living arrangements. Because things changed between us, I would like to move in with you here. I much prefer living with you while we can be together. I won't need an apartment of my own."

I thought, *Drax old boy, what have you got yourself into? What about Maria?* "Oh my God, Maria," I said out loud. "What am I going to tell Maria?"

"About what? What about Maria?"

"I'm rather involved with Maria. Hell, you know all about that. You were there."

"Yes, and I think that is wonderful. In keeping with your culture, you should plan to marry her when she has recovered. She is a wonderful person. I care for her a lot."

"Leura, I am experiencing extreme difficulty adapting to your culture and the way you deal so freely with sharing your sexuality."

"Do you not understand what I told you before? In my opinion, your sexual behavior is bizarre. You obviously enjoy sex tremendously, yet you are bound by all these, what is your word—taboos about it, strange, unreasonable taboos. We Scentar love and make love simply because we love. It is purely good and enjoyable when it happens between two people who love each other. If I lost you, and never loved another man, I would never enjoy sex again, ever."

I was incredulous. "You mean to tell me I was the first person with whom you had sex?"

"Since I became of age and able to conceive, yes."

"What does that mean? I'm getting confused—again."

"All young Scentar go through sex training over a period of a year or so. It is rather intensive and enjoyable training. This is done long before either male or female has matured sexually, before conception can take place for obvious reasons. A single male is matched with a pair of maia for the training. The match is a free choice agreed upon by all three. We are taught all of the various techniques of making love and then practice as much as we want for the last half year. We usually stay with our original partners the entire year. A few stay with those first partners, bear children after they are mature, and then bond. Maia and I will never see our partner, Kelan, as he remains at home, on the other side. Though in a way we loved Kelan, it was not the same as with you. We cared for him and enjoyed the love making and his company, but this was before our time of sexual maturity. You are the first male I ever *loved*, really *loved*."

"I don't think I will ever be able to come to terms with your sexuality, but at least I am now beginning to understand. That's a start. I promise to work on it."

"Do you think you could ever love me, as I love you?"

"Leura, I am certain I loved you since our first escapade right here on Scentar Seven. I doubt those feelings will ever change. It's a complicated mixture of emotional and physical attraction I seem to have no control over."

A powerful and passionate emotion passed through me, and I practically dragged Leura to the bedroom. She of course went willingly.

Afterwards, when we were again sitting at the kitchen table, I asked her about the feather. "I remember what you told me about the crystal feather, but can you tell me more? I took it to a friend of mine who is a jeweler and he was amazed. He said it was an unbelievable piece, and of tremendous value in our world."

"Physically it is a valuable item in our universe as well, but not as uncommon or valuable as in yours. Our jewelers carve many of these stones with a powerful electric carving system. Symbolically, it is exactly as I told you, a symbol of fidelity, a special fidelity, my promise to you if you will. It is difficult to explain in Human terms. The closest to your understanding would be to say, I will always love you, or, you will always be in my heart. I gave four of these in my life, One to my mother, one to my father, and one to my mother's maia. All of them were given before Maia and I left for your universe. The one I gave you is my fourth and was not given lightly."

I was overwhelmed. "What can I say? It is definitely a symbol I will treasure. I hope I am worthy of such a gift."

Leura reached over and touched my hand. "You are more than worthy. You at last accepted our cultural idea of love so different from your own. This is more than I ever hoped for."

"I can hardly believe how my feelings about you changed. I despised and distrusted you when we first came to Vega Five. Yet you continued treating me kindly and with respect."

"That's because the real you, who you are inside, is emblazoned on my psyche. I understood why you were so angry. From a Human point of view your behavior was natural. There's another little secret I'll now share with you. We injected a tracker in your rear when we were in Cleveland. We had no idea where you might go, and we wanted to make sure we could follow you, for your own protection."

"You put a tracker in my butt? I should be angry once more, but don't feel like spending the effort. Is it still there?"

"We removed it the same time we removed the Segwah *bomb*. Remember we supposedly gave you an injection *to prevent infection*? We were removing the tracker instead."

"Now that you mention it, yes, I do remember. Pretty sneaky."

Starting then, we shared my apartment for the entire term of my stay there. She had convinced me her ideas about love and making love were better than my old ones. I was a happy convert.

Chapter 41 - Some Education, Science and Otherwise

Things got off to a rocky start after the three others were introduced to Professor Clauson.

At her first chance, Samantha took me aside, "Drax, you slippery rascal, I heard you were involved in this crazy, off-world caper when I was first asked if I would join the program. Your name alone convinced me to become a member."

"Sam, I hope we can keep this on a professional level. This is important work. I wouldn't want anything from our past to make things any more difficult than they are."

"Come on, Drax. I'm here to learn and will work hard in class and with any assignments. But when school's out, and assignments are finished, I like to play. I doubt we will receive any assignments the first day, so why don't you meet me after class. We could go to my place for some special wine I brought with me. Don't you remember our wine?"

"Sam, that was a long time ago. I'm a different person and in a committed relationship with a fantastic woman. Thanks for the invitation, but under the circumstances, I cannot accept."

"Who's the lucky lady? Tell me."

"I'm sure you'll find out somehow, so good luck."

"Not even a hint?"

"She's female."

"Okay, Drax, I'll back off, but if things go sour with your sweety, think of me. I'm ready, willing and able."

I was glad we were out of earshot of the rest of the group during our little conversation. When Leura spied us talking, she mouthed, "Is she the one?"

I grinned and shook my head affirmatively. Leura rolled her eyes and made an artificially obvious grin.

The first three days of schooling went off smoothly. We covered a great deal about energy conversion from EMF to gravity and back. We also dealt a bit with the equipment. During the discussion of equipment at Eegis, Leura slipped, referring to me as Drax rather than Dr. Syl. Sam caught the slip, and turned to me. When our eyes met, she mouthed, "She's the one, right?" I couldn't help but grin and when I did she mouthed "Wow! Some dish. You are a lucky man."

She would want to grill me after class, so I waited for her to save her having to run after me.

Her first words were, "I am impressed. Your lady is a Scentar, and a high ranking one as well. How did you manage that? Please tell me."

"It was one of those things that happens. Who could guess why? I certainly couldn't."

"I'm dying to learn one thing. Are you compatible?—Can you—does she—how do you manage—you know, making love She's an alien species for God's sake. Is it different?"

"Why don't you ask her. She's the expert."

"She's the expert? You mean she's expert at making love?"

I laughed heartily. "Take it any way you want, but ask her. She will not be offended in the least and will provide all the juicy details if you want. I am serious."

"Oh, I couldn't do that. I would be too embarrassed."

I had to rub it in. "You'd be missing a lot of explicit sexy details from the female point of view if you don't ask. She'll be here in less than ten minutes, so stick around and ask her anything, absolutely anything."

Sam looked around quickly, muttered something about intimidation and then took off at a rapid walk for her apartment. For the rest of the course, Samantha Grundig avoided me as though I had the plague. I almost felt sorry for her.

For the next three weeks, we talked, ate, and slept gravitational force conversions. It was intense, but we were learning some different things about EMF to gravity conversions and the equipment used in these conversions. I also learned how our system at Eegis worked, and why it was so dangerous. We had no formal class each Sunday, reserving the day for catching up on anything not made clear during class. We also took care of personal things like laundry, or even catching up on sleep.

Leura said, "I will work late Saturday to be prepared for the next week's work. I'll be home about eleven, so don't wait up for me. Keep the bed warm and I'll give you a special treat when I come home, a very special treat."

I read until about ten when I turned out the light and went to sleep. I was awakened when a warm, soft body crept into my bed and cuddled up to me. True to her word, Leura had a special treat for me, making love several times, passionately and intensely. I slept like a log afterwards.

*   *   *

When I awoke, it was late. Leura was still holding me as I looked up. I was startled to see a silhouette of someone sanding in the bedroom doorway. A familiar voice came from the silhouette.

"You have now met Maia." the voice said while a powerful sensation of warmth went through my body. I sat bolt upright, untangling some arms and watched as the warm body next to me stirred and opened sleepy eyes.

Another familiar voice came from the body next to mine, "It's nice to meet you, Drax."

The silhouette in the doorway laughed a warm, friendly laugh and said, "Drax, I'd like you to meet Maia—Laura. Welcome to Scentar family life." She jumped onto the bed, gave Maia a big hug, and said triumphantly, "We did it!"

I had been snookered and loved it. "I can't believe you would do such a thing, but now I'm pleased you did. How can I tell you apart? Even your voices are identical."

"We hope you are not angry. We thought this a good way to pass those remaining taboos still lingering in your head," Laura said.

"We know you can't tell us apart, so we'll let you know whenever you are confused. We've been doing those kinds of things our entire lives—and I'm Leura."

They were like two little girls together: two impish, conniving, happily squealing little girls.

"Okay, you two. You taught me an unusual lesson, and I'm impressed. I'm beginning to understand something of how your family structure works. In spite of all the initial misgivings, I think I'm beginning to like your way of treating love and making love. Still, it will take some getting used to. I want to ask one question."

"What?" they said in unison.

"What happens now? Where do we go from here? I'm lost."

Leura explained, "Nothing changes. We each continue our lives as before. When we can be together, we are. When we must be apart, we are simply apart. While Maia and I are both here on Stentor Seven, one of us will stay with you, one will stay at the other apartment. When I leave to go back to Vega Five, Laura will be with you for as long as you want, until one of you leaves. Should you want to be alone, or should either of us want to be alone for whatever reason, that person will be alone. It's simple. The same will be true on Vega Five should we all be there at the same time."

"You make this interaction, the sex, everything, seem so—well—so natural, so normal, a it just happens like waking up in the morning or having lunch."

They hugged each other and said, in unison, "He gets it, finally."

*   *   *

The rest of the schooling went smoothly with no hitches. I learned a great deal more of the culture and education of the Scentar and more details of why they can never return to their homes. They are literally trapped here and must live out their lives in the human universe.

When Leura's five week section was completed, she returned to Vega Five and Laura took over. We started in on the new physics and the associated math. The physics was all new to me and the other humans. Human scientists had never figured out the relationship of the various forces and gravity, or how to convert one into the other. It took some time getting used to the radically different physics of gravity and how these forces interacted with the other known forces. It didn't take me long to realize we were on the right track with the Eegis project. By the fourth week, I realized why Leura had said this training would do in weeks what would take years of effort by our group of Humans. We learned in days a few key bits of basic knowledge that would take years to find on our own. This was an entire new field, and we all soaked it up like sponges.

Chapter 42 - An Internal Truce, and a Big Surprise

Eight weeks of intensive study and we were moved to a new, advanced program with several new professors. Her teaching over, Laura returned to Vega Five, and I was on my own.

Professor Arlan Zumcort led the team handling the next phase of our training. Professor Zumcort's expertise was engineering, and specifically, the engineering of gravitational energy projects. He was familiar with what we had done in the Eegis project and promised we would learn what not to do in the future.

The first words out of his mouth on the first class were revealing. "You all will learn as fast as we can teach you these new concepts. When you are ready, you will join my team in our facility on Vega Five, where we will successfully design and build a device to save two universes from annihilation." There were no *ifs* in the lecture. Professor Zumcort made it obvious he would accept nothing but success. I liked his frankness.

The end of the first week in the new program, Sam stopped me after the last class of the day. It was the first time we had spoken on a personal basis since she began avoiding me. "Your little lady is versatile. First she teaches a sort of sociology course about their culture, then she teaches some sophisticated new physics and math. I am impressed."

I was certain she and the others did not realize they were twins. To them, the two of them were a single person. I was amused, but decided to let them continue thinking what they had. No need to rock the boat. I smiled, "Yes, she's talented, a highly honored, high ranking Scentar, an R-8."

Sam's brows accented a curious scowl. "An R-8? What's an R-8?"

"An R-8 is an educational and experience based ranking within their social-educational hierarchy. She's one of the highest ranking Scentar on their Vega base."

"How did you manage to snag such a prize? Not only is she a high powered intellect, with a lofty position, but she is drop-dead gorgeous as well. Most of the Scentar women are beautiful, but she's a standout even among them, and her body. I can't believe how she moves—like a cross between a cat and a snake. Her movements are a thing of beauty. Are you hiding a talent I should know about?"

I laughed. "No, I'm the same old loveable me."

"Since she has gone back to Vega Five, what will you do for companionship?"

Sam had a one track mind. "Sam, I am currently enjoying more female companionship than I can handle under the circumstances—maybe much more. You are a nice person, but anything other than a professional relationship between us is not possible. I am consumed in solving this important problem we are working on. Please leave it at that."

Sam laughed. "Drax, my friend, I believe you take life too seriously. You are much too uptight about things like women and relationships. If you ever decide to loosen up, give me a call. I could help. Otherwise, I will never broach the subject again, ever. Anything other than a professional relationship will be 100% your choice. "

"Sam, you have no idea how wrong you are, and I'm not about to enlighten you."

"Drax, you were a challenge for me since we first had our little fling. At your request, I'll park my attack vehicle until this whole thing is over. I promise. Professional friends, okay? . . . I mean it, really."

"Okay Sam. We do need your quick mind and physics understanding. I'll wager you understand the gravity, EMF relationship better than any of the rest of us right now. If we can stick to business, we may be able to solve the rift problem, so we won't be annihilated."

"This bothers me. Why can't the Scentar solve these things on their own? They have the knowledge, don't they? . . . Well, don't they?"

"Laura is the only Scentar physicist on Vega Five who understands the physics of gravity/EMF interchanges, and few of their qualified engineers are here. It would take a year to move some here from the other side—their universe. It's tricky to explain, but believe me, it's the truth. Also, the Segwah engineers who designed their shield will not be available soon enough, so we must do the job. That is the reality. We must learn how to design a Segwah shield of a thousand times the power of the one here. It is a brand-new technology even to the Segwah who are using it. Since we only possess the one system, we can't risk deconstructing it to learn how to scale it up by a factor of a thousand."

"Why am I learning this from you now? Shouldn't this have been explained early during our first training? Also, when will we see this little gem?"

"Because of the time factor. We didn't want you thinking beyond where you were studying until you had all the background and prerequisites in hand. You understand how technical education works. We will start dealing with the shield design studies starting tomorrow. It is my understanding that as soon as they think we are qualified, we will go back to Vega Five and see if we can design and build this monster shield generator. Then and only then will you be able to examine the existing Segwah shield system."

"This will be a real challenge. From what you explained about your experiments at Eegis, we're going to need some breakthroughs in engineering such a monster."

"Don't forget, added to the technical difficulties is the tenuous peace between the Scentar and the Segwah. I'm sure the Scentar military want to get their hands on the details of the shield as much as the Segwah military want them not to. It's the only place where Segwah technology is ahead of Scentar, and I'm sure they would like to keep it that way."

"How are we going to manage a design/build on such a large scale and keep their secrets with Scentar workers all over the place? That seems to me to be a bigger challenge than designing the new shield system."

"You could be right. Professor Zumcort said something about separate engineering groups dealing with separate functions. Unfortunately, everything must come together in the end."

I was beginning to feel good about Sam. She appeared to be getting with the program, and was an up-front person, sometimes even an in-your-face person. She told it like it was. You always knew where she stood, and besides, there was nobody who was better at new and different physics concepts. She was also exceptional at engineering ahead of the learning curve. She and Zumcort would keep us centered on realities. After eight more weeks of hard work, Professor Zumcort thought we were ready to return to Vega Five and tackle the design/build.

The return trip to Vega Five was uneventful. When I arrived, an excited Leura met me at the port with a porter.

"Hop in. I've got a big surprise for you."

"What is it?"

"Don't ask. Wait and see."

Her irrepressible smile and near manic demeanor told me something wonderful was up. I thought it had to do with Maria, but I said nothing. I didn't want to dampen her enthusiasm about surprising me. Then she headed the porter away from the Medical Research Building toward the living quarters area, so it wasn't Maria. We pulled up to one of the apartment complexes where she parked the porter.

"Wouldn't you like to see your new living quarters? This is where you'll be staying while you work on the shield system. It's no more than a kilometer from the assembly building. You could walk there from here in a few minutes. Grab your bags."

She hand printed the door, and we walked right into a neat little apartment, a bit larger and better equipped than the one we had on Stentor Seven.

"Well, do you like it?" she asked with a broad grin.

"The apartment is nice, but it's not what you are so excited about."

"Come with me," she said as she walked through the kitchen and out the back door.

She continued across a small yard to another apartment about thirty meters from my place, walked up to the door, opened it and motioned me to follow. Once inside she led me through the kitchen to the living room where she raised her hand and motioned me to stop.

"You've got company," she said to someone in the living room, then motioned me to follow.

There in a recliner sat Maria, a whole Maria with a complete body, her lap and legs covered by a blanket. I was overcome. I could not speak and froze. My eyes filled with tears of joy.

Leura cautioned, "You must be careful with her, Drax. She's only been out of the womb for about two weeks and is only beginning to understand and control her new body."

Maria grinned and motioned me to come to her. "Well, don't stand there gawking. Come give me a kiss, but be careful with the hug. Most of my new body is quite tender."

"Okay boss. Damn! It's good to see you whole. Damn, you look good." I remained frozen where I stood.

"Leura, will you please drag the idiot over here, so I can hold him?"

My feet began to move, and I was soon kneeling by her chair sharing hugs and kisses. "How do you feel? Can you walk, stand, what can you do? How long before we can go mountain climbing?"

"It will be a couple of months before she can do anything strenuous, Drax," Leura said. "She has to learn to walk all over, like an infant. She must also build up her muscles by exercise which won't be easy at first as she must toughen her new skin in the process. This preliminary phase will last at least six weeks. By then she should be able to walk, but will still be quite weak."

"I'm beginning to be able to support part of my weight. I hold onto my walker with my hands and try to stand, but my legs still won't fully support me."

"We didn't know how long recovery would take since you are the first Human we placed in the womb. From what happened thus far it will require the same amount of time as with a Scentar. Believe it or not the limiting factor for both is the skin. Skin takes about six months to reach maturity. Before then it is prone to abrasions and even tears. Think of your new skin as the skin of an infant, soft and easily damaged," Leura said. "When you start to try walking you will wear protective covering all around your middle where you grew new tissue. Even the original skin on your legs will be tender from being in the liquid in the womb."

Maria laughed. "Drax, you should have seen my toenails. I needed a pedicure when they took me out. They were several inches long, soft, and floppy from being in liquid. I had to laugh while they were being cut they looked so funny."

I tried to picture them soft and floppy. "Other than the toenails, what else happened when they took you out?"

"Between Lois, my physical therapist, and Leura, I've not been alone for a moment. Leura made arrangements for this apartment. Then she moved in and stayed with me, only leaving when Lois was here. Today, while she went to get you, Lois rearranged her busy schedule and came to stay with me. She had to leave to see another patient when you came in."

Leura smiled. "We've become dear friends. Maria is like another maia to me. It's funny, but if you remove the letter r from her name, it leaves Maia."

I let that resonate through my mind conjuring up many interesting scenarios which I did not share. We talked for several hours afterwords. We helped Maria to her walker several times for her scheduled exercise. I noticed her legs were little more than skin and bone. Late afternoon, Lois arrived and took Maria through a number of leg exercises, massaging her legs between each series. While Lois was giving Maria a bath, Leura and I fixed dinner for the four of us.

After dinner and more conversation, I went back to my new apartment to unpack. A large box had been deposited in the living room. Attached was a terse note from Professor Zumcort. "READ THESE - be at the Assembly Building at 0800 tomorrow."

I opened the box and found four packets of papers. One was labeled, *Control system* another *transmitter* another, *power connection* and the fourth, *mounting structures*. I would not sleep much tonight.

Chapter 43 - Working on the Project

The engineering crew on the project consisted of four Humans, a dozen Scentar, and Jemrah. The Scentar included Professor Zumcort and his three cohorts, Dr. Doorla Mark and his group along with a machinist and several fabricators. All but the workmen were theory engineers, not used to dealing with real world problems. This made for some interesting conflicts that at first slowed our progress to a crawl. It was obvious Sam had the best practical engineering mind of the entire group. She was ahead of the rest of us. Zumcort, bless his genius, abdicated his leadership position in her favor. He did it nonchalantly one day.

"Dr. Grundig, it is obvious to all of us you should be driving this project, so I am handing the leadership role over to you . . . As of now."

Sam winced. "Professor, you just gave me one of the greatest compliments I ever received. I will do my best to live up to it."

I was a bit afraid her straight up, in-your-face style might anger some of the Scentar, but it soon became obvious they liked it, because she was usually right. Even the fabricators and machinists liked her. She made a few changes in the team organization, and we were soon progressing faster than before.

By the fourth week, many of the components of the four sections had been designed and fabricated. Putting the parts together took another three weeks. Within a month, we would be facing the daunting task of assembling the sections together, downloading the software from the existing shield generator computer, installing them in a ship, and testing our creation. Things got a bit dicey when it came time to download the software from the Segwah shield control, the most essential and proprietary part of the entire system.

Captain Woolgah informed me his superiors would not let him release the software until they were assured the Scentar military would not gain access to it. This ground everything to a halt. After a two-day effort, we came up with a solution the Segwah accepted. The software would be downloaded to a security chip which would remain in Captain Woolgah's sole possession at all times.Because of this, Captain Woolgah would be an integral part of the new shield system, and the sole possessor of the encryption code needed to operate the shield. He was not to let anyone know this code, not even his second in command. This made things difficult, but possible.

Another requirement was no memory of any kind in the system. It was all to be on the chip which was to be removed at all times other than when the shield was in operation. This meant there could be no connection between the Gelwah's computers and the shield's, and in particular, no wireless capabilities. In the end, this isolation did not seem to pose any problem other than a minor inconvenience.

As soon as all of this was dealt with, the software was downloaded and Captain Woolgah secured the chip. Not everyone was pleased with the security measure. With my team being responsible for this installation, we knew it had to be designed for the particular ship we were to use. We couldn't do much more until we had a ship and as yet no suitable ship had been found. It was at this point that my friend, Captain Woolgah walked into my office in the assembly building and sought me out.

"Drax, my friend, I understand you are having a problem finding a suitable ship for your mission. I also believe you still lack a crew to operate the ship if you found one."

"How did you discover that information?"

The captain grinned. "I am in a position to understand exactly what is going on with this project, but to the public it is another matter. There is much speculation about what is happening in this building. Everyone knows the purpose, but the reality is subject to many rumors. These run from a big fake show to a suicide mission and include much in between. Recently, a group of Scentar came forward who don't want the mission to get off the ground, literally. Something about this all being staged for political purposes, a hoax if you will, and the tear doesn't really exist. They can sound convincing."

"Well, the tear is real. I've been shown the data. I learned a lot about it during our training on Stentor Seven. The new physics we were taught indicates your Segwah shield may be our only chance for survival. It's the only tangible and available system with enough gravity wave power to repair the tear we could possibly create in the time we have."

"No need to convince me. I learned enough about inter-universe travel to know, or at least understand something of this tear and what might happen. For this reason, I came to offer my ship, the Gelwah, myself, and my number one, Jemrah, to take this mission on and try to repair the tear."

I hardly knew what to say. "There are great risks and one big probability of a major problem for any who undertake this mission. Hell, your universe is in no danger. Why would you even consider such an offer?"

"Drax, I've been a warrior for most of my life. Destroying things and killing people are not inspirational or even heroic actions. I am used to great risks. Doing so for the benefit of others rather than their destruction is a far loftier aspiration. I rather like the idea."

"That's an interesting concept. The only thing is the major problem I mentioned, a danger of which you may be unaware. It's only theoretical, but the probability of such a happening is considerable."

"And what is the danger?"

"Because of the powerful gravity waves passing though the ship when the shield is activated for long periods and at the junction of the two universes, there may be some time dilation. We don't know how far, but the ship could jump into the future. When and if you return it could be to a different future time."

"That sounds rather enticing," the captain said with a laugh. "Think—I might even meet my descendants of several generations. How many people find the opportunity to do such a thing? I'm looking forward to this mission. It will be a rewarding challenge."

"Captain, until this moment I never considered if you had a family. Any reason why you never talk about them?"

"No reason, Drax. It most likely never came up. Yes, I have a wonderful family, a terrific wife named Meernya, and two boys, Char and Denbo. They are my pride and joy. Both boys are young men now and on their own. Char will soon graduate from the same military academy I attended, and Denbo is a musician, a good musician."

"You sound like a proud father. How often do you see them?"

"Not often, but for long periods of time. Our military sends us on assignment for rather long periods, two to four of your years depending on circumstances and need. Between assignments, we are usually at home with our families for at least one or two of

Chapter 44 - Handling an Unruly Mob

Two days after the conversation with Captain Woolgah, the shield generator was ready for its first test. Everything was set up to run this test out in the field north of our building. All we needed was Captain Woolgah to insert the chip into its slot in the control box. I held the wireless remote control. We stabilized the frequency to generate a field about thirty meters across, but were not sure precisely where the shield double surface would be established. But where was Captain Woolgah? He was never late. I called his communicator with no response. I called Jemrah and received no response from him either.

Our entire group of seventeen began speculating about what could be going on, then someone pointed to the north where several people were running toward us. These two were soon followed by a group of at least fifty, all headed our way. In the center of the crowd and surrounded, walked the two burly Segwah. I saw no evidence of weapons, but the crowd was noisy, obviously agitated and in a foul mood, shouting harsh words and epithets.

"Everyone back into the building," I shouted to our team. "Take your equipment and papers with you and lock the doors. Hurry." All but Professor Zumcort complied. He decided to stay there with me. To be sure, I loosened the flap on my breast pocket where a tiny LK nestled. I would be prepared for whatever happened. The lead runner started across a walkway about twenty meters from where we stood.

"Stop right there mister and tell me what's going on."

"What are you going to do to stop me?" was the surly reply as I took out the LK and kicked up some sod in front of him.

"Take one more step and you will go flying like the sod."

He stopped. "You won't be able to stop us all with an LK," he jeered.

"Maybe not, but several Galbos in the building behind me will. Stop! . . . All of you! . . . Stay on your side of the walkway."

"We are unarmed. You wouldn't fire on unarmed people, would you?" One obvious leader of the group shouted as he moved cautiously to the path.

"Step on the path if you want to find out, idiot. Are you their leader?"

"One of them," he replied. "We are a group of concerned citizens trying to stop an evil."

"Bull! You are an unruly mob who want to take the law into your own hands. You will be treated as such by me until I know better. First off, let the two Segwah go so they can come over and stand with us. Now!"

"We couldn't release them."

"You will or we'll begin picking off members of your group one at a time until you do."

"You wouldn't."

"No? Try me. Now, let them go."

One of the Scentar stepped onto the path to test me. He shouldn't have tried it. I hit him with enough power from the LK to knock him out for a few minutes.

"He means it fellows. Let's hold our ground."

"You do not understand what one angry Human confronted with an unruly mob of aliens could do, do you? Free those two! . . . NOW! . . and then I'd like to know what this is all about."

Both Captain Woolgah and Jemrah were laughing as they crossed the path and ambled over to where we were standing. "Drax, I can't believe how fierce you sounded," the captain said when he got close.

I grinned. "Well, it worked, didn't it? No blood was spilled."

I turned to the somewhat subdued group. "Will one of you please tells me what all this nonsense is about, so we can continue with our work? . . . You . . . the so-called leader . . . will you at least **try** to tell me what you hope to accomplish? I'm still in the dark."

"We don't believe there is any such thing as this tear you are supposedly going to fix, or that it poses a danger to us."

"Are you a physicist? Or a cosmologist?"

"No."

"Well, I am, and I've studied this phenomena thoroughly. It is a real and present danger, to all of us, a deadly danger."

"Why should we believe you?"

"I don't care if you believe me or not. I want you to go and stay out of our way, so we can do our thing and prevent this nonexistent calamity from happening."

"Supposing your experiments make things worse."

"How could such a thing happen?"

"You'll be messing with natural laws . . ."

"You mean the laws of physics?"

"Well, yes, I suppose so."

"Each of you messes with the laws of physics each time you move through a portal, even when you cook breakfast at home. Did you realize that?"

"Not true, is it?"

"Absolutely! Would you all like to see a demonstration of our device, right here and now? It will be perfectly harmless, guaranteed."

A considerable chorus of mumbles and grumbles came from the group. Then the leader asked, "Are you sure it's safe?"

"If you all stand behind us and don't move around I guarantee it will be safe."

Another chorus of mumbles and grumbles led to agreement. I motioned our group to come out and had them set up the equipment once more. When everything was ready I said to Captain Woolgah, "If you would contribute your key and initiate a count down, we can get on with it."

The captain shook his head and replied, "Drax, don't ever let me tell you something cannot be done. You accomplished the impossible. I do hope it works."

I offered a caveat to those from the mob. "This is a reasonable experiment which should work as planned. However, something could go wrong, so please bear that in mind. That is why we want all of you to stay behind us when we fire this thing up.

"Are you ready, Captain?"

"Ready, Drax."

"Five, four, three, two, one, fire!"

A brilliant flash of blue light was followed by the loudest crack of thunder I could imagine. The sound concussion and echos from the surrounding buildings battered us for several seconds, then all went silent as the echos died away. We were unprepared for the shock wave, and many were knocked down. There in front of us was a silvery-gray hemisphere about thirty-five meters in diameter with wisps of steam rising from around where it met the ground. The ground around the edges was raised several feet above the surrounding surface. The hemisphere above ground was obviously the visible part of a complete sphere continuing underground.

I turned to Captain Woolgah. "I think all further tests will be conducted out in space where there is no air or other material in the way of the shield."

The captain shook his head in the affirmative. "Drax, I believe your statement to be a gross understatement. This new shield is several orders more powerful than the original, even at the low power level we used. That made for some unusual results."

Most of the people had picked themselves up while shaking their heads in disbelief. A number of them had some partial temporary hearing loss.

"What do we do now?" the leader of the protesters asked.

Captain Woolgah tried not to laugh. "Well, my friend, I suggest you and your group of troublemakers go far away and let these people continue working uninterrupted. They are working hard to save your universe from total destruction. As you go, do not touch the shield surface as it will likely suck the heat out of whatever part of you touches it and at an astounding rate. Look, the rivulets of condensing moisture are freezing into slender icicles."

I asked, "Captain, will you turn it off please?"

We both felt and heard a loud thump as the shield holding the bottom hemisphere of soil and rock ceased to exist and dropped the entire mass the thickness of the shield proper into the space it had previously occupied. This startled the mob who began to walk away. I wondered what the result of this observation would be on the future of the anti crowd. I was certain this was not the last we would hear from them.

"Well Drax, did your first run go as planned? Was it a success?" Captain Woolgah said as he retrieved the chip from the control. "What I'd like to know is how it will perform when mounted in the Gelwah?"

"I think it will be our second test. There is another concern that showed up in this test and that we will necessarily deal with."

"Oh? What?"

"The power load on the electric buss. Even in this small test the busses became red-hot. We may need to revise the buss section of the hardware. We must find out why the current load was so high. If we had used even a third of the power we plan on using on the rift, those busses would melt. We cannot allow such a happening. Somewhere we missed something important in the load calculations. I'll wager it is off by a factor of at least ten, even a hundred."

Chapter 45 - Serious Problems Dealt With

After Captain Woolgah left to return to his ship, Sam and Professor Zumcort cornered me and asked me to accompany them to the conference room in the assembly building.

When we were all seated around the table, Zumcort began. "We will begin with a couple of big problems which must be dealt with, and soon. First we must protect ourselves and our equipment from the mob who want to stop what we are doing. This organized effort to cancel or disrupt our program must be dealt with and quickly. We must take a defensive stance by being prepared for future actions by the group. The ability of our security service to handle these types of incidents is minimal at best because they were never before needed in such a capacity. I will contact General Straglo for assistance from the military. I will ask him to post a military guard around the assembly building until our work is completed and the shield is installed in the Gelwah. "

I recalled the battle at the fountain. "Is this group related to those who attacked us at the fountain? Your security forces were deeply involved on the wrong side in that battle. I wonder if they can be trusted."

The professor was nonplused. "Good point. Our military intelligence should have enough information to know. I'll ask General Straglo when I talk with him as soon as we finish here. The cause of the buss problem is unknown and might even be more dangerous."

I asked, "Where did all the current come from? Not from the power source or it would show up on the current flow diagrams. The only place it did show up was through the buss, but that is impossible. There was no indication of any excess power entering the buss from either the primary or secondary coils of the EMF transformer or the D-Grav converter. So how did this huge current ever enter the buss and how can we prevent this from happening in the future?"

Sam chimed in. "We will address those questions at the meeting I scheduled for after we finish here. Let's head for the small conference room. The others should be there by now."

When the meeting of our group convened, Sam named this the first priority for everyone. If we couldn't solve it, the entire project would be in jeopardy. Together we pored through the data from the test for the rest of the day. Then in the middle of the next afternoon, Sam pointed at the current flow reports.

"Check out this expanded plot of current flow through the buss. It is definitely not what one would expect. It indicates a powerful flow of current within the buss for a short period of time. The current could only be a strong eddy current staying in the buss because it had no place to go. My guess is it was a low voltage eddy of tremendous power, much like a plasma. That would explain why the buss got so hot. Do we have a sound level plot covering the same time? I'd like to compare the two."

I realized what she was looking for. "Sam, you may be onto something. I think we can fairly accurately calculate when the huge clap of thunder hit. It was a few milliseconds after the shield was activated. The sound contained a lot of energy. The buss was isolated from the power source the instant the shield was activated., and before the thunder clap. So how was it converted into electrical power in the buss? "

"Well, Drax, we'll just need to figure this out, won't we?"

"Somehow, Sam, I think you already figured this out. How about letting us in on what you think happened?"

"Drax, you say the nicest things. What's in it for me if I share?"

"How about the undying gratitude of two civilizations?"

Sam rolled her eyes and shook her head. "That's a large and powerful motive, not to mention staying in existence."

"What about the power surge? What do you think caused it, and what should we do?"

"I believe it was the shield itself. Isn't it much like a large gravitational capacitor? Would it not be possible for the compression wave of the thunderclap to generate a rather large gravitational surge? We all were impacted by the thunderclap. It expended a lot of power in an extremely short period of time. I believe the physical impact of the sound energy on the two standing gravitational waves of the shield generated an intense resonance of some sort. This energy then coursed back through the buss as electrical energy, at low voltage. That powerful current had no place to go outside of the buss, so it converted to heat. I see it as a nonproblem as long as we don't activate the shield in an atmosphere. Since all other uses of the shield will be in the vacuum of space, I doubt it will happen again. I am convinced the sound energy was expressed over such a short period of time, none of the matter it struck was damaged. Otherwise, we would all now be deaf from damage to our ears."

"Then you agree with my first assessment?"

"Basically, but not precisely. I would love to know exactly what occurred, but I'm afraid that is beyond the scope of even the new knowledge we have. I doubt we will ever be able to duplicate the phenomenon we witnessed. We will only deal with it theoretically. Besides, it most likely will not be an issue if we only test in the vacuum of space. I say lets move on."

The consensus of the group was agreement, so our next step would be to install the shield system in the Gelwah. We still hadn't engineered the power connection between the Gelwah's D-Grav section and the shield generator. This will be our next phase.

*   *   *

Three days later the Gelwah with the shield system installed was perched on the lawn beside the assembly building awaiting the go-ahead to test. there was a large crowd of protesters being kept well away from the ship by General Straglo's military guard. The entire group who developed and built the new shield generator boarded the Gelwah to join Captain Woolgah and First Officer Jemrah. They were all eager to test the shield.

The Captain and his number one greeted them with a hearty, "Welcome aboard!"

First Officer Jemrah spoke. "I believe there is enough room for us all on the bridge, so follow me."

As they walked onto the bridge, the Captain said, "This is a military vessel with enough personnel stations so each of you will have a seat. All of the weapons stations are shut down, so no one can accidentally do anything harmful. The only active stations will be my helm station, Number One's navigation console, and Dr. Syl's engineering and shield control station. Everything else is inactive. We will each see a full view of the combat display screen where we hope you will see nothing—no light at all because the shield will be set to deploy approximately 100 meters beyond the farthest reaches of the ship. It will be in the vacuum of space with no matter of any significance to create problems. When the shield is deployed, all the stars and any other celestial objects in view will disappear. You will see—nothing. If that happens, our test and our mission will be successful."

"Please take your seats. We will be underway shortly," First Officer Jemrah ordered. "Navigation is set to take us to a safe orbit around Vega Five where we will conduct the first test. Captain, navigation is set and locked, welt drive is on standby, and lift off sequence is ready."

Captain Woolgah smiled broadly as he ordered, "Engage!"

About three hours later we arrived at our assigned location and fixed the ship in orbit.

"Dr. Syl, the ship is yours," Captain Woolgah said.

"Thank your Captain. The D-Grav section is at full power. Jemrah, will you please confirm my actions verbally?"

"Yes, Dr. Syl."

"I am connecting the D-Grav section to the shield power input—now!"

"Check!"

"I am now powering up the shield generator."

"Check!"

"I will activate the shield when I reach zero on the countdown. I hope we are all ready. Three! . . . Two! . . . One! . . . Zero!"

The only sound was a faint low frequency groan-like noise as the D-Grav section was pushed to its maximum power output. The peppering of stars filling the screen earlier were all gone and the screen was blank. After one quiet moment, a cheer welled up from the group, a cheer of self congratulation for a job well done.

"We did it!" Drax shouted enthusiastically. "We all worked together and did it."

After things quieted down, Captain Woolgah spoke. "I know you are all elated, but I must remind you, this is but the first of several tests we must make before we will be ready for our deep space journey. The equipment has to be carefully analyzed to make certain there was no internal damage. What else needs to be done, Dr. Grundig?"

Sam stood up smiling broadly. "Actually, the test couldn't have been any better. None of the instruments indicated anything outside of acceptable parameters. In particular, the buss temperatures remained well within an acceptable range. We will need to go through all of the instrument logs carefully to see if there were any problems there. Once those are oked, we will be able to proceed with the rest of the tests. I am a bit concerned about the low frequency sound made when the D-Grav system was connected. I did not expect any sound. Segwah engineering will need to investigate this new sound. I suggest checking for anything even a tiny bit loose. It is probably nothing, but it will bother me until we know the source. Captain Woolgah, will you ask your engineering people to check thjngs out and let me know what they find?"

"Certainly. There should be a report in your hands by tomorrow noon."

"Excellent. If we go back down to the surface we can examine some logs and test some equipment. Captain, I am through for now. Let's go home."

Chapter 46 - Final Preparations I

True to his word, Captain Woolgah's report was in Sam's hands before noon. He complimented her for her assessment of the D-Grav problem. A single plate in the stack had cracked, and the resulting vibration made the noise. The broken plate was replaced, solving the vibration problem. By the next week, all tests had been completed successfully. The Gelwah and shield were ready to go. All remaining to be done was provision the ship and load fuel for both the D-Grav section and the maneuvering and lift thrusters. Lift off was schedule for 33.64.21.0500 star date/time, two weeks away.

When Drax returned from the final test, he headed for Maria's apartment. He had been so engrossed in work on the shield he hadn't seen Maria for more than a week. He did know she was progressing a bit faster than was expected. When he walked into her apartment, he was surprised to see both Leura and Laura seated in Maria's living room with Maria.

"What's this, a ladies club meeting?"

Maria smiled pleasantly. "No, this is a meeting of the take Drax apart and put him back together club."

"Well, you three should be good at that by now. I know there is no way I can defend myself from you."

Leura became the first to be serious. "We were simply trying to decide the best way to handle your coming voyage. That's not a pleasant prospect for any of us, especially Maria."

"Why? The voyage round trip should take 60 days, plus or minus a few. No big deal."

"Yes it is a big deal, because it will be a lot more than sixty days for us," Laura said. "I've done some figuring, and none of us are encouraged by my results."

"Oh? . . . How so?"

"I figure the earliest you could be back would be fifty-seven of our years. and only if everything goes perfectly. Any kind of difficulty or malfunction of the shield system and it could be a lot longer—maybe never. I don't think Maria needs to face that prospect."

"Well, I don't have a choice. I must go. I'm committed. We are taking two brave Segwah whose universe and nothing in it are threatened by the rift. Still, they volunteered to go on this mission. I couldn't let them down."

"Then how about you take me with you?" Maria asked pointedly. "You are going in a ship normally holding how many, two hundred, three hundred individuals? As I understand it, even you will only be needed for a few hours during the entire trip. and the others? Once the course is set, there will be virtually nothing to do."

"Impossible. Women are not allowed on Segwah ships—ever—their rule, not mine."

'We'll see about that,' Leura said. "I have a great deal to say about what happens on this base, and I am going to use my considerable power to put Maria on the ship. Think about this, it is only Segwah women who are forbidden to go aboard their ships. Their law is so worded. Incidentally, that is why the three of us were meeting here, to figure a way to put Maria on board the ship with you."

I couldn't help but laugh. "You think you can do it, don't you?"

I was greeted with three determined yeses. Then I said, "If anyone could pull off such a stunt it would be you three. I know one thing for sure."

"Oh, what?" one of them asked.

"I always want to be on the same side of any controversy as the three of you. I never want to be your opponent in anything. Realistically, is Maria strong enough for such a trip? I mean . . . isn't she still fairly frail and in therapy?"

They all laughed. Leura turned toward Maria and said, "Stand up Maria. Take off your robe and let this blind man see how you've changed while he's been occupied with saving our universe."

I could hardly believe my eyes. Maria stood there in one of Leura's clingy red dresses that left nothing to the imagination. Her once emaciated legs were now shapely and well muscled. She seemed to be in excellent physical condition.

"That's why I kept wearing my robe when you were around. I wanted you to be surprised when you finally saw the real me. For the last eight weeks, they kept me on a special high-impact diet and exercise program in the high gravity therapy and training room. I feel wonderful. I regained all of my weight and strength, maybe even more than before."

"I'll say this . . . you sure look spectacular . . . and beautiful. You are positively radiant."

"Bravo!" the two Scentar ladies shouted in unison.

Then Laura said, "The man's eyes are now open. I think it is time we left these two to their own devices. Maia and I are going to see what we can do about getting Maria a ride on the ship."

After goodbyes, the two of us sat and looked at each other for at least ten minutes in absolute silence. It was a powerful emotional experience. I could not believe how beautiful Maria was, sitting there in Leura's dark red dress. Finally, she reached over, gently took my hand, and led me to the bedroom. As we walked in, some familiar music was coming from the sound system. I couldn't resist an observation.

"Scentar music - the red dress - satin sheets - your moves - it looks to me as if you've been getting some training from those two Scentar ladies."

As she pulled me gently down on the bed she said softly, "That's a tiny bit of what they taught me."

*   *   *

I awakened to an empty bed. The satin sheets, the smell of fresh coffee, and the humming of a familiar female voice coming from the kitchen relieved my moment of near panic. I grabbed my robe I found carefully laid out on the bedside chair and headed for the kitchen.

"How'd my robe get here?" I asked.

"If you check around you will find all of your things are now right here in **our** apartment. I will assume these new arrangements are to your liking or do you want to move back across the yard?"

"This whole thing was cooked up by you three conniving ladies, wasn't it?"

"We sort of worked it out together."

"My Gawd! Snookered again. Is there any part of my existence that at least one of you three hasn't controlled for the last ten months?"

"None that I can think of. Don't you love it?" Maria said with an impish grin. "Be honest, Drax. You are over all those negatives you were saying about Leura, now aren't you?"

"Yeah, you are right. By the way, what did she tell you about me?"

"Everything!"

"Everything? I mean, everything?"

"Down to and including how she and Laura tricked you into making love with Laura, and how you reacted in the morning. That was so you. I laughed so hard my insides hurt."

"You weren't . . . or aren't angry or upset?"

"Why should I be? Those two taught me—you might say brainwashed me—into understanding and believing in their cultural attitude about sex and making love. I think it is beautiful. I became a total convert."

"I'm still a bit nervous about their actions around you. It's . . . hard to get over those old sensitivities . . . very hard."

"I must admit, I have some strong possessive thoughts and emotions about you. I think it's instinctive. For instance, I know those two are each going to want to make love with you. That bothers me a little. I will get over it when it happens, and it will happen. Their instincts are strong, and their culture teaches it is a good thing, not bad as our does."

"I could solve the problem by telling them my culture doesn't allow it."

"Please don't. Leura might understand. She's a student of human culture, but I'm sure Laura wouldn't. She would be hurt. I couldn't bear her being hurt."

"Well, maybe it won't happen, then there would be no problem."

"Oh, it will happen, I'm sure. I've gotten to know and understand those two quite well. We spent lots of time together. Besides, they know they will never see you again, ever. So be kind and loving with them. They are going to miss you terribly, as will I if I am unable to go aboard the ship.

"It's hard for me to see myself in such a situation—so cared for—probably because of the situation when I was growing up. Still, I know I will miss them as well. You know, that never registered on me until this minute. Can you believe it never crossed my mind I might never see any of you again. How terrible. I never saw it coming until this moment. How could that happen?"

"You are so preoccupied with the shield project you've put everything else in your life on hold. It happens."

"Captain Woolgah. He has a wife and family."

"What are you saying?"

"That Captain Woolgah has a wife and family he will never see again. That too never dawned on me until this moment. I forgot a lot of important things, really important things."

"It's your dedication to this project. You are so focused you pushed all other considerations to the back of your mind."

"Not really. I've also been dealing with my relationship with you, Leura and Laura. Another major concern and focus of much concentration, in addition to the project. Another thing, I've got to do something about Captain Woolgah."

"But realistically, what could you do?"

"Realistically? I could try to put Captain Woolgah's wife on the ship with us. His boys are grown and lead their own lives. I wonder . . . would she even want to go, to leave her boys and friends and never see them again?"

A thoughtful look crossed Maria's face. "That would be a tough call for anyone. Maybe you should talk to Captain Woolgah about it."

"There's the problem of women, Segwah women on Segwah ships. It might be impossible to bring her here, let alone put her aboard the Gelwah."

"It's at least worth a try. Besides, it would be nice for me if another female was aboard for the trip."

"We don't have much time. I'd better get in touch with Captain Woolgah right away. Two weeks is a very short time to make arrangements, let alone bring her here even if the captain can manage it."

Chapter 47 - The Opposition Grows Nasty

About an hour later I arrived at the Gelwah only to find a large and hostile crowd of Scentar had overwhelmed the military guards and was gathered beneath the ship. The guards were under orders not to injure anyone, and so were overpowered by the huge crowd. Members of what became a mob were shouting and blocking the movement of the cargo carriers and preventing the transfer of supplies onto the ship. The access ramp had been closed, so there was no way I could get in. I called Captain Woolgah on my com unit.

"I see you are facing a slight problem, Captain."

"Yes, Drax, it is more than a slight problem. This crowd has been here since before dawn. Their leaders are threatening to block all efforts to deliver supplies for the mission. I contacted General Straglo and Chief Delgo who are trying to work out a peaceful solution. The organized resistance to the mission seems to be growing. They are gaining many members, some high in Scentar hierarchy and our negotiations are going nowhere. Right now we are considering several places where we can supply the ship in secret. Fortunately, none of the essential supplies are in the two transporters the crowd has surrounded. I'm afraid this may delay our departure. As a last resort, we could portal the supplies aboard, but that would take a long time, more than we can spend "

"Captain, there is something rather pressing I need to discuss with you in person."

"Couldn't we do so over the com system? As you can see, I am currently occupied with necessity."

"I would prefer to discuss this in a private, face to face meeting. It is personal and could be important to you."

"Hold on. General Straglo is trying to contact me."

I waited anxiously for about ten minutes during which time I moved away from the crowd. They hadn't connected my lone figure with the ship as yet, and there was no need for me to press my luck. Captain Woolgah's voice was on my com unit.

"Drax."

"You got me."

"We found a location to put the ship where it can be supplied. You'll need an air car to get there. Switch to coded channel A7 and I'll give you the location in about five minutes. There are ears out there that might be listening to our conversation on this channel. Oh yes, I wouldn't stick around if I were you. There's no telling what the crowd might do when we lift off. Talk to you later."

"Okay, Captain. Will do."

I headed over the hill toward the assembly building. Once inside, I headed for the loading dock where air cars were available. All I would need would be a pilot. I called Leura to explain the situation and ask her to find me a pilot I could trust.

"I'll be right over," she replied to my request.

"You? Why you?"

"What's the matter? Don't you think you can trust me? I'm a qualified air car pilot, and I can be there quicker than I could find another."

"Of course I trust you. I . . . oh what the hell. I'll see you when you are here. I'll be waiting in the lounge next to the loading dock."

While I waited in the lounge, Captain Woolgah called and gave me the location. He explained it was a flat, cleared, hilltop, surrounded by forest, about 150 kilometers north of the base.

"We chose the site because there is no easy way there in a ground vehicle or by foot. We will transport the supplies by air car."

"Couldn't they also get there by air car?"

"That is highly unlikely. It would take a large number of air cars to transport even a small crowd. If they try, we can keep their air cars from landing anywhere on the hilltop. Of course, loading supplies by air car will delay our departure by at least a week, or as much as two. We should still have plenty of time to rendezvous with the end of the rift."

"Okay Captain. We'll play the hand we've been dealt."

I heard the Captain's laugh over the com unit. "All right, Drax, you just used one of your little idioms I cannot decipher. Plain English, please."

"Sorry! I see you are not a poker player. If you were, you would be a damned good one. It is a generality meaning we will need to deal with the situation not of our making—one fate has presented us."

"Yes, I understand. Now I must lift the Gelwah off the ground without injuring any of those idiots beneath us. I imagine we will be there long before you arrive. Call me when you are close, so I can tell you where to meet me."

"Will do. Leura is coming to the assembly building to take me there. I expect her any moment. I am guessing we will take an hour to get there. See you then."

It took half an hour for Leura to check out the air car before we were on our way. About fifteen minutes after we left, I spotted another air car below and behind us. We were being followed.

"I'm afraid we picked up company, something we definitely do not want."

"Look around for a hill or valley where we can hide from them for a few minutes."

"You have a plan?"

"Yes," she said, handing me a Galbo. "We will hide for a moment and they will come after us. With luck, they will fly right over us. I will hold the car steady while you hit their thruster section with a Galbo blast. Without thruster power they will be able to move up and down but not laterally, so they can no longer follow us."

"This is the first time I ever saw you with a weapon."

"I thought it might prove useful. Who knew what we might run into? Right there!" she said suddenly, pointing to a dark stripe in the forest. "We can duck into the valley and back up against this side, close to the trees."

"What if I miss and hit the body of the car?"

"You won't miss. I've seen you shoot, remember? The Galbo is set for a tight beam, so aim for the black tube at the rear of the car. One hit will destroy the thruster. They'll need to call to be towed in."

When she stopped the car next to the trees, she opened the canopy.

"They should be here soon, so be prepared."

I stood and braced myself against the edge of the opening, pointed the Galbo up and waited, and waited.

"Do you suppose they are suspecting what we are doing and are waiting us out?"

"Don't worry. They'll be here soon. I can hear their engines."

No sooner had those words been said than the air car came slowly over the trees close to where we were. As soon as I had a clear shot, I blew the thruster nozzle right off of their air car.

"Now let's head out," Leura said as she zoomed right past their faltering air car, flew down the valley and then climbed at least a thousand meters above the forest and headed west. "I'm going to take a circular path to see if any more followers are out there before I head north."

Suddenly she headed down once more. "I didn't see anyone when I ran a sweep, so we can head straight for the Gelwah. I think maybe we should stay as low as possible and use a zigzag course for most of our trip. That way no distant spying eyes will be able to track us, if there are any out there."

It was a full hour before we spotted the unmistakable shape of the Gelwah sitting atop one of the small mesas sticking out of the surrounding sea of trees. Leura dropped the air car down near the tree tops to approach.

"Down here I doubt any prying eyes could find us. There may not be any, but you never know."

"What are these mesas anyway? They are unusual geological formations, all the same size and shape."

"Vega Five had several frozen periods like your Earth. Those flat mesas are actually drumlins."

"I've seen drumlins on Earth, but they were round and not flat like these."

"That's because there was a different kind of ice sheet moving rather quickly over this area many years after the first one that formed the drumlins. This ice sheet cut the tops off of each hill like a giant bulldozer. If you look closely, you'll notice each one is more elliptical than round, and all of them are extended in the same north-south direction. That's the direction the ice sheet bulldozed the tops off of the drumlins."

"You're a fount of information. How'd you learn all that stuff?"

She laughed. "I'm a botanist, remember? Part of my studies involved geology and the various ages of both Earth and Vega Five. Surely even you know about Earth's ice ages. They are no great mystery, at least a general understanding is not. You remembered about drumlins. That's basic, general knowledge"

By this time we were within a few hundred yards of the mesa where the Gelwah was parked. I could see the top was flat and about fifty meters above the tops of the trees in the surrounding forest. The Gelwah sat alone atop and in the center of the mesa. My com unit suddenly came to life.

"Drax? I assume you are in the air car. You shouldn't sneak up on us. We might have mistaken you for an intruder and blasted you."

"Come on, Captain. You had to read the air car's ID and known Leura was piloting. Don't give me that baloney."

"So it is," the Captain said with a hearty laugh. "A little joke to let you know I am not without humor. Park the car near to the ramp, come inside, and enlighten me about this mysterious personal question. and bring your lovely pilot with you."

In no more than ten minutes, one of the crew was leading us toward the bridge. Shortly we exchanged greetings with Captain Woolgah before being seated at the table in the Captain's private dining room next to the bridge.

"Drax, you now have my undivided attention and intense curiosity. What is the mysterious personal question requiring this private meeting?"

Before Drax could answer, Leura spoke. "Captain, remember our spirited discussion resulting in your agreeing to let Maria aboard your ship for the mission?"

"How could I possibly forget? I'm still reeling from the verbal onslaught of logic and emotion. You and your sister, your maia, are a powerfully persuasive pair. You overcame millennia of Segwah military protocol and tradition that was ingrained in my being since I first entered the military. Does your question relate to why you and Drax are here?"

"Yes! I wanted to remind you of our earlier conversation as much of what we discussed will relate to what Drax is about to say. and Drax, I hope you don't mind my little intrusion. I thought it might help."

Frankly, I was a bit pissed. No, I was extremely pissed. I would now need to direct my words differently than I had planned. I glared at Leura as I spoke to Captain Woolgah.

"I want to talk to you about your wife and family. I know this could be a sensitive subject under the circumstances, but it could be important."

"You are right. It is a sensitive subject. In fact, I have been doing everything in my power to bring them here, so we could spend a few days together before the mission leaves. If I succeed, this will be the first time in our history where a civilian has been sent through the universe portal. It is a big deal indeed. I received word they are coming to the Segwah universe portal as early as the day after tomorrow. Both Meernya and I have mixed emotions about this since it could mean a distressing parting when we do leave."

"That's wonderful news," Leura said. "I'm so happy for you."

"Actually, I used the same argument you used on me, that the Gelwah was not in the Segwah universe, so Human rules applied rather than Segwah. This caused a stir among the Segwah military, but finally, even they agreed to it."

I shook my head in disbelief. "Most of my plan has already been put in motion and I haven't even started explaining it. I might as well just blurt it out. Captain, why don't you take Meernya with us on our mission? That is of course if she would want to go."

My words were greeted with a long, stony silence. At first I thought it best not to speak, but as the silence continued I decided I must say something. "Captain? Did I say something wrong? I meant only good will for you and your wife. I hope my intentions are correctly understood."

For a moment the captain looked distressed. Finally, after another long silence, he spoke. "My dear friend, Drax. I understand your good intentions. The thought that it might be possible for Meernya to go with us never entered my mind. My thoughts are still racing since you proposed it. Many questions are rushing through my head in rapid succession. Would she even consider going? What about our sons? How would they react to losing both parents from their lives? How would Meernya take to living on a star ship? She's involved in many activities and has many friends. How would she feel about leaving all of that forever? It is a complicated situation. I would not even think about broaching the subject to her until I gave it some serious thought."

Many of those same thoughts had also entered my mind. "I thought of your wife when the ladies suggested Maria go with us. I decided then and there to talk to you about it at the earliest possible time. This meeting is the result."

"I will give it some serious thought and come to a decision before they arrive. Should I decide to pose the question to Meernya and our boys, I will let you know the results when they are decided. In the mean time, I must finish provisioning the ship. The first air cars and their cargo should be arriving shortly. I'll walk you to the ramp as you leave. Things are about to be very busy around here."

By the time we reached our car, the first loads of cargo were arriving. We spotted several approaching air cars as we headed south for the base. The delivery of supplies was beginning.

Chapter 48 - The Mob Gets Ugly

We were near base when we received a com call from Laura. "Where are you? Things are a bit ugly here. The mob was angered when the Gelwah lifted off, so they took their anger out on the guards. Chief Delgo called up his entire military guard force to confront the mob and rescue the guards, several of whom were injured. General Straglo is marshaling the base military to back up the guard forces. We all hope things will not get out of hand and turn even more violent."

"Thanks, Maia. We'll stand by and let you know when we are close. Where are you now?" Leura asked.

"I'm in the Porter Building. The mob has moved from where the Gelwah was to the nearby assembly building. I can see from here that they've surrounded it. I also see there are several leaders using hand-held speakers to direct them and incite their anger. This situation may be getting out of hand."

"I hope things don't turn violent. Should they head your way I hope you leave and head for safety before they get there."

"Don't worry. I will. I'll keep you informed, so you'll know where to set down safely when you arrive here."

It was hard for me to believe the normally peaceful and well-behaved Scentar could act in such a way.

"How is it your people can become violent so quickly?" I asked Leura.

"Scentar can be quite emotional, even more so than Humans. Once they get an idea in their heads it is difficult to dislodge. Certain charismatic individuals can use these emotional factors to move groups to do their bidding. Our history is peppered with similar types of incidents. Some promoted good things, but many others were purely mistaken or even evil efforts. Right now Laura and I are working with the council to find out who the leaders of this resistance are."

"Do you have any ideas?"

"Keltra Jung, Leandra's political opponent in the last election is my number one suspect. She ran on an anti-science platform and came close to winning the last election."

"Strange, I never even considered your political situation. What do you mean by *anti science* platform?"

"You might not know, but scientists—at least those working in the hard sciences, math, physics, chemistry, cosmology, gravity, and such—are a small minority in the Vegan system. Even including the life science people, they are vastly outnumbered by technicians, construction workers, all kinds of laborers and those government bureaucrats. There are as many social workers as scientists. If not for the large number of the military, Leandra would never have been elected."

"I can hardly believe what I'm hearing. It sounds like the good old USA."

"We do know this organized effort is being led by a few highly placed and influential individuals. We hope it will not take us long to find them out. How to deal with them will be another matter that could create major problems and interfere with the mission."

"We learn something new each day, don't we? This resistance to our mission, this rebellious resistance, is irrational. Don't your people have confidence in what we tell them?"

Leura's musical laugh preceded her words. "I was laughing at the thought of one common Human expression that describes the answer. They are only human."

We both had a good laugh over that, but it did get her point across. Then we passed over the plaza and approached the assembly building.

"Damn! There must be thousands around the building. This seems to be escalating to serious proportions. I wonder who's inside? I hope they locked and barricaded the doors."

Leura headed the air car toward the Porter Building. "I think we had better set down on the other side of the Porter building, where the mob won't see us. I'll put it right near the door. Should they head our way we will be able to leave before they get here."

Before we could step out, Laura burst through the door in an obvious hurry.

"Stay in the car," she shouted as she ran toward us. "I'm coming with you."

When Laura got in, she directed Leura to head for the Administration Building, saying, "General Straglo has requested all civilian officials including all members of the rift repair team go to the main conference room in the Administration Building. He is in the process of deploying a military guard with instructions to build and expand a perimeter and eventually push the mob out of the complex."

"That sound ominous," I said. "Any obvious military presence could turn this into an insurrection. I hope things don't go that far."

"So far the only violence has been minor injuries to two of the guards who were roughed up by the crowd. Also, there has been no use or even display of weapons of any kind."

I was alarmed. "I hope it stays that way. I also hope use of the military doesn't result in an armed confrontation because of their weapons. All I can think of is the attack at the hotel. As Captain Woolgah said then, Galbos at close range can kill a lot of people in a short time."

Leura set the air car down on the pad in front of the Ad building, and we streamed out and into the lobby through lots of Scentar military personnel. We were greeted by a guard who, upon recognizing Leura, directed us to the conference room where General Straglo was conducting a meeting.

"Great, all of the scientists are here," the general announced when he saw us come in. We sat down among about 40 individuals as General Straglo got to the point.

"I have some important and disturbing new information about the uprising. We now know Keltra Jung is the dictatorial leader of this revolt. She is a long time bitter political opponent of Archon Leandra, and an outspoken critic of the scientific community. She and a cadre of militants, including a few dissident military personnel, used their angry mob to take over the broadcast facilities in the communications building by force. There are an unknown number of minor casualties. Our own forces, led by Lieutenant Lespa Respala under orders from Chief Kropa Delgo, surrounded the facility and are negotiating to move the injured from both sides out to medical care."

"How long ago?" a voice shouted.

"About two hours ago the mob charged into the facility and overwhelmed the few guards. They shut down all TV broadcasts and then switched to Keltra speaking to her mob in the main hall. She has been ranting on and on for at least forty minutes, making ridiculous and false charges against Archon Leandra and our group of scientists. There is no doubt her ranting will reach many sympathetic ears among the many lower level workers and bureaucrats. She is using the rift repair project as her point of attack. She demands it be terminated, that Archon Leandra step down, and that she be made Archon by acclamation. Her words are pure fiction filled with hate and moving emotional appeal, but most of those watching or listening do not understand."

Leura stood up. "Is anything being done to shut down the broadcast? Keltra is using her considerable emotional appeal to sway those with little or no actual understanding of the situation to do her bidding. As long as she can reach more and more people her power will grow. I think our first priority should be shutting down her broadcast."

"We worked on that since she started, but it is not so simple," the General said. "We shut off power to the building, but the emergency power system came on. We considered blasting the antenna, but then how could we reach the people once we regain control of the station. An assault on the building is being considered, but such action might cause massive casualties."

I indicated I would like to speak. "Yes Dr. Syl."

"Is there an exposed cable to the antenna, and are there any guards with weapons on the roof?"

"I will check and find out. What did you have in mind?"

"If an air car went over high enough and then dropped vertically onto the roof it would not be seen from inside the building. It shouldn't take long to cut the cable and silence the broadcast."

"Greelo, you know all about the antenna. What do you say?"

Greelo, chief of the entire communication system, stood to speak. "The antenna would be vulnerable to such an attack, but I suggest a slight change that is easier. There is a junction and control system in a rather compact cabinet at the base of the antenna. Take out the box with a Galbo blast, and the broadcast would be stopped. We keep at least one and maybe two spare boxes in the store room. the box could be replaced in no more than fifteen minutes and the station would be operational. It would need to be a close and accurate blast so the box connections are not damaged."

General Straglo picked up his private communicator. "I was just informed no guards are on the roof at present. Lieutenant Respala will dispatch a team to blast the box. Greelo, do you have any further instructions?"

"An accurate and concentrated blast striking the upper right corner of the box as viewed from the front would be best. That would destroy its function but not damage the connections."

"Lieutenant Respala will so instruct our sharp shooters. Thank you, Greelo. It should take no more than forty minutes unless the situation changes. We'll know they succeeded the instant her broadcast ceases. Now our Archon wants to speak."

Archon Leandra stepped to the dais. "I must warn you not to underestimate the ability of Keltra to gain and motivate followers. She is an eloquent and moving speaker. Her social and motivational skills are impressive. Combine that with her clever abrogation of facts and logic and she presents a serious threat to the political stability of the entire resident Scentar population. She is a dangerous individual who seeks only power for herself and a small cadre of dedicated supporters. She is fomenting and amplifying some cultural suspicion the public has of science and of all scientists—ideas and people they do not clearly understand. It is my opinion trying to topple her by force will only strengthen her politically. The only chance to be rid of her is to convince the public of what she is and what she wants. That will not be easy with a general populace suspicious of our motives and actions. We neglected doing a thorough enough job of educating the public about the rift, its possible consequences, or what we are doing to prevent an unbelievably immense calamity."

I turned to Leura. "I can see why she was elected. She's a good motivator herself, and she has truth on her side."

Leura became serious. "You are right. I only hope we can see the Gelwah, you, and the crew, off on this mission before things are out of hand."

After the Archon had completed her speech, Chief Delgo stepped up to the podium and explained what was being done to protect all of the buildings and the people in them, and help bring back some degree of order. After he was interrupted by his com unit he reported, "I was just notified our soldiers successfully disabled the antenna as planned. No one appeared on the roof, so there was no interference. Our two volunteers came back intact and without injury."

This brought forth a loud cheer from the group. Chief Delgo resumed his interrupted explanation. "A guarded perimeter has been established around the broadcast complex to keep more protesters from going inside. We will maintain this force letting anyone out, but no one inside of the line. At this point, the only protesters who will be detained are those suspected of committing violent actions. This guarded perimeter will gradually be reinforced and expanded to include the entire central complex of buildings. This will remove all protesters from the complex and will calm and defuse the situation. Are there any questions?"

One of the group asked, "What about those inside the broadcast building? They could do a lot of damage and maybe even fix the antenna and restart their broadcasts."

"Our negotiating team is about to enter the building after several loud announcements. They were told the team has armed escorts who will not fire unless attacked. A few members of the team are armed with Galbos they will only use against an attack with Galbos. The rest of the team are armed with LKs set on stun. We do not want anyone hurt. The protesters were also told they are free to leave when and if they want to, but once outside the perimeter they will not be readmitted. They were assured there will be no reprisals if they leave peacefully."

The group posed several questions. "Do they possess weapons, and if so, what will the team do?"

"So far they used no weapons. We do not know and are not assuming they do or do not possess weapons. Any weapons found will be confiscated. We are hoping for a peaceful resolution."

"What will the team do if the protesters refuse to leave?"

"The team is backed up by at least fifty regular troops who will enter the lobby and stay there unless needed. We plan to search the entire building room by room after blocking all means of exiting the building. There will be four soldiers covering each exit including the tunnel. Our hope is that the overwhelming force will motivate the protesters to leave peacefully."

"What if they don't?"

"Let's say we will do everything we can to persuade them to leave on their own. If they don't, we will use whatever force is required to take them out of the building and lock them up in a jail cell. That, of course, is a last resort."

"What about Keltra? What do you plan to do with her?"

"As far as I know she has not yet broken any laws, taking over the broadcast building not withstanding. If she leaves without resistance, she can walk away free and clear. If she puts up a fight, she will be jailed like any other law breaker."

"How soon will all of this happen? How long do you anticipate it will take to clear the building?"

"Barring any serious resistance I think the building will be cleared in less than an hour. If our forces meet with resistance, and especially if the protesters use weapons, it could take much longer . . . Wait . . . Lieutenant Respala, the leader of our troops clearing the communications building is reporting to my com unit. I'll switch his report to the main view screen."

The view screen showed soldiers flooding into the lobby of the building and civilians running out. Lieutenant Respala spoke, "We met little in the way of resistance. Everyone we've encountered seemed eager to leave. We learned from some of them that Keltra and fifteen or twenty of her loyal supporters are barricaded in the main studio on the top floor. Our men haven't reached the top floor yet. Our plan is to move as many as we can spare onto the floor below, then use the stairs to access the top floor quickly. We will move up silently and hope to surprise them. It should be over quickly without anyone getting hurt. That of course, depends on what resistance they put up."

Chief Delgo replied, "Will your troops be able to operate a com unit, so we can see what happens when you enter the top floor? We would like to follow their actions on our display if possible."

"I'll ask my lead men if they can do so, but they may be busy if there is any resistance."

"Don't take any unnecessary chances to do this. I think our people here would like to see your men in action, how carefully they deal with these protesters."

The scene on the view screen switched to a stairway filled with soldiers, some armed, some not. A new voice spoke softly. "This is Sargent Quall. We are positioning our men to burst through the door into the top floor hall. The studio door is about sixty steps down the hall to our left. We are sending a few men up in the elevator as a ruse. A few seconds after the elevator doors open, we will break down the door if necessary, to gain access to the hall."

The men quickly opened the door without having to break it down, burst into the hallway and ran down the hall to the studio door. The com unit man followed, so all the action was shown on the view screen. They soon determined the door was locked and barricaded from the inside.

Sargent Quall spoke in a commanding voice. "Break the door down. They know we're here in force, so be prepared for possible combat, maybe weapon fire."

The door was soon down, and the furniture that had been against it was pushed out of the way. About thirty soldiers poured into the room and surrounded a tight huddle of fifteen civilians on the raised stage. There were only four men in the group. All of the women but Keltra were obviously pairs of maia. No one appeared to be armed. Keltra stood and spoke.

"We trained several cameras on this room to record the violent actions of government troops crashing in on a peaceful protest demonstration. All of this is being broadcast, so the public will know."

Lieutenant Respala entered the room as she made her last remark. "I hate to disappoint you, Madam Keltra, but there is no broadcast. The antenna was taken off line at least an hour ago. Now, if you will all peacefully take the elevator down and exit the building, no charges will be made against any of you. That includes you, Madam Keltra. However, each of you will be barred from any access to any kind of public communications for the foreseeable future. You will also be kept outside of a perimeter being established by our military around the entire complex of government buildings. We will maintain the peace and security of this complex using such force as is required. We will act only where we determine there is a threat to such security."

Madam Keltra was not pleased. "Young man, your insolence and disrespect for my person and position on this base are noted. We will tell everyone about how badly you treated our group of peaceful protestors. We will also let it be known about your illegal censorship and efforts to keep us from being heard."

Lieutenant Respala spoke cheerfully. "Madam Keltra, all of the actions of my men, and myself, here in this building, were recorded along with your responses. I think those records will prove to the public that we acted with restraint and even kindness to some provoking incidents and language from your protesters. There was no bad treatment, no censorship, no effort to prevent you from being heard. In fact, the administration of Archon Leandro offered numerous times to debate you in a public forum whenever and wherever you wanted. Instead, you chose to occupy and control the Communications building, shut down the programs and news that were being broadcast, and substitute your own programming, all in defiance of the law. When the antenna is operational in less than an hour, all of these recordings will be played for everyone to see and hear. We are pleased to let them, the public, watch, listen, and make their own decision as to who is right or wrong."

Madam Keltra was angry and frustrated. Things had not gone anything like she had planned. "All I can say, Lieutenant, is that you and your masters haven't heard the last from us. We can and will stop this ridiculous and expensive effort to fix a nonexistent problem. Then, when I am elected Archon, we'll put the Segwah in their proper place. You will see."

The lieutenant's exasperation got to him. "Everything the members of your group of ignorant malcontents has tried has failed miserably. To me you are like a group of carrion flies, easily swatted and forgotten, a minor inconvenience to the vast majority of citizens and to the government. You and your efforts will be soon forgotten. Now move along and exit our building."

"And what if we refuse to move?"

"I have no time for more conversation. Our forces are all equipped with LKs set to stun. Any person refusing to exit the building and move out beyond the perimeter we established will be rendered unconscious and carried out beyond the perimeter. An hour or two later they will awaken outside with a fierce headache. The choice is up to you. Walk out peacefully or be carried out unconscious. It matters not to any of us which you choose. You will all be beyond the perimeter in less than an hour."

After he had finished, he turned and walked quickly away, leaving the speechless protesters facing an army with LKs at the ready. True to Lieutenant Respala's words, all of the protesters were outside of the perimeter in less than an hour, even those few who were carried out unconscious. Madam Keltra wisely chose to walk out peacefully and without incident. The perimeter was manned by a substantial and well-armed force. This denied them access to any and all of the buildings in the government complex. Those not employed in the complex, but needing access for any valid reason, were screened and, if permitted entry, were accompanied by an armed escort. Chief Delgo was taking no chances.

Chapter 49 - The Woolgahs Make Their Final Decision

33.52.21.0900 (Stardate/time)

Captain Woolgah paced nervously back and forth in the transfer room of the Gelwah universe portal. His family was due to arrive momentarily and he was unsure of what would transpire next. Meernya had been uncharacteristically secretive during their latest communication and the captain didn't know why. He did know that something was up, something outside of his area of knowledge. That disturbed him.

A bright, blue-green flash, a large ring of even brighter energy, and then the open portal appeared. There was a rush of air as the pressures equalized. Standing in the center of the ring, Meernya and two striking, young Segwah strode into the room and up to Captain Woolgah. Tears of joy and soft words emphasized the powerful feelings of the moment. Though at first they spoke little, the emotional reactions of their being together at this crucial time broke over them repeatedly, giant waves breaking on the sea shore of their being. This was a family with strong ties of love.

Typical of Segwah women, Meernya was a bit smaller than her men. Obviously rather burly and well muscled compared with human women, she was dainty and feminine next to the males. She dabbed the tears from her eyes. "We've several surprises for you, Grala, several big surprises. Quickly now. We must step back against the side wall."

An enormous cargo truck rolled through the portal driven by a Segwah soldier with another soldier in the cab. When the truck stopped it filled the room. The portal powered down.

The older son, Char, spoke. "Father, we brought some special things of yours and mother's. The two Segwah soldiers in the truck are going to help us unload before we return home. I'm sure this is a bit confusing, but you will understand shortly. Can we open the transfer room doors and free all of us and the truck out of these cramped quarters?"

The captain was not used to being in the dark about anything. "Will you please let me know what this is all about? What's in the truck? I thought you would be bringing some things for the trip, but this truck?"

Meernya smiled and took her husband's hand. "Once I decided to go with you, thanks to the boys' encouragement, our planning for the trip took off. It developed a life of its own. Our son, Denbo, the architect, came up with the idea of remodeling the empty officer's quarters of the Gelwah. Denbo, you explain."

The taller of their two sons, tall and slender for a Segwah, unwound expressive hands and began. "At first I started picking out your things, those I was sure you would enjoy having with you. The next thing I knew we were dismantling your complete study, bedroom, bath and sitting room from the house. They are packed in the truck. I then redesigned the empty part of the officer's quarters to hold them as they were at home."

"Won't that add to our tight schedule? We do have a deadline you know."

Meernya put her arms around his neck. "The boys assure me they can do the job in no more than four days. The two soldiers were chosen because they are construction workers. Since they will be working in an unused section, their work will not interfere with any other preparations for the trip. Think. It will be like home. You will have all your favorite things in your old study."

Denbo spoke up. "Oh, and Father, the material we will remove from the crews' quarters will weigh exactly the same as the material we are adding so you won't need to recalibrate the balance of the ship, at least not for the changes we will make."

The captain smiled. "It seems you thought of everything. I am so proud of you . . . all of you. We must go up the main deck, immediately. There are some people I want you to meet before we deal with your cargo. I'd like to meet your two soldiers. Tell them to leave the truck and come with us. I'll ask part of the crew to move the truck up to the officer's quarters."

The two soldiers, Corporal Quervo and Private Solas, were introduced to the captain and soon all were headed up to the main deck and the bridge. First Officer Jemrah joined with the captain. The two of them conducted an instructive tour of the main parts of the ship. They finished at the officer's quarters where the truck had been delivered.

Denbo soon began to survey the empty section of the officer's quarters. "Father, for us to finish in time, I think we should start on our remodeling project immediately. It's still early afternoon, and we can accomplish a lot before dinner. We made detailed plans for how and when to proceed in a D-board in the truck. It's all laid out from the removal of the existing walls and fixtures to the placement of the last piece of trim in your study. Would it be possible for a few members of your crew to help in the demolition and removal of waste? That would speed up the process."

"With most of my crew on standby during the provisioning process, I'm certain that can be arranged. Jemrah, will you see to it?"

"Certainly Captain. I was thinking. Members of the maintenance crew would be most helpful. I'm sure they would rather be working than waiting."

"Excellent. The construction men will be staying down the hall. Tell the crew to show them to their rooms and handle the luggage. Please move Meernya's things into my cabin."

"Yes, Captain."

"Dinner is at 19:00, in my private dining room on the bridge deck. I will expect all of you to be cleaned up and dressed properly for the occasion. There will be a number of special guests there, people I want you to meet. Now we should all be on our ways. Time is precious, and we must make the best of what time we have."

Meernya spoke to the captain as they started walking to his cabin. "Grala, I must talk to you about some problems we had getting clearance for your ship both to go on the mission and to take two female passengers. Your son, Char, handled the problems with aplomb. He's quite a clever negotiator."

"What kind of problems? I thought everything was approved."

"Right when we began trying to get approval, we were informed the Gelwah is a military ship on a specific Segwah mission. Under regulations, there was no way it could go on the mission without specific council approval overriding the military controls. When you first put in the request, there was quite a stir. Our son spent a lot of time arguing that the military combat mission was no longer viable. He emphasized that drastic changes were made when we signed the peace treaty with the Scentar. These changes placed civilian authority over the military. He won out handily. This is why you received permission to conduct the mission."

"I was not aware of Char's help, but it is deeply appreciated."

"Then an even larger problem, taking civilian women aboard a Segwah star ship, ran into some determined military resistance. At first, we thought that since it would be operating in the Human universe, Segwah rules would not apply. The military refused to budge. Admiral Sendra said, 'No Segwah military vessel has ever held women during a mission. This rule cannot be changed or abrogated. No women, ever.'"

"Char then made a bold offer. I think it was a stroke of genius. He proposed the military decommission the ship and sell it to the humans. His basic suggestion was to sell it as a derelict to the Eegis Project of Earth. He even sent an envoy to negotiate with them for the transfer of title. It took a bit of time, but the final documents were signed before we left. I brought them all with me."

The captain was shocked. "What does that mean for me and the crew? Are we now without a ship? Our commission and enlistments are all with the Segwah military. What happens to those things?"

"Char found and invoked an ancient military protocol named *foreign assignment*. Under those rules, the Segwah military has assigned you and your crew to the Eegis Project. You will all maintain your commissions and enlistments as they are, but control and pay will be administered by the Eegis Project. They agreed to maintain all Segwah rules and regulations except for limits on personnel. They may, if they wish, permit females on their ship for any mission they choose. Members of the Segwah military are happy as their protocols remain intact. We are happy since Maria and I are now free to go with you on your mission. The Eegis Project people are all happy for their involvement in such an undertaking. and I am impressed with our son's ability to solve a difficult problem. Now I believe we should all unpack and prepare for dinner. I look forward to meeting your *special guests*."

The captain stood dumbfounded, but finally found his voice. "You are amazing, all of you. I will make sure the Scentar are made aware of your skillful efforts. We will celebrate your success at dinner."

Meernya looked at her husband. "Please don't make a big thing of this. Let it come out naturally during conversation. Both boys would prefer not to be so much in the spotlight. It was a personal thing for each of them, and for me as well. We had lots of help from both Segwah and Humans. There were many others who took part in all phases of this effort. We are pleased how it worked out."

"As you wish," Captain Woolgah said with a grin. "I will keep my bragging about my family down to a low rumble."

Chapter 50 - Introductions and a Farewell Dinner

The dinner in the captain's private dining room of the Gelwah was attended by a total of sixteen. In addition to the four Woolgahs, were three other Segwah, First Officer Jemrah, Corporal Quervo, and Private Solas. Humans, Dr. Draxel Syl, Dr. Marty Cohen, and Maria Mendrex were joined by six Scentar, Leura Clauson, Laura Claiborne, Archon Leandra Gordon, Assistant Archon Louandra Gordon, General Lairn Straglo, and Chief Kropa Delgo. All of the military men were in their striking dress uniforms. The civilians were all in comparable formal attire, women in beautiful gowns and men in the formal wear of their own culture. There was a period of introductions and socializing lasting more than an hour when strangers became friends. When they were all ushered to their seats by the serving crew, Captain Woolgah stood to address the group.

"I am pleased you are all here. This is the most amazing gathering I have ever been in during my entire life. Consider, a short time ago our human friends had no inkling any of this even existed. Their entire world was on their one small planet. Now we three species are gathered in a Segwah star ship, on a Scentar base, in a star system in the Human universe, far from the Human's only home on Earth. The Human universe is alien to both Segwah and Scentar. Even more amazing is the peace that has come between Segwah and Scentar after thousands of years of bitter warfare. I know there were many involved in bringing about peace, but my dear friend Dr. Draxel Syl was the catalyst that started us down that road and refused to give up until the peace was secured. Accordingly I wish to propose a toast to a lasting peace and to Drax for his efforts to a peaceful end."

After glasses were raised in the toast and many agreeing comments offered, they all sat except for Drax who remained standing. He also then addressed the group.

"Thank you Captain Woolgah. I believe your wisdom and actions were a major part of the peace you spoke of. Now you are embarking on a voyage of mercy, a voyage to save, not your own universe, but two others including one where your once lifelong enemies live. You could simply go home and let nature take its course. Your life would not be affected in the least. Instead, you volunteered yourself, as did First Officer Jemrah and your wife, Meernya, You dedicated your ship and your leadership, to a mission with great danger, a mission that could cost you your future and possibly your life, as well as your wife's. Your mission, if successful and I think it will be, is to save two entire universes and all of their inhabitants from total annihilation. You, your family, and Jemrah are giving up a great deal, making an unprecedented sacrifice, simply to try to save all of the rest of us from being destroyed. I hope everyone in all universes, will understand and know of your unprecedented gallantry. So, I propose a toast to our courageous Captain, his loyal wife, and his stalwart sons."

After Drax's toast and the many comments, there were several other toasts. Archon Gordon gave a particularly emotional toast of thanks for all involved in the mission and in particular, the Woolgahs. After the dinner, Meernya and Maria spent significant time together. They would soon be living together for at least several months, and each wanted to know the other better.

During one of their conversations, Meernya brought up their similar names. "I wanted to know as much as I could about you before we met, so I researched your name in the Human database Grala provided. In the ancient languages of your culture, the root words, those we believe evolved into the name Maria, were ancient Egyptian names, Mry, meaning, *beloved* or Mr, meaning *love*. I was amazed, because my own name, Meernya, has a similar origin, Meeria, in our ancient languages. Meeria is described as meaning the equivalent of your *beloved* in our native tongue. So you see, our names are similar, at least they come from the same root meaning."

"That's amazing. I hope this means we will get along famously. Being together for months in the confines of a star ship could put a strain on any relationship. I see us both as independent, take-charge types who might come into conflict. We will develop some ground rules to prevent such a thing from happening. We'll need to find ways to decide who is in charge of what, so we won't be stepping on each other's toes."

"Perhaps we should learn and use some of my husband's military protocols. They were developed to keep peace when men are confined over long periods. I see no reason why they would not work for the two of us. Lets check into that before we leave? I think it best that we set some of your *ground rules* before we come into conflict, not after."

"Great idea. I think we will get along well. We are at least like-minded about rules."

It was late when the party broke up and people headed for their homes. The next several days would be a busy time for them all.

Chapter 51 - Final Preparations II

The next ten days were hectic for the Woolgahs. There was the loading of provisions for the trip, and the remodeling of the officers' quarters with the installation of the Woolgah home. The home installation went smoothly, but it took five, not four days to complete. Upon the completion, Corporal Quervo and Private Solas were portaled back home with their truck. Captain Woolgah and his wife spent as much time with their two sons as they could spare right up until departure of the Gelwah. These were emotional times for them considering their divergent futures.

During this same period, Drax and Maria had two weddings. The first was on Vegalan with all of their Scentar and Segwah friends in attendance. The second was held in Pasadena with many of their human family and friends. Maria met Drax's brother, Ori, while Drax met Maria's three sisters, who wept constantly from the joy of the wedding and the sadness of the parting. As Maria's oldest sister, Susan said, "It is so final, I'm torn up completely. We all live on, but will never see each other again."

When Drax and Maria portaled back to Vegalan, they found Leura anxiously waiting for them at their apartment. Serious concern marked her face.

Leura explained. "Keltra and her followers served an ultimatum. None of us, including Archon Gordon know if they can do what they threaten or not. They provided no details. Here's her ultimatum. It was posted all over the areas outside of the complex from which they were excluded." She handed a copy of the notice to them.

To all concerned Scentar. Your stated goals and purposes have not been ignored. Your faithful leaders possess the capability of stopping this false and foolish mission of the elitist scientists. Should the Segwah starship, Gelwah, manage to lift off, it and all those on board will be destroyed unless they abandon the mission. If the Gelwah persists and is destroyed, then the entire central government, including the buildings in the zone of exclusion, will also be destroyed along with the false political and military leaders remaining in those buildings. Then I, the true Archon of Vegalan, will take control of the government and meet all of your needs.

Keltra, true Archon of Vegalan and its associated worlds.

Drax looked puzzled. "Isn't that all bluster and noise? Surely she doesn't possess that kind of power or capability."

Leura wasn't so sure. "All it would take is one Scentar star ship in their hands and commanded by a Scentar who believes all the emotional stuff she's been spreading. There are at least seven of those Scentar ships that portaled here to protect against a Segwah attack, maybe more. I'll ask General Straglo. He would know. He might also know if any of their Captains might side with Keltra, and who they might be."

Leura immediately contacted General Straglo with her com unit. "General, how many Scentar starships are here in the Human universe, and where are they?"

"Leura, are you in a hurry? It may take some time for me to locate the ones not in our base."

"You could say it's imperative. We're trying to run down a possible threat from Keltra and her followers. If you haven't heard, they made public a direct and specific threat."

"I'm familiar with their threat from the notices they posted. We've been gathering new data about her supporters on a daily basis since the broadcast incident. We found there are a lot more of them than we suspected earlier. As soon as we started scanning seriously, they went underground. We should be able to dig them out, but it will take some time. After your question we will concentrate at least part of our efforts on starships and their officers. There are six known Delfro class starships in the human universe. Those are the only warships with weapons that could inflict any kind of damage. There is a remotely possibility others were portaled here without my knowledge, but that is unlikely. I'll be back to you if and when we find anything of interest."

"Thanks, General."

*   *   *

It wasn't long before Leura's com unit responded with General Straglo's voice. "Leura, four of the six Delfro class starships are on the ground at our base. They are on standby and their crews are on leave. The other two, the Intreba, and the Burbya are out. The Burbya is currently orbiting Stentor Seven. The Intreba is on a shakedown run after the installation of new drive engine stacks. Captain Belvra is on the Burbya. He's an old friend of mine and quite reliable. I know little about the captain of the Intreba, Raoul Saras, But will soon download his personnel records. I'm guessing he and the Intreba are the only possible threat. I've started a search scan for her, but with no results as yet. There are five unarmed cargo ships here, all but one are out hauling cargo around the Vega sector. That one is in the shipyard for repairs and maintenance."

Drax replied, "General, as you know we are scheduled to lift off at 0600 tomorrow. Please let us know if you find Intreba, and what she is doing."

"Will do Dr. Syl. You know don't you, there is nothing we can do, no action we can take against her and her supporters unless and until they break the law, and so far, outside of threats in words, they took no illegal action since they occupied the broadcast building. They broke no laws since that action."

"Yes, I'm familiar with how that works," Drax said. "It holds true right up until the Intreba blows us out of the skies if she decides to."

"Not correct, Drax. The action of powering up a disrupter array in preparation to fire is considered an act of aggressive war the same as if a weapon had been fired. Such action would justify the firing of any weapon in self defense, including a Galbo cannon."

"How long does that give a ship being attacked to load, aim, and fire their own weapons. I'll wager powering up a disrupter array doesn't take anywhere near so long. Also, couldn't a disrupter array be powered up ahead of an attack and kept at the ready until needed?"

"To the contrary, my friend. A disrupter array takes at least four, and maybe six minutes to power up. Once powered up, the array must be fired within no more than ten minutes or the power will discharge harmlessly on its own. During the time it takes to fill a charge, a Segwah starship could load aim and fire their Galbo cannons at least five times. One accurate hit on a disrupter array would disable it before it could be fired. With a fully charged Galbo cannon, a ship could aim and fire in about seven seconds. A sudden Galbo cannon attack would be much more difficult to respond to before being struck. Of course, your new Segwah shield would protect a ship from either type of attack. Ask Captain Woolgah. He knows."

"Well, General, let's hope it never comes to that kind of scenario."

"I certainly support your hopes, but that all depends on how committed our enemies are to stopping us. and Drax, good luck on your mission. We are all deeply in your debt."

"We'll take all the luck we can get, General."

"Now, if you will excuse me, I have much to do to keep things under control until you lift off."

"Good bye, General."

Many teary goodbyes were shared by many sad hearts during the hours remaining before lift off. It was definitely not a bon voyage celebration.

The whereabouts of Intreba remained unknown at the time of lift off.

Chapter 52 - Leaving on a Trip to Save Two Universes

From the log of the Segwah starship Gelwah, starting decadate 33.62.21.0600 (Stardate/time)

Captain Woolgah successfully lifted the fully provisioned Gelwah from the mesa where it stood for the last few weeks. At full power acceleration, they quickly left Vegalan behind and were soon leaving the Vega sector, reaching maximum welt speed in less than ten hours. Aboard the ship were four others, First Officer Der Jemrah, Dr. Draxel Syl and his wife, Maria, and Captain Woolgah's wife, Meernya. The men were the absolute minimum number required to operate the ship and its special instrument. While underway, the women would receive training as backups on the ship's controls and on navigation. As Drax pronounced several times, "You never know what unusual situations might occur." For the most part, they would concentrate on housekeeping, meal preparation, administration, and other nontechnical duties.

After decades of warfare with the Scentar, Captain Woolgah was struggling with his new peacetime role. The peace treaty between the Segwah and the Scentar had held for nearly ten months after millennia of bitter and deadly fighting. Negotiated cleverly by his Human friend Draxel Syl, the peace was good for all parties.

✻   ✻   ✻

33.64.13.0600 - Two days at max welt speed behind them, and with his first officer at the helm, Captain Woolgah was relaxing in the sitting room of his old home with Drax, Maria and his wife, Meernya.

"I can hardly believe how pleasant it is to have these rooms from our home aboard and to be sitting here with the three of you. Ours sons certainly did accomplish a lot." Meernya was obviously pleased.

Captain Woolgah looked at Meernya. "Yes, they certainly did. I could hardly believe what they were telling me every day while we were trying to put all of this in order. Char kept getting rebuffed daily in his efforts to get us aboard. Then, all of a sudden, it was done. I didn't even want to ask how, but found out it was all done through channels legitimately."

"I would expect no less from sons of you two." Maria said, smiling. "You folks are amazing. Here we are, out in the middle of nowhere headed for who knows what at maximum welt, and yet within the comfort of your lovely home. It's incredible. I understand we will spend several days of boring travel before we reach our destination."

Drax grinned. "Who says it will be boring? How could any trip with such charming and brilliant companions including two delightful women ever be boring? I am looking forward to many deep and satisfying conversations. Our good Captain showed me the ship's exercise and recreation facilities. I for one would like to try my hand at some of those Segwah games and competitions."

A call from the bridge interrupted them. First Officer Jemrah reported, "Sir, there is a Scentar ship following us. It left from near the Vega system about twelve hours after we left. At first they were vectored substantially away from our path, but recently they shifted heading and are now on an intercept course."

"I will be there immediately. Drax, will you come with me? Please excuse us ladies, duty calls."

When he reached the bridge, the Captain asked Jemrah, "Did you identified the ship?"

"No sir, their ID system does not respond. Their Iway pattern tells us they are a Delfro class warship. That's all we know at this time."

"The Intreba I'll wager. Drax, their ship might be faster, but the Gelwah could easily outmaneuver it in virtually any combat situation. I wonder why they are chasing us? Jemrah, set navigation control for course change to one hundred-twenty degrees Y, forty degrees Z and 0 degrees X and hold that course change until they are within hailing distance. I'd like to talk to them."

"Yes sir! I estimate hailing and active combat range in about three hours."

"Hail them when they are within range and be prepared to make the course change on my command. I don't want to give them much of a chance to fire on us."

✳   ✳   ✳

33.64.16.0900 - "Hailing now, Captain."

After about a minute the Captain said, "They don't seem to want to answer our hail. Lets change our heading—now!"

"Done Captain."

A few minutes after the course change Jemrah remarked, "Our move surprised them. I estimate they will take several days to find us and be back within combat range again."

"Thank you, Jemrah. We will continue on the new course. It will take us to eighty degrees Y, sixty degrees Z and ninety degrees X. Then in fifteen minutes, reverse the procedure plus five degrees in each plane."

            *   *   *

33.67.09.1500 - Captain Woolgah at the helm spots the Scentar ship approaching. "Jemrah, the Scentar ship will catch us in about eleven hours. Let's be prepared for another evasive maneuver like the last one."

            *   *   *

33.67.20.1500 - Jemrah reports. "Sir, the Scentar ship will be coming within combat distance in about fifteen minutes."

"This time, on my command, repeat the last maneuver with a plus five degree correction instead of minus five. That will put us back on our original course."

"May I ask why the same maneuver we did the last time?"

"That's because they won't expect it. They will be set up for the opposite maneuver and overrun our position by several days. By the time they figure out where we've gone we will again be at least two days beyond them."

"Do you want me to try hailing them when they come close enough?"

"Not this time. They didn't respond last time so let's see if they will hail us now if we remain silent."

"Yes Captain. Uh, May I speak freely sir?"

"Certainly! What's on your mind my friend."

"We are on a critical mission to try to stabilize a slowly growing tear in the space time continuum, a positive thing for all Scentar. Is that not correct?"

"Yes, of course."

"And this tear was started by crude gravity wave experiments conducted at least in part by our friend Drax, here, was it not?"

"Jemrah, what are you getting at?"

"There is no direct Scentar involvement in this mission. Segwah technology in the form of our new gravity-based defensive energy shield is the only system available that can possibly repair that tear and stop its propagation, correct?"

"Damn! Jemrah. You know that is an unproven theory. The Scentar, even with their understanding of inter dimensional rifts, admit they are guessing. You know quite well the dire consequences. If we do not repair the rift, our universe will be the only known one left and virtually all Scentar and humans will be gone forever."

"Yes, Captain, but such being true, why would a Scentar ship follow and possibly try to stop us? It makes no rational sense, none at all."

"I don't know, Jemrah, but it seems Keltra and her followers are continuing to behave completely irrationally. Why they are is beyond my understanding, but until now, they have only been a nuisance. The times they were within combat range they did not fire anything and they certainly could have. We must see to it they do not come within combat range again until after we've reached the end of the rift and engaged the shield."

"They know where we are going. Couldn't they portal to where the rift is and wait for us there?"

Drax replied, "They must know as we do that using a portal so close to the rift could trigger the gravitational collapse we are trying to prevent. Surely they are not so stupid. Of course, that would merely be one more irrational action, completely incomprehensible to me. They could do anything. Should they do so, and the worse happen, we would all be annihilated. I wish we understood what their game was."

❖   ❖   ❖

33.67.20.3000 - "Captain! The maneuver is complete. The Scentar ship is now far off our course. It will take them at least a day or more to catch us."

"Thank you Jemrah. One more course change to lose them again and we will be there. We should be in position to deploy the shield in about forty-two hours.

"Then we'll know for certain your gravity wave damping theory is correct." Drax said. "If not, we're all in deep doo doo."

Captain Woolgah laughed. "Drax, my friend, your colloquialisms are quite colorful. I'm beginning to *get* them as you say. It's good to bring out some humor during this serious business. It helps to relieve the tension."

Jemrah, the serious one, added, "Unfortunately, if it doesn't work or if we miss the spot, the Gelwah with us in it will not survive."

Drax commented, "Then we had better not miss." adding, "Jemrah, don't be so encouraging and optimistic."

Captain Woolgah smiled. "Better not miss indeed. My good friend, your words are a gross understatement. Now let's check over the shield generators to make sure they will be fully functional when we need them."

❊　　　❊　　　❊

33.68.05.1209 - Jemrah shouted, "Captain! The Scentar ship is within half an hour of reaching active combat contact. But that's impossible."

"Those fools. They acted irrationally and used their portal. That's the only way they could reach their present position so quickly."

"If they used their portal with no ill effects, why don't we portal to the end of the rift and be ready to activate the shield immediately when we arrive there?"

"Far too risky! They acted stupidly." Drax said with disgust.

The Captain added with disdain. "They must now be in maximum welt drive. Reverse course and they will blast right past us. When they do, reset course for the end of the rift. That should give us the ten hours we need to reach the optimum position at the end of the rift using welt drive. Once we operate the shield they won't be able to touch us."

"Yes sir! Captain."

Chapter 53 - Madam Keltra's Last Stand

From the Log of the Segwah Star Ship Gelwah, Starting Decadate **33.68.05.4200**

Captain Woolgah ordered from the Bridge. "Jemrah! Cut the engines, and prepare to engage the shield generators in seven minutes. We will then be at the optimum point to engage the shield around the rift."

"Yes sir!"Jemrah answered and a few seconds later said, "Captain, the Scentar ship is directly in our path. Four minutes to impact."

Drax cursed. "Damn. Those stupid fools could destroy us all, them included."

Our com system display lit up with incoming on the screen. Madam Keltra was standing next to the captain. "Captain Woolgah, this is Captain Raoul Saras of the Scentar star ship Intreba. You are ordered to stand down. Abort the mission. I repeat, abort the mission."

"And on whose authority do I abort this mission?" as he spoke, he signaled Drax to hold on to the shield control.

Keltra screamed, "On my authority, and because we are training massive disrupters on your ship. If you do not do so, we will obliterate you."

"We will comply. Give me two minutes to shut down the deployment series. It will take fully two minutes."

"Granted. But not a second longer, Captain."

Captain Woolgah shut down the com unit, and issued rapid fire orders to Jemrah and Drax. "Set sensors to activate the shield generator the instant they start a firing sequence, not before. Set the envelope to include the Gelwah, no more. The shield should not only stop anything they fire at us, but should brush their ship aside like a toy when we impact them which we will on this course. They've never faced our shield before, and don't realize what it can do. Any kind of energy poured into the shield is absorbed by the shield and strengthens it. That includes all inertial energy. When we hit them, they will bounce off the shield like a rubber ball. I doubt anyone on their ship will survive the sudden huge acceleration. We will experience no acceleration in the impact."

"Yes sir!" Jemrah said with a smile. "What about the rift?"

"When you know we cleared their ship, Drax will cut the power to the shield and reset the control to the original pattern. We should be near enough to the rift in less than five minutes. We must activate the shield before the Gelwah comes under the influence of the rift's powerful gravitational distortions."

"They're firing sir," Jemrah announced as the sensors activated the shield.

*   *   *

Aboard the Intreba, Madam Keltra was berating Captain Solas. "Why shouldn't we portal to jump ahead of them? You don't believe that drivel that portalling a ship might activate the expansion of the rift, do you?"

"Not really. It's . . . why take the chance?"

"That could be considered insubordination, Captain, even close to mutiny. Did you forget who is running this mission? Maybe you also forgot who made you the Captain of the Intreba. Now, portal to the coordinates directly in the path of the Gelwah, and let's be done with them."

"Yes, Madam Keltra, I will execute your orders."

"As soon as we are there, hail them, and issue the ultimatum."

"Yes, Madam Keltra. Helmsman, execute the standing portal order on my command count. Three . . . two . . . one . . . execute!"

*   *   *

As the blue glow died, the Gelwah appeared in the forward view screen. The helmsman sounded an alarm, "Seven minutes to impact on our present course."

Keltra, standing next to the captain, shouted, "Hail them, and issue the order."

"Captain Woolgah, this is Captain Raoul Saras of the Scentar star ship Intreba. You are ordered to stand down. Abort the mission. I repeat, abort the mission."

"And on whose authority do I abort this mission?" Captain Woolgah asked.

Madam Keltra shouted, "On my authority, and because our massive disrupters are trained on your ship. If you do not do so, we will obliterate you."

"We will comply. Give me two minutes to shut down the deployment series. It will take at least two minutes."

"Weapons control, prepare to fire the disrupter display at the Gelwah on my command, or in two minutes and ten seconds if the command is not given."

"Aye, Captain."

Captain Saras turned to Keltra. "We will have less than five minutes from firing the disrupter until the remains of their ship impacts us. It will be tricky avoiding some rough going."

"I think we can handle a little rough riding. I assume the shields will prevent any serious damage."

"If we put the shields up quick enough. Once the disrupters are fired, it takes several minutes before any of the engines are operational. Until they are, the shields are inoperative. They are set to come up as soon as the disrupter array is fully discharged. It will be close."

"Those fools. Don't they know they will be destroyed? I was certain they would not go this far."

"Madam Keltra, are you now having second thoughts? It's a bit late. The disrupters will fire in ten seconds. - - - five . . . four . . . three . . . two . . . one . . ."

An instant before the disrupters fired, a large grey sphere replace the Gelwah in the view screen. There was a blinding flash when the blast hit the sphere, but the sphere was unaffected.

"What in hell is that?" Captain Saras shouted.

His helmsman shouted, "I have no idea, but we will impact it in about three minutes, before we will be able to take evasive action."

Captain Saras shouted, "Full power in reverse. Execute!"

After a few minutes, the helmsman responded, "I'm afraid it will take longer for the engines to power up than for us to reach the sphere, Captain. Prepare for impact. Force unknown." Those were the last words spoken on the Intreba.

*   *   *

The screens on the Gelwah went black, no impact was felt, and there was no sound for two minutes.

Then Drax reported, "The shield is off and reset as you requested. We are fifty seconds from optimum position."

"Great work, both of you. I see no sign of the Scentar ship. I wonder what happened to it?"

"Prepare for shield activation, Drax," Jemrah said as he brought the coasting ship to a halt with a retro burst.

Once more, the screens went black as Drax activated the shields.

"Now what do we do, Captain?" Jemrah said as he looked at the captain and Drax with a big grin on his face.

"You know exactly what we do. We park here for fifty hours, and hope it works. Our storage has enough fuel to power the shield for at least seventy more hours, but our Scentar scientist friends promised us fifty will definitely do the job," Captain Woolgah said, grinning. "I don't know about you my friends, but I am going to take this opportunity to catch up on my sleep, and spend some time with my wife. Drax, I suggest you may want to do the same. Jemrah, you could use some sleep as well. We've earned our rest, and we can't go anywhere or do anything now anyway."

*   *   *

33.70.00.1009 - Captain Woolgah, Drax, and First Officer Jemrah finished their two-hour workout on the exercise machines, and stepped off the platform. Then they showered, dressed, and walked together toward the bridge. Meernya and Maria were invited to join them on the bridge.

"My friends, it's been fifty hours since we deployed the shield. If this hasn't closed the rift, nothing ever will. Power the shield down and we will see where and when we are."

"When? Captain?"

"Yes, my friends, when. We are dealing with unknowns here, unknowns based on sketchy theories of a bunch of theoretical scientists who deal with gravity and gravitational rifts in their computers. We're the ones who risk life and limb to test those theories in reality. I'm betting we will be in for a few surprises when we drop the shield."

"Is that why you insisted the entire crew stay behind?"

"No need to risk lives unnecessarily. The five of us are enough crew to handle this mission. I thank you all for volunteering."

"Every man aboard the ship volunteered. They are loyal. Thank you for choosing me. It is a great honor."

Drax echoed Jemrah's comment, adding, "I hope we survive to tell others of this effort and of good results."

"The honor is mine to have such men as you two by my side along with these lovely ladies."

"Thank you sir."

"Here we are. Let's see what happened. Shut down the shield."

"Yes sir!"

In seconds the shield was gone. All they could see in the display was blackness. Not a single light, star, galaxy or other visible object could be seen.

"Well, Jemrah, where can we be? Activate the position search system."

After several tense moments of waiting, the system reported "location unavailable."

"Captain, I don't like the sound of that."

"I don't either. Prepare the basic portal for transport to a known position in the Human universe. That should be where we were."

"Yes sir!"and after a few minutes at his console Jemrah reported, "Ready sir."

"Execute."

The blue glow gradually engulfed the bridge then slowly died away. It was not a good sign.

"Well, Jemrah, the portal couldn't find the destination coordinates. At least we know we are not in the Human universe. Let's try our own. Set for home base."

Once more Jemrah reported, "Ready sir."

"Do it!"

The blue glow again grew bright, and then died slowly away.

"That leaves only the Scentar universe. I hope this is it."

The blue glow intensified then died away.

"Damnit, Jemrah, we are definitely outside of any known universe. We'll use the universe portal, and I don't want to use the power it will require. Check our power reserves."

After a few moments at the console, Jemrah reported. "Portal power is down only 20%, sir, steady at 80%. We used much less power to generate the shield than we thought we would. Welt drive power is down to 55%. System power is only 22%. Weapon power was never used, and is at max."

"That's good news. Now check the transfer conduits to make sure we can transfer power if necessary."

"Yes sir."

It took Jemrah no more than ten minutes to set up the tests, execute them and report. "All tests are positive, sir."

"Good. Run some forward impact weapons fire test on visual with trajectory analysis."

"Sir? The purpose?"

"I know it's a strange request, but I want to check out one of my suspicions. Fire when you are able."

Within seconds, Jemrah fired the forward impact guns with tracer rounds. The tracers did not go straight, but curved sharply up and to port, and went quickly out of sight.

Captain Woolgah barked an order. "Set a course for a turn, 90.30.150 and give me full welt drive as quickly as possible. We're in the grip of a massive gravitational force and close to its event horizon."

"Captain. It is possible that when we collapsed the rift, the result was the creation of a black hole. My calculations indicate such a possibility," Jemrah said quickly.

There was a noticeable jolt of the ship as the welt engines powered up. This was followed by surging vibrations. The ship groaned and creaked as if it were being twisted and stressed physically. He watched the display for any sign of light.

"Repeat the forward weapons test, now!"

This time the tracers made a much wider curve directly upward.

"Change course minus 45.00.00, and maintain full welt."

"Yes sir! - - - done!"

"Repeat the weapons test."

"Done."

This time the tracers went straight ahead with no curvature until they burned out.

"Thank you, Captain. That was close. We were about to fall into some kind of event horizon, weren't we?"

"Right on the money," Drax said. "Now, look at the display, the view outside. What a beautiful sight, all those points of light."

"Give us another position check," the captain ordered.

"Yes sir," Jemrah said with a smile, "Yes sir indeed."

A few motions at the console and Jemrah reported, "It still indicates the location is unavailable, sir."

"All right my friend, repeat the same jump sequences with the portal as before, and see what that gets us. Before we do so, cut the engines. No sense in wasting fuel."

"Yes sir."

Engines were cut off, and the sequences run. The result was the same as before.

Jemrah looked at his captain and said, "We must be in another universe in a still different dimension from the three we know of."

"Or possibly we are still in the Human universe but at another, later time."

"Of course. The result would be the same, wouldn't it?"

"Yes! Out of curiosity, do a search for known objects, million kilometer range. We might pick up something."

Jemrah executed the search command, and the image of a ship appeared on the screen. It was the Intreba, and she was distorted.

"Distance?"

"About fifty thousand kilometers, Captain, and we are approaching. She's within hailing distance."

"Hail the Intreba, Jemrah."

"Yes sir."

The display flickered, but there was no answer.

"Give us a close up view, Jemrah."

"She's derelict, sir. Looks to be badly damaged."

"Yes, Jemrah, she's misshapen. Look at all those pock marks on her outer hull. It appears she has been here a long time and received many meteor strikes after her impact shields quit working."

"Captain, it would take at least a hundred years to receive so many meteor impacts. I think you were right about another time."

"All Scentar ships carry flight recorders as do ours. Those recorders also use permanent atomic clocks that run virtually forever. I wonder if we could find theirs and remove it?"

"Sir, if we could find and remove the recorder it would tell us a lot about what happened, and possibly where we are."

"Our current trajectory will take us within about ten-thousand kilometers. When we reach that position, set a corrected course to bring us alongside Intreba. Find out how long that will take."

Jemrah adjusted the controls and did a few calculations. "At minimum power use, it will take about five hours. I assume you don't want to use any more power than necessary."

"Correct. Until we know more about our situation, we have a lot more time to spare than power. We don't know when or how we might get home."

Chapter 54 - Aftermath of the Meeting with Intreba

From the log of the Segwah star ship Gelwah, starting decadate **33.70.05.3000**

Jemrah reports, "Captain, we are in sync with Intreba about a quarter of a kilometer off her starboard bow."

"Thank you Jemrah, and well done. Now let's see if their atomic clock is still working. Set the energy scan for the lowest emission, and scan Intreba. If we find anything, we'll then figure out how to get it."

"Sir, three small energy sources showed on the scan. From its emission signature, I know the forward one is the atomic clock. I can only wonder what the other two are. There are no life signs whatever, and there is no air in the ship, only the vacuum of outer space."

"Is there a hatch forward near the clock?"

"Better than that, sir. The flight recorder is in its own easy access tube that can be opened from the outside. The Scentar at Vega Five showed me when I took a tour of their ship. I can put on a vacuum suit, and take a scooter over to remove the recorder. I'll need a Darium cutter to open the tube because we lack a key."

"Do it! Drax and I will keep watch in case something goes wrong. Check to make sure our com units are working before you leave the airlock."

"On my way, Captain."

While Jemrah prepared to go after the flight recorder, Captain Woolgah and Drax started searching Scentar ship schematics to try to find out what the other small sources of energy could be. They had examined energy sources on three Scentar ship plans when Jemrah clicked his com unit.

"All set, Captain. Air lock is open, and I'm ready to go."

"Good luck my friend. Don't take any chances. I can't afford for you to be injured. Come back to the ship immediately should you sense anything that doesn't seem right."

"Yes, Captain. I'm out of the airlock, and on my way."

Captain Woolgah said to Drax, "While I continue searching these schematics, please follow Jemrah and the scooter. Let me know if you see anything amiss."

Soon the bright white flashes of the Darium cutter told him Jemrah had found the flight recorder tube, and was working to extract it. About an hour later the com unit signaled.

"I've reached the recorder," Jemrah reported. "It's going to take a while to cut it out. Both the outer and inner hull shells are crushed in, the tube is badly mangled and the recorder itself is jammed into the bulkhead it was attached to. I would say I'm about half way finished with the cutting. You will need another hour at least, to free it and carry it back."

"No hurry, Jemrah. Make clean cuts, and don't leave any jagged edges that could catch and puncture your vacuum suit. While you are clearing the recorder, I'll search the Scentar ship plans to try to find those other energy sources. They must be significant sources or they wouldn't still be active."

"Yes Captain. I'll let you know when I free the recorder."

*   *   *

With that Captain Woolgah went back to studying Scentar ship plans. True to his estimate, Jemrah called about an hour later.

"Captain, I'm about to cut what seems to be the main power cable to the recorder. I don't understand why it is so big, about the size of my wrist. Once I cut through the cable, the recorder is easily removed."

"Jemrah, be careful. I know no reason why there should be any power cable to the recorder. They maintain their own separate power source inside the box. Maybe it's a security lock or hold down. Wait a minute. Here is a diagram of a flight recorder installation as you describe. I think I also discovered those two power sources."

"Captain. I'm cutting the cable now. It's hollow."

The display of the energy sensor lit up with a brilliant display. At the same instant, the captain realized what they were.

"Fusion Bombs! get out of there now!" He shouted over the com unit. "Drax, set the shield envelope to include up to the surface of the ship right where Jemrah is."

He and Drax watched the display. The instant Jemrah mounted the scooter to head back toward the Gelwah the captain shouted, "Activate."

In one fluid movement Drax set and activated the shield envelope to include Jemrah. In the instant before the shield deployed and everything turned black, they saw the hull of the Intreba turn white hot.

"Jemrah!" the captain screamed into the com unit. There was no answer. As the captain and Drax bolted for the door to head for the airlock, the com unit popped. Jemrah's calm voice stopped them in their tracks.

"Yes Captain? What happened? I had started for the airlock when everything turned black. I had a hard time locating the com unit in the darkness. Please turn on the airlock navigation lights so I can see to enter back into the ship?"

Captain Woolgah slumped into the nearest operations chair on the bridge in immense, soul-wrenching relief. "I'm sorry, Jemrah. The lights are now on. Please come aboard as quickly as possible, and come to the bridge. We were all tremendously lucky."

"Yes? How's that, sir? and why did you turn on the shield? I assume that's what happened."

"I'll explain when you return to the bridge."

❊   ❊   ❊

Half hour later, Jemrah walked onto the bridge carrying a large metal cylinder with several feet of a large diameter tube hanging out of one end.

"What happened, Captain? I had started the scooter back toward the ship when everything went black. Why did you turn on the shield?"

"Those two energy sources we couldn't identify? They were two fusion bombs connected to the flight recorder with a waveguide trigger. They used a similar long-lived atomic power source like the one in the flight recorder. When you cut the waveguide the bombs were triggered to go off. I realized what was happening when the energy sensor display lit up as the firing mechanisms energized and set the bombs to explode. I tried to tell you what was happening, but couldn't connect with your com unit. Drax set the shield to include the space you were in, and turned it on the instant you were clear of the Integra ."

"Was it that close?"

"Here's how close it was. The hull of the Integra turned white hot no more than a nanosecond before the shield deployed. Which reminds me, why didn't you respond when I shouted 'fusion bombs' over the com system?"

"I had to turn off and stow the com system in order to pull the recorder out of the ship, it was that tight. As soon as I boarded the scooter, I turned my com unit on and heard you screaming for me. I was only a few meters away from the Intreba when everything went black."

"That was way too close. I'll wager we benefitted from those bombs, and their energy fed the shield and filled storage."

"I'll check power storage." Jemrah punched a query into his console. "You were right. All energy storage systems report full."

"Good! Turn off the shield. Then let's examine the flight recorder clock, and see what it tells us."

"Damn! Captain, check the display. All those incandescent objects must be the remains of the Intreba. They're all rapidly receding from us."

"That's the result of being at the center of an explosion while protected from it."

✼   ✼   ✼

33.70.08.1735 - It took two hours of extremely careful effort to remove the flight recorder from its heavy protective cylinder. The record showed the ship had jumped three times since leaving Vega Five, had sustained a sudden acceleration of forty G's, and nothing after that until the recording space filled and data recording ceased. No living being could survive such a sudden acceleration.

Captain Woolgah looked up at Jemrah. "Whatever those Scentar wanted, whatever their mission or purpose, we will never know. The impact with our shield killed all of them instantly, and whatever records they had were incinerated when those bombs went off. There's another shocker. The atomic clock indicates we jumped 126 years into the future. That's why the locator couldn't tell us where we are. The data base of celestial objects is very much out of date. Those objects all moved quite a distance since we jumped."

Jemrah entered some information on the console, and queried the locator once more. "I've updated the data base. Known movements of those baseline objects should provide us with a fix. There! At last we know where we are."

"And when!" the Captain said. "We're slightly more than ten million kilometers away from where we sealed the tear. We're also about fifty days from the current position of Vega Five. We moved apart considerably during those 126 years."

"Do a dimensional gravity scan to see if the tear is there."

After a few moments, Jemrah said, "No sign of any disturbance, sir."

"I guess that means we should head back to the base on Vega Five. Set the return heading to the new coordinates and let's go. I'm wondering what we'll find after being gone more than a hundred years. It should be interesting."

"No one there will know us," Maria said. "I wonder if anyone will even remember us."

Drax grinned. "At least we'll have a clean slate and no enemies."

Chapter 55 - The Heros Are Welcomed Home

From the log of the Segwah star ship Gelwah, starting decadate **33.72.06.1735**

Approaching Vega Five orbit, Captain Woolgah speaks. "Jemrah, open up a direct channel, and see what we can find out."

"Yes sir, Captain."

The display held a background full screen shot of Vega Five from the Gelwah forward cameras.

"There seems to be no response to our signal. Send out a frequency pattern call, and zoom the camera in close on the base location."

"Yes, Captain." The display filled with an expanse of green vegetation with a tall, black tower. Atop the tower was a fairly detailed model of a space ship. "What the hell is that?"

"Unless I miss my guess, Jemrah, you are looking at a model of our ship, the Gelwah. Are you getting any confirmation of our signals?"

"Not yet, sir. Wait. there's something digital coming in. It's in human English requesting we identify ourselves. They do not recognize our ID signal."

"Switch the display and communications to their frequency."

A disturbed and obviously human face displayed on the screen. "Please identify yourself. Your ID signal is unknown to us."

"This is Captain Grala Woolgah of the Segwah star ship Gelwah. Aboard with me is First Officer Der Jemrah, Dr. Draxel Syl, his wife, Maria and my wife, Meernya. There is no one else on board. We left the Scentar base on this planet more than a hundred years ago on a critical mission which has been accomplished."

"One moment please" was followed by a long silence as the face on the screen looked off to his left. After at least fifteen minutes the face on the screen turned to the camera. "Please enter security orbit D for David, and wait for further instructions."

The captain smiled. "If you will provide me with the vector and coordinates for security orbit D, I will comply. Who are you please?"

"One moment, Captain. We're not accustomed to providing such information as it should be in your ship's navigation data banks. My name is Charles Sung, and I'm a security officer on Vega Five."

"Our navigation data banks have not been updated in more than a hundred of your years so it's no wonder they are out of date. If you put our ship on visual, you will note it looks exactly like the one atop the huge black tower near your base. That is no coincidence. Now please provide us with the requested navigation guides so we can comply with your directions."

The display went blank for a few seconds. Then a different and smiling face appeared. "I am Grace Shelbourne, Governor of the Vega Five territory, the oldest Human outpost in the galaxy. I want to take this opportunity to welcome you back, Captain Woolgah, and apologize for your earlier treatment. Your return is miraculous and quite unexpected."

"Thank you Governor Shelbourne. It is good to be back."

"Is your ship capable of landing on the surface without assistance?"

"Tell us where we can land, and we will do so unassisted."

*   *   *

It took less than an hour to land the Gelwah on the broad grassy area near the tower and next to the road circling it about a third of a kilometer from the tower itself. It took another hour to shut down all flight equipment, and prepare the Gelwah for ground access and control before they could exit for any length of time.

By the time they lowered the entrance stairway, a crowd had gathered from all directions, running across the grass and along the road. A military detachment had surrounded the legs of the Gelwah, and held the crowd back. As the entrance staircase lowered from the nose of the ship, a group of small busses or "porters" pulled down the road. They wove their way through the crowd and stopped near the staircase. Two women and three men stepped out of the first porter, and walked over to the staircase as the five travelers came down the steps. Media cameramen and reporters tumbled out of the other busses, and virtually fell over each other getting in position and set up. It was an historic occasion.

As the two Segwah officers stepped on the grass, the taller of the two women spoke. "It is my great honor as Governor of Vega Five, to welcome back five historic figures from the past. But for their courage and daring in a successful mission of great danger, none of us or even our universe would exist. Welcome, Captain Woolgah and Meernya, First Officer Jemrah, and Dr. Syl and Maria. Welcome back to your adoptive home. In our history books, we all read about two dedicated Segwah soldiers, their human associate, and two brave women who risked their ship and their lives to save both the Scentar and Human universes from annihilation. All the more amazing is that the Segwah home universe was not threatened, and the Segwah could have gone back there and lived out their lives without danger."

The crowd applauded, and stomped their feet in approval. They also called for Captain Woolgah to speak.

The captain looked at his crew, smiled and addressed the crowd. "Madam Governor, citizens of Vega Five, believe me when I say emphatically, we are pleased to be here. We are especially pleased you chose the Segwah foot stomp to honor us. According to our clocks, it was sixty-six days ago we left this spot on our mission. During the same time you experienced more than a hundred years. This will take some getting used to on our part. I'm sure we will have much to share with each other in the future. Right now we are exhausted from the rigors of flight deceleration and maneuvering into orbit."

After much hand shaking and greeting of members of the crowd who responded with a few Segwah stomps, Governor Shelbourne turned to the travelers with a big smile. "We thought you would be exhausted from your ordeal so we arranged for you to stay in the VIP suites at our finest hotel. We will hold any debriefing and celebration until you are refreshed and ready to enjoy our hospitality."

At this time Captain Woolgah took the hands of his first officer and Drax, and held them high, saying, "We may be tired, but I want to say something important about First Officer Jemrah before we go to the hotel. It is something the history books may not mention. I now publicly acknowledge that First Officer Jemrah was the one who first conceived the possibility that our gravity-powered shield might repair the damaged space/time fabric. He conceived of this entire mission. Working with Dr. Syl and his associate, Dr. Martin Cohen, they developed the basic design of this mission. True, Scentar theoretical physicists confirmed Jemrah's concept and calculated the details of the mission, but this man initiated the entire project. That such a man would choose to remain my first officer when offered a command of his own was the greatest compliment, honor, and reward I ever received. No man had a better or truer friend."

Jemrah was a bit embarrassed. "Thank you, Captain. To hear such words from you brings me great joy. You will always be my friend, my mentor, and my Captain. I'm not good with words, but I must say we lost all of our friends and most of our families, save each other. True, we will make new friends, but to lose all one's friends and family in two months brings great sadness to my heart and I'm sure to Dr. Syl's and my Captain's as well. Thank you all for being so kind."

Drax was the last of the three to speak. "To accomplish such a mission with men and women like these, was a humbling event. I am also greatly honored to call them true and loyal friends."

Governor Shelbourne said. "This day has been a day of unprecedented revelations, happy and pleasant revelations. Now let's take you travelers to your hotel and some rest. This will also give us the opportunity to prepare a proper welcome along with a few surprises for you. We are planning a reception tentatively scheduled for a week from today. We will need time to make the arrangements."

A few more handshakes, cheers and foot stomps, and the group headed off to the hotel in the porters.

Chapter 56 - Revelations

During the next week, all five of us met with numerous dignitaries and were introduced to many of the humans who now manned the base. It was a busy but exhilarating time. The day before the reception, the captain and I were relaxing in the hotel bar while waiting for the rest of our group. I couldn't help but make a comment. "All this hoopla is great, but a lot more exhausting than running around the galaxy in a star ship."

"Right you are, Drax my friend. I am not usually overjoyed at meeting with large groups of people. I much prefer smaller, more conversational groups."

"I must admit, all this attention and popularity has its perks, this hotel for example."

"Don't get too accustomed to the attention though; we'll soon be part of the crowd once more."

"Yes, Captain, but now our public calls. I see our ladies are being escorted by your first officer to the entrance. Unless I miss my guess, that means Governor Shelbourne and her entourage are about to pick us up for the afternoon reception."

We all rode in one porter with the governor and her aide. The governor spoke. "We organized an unusual reception in your honor. This is being held at our life research facility which incidentally was funded by generous gifts from Humans, Scentar, and Segwah alike in memory of the three brave adventurers who saved two universes. The full name of the building is, The Woolgah-Jemrah-Syl Life Science Research Facility."

"Thank you for the opportunity to relax a bit before the reception. I assure you we appreciated your thoughtfulness," Captain Woolgah said. "It is wonderful to have the opportunity to meet new people and make new friends."

I said, "I must say the Captain precisely expressed my sentiments."

Maria said, "I'm sure each member of our group feels the same way."

The Governor said, "Do you remember the friends who said good-bye when you left? Our historical records indicated there were many at your departure. Those who were there to send you off included the crew of your ship, and a number of dear family and friends."

"Of course we do. We will miss each and every one of them. We will miss our two sons. I'm sure there will be pain from such a loss for a long time," Captain Woolgah replied as the porter pulled up to the Life Sciences Research building.

When we walked inside, Governor Shelbourne guided us to a large reception room where the trappings of a major reception celebration were laid out, and a large number of people were gathered. The Governor walked to the podium to address the crowd.

"Welcome ladies and gentlemen. Thanks for coming to celebrate the miraculous return of five of our most cherished heroes."

The governor continued recounting our departure and the acknowledgment that the efforts had succeeded. Then there was the agony of waiting, not knowing when or if we would return. She then described the purpose and mission of the research facility.

"Some important and successful research has been accomplished in this establishment by the fine people from all three universes who worked here over the years. One major accomplishment happened soon after our travelers left on their mission. This success was in the Life Stasis project. This project was to develop the means to suspend life activity for long periods, mainly for those with incurable fatal diseases or serious injuries. Everyone hoped that once treatments were perfected, those suspended could be awakened, healed, and cured. Of course, this was not the only way the process was used.

"I would now like to introduce a group who chose to be suspended not for health reasons, but for another that should be obvious. Let me introduce members of this group who were awakened soon after our heros arrived. They spent the last few days readjusting to being awake after more than a hundred years in Life Stasis. They are thrilled to be here at this reception today."

As the echos of her words died, the dividing wall at the north end of the room split and folded back to the sides of the hall revealing a large group of Segwah individuals.

The governor continued, "Let me present to you all and especially to our heroes, the entire crew of the star ship Gelwah."

Captain Woolgah and First Officer Jemrah were soon greeting their old shipmates. After some time, the greeting began to slow down. When things quieted, Governor Shelbourne called out, "Captain Woolgah, would you and Meernya please follow me this way? There is another group that required considerable effort in a short time to contact them, and transport them here for this occasion. They are waiting in this next room."

When she opened the door, the governor said, "Captain Woolgah and Meernya, I would like to present you to most of your descendants. I'm quite sure this is an unexpected pleasure for you both and for your family as well. I will leave you to become acquainted. I feel certain you will have much to share with family, to learn and enjoy."

Governor Shelbourne returned to the main hall and found Maria and me. "There you are," she said as she walked up to us. "I hope you are enjoying the reception."

"We are," Maria said. "I shouldn't speak for Drax though."

"You've organized quite a party in such a short time. I'm impressed." I looked around at the people gathered in the hall. "Wait a minute. I just this moment realized there are no Scentar in this crowd. Why is that? Where are all the Scentar?"

Governor Shelbourne responded quickly, "Only a few thousand Scentar remain out of more than a million. Most of them are at least a hundred and twenty years old. The only exceptions are those born here with two Scentar parents, and there are not many of them. You couldn't know that within ten years of when you left on your journey, Scentar stopped coming into the Human universe. With humans trained to run the base, they gradually took over all operations. Because of the combination of humans learning Scentar technology, and the success of the peace between Scentar and Segwah, Scentar were no longer required to go through the drastic and dangerous adaptation process, so they stopped coming. Those who were adapted couldn't go home so they grew old and died here."

"So where are those few remaining Scentar? Why aren't there any of them here?" Maria asked.

"In good time, Maria. While Captain Woolgah and his wife are becoming acquainted with their family, there is someone I would like you two to meet, actually, a number of people."

"And who might they be?" Maria asked.

"Since I would like to see you enjoy an extremely pleasant surprise, I'll let you meet them first. Come with me to the next conference room."

As we walked toward the conference room, I wondered who they could be. We entered a small room off the main hall. When we entered, we found chairs positioned around a small table. Seated in one of the chairs was an elderly Scentar woman with long snow white hair. As she rose to greet us, the expression on her face and those dark eyes were unmistakable.

"Leura? Is that really you?" I asked as the tears of joy flowed.

Maria was equally overwhelmed. "How can this be? You must be more than a century and a half old," she said as they embraced.

There were hugs, kisses, tears, astonishment, unbounded joy—all the unspoken expressions of love. During a long time when no one spoke in words, looks, and body language alone spoke volumes.

It was the governor who broke the silence. "I am certain there is much you would like to share in private. I will leave you three together and return to the reception. Please sit and reacquaint yourselves. Take all the time you want."

When she left, we sat for another silent time, looking at each other. This was positively delicious. Leura broke the silence. "I never dreamed I would see you again. During all the years since you left, I kept hoping you would return. I'm so sorry Maia is no longer with us. She passed away about twenty years ago."

Drax shook his head. "We expected never to see you. How can this be?"

Leura smiled. "You undoubtedly didn't know that the average Scentar lifetime is about one and a half times the lifetime of humans. In the short time we were together before you left, the subject never came up."

"Still, few humans live to be a hundred," Maria said. "You must be past one hundred and fifty."

"One hundred and fifty-three to be exact. I am happy to be alive and in good health for my age. I am most fortunate, more so than Maia. I miss her so terribly, and wish she could be here for your return. Please, accept that as reality, and let us go on to some more pleasant, beautiful, and unexpected experiences, some you couldn't imagine."

Surprise bloomed on Drax's face. "Oh? and what might these surprises be? Finding you here was quite a surprise. I can't imagine a greater one."

"There are nearly a hundred people in the next room waiting anxiously to meet you. Be prepared to be amazed. Follow me."

We walked out into the hall and to another larger conference room. When we entered the room a loud cheer arose from all of those assembled. The faces of a number of the men, women, and children looked vaguely familiar to me.

"Who are these people?" I asked.

Leura raised her hands to silence the excited conversation and comments. "I told you all this would be an emotional moment, particularly for our two honored returnees. Drax and Maria, I remember telling you we believed there was no chance of conception between Human and Scentar. We were wrong. Shortly after you left, both Maia and I discovered we were pregnant. These individuals include nearly all descendants of those children, and your four daughters, Drax—yours and mine and Maia's.